FIREBOLT

SGT. HAWK BOOK FIVE

PATRICK CLAY

ROUGH
EDGES
PRESS

Firebolt
Paperback Edition
Copyright © 2022 Patrick Clay

Rough Edges Press
An Imprint of Wolfpack Publishing
5130 S. Fort Apache Rd. 215-380
Las Vegas, NV 89148

roughedgespress.com

Paperback ISBN 978-1-68549-136-9
eBook ISBN 978-1-68549-135-2
LCCN 2022941283

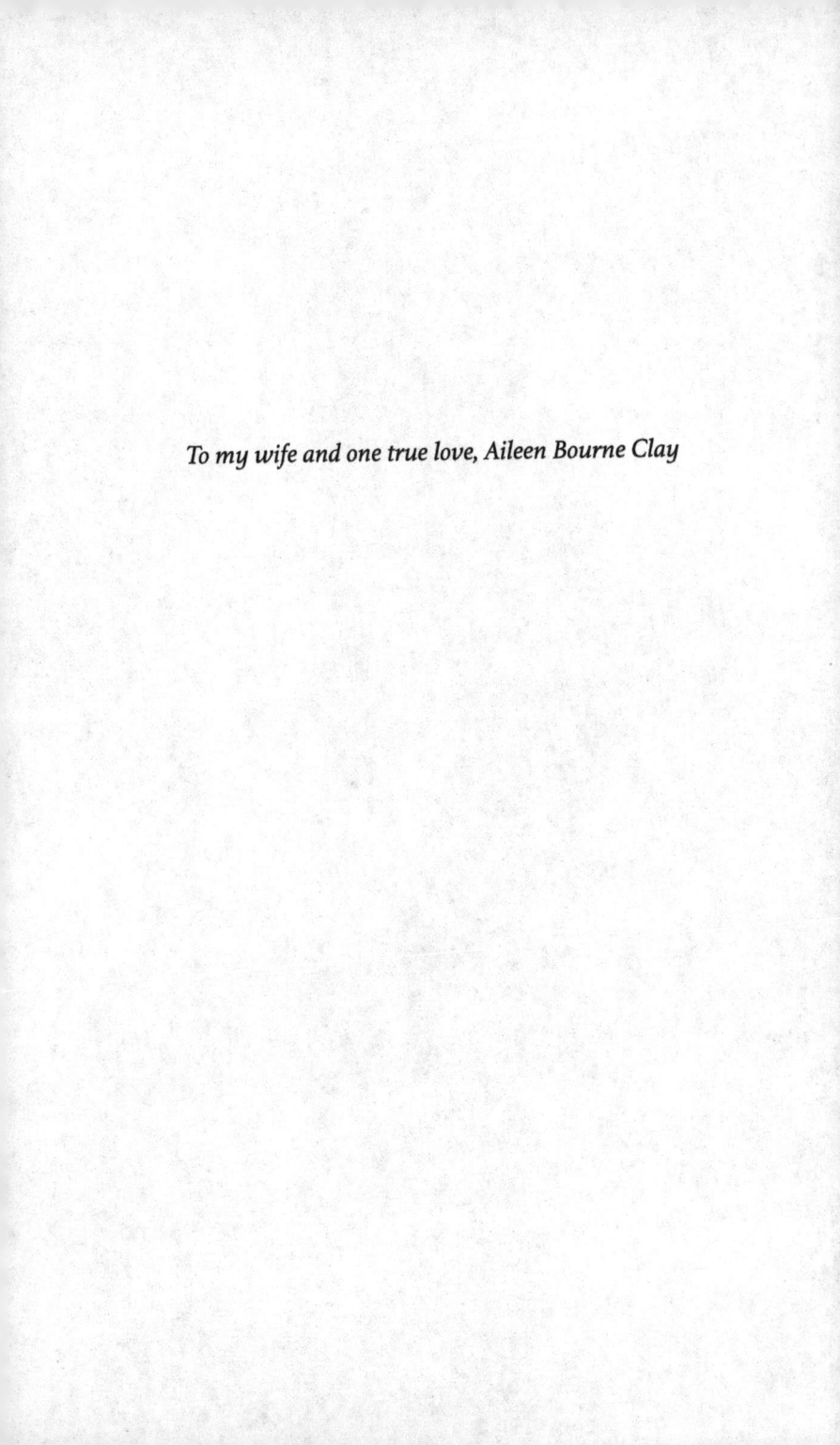

To my wife and one true love, Aileen Bourne Clay

FIREBOLT

1

THAT A MAN LAY DOWN HIS LIFE

THERE ARE THOSE WHO EXCEL, AND WE ADMIRE THE virtue in their triumphs, until that is, they triumph over us. Then we recognize that what we mistook for virtue was only commonplace evil, and not worthy of admiration, or very much at all.

His eyes squinted at the yellow sky, falling gradually to the brown earth. He saw nothing of concern, but James Hawk looked over his shoulder frequently now. He distrusted peace, he expected something. Peace was death sneaking up on you. It was about time for it, again. Maybe from up there.

"To face such a man in the sky would be to die," said the company's islander scout. He said it with a note of pride. He spoke of Isamu Zanji, one of the greatest Japanese fighter pilots. The scout was a resident of Cokoni, long a possession of Japan. The people living here had close ties to the Empire. And now the American Marines had come to their island to capture Zanji, a national hero.

"Well, we ain't facing him in the sky," said Sergeant

Hawk. He lifted a ration tin off the canned heat and set it down quickly. He opened his canteen and nuzzled a cradling spot for it in the thick wet grass. "Way it looks, we ain't gonna be facing him at all," Hawk added. The scout smiled with pleasure at the admission, and studied the flaming eyes in the American's cold face. It would be better for Zanji, the scout decided, if he remained in the sky, and did not interact with men like this.

Captain Hermsdorf walked down the high hill in front of them. Hawk watched him the whole way. The captain stopped behind Hawk, so that Hawk would have to turn around to see him. "Saddle up, Sergeant, we're moving out." The captain put his hands on his hips.

"Sir? That was a short break." Hawk was irritated. The rations had arrived late and were in both insufficient quality and quantity.

"Shake a leg. Nobody told you to set up house-keeping."

"Aye, aye, sir."

The captain strode off with his hands still on his hips. Hawk stuffed half of the meat portion of the ration into his mouth and chewed roughly. He stood and shouted the change in plans to Sergeant Kreski, some yards away. He screwed the cap on his canteen and noticed the scout, Koichi, staring at him. The young man was always watching him.

"The captain moves too fast," Koichi said. "In too big a hurry. A man must move slow in this country. He moves fast, into something bad."

"Ah, that goddam son of a bitch," Hawk snarled, dropping his helmet on disarranged sandy hair. But he knew the urgency of the mission. Zanji was worth a lot of missed meals to the American military. Some even thought he was worth a lot of dead riflemen. The enemy ace had downed eighty-four Allied planes, as well as a few ships. He had killed a lot of men, but what was worse to the American mind, was that he was costing the Allies a lot of money and materiel. When riflemen died, they didn't take a fifty-thousand-dollar airplane with them.

After Zanji crashed his Japanese Naval aircraft onto the prefecture of Cokoni, his fate was sealed. American intelligence intercepted messages relating to the enemy's frantic rescue plans for the ace. The U. S. Marine Corps reacted swiftly, sending a retread regiment to the island to put a stop to this. Cokoni presently served no strategic purpose, other than its harboring of Zanji. The Americans occupied the strips of beaches surrounding the island. Fighting men thoroughly surrounded the wild interior. Zanji, however, remained safely ensconced somewhere in the unknown badlands of the island. The increasing amount of time the siege was taking, and the ever-present possibility of an escape, brought down the order for a sweep of the sinister terrain. Cokoni was big and bad. It comprised nearly six hundred square miles of mountains and peculiar high-altitude jungles. It would not be easily swept.

That was the big picture. Sgt. Hawk was in the little picture, where things were never as clear or clean. The men were getting to their feet. Hawk sent his friend, Joe Canlon, out to the point. He usually watched out for Joe, they had been through a lot together. He could always find someone else who needed a new perspective on life for point duty. Hawk figured it would be better for Joe to take the job now, while things were quiet. You could never be sure of how quiet things might be later. No one would accuse Hawk of favoritism. Joe certainly wouldn't. This was all in the little picture, where you could get yourself killed.

Hawk's third platoon took the lead in a sluggish skirmish line that was climbing a grass-patched ridge of blue rock. Reports indicated that enemy paratroopers were being periodically dropped into the mountainous jungles. They were not going to give Zanji up without a fight. Hawk had heard the report, but he didn't believe any of it. He had never seen enemy paratroopers anywhere else, and that was good enough support for his stubborn opinion. His superiors believed it, however, and were already having their doubts about the wisdom of the sweep. They were making more conservative plans to strengthen the beach defenses, denying their prey access to the ocean. Searchers could rattle around forever in six hundred square miles of wilderness.

Hawk's nerves were calm and his body at ease with a focus on the physical task of climbing the ridge. He knew it was a time to beware, but you can't stay tense all of the time. Sometimes you have to get where you're going. After so many hours, days, weeks and years, even tension can get boring. Some called it fatalistic, some called it bored, but it all looked the same: a dangerous man on a dangerous move. His fiery blue eyes scanned the crest of the ridge. Captain Hermsdorf was nearly to the top. He snorted at the captain's broad back and bit into another handful of meat. His shirt hung open and his sleeves were rolled up over hard biceps.

Hawk's nerves snapped suddenly taut. An echoing hammer of fire beat furiously beyond the top of the hill. Hermsdorf flattened. Hawk stopped chewing. Joe Canlon was somewhere over the top of that hill.

"Occupy the military crest!" Hermsdorf shouted. He held both hands on his helmet and clung to the earth. The hardened men of third platoon looked at their captain and then at one another. They continued climbing at the same steady pace. Hermsdorf was several yards below the crest, or the military crest. Hawk ran up the resisting incline, passed the captain, and dove onto his elbows. He crawled higher to look over the summit.

A wooded valley lay between Hawk's ridge and the next ridge. A hillock loomed through the trees some three hundred yards away. Machine gun fire came from somewhere on this side of the hillock. It danced about like a diamond mirage through the screening leaves. Hawk did not see Joe Canlon.

"What is it?" Hermsdorf demanded.

Hawk's eyes narrowed as he swallowed his rations. That would be all he would eat today. "A pillbox. I don't see Canlon."

"Canlon, hell," the captain replied. "I got a company here. You men spread out. There is a Jap pillbox up there," he announced.

"Joe!" Hawk bellowed. There was no answer. "They got him or he's afraid to give himself away," Hawk said. He turned over on his back and lay staring at the silver blaze of sun overhead. A peaceful sky hung low over the brutal and vicious earth. His lips tightened. He drew back the bolt of his Thompson. "Joe!" The machine gun fire was his only answer.

"Shut up, Hawk! You're giving away our position. What the hell good does it do to have a point man if you're going to yell your guts out?" Hermsdorf snapped.

"Jap sons of bitches," Hawk muttered, although he may have been mentally attaching the title to someone a little closer. He rolled over and peered across the draw once again. A third platoon corporal, Connie Jackson, crawled up beside him.

"Are we going to do something about Canlon?" Jackson asked. He spoke with a soft South Carolina accent.

"Goddam right."

"You waiting on the captain?"

Hawk sighed. "No." He took out a block of chewing tobacco and took a bite. "It's quiet. They might've got him. He could've walked right into it." His teeth anxiously squeezed the liquid out of the tobacco. It rolled beside his tongue, offering no comfort.

The machine gun rattled angrily. "Then what the hell are they shooting at?" Jackson asked. Hawk spat. Good question. A good sign. He looked down where Hermsdorf had been. He was gone. Hawk's tragic-stricken eyes searched the slope like a gun muzzle for his company commander. He finally spotted Herms-dorf, already near the bottom of the ridge. The machine gun spat several times, to remind them of their critical predicament.

Hawk nodded down the slope. "I think he's calling for artillery or setting up the mortars on that gun."

Jackson squinted. He saw no indication of either. "Or he's going to the officer's club for a toot."

"Yeah, well, either way, I gotta get to Joe pretty quick."

"I'll go with you." When Jackson began awkwardly discarding equipment from his back, one of his friends, Tony Smith, recognized the situation from below. He quickly ran to the other two.

"What are you guys doing?" Smith asked.

"We're going after Canlon, before Hermsdorf shells him," said Jackson.

"Why, hell, that's nuts. You can't do that. I'll go with you." Hawk did not like the idea of being joined by the other two. The considerations were too many to contemplate for now. When you did the right thing in these situations, there would always be a lot of second guessing later, by men who seldom did anything, much less the right thing. Hawk kept quiet and did not object to their help.

The three men slipped over the top of the ridge in the fluid manner of stealthy reptiles. They breathed heavily as they skidded in a half-controlled fall down the other side. A tornadic line of bullets, interspersed with fiery tracers, erupted on the rock above them as they reached the bottom of the slope. The dust from the explosions was blown away by a tumbling surface breeze. The men peered up from the rock beneath them, three turtles hiding under their steel shells. The ground smelled like radiant heat.

"Well...they know we're here," Hawk said. Sweat from his eyebrows blurred his vision as he tried to look through the tangled trees. Beyond the trees lay the bunker. Apparently, within the trees, somewhere, lay Joe Canlon. Hawk rubbed the bristly blond stubble on his jaw. No need for caution now. All the cards were on the red hot table.

"Joe!" Hawk screamed.

While Hawk felt no need for caution, from his own perspective, Joe Canlon was not quite as sure. Finally, he made the decision to respond. "Over here!"

"Okay. He's all right," said Hawk. He jerked the Cutt's compensator of his Thompson toward the sound of the voice.

"You hit?" Jackson called.

"No. Pinned down! Can't move an inch!"

The three rescuers crouched and moved into the dubious shelter of the trees.

"We'll get him out. Use a little distraction," said Hawk. At this point, he had no intention of attacking the enemy fortress. "We gotta move fast before the shelling starts." The shadows of the leaves played across the top of his camouflaged-colored helmet cover. Wet leaves were thick on the ground, dead, but too moist to crackle. The softer sounds were not as important now, as everyone's hearing was half numbed by the noise. The trees were slender, and the trunks were splotched with a white fungus growth. The whiteness resembled paint that had been slapped on too heavily. It smelled dungeon-close in the gloomy wood, and Hawk could already taste the burnt metal of too much spent ammunition.

They wound through the covering trees with scarcely a sound, their faces glowing inside the dark shadows of the helmets. Upon reaching the end of the vegetation's seclusion, they could see the enemy emplacement with startling clarity. Fifty yards ahead, between them and the pillbox, leaned another small stand of trees, growing thickly together out of the rocky soil. Hawk bent forward, touching a hand to the ground. He could make out the shape of Canlon's helmet near the front of the clump of trees, closest to the enemy. The helmet was as close to the ground as it could get. Hawk found it difficult to see how the machine gun could miss Joe. Canlon must have found a blind spot in their field of fire; but not quite blind enough.

In the silence of the deadly predicament, Hawk, Jackson, and Smith became hyperaware of one another. Their drab, herringbone twill fatigues became unique in the way they were worn and fitted. Every fleeting expression conveyed a dozen emotions. They would be counting on each other. They each had the greatest respect for the other, just for being there. This was where trust would be tested.

"We cain't get across that," said Hawk. "He can't even fart without getting plugged." Jackson eyed the pillbox. It was disguised with living plant life. Only the dark window was clear of brush. He could see the rim of a funnel-shaped flash guard. He well knew that behind these smaller types of funnels hovered the heavily ribbed barrel of a 6.5 mm machine gun.

Hawk studied the concealing plants with their bizarre tropical shapes. He ignored the green geometric wonders as commonplace, until something like this happened. Then nothing was commonplace. Something might turn out to be important. For the moment, he was an interested tourist in the lowest circle of hell. Unhurriedly, he rubbed his face with the Thompson barrel, studying the problem given him. The bunker must be a big one. The hill probably consisted of solid reinforced concrete. The Japanese were not waiting for three lightly armed men. They were ready for ships, planes, tanks, and a hail of solid steel. Hawk spat. He looked thoughtfully at the ground for a moment. He became fully aware that he had no business doing this.

"Y'all get yourself some cover. Joe never got the chance, so look out. Then we'll lay down a little fire and see what happens. See if he can move any, with us shooting at them."

"How about the back?" Smith asked. The three turned simultaneously and looked at the forbidding growth and uneven rock all around the emplacement. They looked quietly back at one another. "I guess not," he answered his own question. It would not take much for the Japanese to cover the rear of the hulking thing. The only way to get around it would be with a wide, time consuming flanking maneuver.

Jackson moved along the edge of the woods, finally crawling behind a solid looking forked stump. Once he gave his position away, the enemy would have a clear shot at him. The stump was green and strong, or it had better be. Smith went farther to the right, to a more exposed position, behind a low rock. Two other rocks scattered in front of him might afford a little extra protection. Hawk dragged himself behind the two of them, to a position on the extreme right. The roll of the ground gave him a slight defilade. That and hugging the ground would be his only cover. But he liked the vantage point. He had a clear shot. They made it to their positions unseen. Hawk heard the gentle flow of air from his lungs. He keenly felt what is was like to be alive and healthy, and as close as you can get to the opposite of both. "Open up," he said in a voice falling flat and ominous in the tree and rock cushioned air.

The two semi-automatic M1s pumped rounds vigorously into the viewport. At this range, bullets flying into the close quarters could do enormous damage. They could also do nothing, as the Japanese were masters at building a maze of walls within such bunkers, in order to deflect incoming fire.

The thirty caliber bullets splintered the coconut log windowsill. Some of the leafy camouflage dropped in pieces to the earth. White spots, like water droplets fading the surface of paper, appeared across the front of the exposed bunker. Without hesitating, showing no shock or surprise, the Japanese fired back—at Joe Canlon. The two sides of the metallic rage contended with one another to be the loudest. Joe remained still and silent, as before. He saw no improvement in his predicament. Hot dust and sprigs of trees whipped all about him. Hawk's Thompson belched lightning, staining the gloomy shade with a fluttering blue glow.

Canlon sensed that the plan was to pin down the enemy long enough for him to escape. His rescuers were not engaged in an attack and destroy mission, if they were merely shooting at the solid concrete. When should he try to escape? That was the life and death question. Joe decided there was no point in waiting. The Japanese would be most surprised and engaged right now. Lying frozen in that one spot had lost all of its appeal for him. He pulled a leg under himself. Timing was everything, when your bodily integrity was at stake. He had picked the right time.

An explosion shook the earth. A grayish-black cloud spewed from the ground behind the enemy fortress. Scalding vapory shrapnel hissed overhead. Joe turned and ran for the larger section of woods, his short, unassuming legs whipping at Olympics-winning speed. One hand was wrapped around the barrel of a shotgun. A slung MI banged against his back. The grim column of smoke hung in the air behind him, like a newly erected natural formation.

"Mortar," Hawk shouted over to Smith. "That won't crack that bastard." His voice trailed off.

"No, but it can damn sure crack us!" Smith answered, concerned about a short round.

Another mortar round fell in front of the bunker. This one saved Joe's life. It jolted and obscured the view of the enemy gunner zeroing in on Joe's back. Hawk smiled and Jackson laughed as they watched Joe near the woods with unimaginable speed, his feet barely touching the ground.

The reckless burst of superhuman speed caused Joe to slip and fall, catapulting him into an extended sprawl. The smoke over the mortar crater began to dissipate. Joe tried to get up and fell again. He seemed paralyzed with terror. His eyes turned pleadingly to his three comrades.

"Hurt his leg," said Smith, inhaling deeply. He stood and ran into the open space.

Hawk gasped at the unexpected development. *Shit, what did he do that for?* He got to one knee. Smith was already halfway to Joe. The machine gun opened up. Hawk watched in helpless awe as the shells ran like smoke from a locomotive's stack across the ground and straight into Smith. It had all happened in a second. Smith spun, droplets of blood spraying the air. His legs tangled and he hit the earth solidly. The trail of fire kept going beyond his fallen body, forcing Hawk to flatten again. He heard the singing soprano of metal beating into the rock behind him. High velocity dust peppered the back of his neck. When Hawk looked up, Joe was on all fours, dragging a leg, still trying to make it to the woods. Hawk pulled furiously on the trigger of his submachine gun, and the muzzle leapt, throwing a .45 caliber barrage into the bright ball of light at the mouth of the blazing pillbox. A prolonged cry squeezed out of the enemy bunker, and the shooting stopped. Canlon threw himself beside Jackson.

One saved, one dead. Maybe Hermsdorf had been right. Nothing felt right presently. Right and wrong, duty and responsibility, loyalty and concern—it was all there somewhere in broken little pieces on a strange, foreign, forest floor. But Hawk had saved Joe Canlon.

"Let's get outa here," Hawk shouted over to the other two. Three mortar rounds sliced out of the sky in rapid succession, shattering the earth atop the pillbox. Hawk looked up after the crescendo of noise passed. The trees had been cleared from the bunker's roof. He could see the massive thickness of the bald structure. The mortar rounds had not dented it.

"Jack-son..." A disembodied voice came from where Smith lay.

"He's alive," said Jackson. "I gotta get him."

"Wait," said Hawk, "you can't get to him." The voice cried out again from the deadly still body. "I got to," said Jackson.

Joe was still dazed. He sat behind the stumps without speaking, an intense expression on his face, as if he were trying to solve an algebra problem. His fingers released the shotgun barrel. His hand trembled.

Jackson stood, his jaw set, and seemed to run forward without a second thought. Hawk winced with dread. Jackson reached Smith before the Japanese opened up. He lifted the wounded man from under the arms. They both disappeared in a cloud of flaming rico-chets. When the firing stopped, there were two motion-less bodies lying across one another. Their clothing smoked. A helmet rocked on the ground. Without ratio-nally thinking it, in that moment, Hawk sensed: *you did this.*

Other Marines advanced cautiously through the woods. They remained under the cover of the sheltering trees. Hawk stared at the scene in front of the pillbox. The humans looked small before the merciless face of the concrete structure. Two dead. It could have been one, it could have just been Joe. That's what point men are for. There would be hell to pay for this.

Hawk spat. He glanced at the men gathering behind him. He saw no rocket launchers, flame throwers, or even automatic weapons. The Japanese machine gun spat a triumphant burst at the ground around the dead men. The dust rose lazily in the sun.

"Ahhh..." Another frightening moan rose from one of the stricken men. The moan turned into a high-pitched squeal of agony. Hawk opened his somber mouth and clenched his teeth. Sweat poured off his face. It sounded like Jackson. Jackson came with him to rescue Canlon. The liability was clear. It was that strange code of ethics among brave men. If either of the two volunteers had used common sense, it would be permissible for Hawk to do the same. Then Hawk could back down. But he didn't want to back down. That was not an option. Aggression was an integral part of his character. Challenges brought reactions, immediate and harsh, from his very soul. He had the whole Marine Corps behind him now. He could have enlisted others, but he saw the problem as his alone. Hawk did not always think things through, but his instinct was usually pretty close to accurate. If they waited, the enemy could blast Jackson once again, on a whim, at any time, and he was not going to let that happen.

"Joe...throw me that shotgun!" Joe looked over at him.

"Don't, Hawk."

"Slide the son of a bitch over!" He ordered, more emphatically. Joe pushed at the muzzle with his shaking hand, using the hand like an inanimate object. The sergeant grabbed the stock with his fingertips.

"You can't do anything. And he's hit bad. He can't make it."

He didn't say that about you, Hawk thought. But he said nothing. Joe looked away, likely reading his mind. Joe continued to study his unsolvable algebra problem. Another moan rose from Jackson. It sounded like Hawk's name.

Hawk squinted and judged the distance. He had let other men die, men who were calling his name. Perhaps that is why he slowly drew his knee against his chest and pulled a grenade off his belt. There was a sucking shriek of noise as another mortar round splashed chips of concrete off the pillbox roof. The trees rattled with the gravelly rain. Hawk was up and running before the echo of the blast died away.

Bullets followed the heels of his boots. They were hungry, but he was faster. He had an unknown purpose and they could only follow. He dropped to his hands and crawled. The trail of exploding shells passed to his right. They seemed to emanate from the earth, rather than from some distant source. He made it to the little clump of trees that had first sheltered Joe Canlon. The

Japanese gunners fired passionately into the under-growth. When the firing stopped again, Hawk got to one knee, hoping that they would need to reload. He would not give them that courtesy. His method of rescue was going to be a little different. He was not going to stand out there wrestling with the wounded men for the amusement of the enemy gunner. He would eliminate the source of the problem. If the Japanese were under the impression that they had a monopoly on terror, they were about to learn otherwise.

In the ringing silence, Hawk walked into the open like the madman that he was. He pumped the shotgun and went into a crouch. The sliding click reverberated inside the enemy stronghold. The muzzle of the enemy gun was pointed haphazardly at the sky. The sound of rattling, like marbles in a can, could be heard across the glade. Reloading was in progress. The flash guard started to move, jerkily at first, and then with a sureness of purpose. The shotgun erupted and Hawk pumped it again. The loud blast blackened the stone above the viewport. Chips of concrete trickled down. The muzzle of the machine gun again fell skyward. Hawk walked slowly forward, lifting one large boot over the other. The bunker was quiet as he closed with it, a lone man stalking a giant stone monster. His eyes narrowed and his steps crunched in the gravel.

"Ahhh," Jackson screamed behind him, and Hawk flinched. The machine gun muzzle jerked suddenly downward, under some sort of human control once again. The shotgun exploded a second time. The ringed barrel of the machine gun disappeared from view. A hideous scream came from inside. Piercing and chaotic Japanese words from the bunker drowned out the cries of Jackson, in spite of the muffling effect of the enclosure. The sergeant bent lower over the shotgun, pumping it once again, never slowing in his forward progress. His face could almost touch his stalking boots. The machine gun barrel jumped into view and spat an opaque bluish-red fire. Hawk felt the hum of lead pass by his head. A track of shells splattered the ground to the right and behind him. He pulled the trigger of the shotgun again. He could see the slug exploding violently within the pillbox. A single abbreviated grunt followed. Hawk's footsteps stopped, he dropped the shotgun, and stood upright.

Joe Canlon could only watch. He kept the same expression on his face. His eyebrows were drawn, and his mouth was open. He finally turned away, either shaking his head in disbelief, or swaying it involuntarily. Cold chills made him grip an unsteady earth.

Hawk stood directly in front of the emplacement now. He pulled the pin attached to the grenade's cotter key. The safety lever sprang free. The pineapple snapped and began to sizzle. He heard men talking and moving inside. In a loose throw, somewhat between side-armed and underhanded, he lobbed the grenade toward the aperture. The missile, looking orange in the sunlight, appeared as if it were going to miss the opening. At the last fraction of a second, however, the grenade developed a mind of its own, and barely cleared the sill, as a high jumper clears the bar. That fraction of a second, and the fraction of an inch, was all it took.

Neon-red noise flashed inside the bunker. Smoke blossomed from the window. A clawing hand on a bloody arm jutted through the viewport, pulled back, and jutted out again. Without looking at any of it, Hawk picked up the shotgun. He walked back to Jackson. "Corpsman!" He shouted. "We gotta corpsman up here?" Hawk bent over. "Hang on, buddy, they're coming."

Sergeant Kreski knelt beside Canlon. He quickly decided that Joe was in one piece, physically. Other men were running forward to grenade the bunker, as Hawk walked away.

"Did you see that?" Kreski asked Joe Canlon.

"Yeah." Joe looked up at him with a pained and unfocused squint. "I saw it."

2

THE BREAKOUT INTO NOWHERE

CAPTAIN HERMSDORF RECEIVED THE ORDER TO STAND AND hold. A suspiciously large element of Japanese ground troops had moved toward the Marine lines. This came as a surprise to command. They were under the mistaken impression that the Americans were going to launch an unchallenged push to support their search efforts. Their adversaries had decided, however, that they were not going to allow the sweep of the island for the downed pilot. It became apparent that protecting Zanji was more important than expected, or it was not the only concern of the enemy. The majority of the regiment fell back immediately to consolidate the beach positions. The beaches were all the American forces needed to hold to accomplish their purpose: the denial of an escape route for the pilot. Portions of the regiment had, however, become entangled in the new Japanese assault.

Joe Canlon overheard Captain Hermsdorf on the radio. "How could there possibly be that many? We are supposed to be beating the bushes for one man, not getting chewed up by the whole Jap Army. Where did they all come from?"

Joe rubbed his broken nose as he figured out the answer for himself. The enemy had come by air and submarine, or otherwise under the cover of darkness. They were pushing outward, from some central location on the island. He could tell that the captain was upset. Just wait, Joe said to himself, until they come after you, captain. Joe still felt the angry heat of the machine gun bullets from the pillbox. He could remember them vividly like the words of an old song, playing over and over through his nervous system. Hawk's heroics had not made him forget. Heroic deeds were not unusual in Marine operations. Today's heroes were tomorrow's Gold Stars.

Still simmering with irritation at the developments, Hermsdorf decided to form a line on a low ripple of land beyond the pillbox. He set up his command post inside the smelly captured bunker. It had not been necessary to significantly damage it. Hawk was located on this new front line, when he got a call on the telephone. Sprack, the Marine manning the phone, gave Hawk ample warning: "It's Colonel Dreisen!" Sprack knew that a sergeant would have little familiarity with such exalted voices. But a certain familiarity was to quickly develop. "Whoa," Hawk muttered in surprise.

The voice crackled starkly at him. "Heard about the pillbox! Get you a medal for it! How's Hermsdorf doing?"

"The captain, sir? Well..."

"How is he under fire? Don't give me any opinions. What did you see?" Dreisen's voice was gruff, always leaving one with the feeling that he was angry. "Give me the facts." Having an underling report on the conduct of an officer was not standard procedure. It indicated a problem with Hermsdorf—or Dreisen. Or some odd relationship. Hawk didn't like being in the middle of such problems.

"I didn't actually see him under fire, sir. Him and me were going in two different directions, see? He called in some mortar fire that was pretty close, but right on target. I might have been a little closer to it than I should have been. What I did, was all my own doing. He didn't do nothing wrong." His words came out in short bursts, each phrase trying to explain the previous phrase, and without trying to put Hermsdorf in a bad light.

"Yeah, yeah. That's what I figured. He contacted me, griping about you. I knew that was bullshit. That company is a mess. We're stuck with him. But listen, the Japs caught us with our ass hanging out. I pulled most of the line back, except for Hermsdorf. Better make sure the kid has a good perimeter, there won't be a line there in about...oh, thirty minutes," Dreisen emphasized. "Watch him and those brown bars for me. I figured he'd be okay for chasing fugitives, but we didn't know all this was going to happen. I just wanted you to know that I know what you're up against up there. I don't want any massacres on my watch. You watch that boy, all right? He's got friends in high places, and I ain't one of them."

"Yessir. I'll do what I can," Hawk answered. What the hell could he do? Better to not ask, lest there be an answer.

"How's the weather up there?" High ranking small talk followed.

"Hot, sir."

"Yeah. Love it. Beats the hell out of Cheyenne. Carry on, Hawk. Working on that medal. Tell your momma it's in the mail."

"Yessir." Hawk had no momma, or anyone else for that matter.

"Oh, and Hawk, I still need that damned pilot, that... that...Zanji. Funny name. It'll be tougher now, but I have to have him. You might turn out to be in a good position, up there. If they hit our defenses, you could run loose and get behind the worst of it, and into the interior. This pilot is very important to me personally. He is a celebrity. Do you read me? Get to the interior if possible."

"Aye, aye, sir." Hawk could not envision himself anywhere but in the worst of anything. Getting behind it seemed unlikely. The call from the colonel was more than reassuring, however. At least the colonel knew what was going on. Hermsdorf was kind of a jerk, but he seemed to have a protector somewhere. In the day to day dealing with the chain of command, however, Hawk did not see how any of this could benefit him. Jerks were pretty common. He did not have to worry about these hypotheticals for long. Real things started happening.

Within two hours, Hermsdorf's company was cut off. The Japanese moved in under a shower of howitzer and 81 mm mortar fire. The Marines facing this wondered how men dropped in by air came so well-equipped. The platoon on the left flank reported sighting tanks. Hermsdorf's weapons platoon had staved off the enemy's probes. Now, they were already out of ammunition. Second Lieutenant Repler passed this message on to Hawk, the platoon sergeant. It was left to Hawk to explain the situation over the phone to Captain Hermsdorf back in the bunker.

"Well, get some ammunition!" Hermsdorf squeaked from the safety of his thick-walled headquarters. "Hold!" Hawk draped an arm over the rectangular body of a hot and hungry thirty caliber Browning machine gun. He looked with exasperation at its crew. He was fresh out of miracles. MI's fired nervously in the background against the threatening advance of various disjointed clumps of enemy assault troops. The Japanese yelled taunts. They were too close already, and in numbers too large.

"We ought to withdraw. We can't hold this without some mortars," said one lightly bearded machine gunner. "Or some damn thing." A 70 mm shell lit the ashen sky behind his helmet. The blood of every man there sharply descended into the centers of their bodies, in a last-ditch search for safety, leaving them cold and clammy.

"Yeah," Hawk agreed. They could accomplish nothing here. He dropped the phone with Hermsdorf still making noises on the other end of the receiver. "I reckon we better drop back a little. Get a tighter front. Maybe they can get some gun belts and crates up here in a minute. This ain't so good." He looked out over the top of the slit trench. They were not dug in all that well, either. This did not look like the hill to die on, in spite of the order to hold. Hawk's command decision, as with most decisions, came a little late.

A group of at least thirty Japanese burst over a rise and swarmed into the last foxhole on the right flank. The Americans could see three of their fellow defenders emerge from the hole, standing and swinging their rifles valiantly. A corporal gave the order to grenade the overwhelmed fox hole. The grenade explosions were sharp and light, by comparison with the crashing behemoths of artillery all around the position. The grenades were more frightening, however. They were close and desperate, and they had killed Americans. But they had killed more of the Japanese. Rifle fire thinned out the remaining attackers. Thankfully, the enemy survivors ran, something that they seldom did.

"I don't see where all them son of a bitches are coming from," said Hawk. He looked around in vain for the third platoon leader, Lieutenant Morgan. It looked like it was up to Hawk to do something now. This was never good, as there was always the possibility of doing something very wrong. "Pull 'em back," he said. "Withdraw!"

The Japanese pounded the confused American flanks as they tried to withdraw. It became impossible to recover the dead and wounded. They backed through the forest, firing at their pursuers all the while. Outnumbered did not seem to adequately describe the situation any longer, it was a mismatch. The fighting retreat eventually ended all the way back at Hermsdorf's bunker. The walls of the bunker whined under the vicious oncoming, but unaimed, fusillade. Hermsdorf ducked out of the shelter's hatch, amidst a hail of fire. His face looked shocked. The first man he saw was Hawk, backing up rapidly, half stumbling, as he fired into a dark evil jungle that seemed to be following him.

'What are you doing here, Hawk? Your orders were to stand and fight!" Hermsdorf had not pictured his front line in his lap.

"Yessir," Hawk said distractedly, spitting a stream of

tobacco juice. He had finally spotted Lieutenant Morgan, running with the rest. It would have helped to have had Morgan dealing with Hermsdorf. Nothing ever seemed to work out, and this was no exception. There was no time for obsequiousness at this point. Hawk had his hands full. "Joe! Get them men in the pillbox!"

Running was not going to work, as they were being outrun. Hawk slung his Thompson and began spreading the word, running along the edge of the clearing as his men emerged one by one from the shadows. The situation was growing increasingly worse, as the Americans began firing indiscriminately in all directions. A howitzer shell careened off the top of the bunker in a glancing skid. A smoking groove remained in the concrete where the screeching shell had skimmed it. Hermsdorf ducked quickly back inside, his urge to command temporarily satisfied. The incredible noise blocked out the cries of individual combatants, but a pitiable human undercurrent remained discernible.

Twenty men or more eventually crowded into the safety of the thick-walled bunker. The others were unaccounted for. The weapons platoon was reported by Lieutenant Repler to have retreated to the beach, ostensibly to be resupplied. Even so, that left around sixty men outside somewhere, without even a rumor as to their whereabouts. Maybe they were all dead. The phone lines had been cut or blown. Hermsdorf knelt in a dark corner, shouting into a radio. Hawk threaded his way through the sweating throng to Corporal Joe Canlon. He winked.

"Stand and fight," Hawk told Joe. Joe looked up at the open viewport, remembering what had happened to the previous occupants of the fortress. They had been killed by one man. That's all it took. Several hundred fanatical paratroopers were outside the walls, drawing tight the noose.

"Get the BAR's up in that port hole," Hawk ordered in the vacuum of authority. A burly scout named Breaux, and two others, stepped up to the windows, their helmets bumping the low ceiling. Under the circumstances, a relative calm pervaded. Hermsdorf dropped the radio and called over the two officers and two sergeants remaining to him.

"They punched a hole in our lines. It's not as bad as it looks. The colonel says that they can roll them back in an hour or so. The companies on our flanks pulled back before we did. That's what happened. We're isolated out here."

Hawk listened quietly. An hour was a long time to be surrounded by a Japanese Army, raging three feet away from your doorstep. The Marine position, as it were, was in the middle of the Japanese lines, and soon to be behind them.

"I heard they had tanks," Hawk said quietly.

"Yes. Don't panic. Let's not spread the word on that. It will be all right. We are getting artillery soon," Hermsdorf assured them. Almost in response to the introduction, one fifty-fives splashed a hell glow in the jungle before them. The pillbox tried to jump out of the ground amidst the great explosions. The men braced themselves against the walls of the fort, as if it were a ship in a typhoon. It had withstood mortar fire easily, but could it hold up under this?

"It'll hold," Hawk replied to their unspoken fears.

After all, no one would know the difference, if he were proven wrong.

American rockets with tails of black smoke slashed low overhead. The Japanese response to the barrage began falling even closer to home. A curtain of mouse-colored smoke blocked the view from the only viewport, as 50 mm mortar fire ringed the structure. Both sides had decided that the area around the pillbox would be an excellent target to shell.

"Jap knee mortars," Hawk commented. The 50 mms were light and easy to carry. The enemy had a lot of them. Hawk could hear an occasional grenade outside, which was of greater concern. A grenade came out of a hand, and the hands had to be pretty damned close by. The Japanese grenades were not as powerful as the American equivalent, but they could still kill you; especially if one came bouncing in here.

Joe Canlon solemnly watched Hawk's face. The man looked unperturbed by any of this. Incredible as it seemed, if anything, he was enjoying it. He was calculating, playing a game, sifting details in his head. Joe knew that Hawk would not simply sit here for long, however. He was *always* up to something.

"Move one of them sandbags so we can see out the back," Hawk ordered. The man who complied with the order, a fellow always willing to do his part, was killed instantly by shrapnel gushing through the opening he had created. Joe cringed from the blast.

That was the kind of shit Hawk was good for, getting you killed, Joe thought. Hawk stepped over the victim and peered out the back hatchway, that had only a dozen sandbags for a door. Blood spread in several puddles on the irregular floor. Hawk could hear the

Japanese barking orders nearby. Smoke swirled outside and tumbled its way into the tight enclosure. A shadow moved through the smoke.

Hawk poked the muzzle of the Thompson outside. He could clearly see two legs moving through the fog. He lifted the butt of the machine pistol against his shoulder and squeezed off a burst into the area above the two legs. The legs snapped back, followed by a grunt as the body hit the ground.

* * *

THE BARs, defending the front viewport, rattled on maximum fire. They filled the chamber with claustrophobic noise. The ears of the men numbed first, to be followed by the numbing of the rest of their nervous systems. Shell casings rolled underfoot. Joe stood near the center of the room, between the frantic chatter of the automatic rifles and the louder hammering of Hawk's Thompson. The deadly jack hammers kept the enemy at bay. Joe thought that he saw Hawk flinch once, with an almost human expression crossing his features, as he faced the enemy outside.

Hawk thrust his face into the blowing smoke. There they were—the tanks! Oversized shadows. Two of them, three of them. They roared by like race cars, ignoring the pillbox, and evidently heading madly toward the beach defenses. He suspected that at least one of them would take the opportunity to stop in front of the bunker and eviscerate the viewport with a point-blank blast from its 37 mm cannon. That's how the Marines would do it. These were cheap looking little tin cans, compared to the stalwart American tanks. They were maybe eight tons at most, with one machine gun right under the short thin cannon barrel. That was all it would take, however, to level Hawk's remaining portion of the Marine Corps.

Breaux could hear the armored vehicles from the other side of the bunker. "Are they stopping?" He shouted anxiously at Hawk. He was the one standing in the viewport, where the blast would enter.

"No. Not so far."

The tanks produced two sounds meshing into one terrifying roar: the groan of the straining engines and the clanking of the bogie wheels. The machines were painted in bright green and brown swirls, making them look like some hideous reptile. The infantry closely followed their armor, bent over their rifles and trying to peer through the smoke.

Hawk picked out a target from his post at the rear door of the pillbox. He coughed and blinked, before finally firing into the smoke and dust, unable to tell whether the man had been hit or not. He succeeded in provoking an overwhelming response, however, as return fire split asunder the sandbags that had been sheltering him. The yellow grains spilled into the red blood on the floor. Hawk struggled to replace the first sandbag that had been removed, as he straddled the dead man still lying there.

The fury of the American artillery increased. Naval guns thundered from far out at sea, leaving random craters where forest had been. The tanks pressed on, dodging and weaving among the irregularly placed holes in their paths. The infantry was not as resilient, having little protection from the ubiquitous shrapnel. Wounded enemy soldiers dragged themselves into the still hot shell holes for cover, finding that sometimes lightning does strike in the same place twice. Joe could barely see the outside over Hawk's shoulder. As Joe watched the last tank pass by, it took a direct hit. Joe imagined that he saw the heavy plug of steel fall out of the sky onto the vehicle. It disappeared into a ball of red-orange streamers, the three crewmen obliterated. The smell of burning oil and diesel smothered the Marines' close quarters.

"Got one," said Joe without any exuberance. He was just observing the facts of this madness. He had no thoughts or feelings. Joe was just here, instead of being somewhere else. Hermsdorf stepped up and passed him to get to the viewport. His helmet bounced off the ceiling.

"Look at all the dead," exclaimed Hermsdorf. Dozens of limp and shredded grey-green uniforms were strewn about the stumps that had been a forest. Three more tanks, huddling together like paranoid ducklings, hurtled by. They drove their rending treads indiscriminately over the dead and wounded. The tanks did not exhibit any interest as to pausing in this corner of hell to inspect the smoldering pillbox.

"We should get those tanks," said Lieutenant Morgan. "They won't be expecting something like that at the beach." He was an experienced platoon leader of twenty-three. Several men looked at him as if he had lost his mind. Others nodded in agreement. "Get your grenades in a pile. We can stop some of those things," he insisted. The men began tossing the bombs into the center of the room. Joe gladly dropped his. He didn't ask why, but there was always the chance of not having to pick them up again. Hermsdorf was quiet through all of this.

It was left to Hawk to challenge the plan. "The colonel said to get that pilot, sir." He edged toward the middle of the room. "He told me to head for the interior if there was any way of getting behind this force. I think we could slip out the back. Engaging tanks might...end up tying us down some, sir."

The men quietly observed the dispute. It was always entertaining to watch superiors make ordinary fools of themselves. Attacking tanks with grenades did not sound promising. On the other hand, anything Hawk had in mind was likely worse. Morgan studied the floor. He had not expected resistance from the sergeant. He trusted Hawk's judgment, but he still preferred his own idea. Hermsdorf had been pretending not to hear any of the discussion. The attention fell on him, however, as both Hawk and Morgan faced him. They were both willing to take a chance on Hermsdorf's choice of the alternatives, which meant neither was very appealing.

"We will proceed toward the interior until further instructions. Communications are down. We have a good opportunity here to slip behind the Japanese. That is reportedly our last word from the Colonel." The captain's order came out well, sounding intelligent and authoritative. Hawk nodded. Lieutenant Morgan shrugged.

Morgan didn't like it. He thought they were likely to run into more and worse resistance. Dealing with the tanks would buy them time until communications could be restored. Hawk saw it differently, he figured that the storm had passed, and that the enemy had few reserves.

They faced nothing but wild country by heading to the interior. If this pilot existed, they might even find him. Hawk's assessment would later prove correct, but at the time, it seemed a dangerous supposition. The men picked up their grenades. Joe turned up one short.

"Scout the outside," Hermsdorf told Hawk. "I agree with you, Sergeant Hawk. Dreisen wants the pilot, and that's our priority. We had to take the pressure here, and the forces on the beach can take it as well as we can." Hawk nodded solemnly. It was then that Hawk suspected Hermsdorf was aware of Dreisen's conversation with him. Hermsdorf had never shown anything resembling confidentiality with Hawk before. The captain's new attitude wasn't exactly respect, but whatever it was, Hawk would take it.

Hawk thrust his head outside and slid between the sandbags, squirming between them and the top of the door. He heard the tanks chugging in the distance, and wondered how Morgan had expected to catch up with them. Only the dead lay outside on the dusty earth. The fire had passed over their sector. *It looks like hell*, he thought. An animal-like shriek came from overhead and something awkward in shape hit him from behind.

A lone Japanese infantryman dove from the top of the pillbox and slung an arm around Hawk's neck. The sergeant bowed slightly under the added weight. He tossed his head like an angry bull and threw the man to the ground. The soldier carried a long bayonet in one hand. Hawk flipped the machine pistol from his shoulder as the man struggled to get up. He blasted several rounds into the attacker's chest. The flashing steel fire lit him up, making him look transparent, and pinned him to the earth. No one could survive the stopping power of such a close range .45 caliber encounter. The victim lay silent. His burnt and saturated Bousyo blouse sank into the mush of his body. The bayonet was still tightly held in his fist. His eyes were open. A round ceramic hand grenade rolled out of his other fist.

Hawk backed away quickly, glancing at the roof of the bunker as he did. Holding the pistol grip of the Thompson in one hand, he backed even farther away. He saw no spewing fuse. He walked back to the corpse and nudged the grenade with his boot. Its rubber cap was in place. Glancing around once more, he stooped and picked up the bomb. He didn't like dealing with the cheap unpredictable things. He tossed it as far as he could. It landed on solid stone with an audible crack, refusing all the while to explode. Checking the roof yet again, he turned until his eyes focused on the distant hills.

"What's going on? Is it all clear out there?" Lieutenant Morgan called from inside.

"No, sir. Don't look like it. Send out two men," Hawk answered.

* * *

TAMATSU TANAGUCHI HAD BEEN OFFICIALLY, but not properly, trained as a paratrooper. In fact, his only preparatory jump had been inside an airplane hangar. His only preparatory landing had been from the back of a speeding truck. Such was paratrooper training in the latter stages of World War II for Tanaguchi. No youngster, he was an experienced combat infantryman, having started his career in the Japanese invasions of China in the 1930s. He found having a parachute strapped to his back a discomforting experience. The Flying Boat bucked as it hit an air pocket. It took a great deal to frighten Taniguchi, but the Imperial Army had finally succeeded. As he awaited his first real jump, the noise and turbulence augmented his fear. With both feet on the ground, he would face any odds. Some men love the air, some the sea, and Tanaguchi now knew that he loved the earth.

The Japanese needed the wily Tanaguchi on Cokoni, and unfortunately, it would take a parachute to get him there. Tanaguchi was the man, or the force, that would be able to get Isamu Zanji to the American infested coast. He would be able to evade the pervasive American patrols. No one questioned that. Though the beaches were held by great numbers of the fanatical American Marines, Tanaguchi could operate in Cokoni's jungle interior forever, or at least until some of the enemy's interest in the pilot waned. Then he could get the ace into a position for an air or submarine rescue.

Isamu Zanji was a national hero, one of the few that the military allowed to the public. The Imperial hierarchy preferred their warriors to be anonymous. At this stage of the war, the failing Japanese morale needed to see Zanji live to fight another day. The newspapers referred to him as The Firebolt. The newly manufactured type of plane that he flew was known as Violet Lightning. The crafty pilot flew this machine as if he had flown it all his life, instead of a few short weeks. All of the bugs had not been worked out of the new plane, and mastering it was no task for a merely average pilot. The plane had yet to live up to Zanji's level of proficiency. That was how he had been forced down on

Cokoni. Machines were fallible, but luckily, Zanji was not. He was alive, but in a place where he could not have been any more useless.

Tanaguchi lit a cigarette. He took the public's adulation of pilots with a grain of salt. He saved most of his respect for the ground troops. The flight today, however, gave him a new appreciation for the nerve it took to fly in the American dominated skies of the lonely and endless Pacific.

It was well established that Tanaguchi was mature, wise, and had an unblemished reputation regarding jungle operations behind enemy lines. The men who served with him, worshipped him, and in return, he kept them alive. It had taken more than his sterling reputation to get Tanaguchi into this affair, however. He had not been sought after in the beginning. He had volunteered for this operation, and when he did, his services were snapped up. The reason that he volunteered for such duty was far from a wholesome one. The reason was Sergeant James Hawk.

Taniguchi was not a degenerate military hack, such as his counterpart, Sergeant Hawk, whose presence guaranteed a successful mission, but with little consideration for caution or cost.

Through a friend in intelligence, Taniguchi had learned the unit to which Sergeant Hawk was assigned. That same unit had invaded the islands of Rechnung and Verhangen several months earlier. Tanaguchi discovered that this same unit had been shipped to Cokoni, although it was well overdue for restaging elsewhere. The Japanese sergeant had taken a safe instructor's assignment in Japan, until through some quirk he might hear where the Marine unit would surface again.

Tanaguchi felt that he had an appointment with that battered regiment. He was not a vengeful man, and he seldom held a grudge. He was stoic and tolerant. But everyone has their limits. Sergeant Hawk had killed his dearest friend, Major Keizo, on the island of Verhangen. Keizo had been a gentle soul, having no business in the soldier's trade. Keizo had been unarmed, and in the process of offering a trapped group of Marines surrender terms, when he was mercilessly shot down by Sergeant Hawk. Kindness had killed Taniguchi's friend, and kindness was something that Sergeant Hawk would never benefit from again. Taniguchi did not know Hawk's name, but he knew his face, his rank, and his regiment. And now he knew where this torn and dwindling regiment was. If Hawk was still alive, Tanaguchi would find him. He knew this would happen. He may have even been right, because the two had already crossed paths before. Their chair-bound superiors seemed to find the sort of situations where the paths of the two men were forced to intersect.

Taniguchi heard the order to jump being given. He remembered looking at the treetops and grassy hills. But later, he would not remember the cold thin air. All he knew was that he was on the ground again, and even if it was the remote Cokoni, it was solid ground. He was on the ground with a mission from the highest Japanese command, one that just might coincide with the greatest mission of his own heart. Tanaguchi had never failed in a mission.

3

THE LOST MONASTERY

The next morning found the Marine patrol leaving its position near the enemy pillbox, and slowly penetrating the unfamiliar jungle. The trees grew densely together and heavy vines connected them. Ferns and thorns made the earth between the trees impassable. The men stuck to the main road leading away from the shoreline. Japanese tank treads had squeezed ripples of mud out of the soft earth. Every man there was thinking that one of the clanking dragons might appear beyond the next bend in the tortuous road.

Captain Hermsdorf preferred the road. Hawk didn't like it, but he made no other suggestions. The radio had worked for a while, but it looked like it might have retired from its military career for now. An occasional squawk raised hopes, hopes that were dashed once a transmission was planned.

Captain Hermsdorf thought of home. He had a baby son that he had never seen. He had a father-in-law with a nice job waiting for him. He knew joining the Marine Corps was a mistake. He was not the first man to make that discovery. It was kind of a running joke from the minute a recruit got off the bus at boot camp. Hermsdorf did not fully realize just how big a mistake it was until he was sent overseas. Now it was too late. Here he was, with men like James Hawk, in what could loosely be called a place, like Cokoni. It frightened Hermsdorf to be away from the United States. As he traveled over the ocean, it had not bothered him much aboard ship. A large part of America was traveling with him. Then his regiment was sent here. The size of his America was shrinking. Today his America was no larger than this patrol. It was a fragile America, compared to the might of the jungle and the fury of the Japanese surrounding it. This America was different. He was beginning to feel the terror of man alone.

Hawk slunk leisurely along, aware of the danger, but not especially cautious. His feelings were nothing like those of Hermsdorf. Hawk really *was* man alone. He was the hobo living under the train trestle. He was the man who came out of the dark, on a stormy night, and showed you how to pull your car out of the ditch. He was the guy passing by, who helped you after a hurricane, and then disappeared—somewhere. But no one helped him; and he had no expectations that anyone ever would. Rejection was about all he expected, not that he cared, or would even have noticed.

Hawk studied the lazy green umbrellas created by the trees above him. Hot white light played along the dark leaves. The earth smelled sour. Very little would have surprised him at this point. Tanks, snipers, mines; anything was possible on a detail like this. A division of the enemy could come rolling out of the forest unannounced. Those on the front line lived with action coming at them from out of nowhere. Most of the sensitive men had been eliminated from the rifle companies, one way or another. Those that were left accepted this unpleasantness, as easily as they accepted one another. And their bond was strong. On the surface, things didn't seem to bother them much. That was their persona. Rough and bitter jokes, and silence.

Hawk was unaware that the enemy had few troops on Cokoni. Like the blind men inspecting the elephant, that had not been his observation. It felt to him as if they had unlimited resources. Of course, he was the man facing those resources. Other troops, stationed on the beach, would remember all of this as a cakewalk. The vastness of World War II inevitably guaranteed that some participants would remember the experience as great sport and adventure. James Hawk was not one of those. He had other kinds of memories, they came at night mostly, and they were not fond.

Hermsdorf stopped the patrol. He sat on a leg and opened out a map. Hawk struck a match and held it to the tip of a long thin cigar. Joe Canlon stopped beside him.

"What are you doing? The Japs could smell that thing in Tokyo." Joe had a hoarse, boxer's voice. He may have had a throat injury as a child.

Hawk threw the match to the ground and smiled without baring his teeth. "Hope so." Hawk was amused by Joe's nervousness. He felt sure that this spot was safe enough. Other men began to smoke. Sometimes Hawk got on Joe's nerves. They had been together a long time, but they still had differences of opinion on the line between caution and recklessness.

"Platoon leaders!" Hermsdorf called out. Morgan

was actually the only man there who bore the official title of platoon leader. They were only remnants of platoons in this remnant of a company. The acting leaders, Hawk, Sergeant Kreski, and Second Lieutenant Repler, joined Hermsdorf and Morgan.

"There's a shrine or something up there," said Hermsdorf. "The colonel told me that a platoon-sized detachment of Japs was seen there three days ago. We better go up and check it out. It should be cleared, but we'll have to make sure. I'll stay here with the BAR men and guard our rear."

You'll guard your rear, all right, they all thought. The captain was reserving a lot of firepower to himself. Morgan, Repler and Kreski said, "Aye, sir," in unison. The one missing voice went unnoticed.

The road to the shrine was straight from this point forward. The establishment should come into view soon. Morgan put 18-year-old Jesse Ruiz at the point. After five minutes of uneventful walking, Ruiz stepped on a mine, within full view of the others behind him. In time, it was a flash, like lightning, or a photograph being taken. Repler and Morgan had just been consuming much more time, discussing the good judgment of choosing to go into the interior, for no resistance had been encountered. The deadly mine could be categorized as resistance. It blew the point man several feet into the air, launching him like so much weighted and sparking fireworks, and nearly cutting him in two. A little smoke lingered.

"Mortars!" Morgan shouted, and waved the men to either side of the road. The distance had obscured most of the details of what had happened. Hawk had not seen it well, but he recognized the sound of the mine. Joe Canlon knew this as well.

"Shouldn't have been on the goddam road," Hawk grumbled to Canlon. He proceeded forward to see if the kid was still alive. There was a gray, swirling crater, and no, he was not alive. Shockingly vivid body parts lay in a random pattern emanating from the center of the blast. Hawk did not like this. He thought of how he should have said something five minutes earlier. *We'll have to gather this up*, he thought angrily. He looked up and saw why Ruiz may have been distracted.

The trail ahead of the crater dropped off a steep hill and down below he could see a gleaming white temple dome. He saw people in colorful robes moving around the compound. The noise left several of them craning their necks toward the road. Hawk turned around and walked back. He felt the eyes of everyone on him, and self-consciously studied the woods on either side of the road, as he slouched back to the men.

"Some kind of monastery thing is up there, sir," he called out before getting very close.

"Where is the enemy, where did that come from?" Lieutenant Morgan called back.

"That was a mine, sir. I guess we better check out the rest of the road, if we're going to be using it. No sense in anybody else stepping on something." Hawk spat distractedly, glancing down at Morgan crouching in the weeds at the side of the road.

The lieutenant stood. "Okay," he said, a little breathlessly. "Ruiz is dead?"

"Yessir. He is dead."

Two men gathered up the remains. Sergeant Kreski and a man named Holley, who had a little experience with mine sweeping, inspected the road, while the others took a break. Hermsdorf appeared from the rear, and the entire patrol moved forward to within sight of the temple. Hawk studied the graceful shrine. If the Japanese had been there, they did not appear to be there now. Of course, appearances could be deceiving.

"Platoon leaders!" Hermsdorf shouted.

"What's this 'platoon leaders' shit?" Canlon asked as Hawk walked toward the captain. "Are you a general now?"

"I think we're playing like we got a company here."

Joe laughed a little. He did not know Ruiz well. That was always good, as it made it easier to get over things. Men in direct contact with the enemy have to "get over" things rather efficiently, in the best ways they can. Joe's laugh was like the braying of a jackass. The peculiar noise caused the captain to look over at him, which immediately silenced it.

Hermsdorf ordered them to surround the temple. Hawk was a little concerned about more mines, but an hour later they had searched the area without finding anything but tracks. The Japanese troops had recently departed, and had not made use of the road. The captain instructed young Lieutenant Morgan and five men to go into the temple proper, and scout it out. Hawk, Kreski, Canlon, Sprack, and Holley won the honors.

"Kind of heavy on you executive officers, ain't we?" Joe commented. Hawk snorted. "We're risking all of our 'platoon leaders'."

"Yeah," Hawk answered. "If only my congressman knew he sent me to West Point for this."

The fields in front of the temple were well tended.

The road ran between two divisions of farmland. Thin men with shaved heads wore robes tied up between their legs. They stood silently straddling furrows of crops and watching the advance of the dirty visitors. The tilled earth smelled fresh.

On general principle, Hawk pushed the safety on his Thompson forward. These guys might look like little old ladies, but little old ladies had trigger fingers, too. He walked next to Morgan, who was taller than the rest. Morgan seemed to be made ill at ease by the sight of this place, which was not entirely unreasonable. It was weird. Canlon took up the rear. Hawk eyed the upper stories of the temple suspiciously. The main structure in the middle was high, three and a half or four stories tall, topped by a rather beautiful and perfect dome of white stone. The decorations on the outside of the building were simple, but one could see the hand of a master artisan in the flowing lines. Two wings branched out from each side of the main building, consisting of numerous columns topped by a flat roof. It had a solid look. Bullet stopping solid.

Hawk wondered why the Japanese had not destroyed this. *They like to do shit like that,* he thought. There may have been a reason, and it may not have been architectural appreciation.

An older monk, evidently a superior of some sort, flowed rapidly down the sparkling steps of the central building. He walked toward the approaching Marines. Hawk noticed that both of the man's hands were visible and empty. Still, the sergeant eyed the concealing apertures that rose above and behind him. Morgan seemed frozen.

"He's gonna strike up a conversation, sir," Hawk told

the lieutenant. "You probably ought to get the men off this road, and check the inside of that joint, pronto. I'll stay out here and shoot the shit with him, if you like."

Lieutenant Morgan nodded quietly to all of this. He had no desire to interact with any locals. Looking more confident now, he motioned the men forward, ignoring the monk as if he were some figment of their imaginations. Hawk stepped toward the monk, to let him know that Hawk would be the person engaging him.

"How do you do, sir? I'm Sergeant James Hawk, United Stated Marine Corps." Hawk had a habit when engaged in formal conversation, of cocking his shoulders in the direction of the person with whom he was interacting, as if he might punch them in the face.

"I am Hai-lon. I am so pleased to know you, honorable Hawk." The monk smiled pleasantly. His teeth were perfectly intact, although he was past his prime. His voice was soft and thick. Hawk could tell by the voice alone that the man was intelligent and gentle. Neither quality meant much to Hawk. *At least the crazy little bastard speaks English*, he thought.

"Yessir. Glad to meet you." Hawk's Mississippi courteousness briefly returned to the surface. He thought quickly of offering his hand, but then thought better of it. He was still unclear on whether these folks were Japanese or mere islanders. His contact with Koichi had not informed him to any great extent on this point. As a general rule, Hawk didn't like civilians at all. He liked knowing that everyone in front of his gun muzzle was a target, and that everyone behind it was on his team. "Been any Japs around here, sir? Uh...Jap soldiers?" Hawk was not smiling. He seldom did. The mere sight of his piercing eyes, hostile posture, and angular muscles frightened most civilized people. The monk showed no alarm.

"A lie is a thing that is just as wrong as a theft, is it not? It robs us of truth, the teller most of all. It would be wrong to lie to you, and most foolish, because you know that they have been here." The monk smiled. "Thirty holy men cannot eat two barrels of rice."

"Yeah, see what you mean," Hawk replied. He had smelled the rice from the road. The enemy had been there recently. "Did they have a pilot with them? A flier?" Hawk got right to the point. He seldom relied on craftiness.

"Oh, yes. A very fine, quiet gentleman of some esteem. Again, a lie is a thing that only harms the soul of the liar. Yes, this great man was here. There were many tales of his adventures in the air."

"Yeah? Sure enough?" Hawk answered in his thick delta accent. "Which way did this esteemed gentleman go?"

"That I may not tell you, for that could result in death. Perhaps even, your own death, you understand? I will not lie, but I will not kill with words. Words are dangerous weapons in the mouth of the imprudent man. It is better that I say no more of it."

Hawk scanned the trees bordering the fields of the self-described holy men. He saw several worn trails disappearing into the dark forest.

"Yes, many roads lead from here," said the monk, watching the cold, killer eyes of the American. He felt certain that this man was capable of just about any atrocity. "All roads on Cokoni lead here and to the relic of Hai-tai. Eight roads you will see, and this the hub of the wheel. Surely, young seeker, you have a map?"

"Uh...yessir. Well, no, I ain't got one on me. You say these Japs are gone now though, right?"

"You are in no danger. They are gone. I assure you, you will be safe here. And you will be our guests."

For some reason, maybe it was the tone of his voice, Hawk believed the monk. He looked at the trees again. Men can be honest, and they can still be wrong. The son of a bitches could be lying out there in the weeds.

"What you got here?" Hawk asked. "A Buddhist deal?" He looked down, avoiding the searching black eyes of the other.

"No. Not precisely. We follow the teachings of Hai-tai, the great holy man of the early Ch'ing dynasty. We trust in the words of Buddha, Confucius, Taoism, and yes, in your own Christ. We are gentle people who believe in goodness."

"Oh. Well, I'll be goddam." Hawk bit off a plug of chewing tobacco. "What I was driving at though, is...are y'all Japs or what? See, far as I can tell, Japs are all over the map on this religion thing."

"By ancestry, perhaps. But we do not abide by the Japanese tolerance of Shintoism with Buddhism. The Shinto reverence for deities involves nature, ancestors, and living souls, such as the Emperor, which is too militaristic and warlike for us."

Hawk spat and nodded, inspecting his boots for a moment. "Like Quakers or something?" They stared at one another. Did the word mean anything to the monk?

"For a comparison, yes," the holy man finally answered.

Hawk allowed himself a grim smile. A harmless old coot. Obviously, full of shit. Morgan returned, his clothes saturated with sweat. The monk looked cool in his thin robe.

"There's about a dozen trails out of here," said Morgan.

"Eight," said the old man. The lieutenant glanced at him, as if he were a roach, and turned back to Hawk.

"It looks like they went down every trail. They split up and went down every trail, to throw us off. It looks like four or five of them went on each pathway." Morgan's eyes looked over the heads of the other two.

"That is true," the monk interjected. Morgan focused on the old man with distaste once again. He turned back to Hawk.

"What's this here *swami* got to say?"

"He says the Jap flier was here. I reckon that's why they split up, so we don't know who he is with. The old shell game." Hawk winked at the monk. Hai-lon smiled and bowed. He didn't know about military rankings. Judging by the gravitas of the two men, he assumed that Hawk was in charge.

Lieutenant Morgan took off his heavy helmet, with the bar clearly marked on it. "Wonderful. Now what? We split up, too, so they can pick us off?"

Hawk shrugged. "It's up to the captain." He did not add: let him make the mistake.

Hermsdorf arrived after receiving the "all clear" signal. Morgan and his five men were eating rice on the temple steps. Several smiling monks were gathered around them.

Something about this rubbed Hermsdorf the wrong way. The captain pushed the monks out of the way and stalked up the temple steps. The holy men looked puzzled. Until now, the Americans had been rather friendly.

"What the hell is this, a Fourth of July picnic?" Hermsdorf stopped in front of Hawk. It looked like any respect he might have held for the sergeant had just been spent. Morgan was left out of the encounter. Hawk calmly relayed what they had discovered.

"Isn't that just perfect," the captain roared. "He won't tell you where they went? And that's supposed to be the end of that, right? Tough shit, American dog?" Hermsdorf looked furiously around at the robed figures. They were no longer smiling. "Which one is the head of this stupid shit?" he demanded.

Hawk looked intently into his rice bowl. Hai-lon stepped forward. "There is no need for anger. I guide these humble travelers, and we are all your servants."

"Don't give me that whiny Jap shit, you son of a bitch! Where is Isamu Zanji? Which way did they go?"

"I am sorry. I have explained why I cannot tell you these things." Hai-lon raised his eyebrows apologetically. The captain's outburst surprised him. He thought this matter had been settled.

Without warning, Hermsdorf struck the monk forcefully across the brow with his open hand. The fragile old man sat down heavily on a step. A couple of the Marines could not stifle a laugh at the ungainly fall.

"Now, I have explained why you *will* tell me these things," said the captain. He was tense. He wanted to get this over with and get out of this deadly jungle and into a desk job in New Zealand. He wanted to see his son. "Where did they go?"

Hawk continued eating. Morgan set his half full bowl down on a step and walked away. Hermsdorf kicked Hai-lon. The other monks squatted down in unison with pained expressions. They rested on their heels and bowed their heads. Hawk shook his head.

"You catch more flies with honey than you do with vinegar, Captain." Hawk said. Hermsdorf turned his wrath on the American. Tension blossomed into rage.

"Is that your home spun wisdom or some Jap proverb, Sergeant?"

"Just a fact, sir," Hawk replied very quietly.

"You're a real smart ass, aren't you, Hawk. That's why you're sitting here while the pilot is probably catching a boat home." Hawk had a short, violent temper. Most of the men knew this. He set his bowl down and stood up. That was all he would eat that day. He walked down the steps and stood before the tall, wide, and thick captain. Hawk had no stomach, no hips and was not quite as tall as the officer. His veined arms, however, were almost as thick as the captain's. They were knotted with hard muscle. And his shoulders were wide.

"The old fella don't mean no harm, sir. He's got this religion thing to stick to." Hawk's clear blue eyes were hooded by dark brows and his downturned mouth said more than the mere words conveyed. Hermsdorf turned his back on Hawk. It looked like he might walk away. Then he kicked the monk again with his huge boot. This time the man cried out. The sound indicated that the blow must have hurt fiercely. One of the Marines, using a cartoon character voice, called out from the back, "Chicken shi-i-i-i-t."

Hawk rubbed his nose, walked around Hermsdorf, and with one hand, pulled Hai-lon to his feet. The monk could hardly manage to stand. "Excuse me, Captain. Let me give you hand there, old timer."

"Get the hell out of the way!"

"Out of the way of what, sir?"

"Out of *my* way!"

"I ain't in your way, sir. Where are you going?"

Hermsdorf doubled his fist and took a step forward. Hawk stood there. Hermsdorf stopped. He knew Hawk was from the dregs of society, with nothing to lose. What did a career or family, or even life itself mean to scum like that? The crazy bastard might hit him back. "You're in trouble, Hawk," he said, pointing a finger into the sergeant's face.

"Yessir." Hawk knew that much long ago. It was probably about the same time as Pearl Harbor.

Hermsdorf spun around to face the others. "All right!" he bellowed, in a tone that must have been fearsome on his old college gridiron. "We're going over every damned one of those trails until we find the right one. In case you have forgotten it, we have a mission here, and it does not involve holding hands with a bunch of lily-livered Japs. Lieutenant Morgan, I want two men to search each trail. Make the assignments. Sergeant, you are under arrest. You will remain here, and Lieutenant Morgan will serve as your guard. The rest of you, get ready to move out." He decided not to stop there. He paced up and down. He then gave a short speech on discipline, laced with obscenities. He didn't sound familiar with the obscenities and the whole tirade came off as ridiculous. The men traded covert and mocking smiles.

With the trace of a smile of his own, Morgan held a rifle on Hawk until the others had left, and the captain was no longer observing. Then he sat down beside him. "You shouldn't have done that," said the lieutenant.

"Probably not."

"I mean, I didn't like any of it, either, but he's the captain. I wouldn't spend one minute in the brig for some flimflamming Jap."

"Don't worry, sir. I won't."

* * *

Two of Hermsdorf's most reliable men spent the rest of the day sitting on the temple's steps. Hermsdorf participated in the search for the pilot himself. He came back that night with nothing to report. The job was too big for the number of men left to him. It was infuriating. Zanji had been that close, and he could not lay a hand on him. Hawk felt confident that the captain would have him back pounding the trail with the others the next day. But he didn't. Hawk remained under arrest. Lieutenant Morgan's services, however, were needed elsewhere. His guard duty was over. Hawk was left alone at the temple. If he were a flight risk, it evidently didn't matter much to anyone. All of this was fine with Hawk, except no one bothered to feed him. The monks kept their distance now. Their leader lay injured in his room as the result of the beating. Hawk followed the shade, moving from one tree to the next on the outskirts of the grounds, napping throughout the day. Occasionally, the thought crossed his mind that the next soldier to stumble out of the thick jungle might not be an American.

The patrols returned at dusk and Joe Canlon sat down beside Hawk, under a tree at the edge of a plowed field. Joe began talking of his tormentor of the last several hours, the captain.

"The guy's wacky. Real get up and go type shit. But he don't know what he's doing. We're just farting against the wind. What the hell did you do all day?"

"Not a goddam thing. I sat on them rock steps over there until I think I got the piles. So, now I'm sitting here."

Joe pulled a piece of well burnt meat out of his pocket. He handed it to Hawk.

"What the hell is that?"

"I don't know," said Joe. "Some squirrel-looking thing. They're thick as shit out there. I cooked it. Me and old crazy-ass Baker just went down our trail and sacked out."

"You need yourself a new buddy. That fella ain't got all his thinking gear strapped down. He'll be the next one getting popped off."

Joe took out some more of the unappetizing matter and began chewing on it. Hawk decided to follow suit. "So, the Captain gets us together and says, we got to go north, we *got* to go north. That's the closest to the ocean. This pilot guy went north, for sure, he says. Gotta go north. Then he marches us all off to the east."

Hawk laughed. Joe laughed. "I seen the bolt on his rifle, it's like corroded green. Bet he don't wipe his ass," Joe laughed some more. Hawk chewed contentedly on the morsel given him, vaguely wondering if perhaps it might be a rat. It had a taste that sort of lingered up behind his nose.

"We ain't gonna find nothing this way," said Joe. "I got to thinking. Say, you find the bunch that has the pilot with them. That's probably gonna be a bad bunch."

"Yeah," Hawk agreed. "They'll have issued all the automatic weapons and grenades to them fellas."

"And they'll be the bad asses. But, it don't matter. We ain't gonna find nothing with this captain guy anyways."

"Nah." Hawk unsnapped Joe's canteen and took a long drink. "It's all horse shit." He closed the canteen with a frown. "Was this a goddam rat?"

"I don't know. He wouldn't say. Anyway, would you believe a rat?"

The next morning, Hermsdorf assembled the men. "Sergeant Kreski has located a farmhouse," the captain announced. "We are *all* going on the central trail this morning. We might pick up some tracks there. The Japs could be at the place. Be ready for contact. All right, get moving."

Hawk lay stretched against the wall of the temple. He studied the shining little specks in the stone of the wall. He locked his fingers behind his head and watched the others prepare to leave. Joe looked over at him with an envious expression. Hermsdorf caught Hawk looking back at Joe, while raising his fist in mock encouragement.

"Get off your ass, Hawk," the captain barked. "You're not going to sit there all day like a king while we walk our butts off."

Showing no surprise, or interest, Hawk stood and dropped his helmet onto his head. He walked over and recovered his Thompson from Kreski, who had been carrying it in Hawk's absence. Joe handed Hawk a canteen.

"He wasn't shitting you about walking your butt off," Joe said. "I got a chapped ass."

Hawk hooked the canteen onto his belt. It was three

quarters full, and sloshed loud enough to be heard for several yards. He didn't care. He did not expect to get within several yards of any interested ears.

"Well, chapped ass, or piles," he sighed, "it's all just a pain in the ass."

"Yeah, but this time he's talking about shooting, too," Joe said. "That's a pain in the ass that you wouldn't have to worry about here."

Hawk shrugged. You could get shot anywhere.

An hour down the trail, Hawk realized the enormity of the task and the reasons for Canlon's pessimism. A man could get tired of this pretty quick, and Joe had been at it for a while. Scores of tributary paths branched off the central trail and into the sweating recesses of the jungle. Some looked like little more than animal runs, or places where water had once drained and created inches deep ditches. Though only eight trails left the shrine, dozens riddled the humid forest. Anything could be lurking and thriving out there. Hermsdorf stuck to the central trail, which resembled an old logging road. The earth was lined with wagon tracks that had been put there when the earth was soft, and had now hardened.

Any sign of the Japanese that Hawk had expected to see had been erased by the passage of the Marines over the main route. Zanji had escaped. This was one of those tasks common to the military. You had to look within yourself and find a reason to explain why it mattered.

Before noon of that day, they came to a clearing. A thatched hut with a nipa leaf roof leaned wearily on the far side of the clearing. Kreski said that it was clear. He gave the thumbs up signal, and the patrol crossed over to him. An old woman sat in the door of the hut chewing the red nut of the betel palm. The door leaned like the rest of the hovel, and the old woman. The whole picture seemed like the top half of a parallelogram. On the woman's lap sat a beautiful white dog. Her arms were wrapped around it, and wisps of its long hair rested on her gnarled and blackened arms. The eyes of the dog were large and brown, with a very human appearance. The creature looked quizzically at the alien visitors, without raising a protest at their invasion of its turf. Its face seemed more alive and animated than that of the old woman. Something about the scene made Lieutenant Morgan feel strange. The dog looked like a white genii in some surrealistic painting. Morgan nervously looked into the hut. When he looked back out, the dog was staring at him. Like a person. Like someone he had known—or, would know. It was odd. Was it *déjà vu*?

"You speak English?" the impatient Hermsdorf asked the old woman. She looked at him without answering. Flies buzzed in the heat. The place stunk. It looked like a miserable place to spend your life, or the next five minutes, for that matter. Hawk studied the surrounding forest, patiently waiting for this to end.

Morgan alleged that he had studied and understood some Japanese. He had never tried speaking it. He uttered some strange sounds that sounded like he was speaking English backwards. The woman looked at him without any light of recognition on her face. Of course, maybe she didn't speak Japanese, or whatever Morgan was speaking. Hawk was amused by her expression and stepped forward to pet the dog. The woman shrank back, the dog remained still and allowed itself to be petted. The woman was likely one of the more primitive islanders, who spoke only Cokonian.

Hermsdorf looked around. He sighed with restrained rage. "You see," he pointed to his eyes, "many men, soldiers," he pointed to his own men. The pantomime went on for a while. The Marines restrained laughs as the woman stared blankly at this recreation of some frontiersman movie. If it does nothing else, the Marine Corps can train one on how not to laugh.

Hermsdorf walked closer to her. "You like that damned dog, don't you?" The captain was visibly angry. People who don't understand, people who pretend to not understand, and people who won't talk to you even if they do understand, can drive anyone to the brink. Especially if you are already at the brink. The woman had probably used this unresponsive tactic all of her life, and had achieved some success with it. This was the day the success ended.

"I bet you'll get the message a lot quicker if I grab that damned..." The captain reached toward the dog. The animal may have had a better command of English than the woman, for it came to life. It bared its teeth, growled and leapt from her lap. It charged Hermsdorf's feet, barking and snapping at his ankles. The captain danced around fitfully. This was so animated and so sudden, that some of the watchers had to laugh. Hawk, however, was not one of them. He watched solemnly.

Hermsdorf finally leveled his rifle and fired. The dog gasped a couple of times and expired, bright red blood streaming across its shining white coat. There was no laughing now. The woman stood and looked down at her dog, with no discernible change in the mask of her expression. The captain nudged the animal with his rifle muzzle. Maybe he regretted it. As he did this, with some sort of inexplicable interest, the farm woman glided over to him, and with unexpected speed and strength, wrenched the rifle from him. Everyone watched in utter surprise, and yet, no one seemed alarmed.

"What in the hell, you old whore..." Hermsdorf snarled. She pulled the carbine upwards and held the muzzle right where the underside of the captain's jaw met his neck. The shot went out the top of his head. His corpse fell like a tree. Several Marines aimed their weapons at the attacker. Hawk took a step toward her and held out his hand with the fingers outstretched. He knew it was a dangerous, and even a pointless thing to do. Most of what he did, however, was dangerous and pointless.

"Hand it back, lady," he said calmly. Their hard eyes met for a long moment. He reached a little farther and grasped the muzzle behind its three-pronged sight. She let go of her end of the rifle and hung her head. Hawk slung the butt of the rifle forward and let it drop with a clatter on Hermsdorf's body. The woman went back to her doorway and sat down. A tear ran down her tough cheek. Her expression was the same. An unbreakable silence gripped the men, as if something had frozen them in time and they could not get out.

"Well..." Hawk said, upon expelling a deep breath. He turned and saw everyone looking at him. His narrowed eyes looked down the trail, one more tragedy reflecting in their blueness. "I guess we ought to bury the dog."

4

THE OFFICER IN CHARGE

IT WAS ON THIS STRANGE DAY THAT YOUNG LIEUTENANT Morgan took command. The strangeness permeated every aspect of the day, and few spoke of the odd incident. All remained on edge, for no definable reason.

As if waiting only for Hermsdorf to die, the radio came back to life. Colonel Dreisen contacted the patrol. He had been trying to reach them for days. Morgan explained what had been going on, and requested that they be relieved or reinforced, as they had little chance of achieving their purpose under the present conditions. Dreisen had a few things of his own to say, however.

The colonel was not upset with them for taking the initiative, and breaking out for the interior. But it was imperative for Morgan to realize that he was in a perfect position to capture Zanji. Perhaps it was by design, perhaps by chance, but the patrol was in the perfect location. Reconnaissance had yet to turn up any movement outside of the general area of the monastery, where Zanji was last seen with his bodyguards. There was activity nearby: small groups dashing and hiding in the undergrowth. One of these groups was suspected to have the pilot. The only other Japanese on Cokoni were entrenched in force on a hilly area near the southern beach. The pilot's rescuers were likely trying to connect with this force. It was the same force that had overrun Hermsdorf, allowing his sortie into the interior. Lieutenant Morgan continued to be isolated by this larger enemy force. The enemy periodically attacked the beach defenses, likely seeking access to the sea, in order to be prepared, if and when Zanji arrived. This was of no concern to Colonel Dreisen. He was convinced that Zanji would in fact head northward, toward some unoccupied area, and escape without any fanfare or aid.

Morgan watched the monks tilling the fields as Dreisen explained his intelligence sources—who were certain reliable and well known Cokoni residents—for all of the air waves to hear. The colonel suggested that Morgan explore his immediate surroundings, and only if failing to find anything there, to go north and likely intercept the fugitive in the interior. The success of the mission of the entire regiment rested on Morgan. Everyone and everything else were now just a backdrop to his operation.

Morgan tried to process the order. This was a lot of responsibility for one with limited experience. If the northern interior was anything like this, they could search forever without finding anything. There was every indication that the interior was actually even worse. Morgan waited until the next day to tell Hawk about the plan. The lieutenant confided in Hawk more than he did in Second Lieutenant Repler. Repler was close to Morgan's age. They had been friendly enough, but now their relationship had changed. Morgan was in charge. They were not co-commanders, and Morgan wanted no co-commanders. They were still friends, things had just changed. Hawk, the perennial peon, was no threat to authority, and the non-com knew a lot, and had good judgment. Repler also tended somewhat toward the Hermsdorf school of command. He thought beating the information out of Hai-lon was an excellent idea. Morgan himself had considered this option. But it was not his style. And Hawk, no man of peace by any means, had been against taking the torture route. So far.

"He's a nice old guy," Lieutenant Morgan told Hawk the day after Hermsdorf's death. "I think Hai-lon really thinks he is doing us a favor by not telling us anything."

Hawk lit a cigar. "Well. He is kind of a Jap, sir. The only difference between nice people and bastards is that bastards aren't very good actors."

Morgan shook his head. "There's a cheerful outlook." The word "cheerful" sort of fell into the air between them and disintegrated. Nothing about this was cheerful. Morgan continued. "I think the *swami* is really...devout. Why don't you talk to him? You two hit it off, didn't you? He likes you. He might come around. Especially since you stood up for him the other day. You're old shipmates."

"I ain't much of a talker."

"We're not interested in what you are. Do it."

"Aye, aye, sir."

Reluctantly, to say the least, Hawk requested an audience with Hai-lon. The monk was still confined to his bed, but he granted the request. A young holy man led the sergeant into a stone-walled chamber on the second floor, devoid of furniture, save for the spartan bed. The aperture to the hallway had no door on it. The bed was little more than a quilt lying on the floor next to the open window. A low candle burned by the bed, although there was plenty of light without it. Restful shadows followed the monk as he sat up to welcome his visitor. A dark blue sky framed him in the window. For some reason, Hawk thought of Zanji in that wide and empty blue sky out there. The monk smiled.

"Please, come in," said Hai-lon. Hawk walked heavily across the immaculate floor, feeling like an obscenity in the cleanliness of the room. A drawing on thin bamboo strips, that had been sewn together, hung on the wall. It was a portrait of an Asian man with a forked beard.

"How you doing there, sir? Looking good. Did you pour some kerosene on them scratches?" Hawk's long and wild hair pointed in every direction. The bald man marveled for a moment.

"I am well. I have you to thank for my life, I fear. Please forgive me many times for not thanking you earlier. You saved me and you did not resort to violence in the face of violence to do so. I have the greatest respect for a man who uses peace as an active force. Only the strongest of men are able to do this. I also feel great sorrow for the turmoil in the heart of your leader. I fear he has great weaknesses."

"Uh, well, not no more," Hawk looked down. "He's done cashed in his chips. I had to do things the way I did because he's an officer and all. It's kind of hard to explain to outside folks. He had the ax on me. We put up with a lot of sh... stuff, to keep things running smooth."

"He cashed the chips? This means he has left you?"

"Yeah. Permanently. Accident out on the trail. Got his head shot off."

Hai-lon closed his eyes. His shoulders drooped. After a few moments his eyes opened again. "Tell me that this was not at your hand, honorable Hawk."

"Naw, naw. Just some crazy thing. It happens. He got caught off guard, kinda actin' a fool. But what I really wanted to talk to you about, was this here pilot fella." Hawk looked seriously into the old man's eyes and wagged his head for emphasis as he said: "They're all hot to trot about that fella. I think you probably ought to just tell them where he went. This is nasty business, here, for a gentleman such as yourself, sir."

Hai-lon was not prepared to so suddenly abandon the subject of the untimely death of the captain, which seemed like an inconvenient subject to his new friend.

"I would that your leader's soul had left this life out of its turmoil. It is the great tragedy that so many leave this way. It is worse during warfare, when the young leave before they have had time to make intelligent choices. They learn the evil side of life too quickly, and none of the good."

"Oh, uh, you talking about Hermsdorf? He wasn't young, sir. They said he was like twenty-nine. And not so good, either. Fact is, he was kind of a jackass. Ain't no sense even talking about him much. I've seen a lot of good men die, sir. *Good* men." Hawk stressed the "good" part, to differentiate these from Hermsdorf. It still bothered him a little, however, that the colonel had told him to watch over Hermsdorf—an unprecedented request. Now, he was just another name in Hawk's good initiative, bad judgment, scrapbook.

"Of that, I am sure. You believe in the afterlife, of

course. You are a Christian. Do you belong to a sect of Christianity? There are so many with such insignificant differences, it has always interested me, how these came about. This unfortunate leader of yours has now gone to paradise, according to your beliefs?"

"I imagine, he went straight to hell," said Hawk, freely voicing his theological opinion.

"I can relate Christianity to Taoism. Taoism teaches a path to truth. But I fear it became complicated by superstition many years ago. Tell me, young seeker, tell me of the beliefs of your soul, tell me how you seek the truth, and goodness, so that I may understand you."

Hawk flushed with embarrassment and rubbed his nose. "Well, I don't really seek it too much. Now, I might run across it sometimes. I never followed religion real close. I guess I am what you call a Christian. That's kind of the American deal. I got baptized one time. Now, I ain't got no papers or nothing."

"I see, you entered this faith as a child and merely accepted it? You were forced to study it by your culture?"

"Naw. I...uh...didn't do nothing as a child. I was kind of ignorant. Not much studying. Or culture. Now if you want to talk about the Bible, I know a lot of the men that can do that with you...chapter and verse...and all."

"Oh, no. I have read the Bible. I want to know of your beliefs."

"Beliefs, huh?" Hawk asked. The old guy was persistently exploring a shadow land that did not exist. Hawk's beliefs were generally circumscribed by the ten pounds of metal holding the twenty .45 caliber rounds by his side.

"You chose your religion as an adult, you must have had some deep conviction?"

Hawk nodded. "Well, sort of." He remembered a good story for the old man. He might like this. He cleared his throat and rocked forward a bit. "I guess everything about me has something to do with the Marine Corps and the war." Hawk opened his palms out.

Hai-lon smiled and nodded as if this were some deep truth.

"A couple years ago I was in this place called Guadalcanal. Bad place. This was like the first big battle, where we stopped the Japs from winning the war. That's where they started keeping me in the front lines all the time. The front lines, you know, is where the fighting is. And there was plenty of it there. The Catholic chaplains, priests they call 'em, was the only ones that would go to the front lines. I kind of respected that. I got to know one of them pretty good, I would take him around and stuff. And so..." Hawk opened his palms again, "he got one in the chest. It was a rough place," Hawk shrugged. "Those are bad ones, you can't make it, or even last very long. He had asked me before, see, if I wanted to be baptized, and I always told him I figured not, you know, sort of putting him off. I never liked that kind of stuff much, ghosts and all that. So, we're laying in a mudhole full of bloody water, and he's dying, and he asks me again. What can you say? He poured a handful of the water on my helmet and said... the words." Hawk sighed and looked out at the gorgeous blue sky. "He told me I should be the one dying, instead of him, since I had a brand new soul. Next thing you know, he was gone. And so, I'm probably a Catholic.

Unless the helmet blocked it out and all. The baptism. Like I say, I got no proof of any of that. Sometimes... sometimes, I remember about that. I'll remember something new about it. This all happened in a few seconds. But I keep remembering more things about it. I remember stuff right before I go to sleep sometimes." Hawk took a cigar out of his shirt pocket. "He was a good man. Good, bad, they all die. He had no business there in that place. Just like you got no business mixed up in this, sir. That pilot has killed a lot of men."

"As have you. But there is good in your soul."

"Well, that's not likely. You can ask anybody about that. Everybody knows I ain't no good. You might think so, but if you could ask Hermsdorf, he could tell a different story."

"This priest that you admired saw the good in you. His faith in that goodness gave him courage. The courage to serve his mission."

"I don't know about that." Hawk felt they were getting pretty far afield now. He had a suspicion Hai-lon wanted to baptize him again, shave his head, put him in a dress, and hitch him to a plow on the farm outside. Hawk had sworn off plows when he left Mississippi. Not much good came to a man behind a plow. The talk of religion made him uncomfortable, like talking about mental illness or something. He decided to get to the crux of the matter.

"The priest on Guadalcanal was a good man," said Hawk. "But he was on our side. There wasn't any doubts about that. You see, we aren't so sure about you, sir."

"War has sides. Mankind does not. Good is what is good for everyone. If I told you this thing you ask, it would be good for me, for I would please you. That I would like to do. But many on both sides would die: you know this."

The old fart is full of mumbo jumbo, Hawk thought. *I ain't gonna trick him into nothing.* He had one weakness, though. He liked to talk. Maybe he would slip up yet.

"You talk about goodness, and doing the right thing, this religion thing of yours..." Hawk began. He was interrupted.

"My beliefs are not a religion. They are a philosophy. Religion depends on magic, and the intervention of the external, a faith in the magical. My beliefs are based on conviction. One may have such faith in the good that there is no need for magic." Hai-lon shifted. "One may progress in life, to a higher state. Have you ever sat alone and at peace?"

"I been sitting a lot."

"Do you breathe, and empty your mind?"

"Oh, yeah, I breathe a lot. Unless I'm asleep and all. My mind...is always empty."

Hai-lon smiled. "I believe you. But your heart is full, honorable Hawk. I fear, all that it is full of, is not good."

"Maybe not. So, is this thing you have, is it a Japanese religion?" Hai-lon's expression saddened.

"You are wise. I have told you that it is not a religion, but a philosophy. And yet, you know the truth. We are in transition. All of life passes through stages. We suffer the same corruption as perhaps the philosophy of Lao-tse, when the followers became superstitious. You are right, honorable Hawk. For now, it is but a religion. We have the relic of Hai-tai, kept in the moonstone. This strengthens the faith of the weaker members and the people of the island. On the anniversary of the martyr-dom, the relic, a bone of the finger, is known to bleed.

This keeps the untutored ones faithful to us, for they still need the magic to value goodness."

"You mean this thing doesn't really bleed, it's a trick?"

"No, it is not a trick. It is quite real. On that day, it is passed from one holy man to the next, and when it bleeds, that man becomes the high lama. I have been that man for twenty years." He shook his head. "It cannot be explained. Does that make it true? I believe it is a barrier to true faith. But how am I to know the hearts of every believer? Someday, all followers will believe in the good through the faith in their heart, and we will no longer need the relic. It will then vanish, never to return."

Hawk sat back, digesting all of this. There were inconsistencies in all of it, but he couldn't identify them, nor did he particularly care to identify them. It sounded like some kind of snake oil business that he did not like. Bird songs came through the open window. Hai-lon closed his eyes. A stray thought crossed the empty mind of the American. Hawk wondered if it were possible that the pilot could still be here.

"I'd like for you to tell me the truth," said Hawk. "But...if you're not, I guess I better go. I'll come back, and talk some more. Maybe you'll see things better."

"It hurts me for you to say this. Please, do return. Perhaps our convictions will change in the near future. Truths are like the winds, are they not, for the young seeker?"

"Mmm."

Hawk stood and left the room. The departure did not seem to have the same friendliness as the welcoming had had a few minutes earlier. A young holy man at the door bowed as Hawk left. A troubled expression crossed that man's face as the visitor's heavy steps pounded down the stairway. He had overheard much of the conversation with the American, and he tried to understand it. He felt that perhaps the goodness of Hai-lon was not as perfect as he had previously thought. He sat, to once again guard the lama's open doorway, his mind far from empty.

* * *

HAWK OFFERED no report to Lieutenant Morgan on the conversation with Hai-lon. There wasn't much to say. It had all been funny business. Morgan, however, knew none of this, and had to finally ask what transpired. The honeymoon period of his command was drawing to a close, with little accomplished. He found Hawk on the ground floor of the temple, in the rotunda under the dome. A refreshing breeze blew through the open area. On the floor of the rotunda, directly under the center of the dome, lay a stone of slab, and on it a small wooden box had been placed. A glassy feldspar cover formed the top side of the box. Morgan had not noticed the box before, but he supposed it had been there all along. In the box sat a yellow bone, the type you might find discarded in your flowerbed by a passing dog. The sergeant was looking down at it.

"What's the *swami* got to say," Morgan began. Hawk saluted courteously, but a little on the relaxed side.

"Oh, just the same old shit."

"What do you think?"

"About what, sir?"

"About getting the flier, goddamnit."

"I don't know, Lieutenant. I been thinking, The United States government is turning out about 300 airplanes a day. Do we need one of those, what'd you call him, a *swanee* to find this Jap?"

"Oh, yeah? And we can afford to lose eighty-four more of those airplanes if that bastard gets away?" Morgan put his hands on his hips. Hawk thought, *where have I seen that before?*

"He ain't talking, Lieutenant Morgan. You can beat him, you can bullshit him. He ain't saying shit. Forget the *swanee*. There has to be another way. Air reconnaissance or something."

"Are we of equal rank or something, or did you just forget to say 'sir'?"

Hawk looked up coldly. "I guess I did, sir. It won't happen again. With your permission, sir." He stepped around the lieutenant to walk away. Hawk was not accustomed to all of this intimate interaction. He did not have the personality of a clerk typist, necessary for daily communication with his betters.

A procession of holy men came down the stairs and blocked his path. They walked in a single file and the man in the lead rang an odd little bell. Hawk and Morgan stood uncomfortably next to one another, watching the formalities. The monks sat on the floor, some distance from the relic. Hawk noticed that he was standing between them and their object of worship. He politely stepped out of the way, having some rudimentary knowledge of what was going on. Morgan, with an uninformed and disgusted expression, did the same. Hai-lon then came down the wide stairs, eventually sitting in a place that faced his assistants. He said something in Cokonian, and looked up at Hawk, while he translated the words. This seemed to make Hawk some sort of guest of honor.

"I take refuge in Hai-tai. I take refuge in truth and goodness. I take refuge in the order." He then said something else in Cokonian and was about to translate it. Hawk was wondering how the hell he could get out of the room, when Sergeant Kreski shouted to them from outside. Morgan and Hawk walked out onto the steps and into the dreamy late afternoon to see the cause of the commotion.

"Paratroopers!" Kreski pointed to the sky. Hawk felt a sinking feeling in his stomach as he looked up. Only two of the great silk awnings floated toward the ground. Hawk watched tensely, waiting for Morgan to give an order, since, as he had been reminded, they were not of equal rank. Morgan said nothing. Finally, Hawk said, "Let's go get 'em."

His Thompson lay nearby. He picked it up and led the four men who had answered his call toward the field, where the two sky troopers were about to land.

One man hit the earth on his feet, flattening a neat furrow, and knocking the loose soil into the air. After his feet struck the earth, he landed roughly on his rump. The other man landed directly on his knees.

"Them's got to be Japs," said Joe Canlon from Hawk's side. "Our guys don't land like that."

"Don't kill 'em yet," Hawk called out. "Find out what they're doing here first." He suspected that they must be trying to rescue Zanji, and therefore must have some indication of the pilot's location. The sergeant was not likely to be as genteel with Japanese combatants as he had been with Hai-lon.

The first man out of his chute appeared obviously to be Japanese. But he wore Marine utilities. Hawk smiled, that meant he could shoot him on sight. Wearing an enemy uniform made them spies. Then he frowned. He couldn't shoot them, because he had to interrogate them. The other man still sat on his roughly treated rump. He fumbled with his chute, and the wind threatened to take him away. He must have been unusually heavy, for he remained rooted to the earth. Morgan shouted in his version of Japanese for them to put their hands on their heads.

"If you sons of bitches shoot me, you'll spend your old age in Portsmouth!" the man on the ground shouted back at him.

"Shit, that's Dreisen," Hawk told Canlon. He recognized the voice. "Go cut him loose." Joe ran from the line of Marines, drawing his knife. The parachutes could draw the enemy. Hawk had the men stay in place to provide cover. The other chutist turned out to be the guide, Koichi. He carried a functioning radio. Hawk was a little relieved. At least, the colonel would tell them what to do. Hawk would not have to worry about second-guessing him, the way he had been having to do with Morgan. Sometimes it is a comfort to have someone to tell you what to do. The Marine Corps never failed to comfort its own. Hawk walked away from the line and over to the colonel.

"Good jump, sir," he said with a wry smile.

"Yeah, busted my ass. Back's killing me. Not bad for an old fart, though, huh? Third time in my life I've done that. Goddam last time, too." Hawk pulled the officer to his feet, and by surviving the pull itself, Dreisen proved that nothing was broken. The colonel straightened out his short, square body. He winced as his bones creaked. He looked over at the monastery.

"What you got here, Hawk, the Taj Mahal?"

"Yessir. Kind of a Buddhist deal."

"Afraid I was going to land on the s.o.b. Why haven't you found Zanji? You better get off your ass. Do you think Roosevelt is paying you all that money to get a suntan out here? Helluva suntan you got there."

"Yessir. It's probably the atabrine."

Joe Canlon finally severed the straps, and the billowing canopy blew across the field. Joe sheathed his knife, as if the task were completed.

"Catch that chute! You sorry s.o.b.," Dreisen shouted. "That's government property, you worthless bastard." Joe looked shocked for a moment and then went stumbling through the furrows with the chute blowing just ahead of him. "And by God, don't come back if you lose it!" Dreisen shouted after him. "Who is that man? Runs like a goddam monkey, if you ask me." Joe failed to close with the sail, as it now blew sideways, feinting away from him. "That's terrible coordination. He moves like something is not right. Young fella, too." Joe continued to provide them stumbling entertainment, never touching the chute until it crossed the entirety of the plowed field and entangled itself in the far trees.

"Mmph, mmph, mmph. Now that's disgusting. That man belongs in the Army, Sergeant." The colonel looked accusingly at Hawk. Hawk did not reply. He didn't know if Dreisen was joking or not. You couldn't fool around with a colonel. He kept a straight face. Joe tripped and fell face first into the chute, but fortunately, no one of note watched him anymore.

"Yeah," Dreisen said, dusting himself off and facing

the sergeant. "Got the report on Hermsdorf. Hate it, hate it like hell. Young fella. I was counting on you, Hawk. Should have watched the boy better than that. Something like that..." Dreisen shook his head.

"Yessir, well, we was in the wilds, with no rules or reason, and guns everywhere, and everybody half screwy. You gotta kinda watch the stuff you do." Hawk trailed off with the somewhat esoteric excuse.

"Yeah, yeah, I know all that shit. Still, that was awful. I have to write letters home about that stuff, you know. I can't just say shit like that to his mother. Thought I better come out here myself and straighten this crap out. Big mess. Big mess. You know, Hawk, this is important. I don't think I got through to you on that. Do you think for one minute that I would be here, if this was not important?"

"No, sir. It must be important."

"You goddam right, it's important. Now tell me, son. Just what in the hell is the problem here? We got the s.o.b. right in our hands, and you men are standing around in circles shooting each other. This is not something that should involve all these casualties. I mean, exactly, exactly what is the hold up here? You know, I have a lot of respect for you, Sergeant. You are one son of a bitch that has been around. But I'm kind of disappointed in this. You mean...they're Buddhist? Like Japanese?"

They began walking toward the monastery. The men looked uncomfortable. They were not the sort of men used to close proximity to a colonel. A Marine colonel could result in some good solid brig time just for amusement. Colonels liked things like buttons buttoned, and the line of buttons lined up with your belt buckle. Silly shit, that had been forgotten for weeks.

"We have eight trails here, sir," Hawk pointed as they walked. He explained some of the difficulties encountered in exploring the forest. Reluctantly, he told the colonel about Hai-lon withholding information. He tried not to, but it had to come out. They walked up the steps of the shrine. The monks continued their prayer service without any interruption to honor their distinguished visitor. Lieutenant Morgan was inside, and he snapped to a sharp attention.

"How ya doin', kid?" Dreisen greeted him warmly, without returning the salute. "Get outa the way, boy, I wanta see the show here. Must be damned interesting if you've been sitting around watching it for two days." Being ignored, Morgan respectfully terminated his salute, and stepped aside. Dreisen watched the reverent ceremony for a moment.

"Primitive. Primitive. Damn shame people in the twentieth century got to be so goddam primitive. What's that piece of crap on the rock there?"

"Uh...that's like their magic gimcrack, sir," said Hawk, quickly summing up the metaphysical significance of the relic. Dreisen closed one eye and aimed the other at the sergeant as he listened. He leaned over, taking a closer look at the moonstone. Finally, in a low voice, he said: "Listen...get me some chow. I'm going to have to talk to you about this. This kind of stuff ain't right. This is against nature." He sighed as if a great sadness had overcome him. "How long are those cue balls gonna squat there?"

"Probably not much longer, sir," Hawk guessed.

"Come see me when they're done. Bring me the

head cue ball, this one that says he knows something about the flier. Now get the grub, and I want the best room in the house. No matter who is in it. And a bowl of water, if it's clean. Shit, do they have anything around here?"

It was after dark when Hawk led Hai-lon to Dreisen's quarters. Hai-lon was on his own now. Hawk would not be taking on a colonel for him. He also knew, however, that Dreisen had just enough class not to beat an old civilian. The sergeant made the introductions, after a fashion. He told the lama to have a seat. The colonel pushed aside his rice bowl, and rubbed his hands on his thighs with enthusiasm.

Dreisen laughed heartily. "How do you get that head so damn slick? What do you rub on those things?" He laughed again. Hai-lon looked at Hawk. Hawk winked and sat down without an invitation.

"Okay, mister," Dreisen's smile suddenly disappeared. "I've been told that you are refusing to divulge valuable information to the United States government. And...aiding and comforting the enemy. Is that correct?"

"Sir, I would hope to comfort all who pass my way."

"That so? You ain't no comfort to me. You're a pain in the ass. How would you like to spend the rest of your miserable life with your ass behind a barbed wire fence in a POW camp, bald head and all?"

Hai-lon considered this for only a moment. "That would sadden me. I would not like to leave this place. My home is the earth, but the greatest need for me is here."

"Damn right it is. You got your palace and your silly jerks feeding you. Look here, bug face, I'm gonna tell it to you straight—this is gonna be real simple, so that even your ignorant ass can read it—you tell me where that goddam Jap went off to, by tomorrow morning, or get your crap packed. They got a tidy little cage for you over on Guam, just recently freshened up. Comprende?"

"I understand. As you know, my answer can be delivered now. You are a man of great authority and maturity, you must see that..."

Dreisen held up his hand. "Stow that bilge for the hill jacks. You sleep on it. See if anything seeps through that coconut head of yours. If you ain't changed whatever mind you got by daylight, you get all these loons bagged up and ready to ship." Dreisen took a drink of water from a canteen. "This nut hatchery is going back to the weeds. You and me are through here. Get your stinking ass outa my sight."

Hai-lon bowed and left crestfallen, without looking at the sergeant. Dreisen waited until he was gone to speak again.

"Lunatics. No excuse for it. Line 'em up and get 'em doing calisthenics eight hours a day. You take a man that sits around thinking all day, he's gonna turn into a nut, like that. Even a savage, like that one."

"Kinda rough on the old fella, weren't you, sir?"

"Damn right. Pissed me off. That...that head in the clouds bullshit. The way you been sitting around here, why, the information he has, probably ain't even worth anything anymore. I'll tell you what else. We can grab that bone thing of theirs and throw it in the ocean. Tell them we'll give it back when they act civilized." Dreisen laughed. "I'll tell them where to dive for it, is what I'll do."

Hawk looked at the floor. "Well, if he won't come through, maybe I could talk to him, and tell him about taking their thing. Just telling him might be enough. I was thinking of something like that."

Dreisen yawned. "Thinking isn't doing. Remember that. Want me to repeat it for you? We'll see. Okay, son. Back's killing me. Think it's time to turn in. I'll see you tomorrow. And watch those officers for me." Dreisen aimed a meaningful eyebrow at the sergeant.

"Yessir." Hawk moved toward the door.

"And Hawk—I'll let you know before I do anything to your old granddaddy there. But, you see, I'm not getting any younger. You don't know about that yet. Time isn't free. This pilot means a lot to a lot of people. He might even kill somebody that you know some day. There's a lot about this you don't understand. You remember that." He clutched at his back with a straining arm. "Everybody gets old. You will, too, some day. And before you know it."

"Yessir." Hawk was not as sure of that as the colonel. In a war, the lives of sergeants and the lives of colonels were lived, or not lived, in a different set of circumstances. Dreisen was stepping dangerously close to Hawk's world, and he might learn a few unwelcome things there for himself. He was going to places where bluster and bullying only won you the honor of being buried a little deeper than the rest of the riffraff.

The night of rest was prematurely disturbed. A ringing bell caused Hawk's eyes to slam open a little before three in the morning. The sergeant had been sleeping outside of the temple. He had done so much open air sleeping, he had come to prefer it. He went inside with several others to find the reason for the unappreciated noise. The monks were awake and gathered around the stone slab that held the relic. Each held a candle, and their faces were dark and menacing. Tired Marines began to gather around them as well. Dreisen eventually staggered down the stairs, fully clothed, one hand clutching behind his back. His closely cropped head had little more hair than did the heads of the monks.

Hai-lon stepped from the group, and walked through the orange glow to Hawk. He ignored the presence of the colonel.

"We have suffered a grave sacrilege," he said, "we ask you to return the relic of Hai-tai, that all men may live in peace with themselves and with one another."

"Somebody got the bone?" Hawk's deep voice, still partially asleep, rumbled through the pagoda. Hai-lon nodded.

"Please, young seeker, make them return it."

"Who...uh." Hawk looked around the stone reflected candlelight. He spotted Dreisen. The colonel motioned him over, to where he had stopped on the stairway. Morgan and Repler, uninvited, walked over as well.

"What's going on here, Hawk? I thought we were waiting a day or so to pull this off?" The colonel was breathing heavily for no particular reason.

"That thing is missing, and they think we got it," Hawk answered.

"Do we?"

"Not that I know of, sir."

Dreisen yawned vigorously, unbefitting the solemn occasion, and scratched a thumbnail through the deep, blackhead peppered creases in his forehead. "Cover them," he ordered, "people that ignorant can be dangerous. Tell them...tell them that we have it. Tell them that we'll give it back when they tell us where the

Jap is. We can't afford to miss this opportunity. This was our ace in the hole. Tell them...that *you* got it. Play it by ear. Maybe one of our boys does have it. Is it worth anything?"

Hawk shifted. He did not like playing a role in this matter. "Me, sir? Why would I...?" Dreisen pointed his hand with the fingers together and shook it at Hawk.

"Go ahead," said the colonel. "Don't act stupid."

Hawk went back to Hai-lon and spoke softly. His heavy delta accent nevertheless filled the chamber with low echoes. Even though he was aware that this was an excellent way to get set upon, he went along with the ruse.

"I'm sorry, sir. I took the thing and hid it. You have to tell us where the Jap flier is, and then we will give it back."

Hai-lon looked long and hard at the sergeant. The monk had the power to read men's faces. He had also noted, by sight only, Hawk's secretive conversation with Dreisen. The monk turned back to his people. He began to discuss the matter with several of the monks. Hawk looked at the circle of Marines standing behind him. He shrugged. The lama returned and looked into the cold blue eyes, lit with the pinpoint fires of thirty candle flames.

"We have agreed that this is the greater evil. It is the greatest evil ever visited upon us. I must do as you ask. The party escorting honorable Zanji took the eastern-most trail into the hard lands known as the Jarok. We tried to dissuade them. There is much danger there. That...is where they went. No one has looked for them there. No one goes there. The trails end in these lands, and how you may travel after arriving there, no one knows. Will you now return the sacred relic of the martyr, as you promised?"

Hawk folded his upper lip down. "Yeah. Yeah, at daylight. We'll get some rest tonight, and tomorrow you point this trail out, so's there is no mistake."

"I will abide by your wishes, and do as you instruct, for I trust you, honorable Hawk."

Hawk walked away without saying anything. He had done worse things than this. Hadn't he? The Marines shuffled in the dim light, larger and more intrusive than the Cokonians. Dreisen walked to the side of Hawk.

"Good work. Got through to the little bastard that time. You'll see. Hope I get hold of that bone thing before they do. That'll be the end of that stupid shit. Next time we see 'em, they'll be worshiping a picture of the Lone Ranger. Get some sleep." Dreisen retreated back up the stairs. Hawk was the last of the Americans to leave the scene of the crime. He did not get much sleep. He regretted the theft. But the way the colonel was talking, perhaps the relic would be better off, wherever it was, away from Dreisen.

The patrol was fitted out for a prolonged march. A sort of holiday atmosphere pervaded in the early morning hours. There was none of the dread the men had before a battle. The contingent was ready by dawn. The sergeant sat against a wall inside the rotunda of the temple, smoking a cigar, the picture of satanic serenity. Dreisen had yet to appear. They couldn't leave without his blessing. Hawk thought maybe the officer might even come along. For a while, at least. The monks appeared for their morning prayers as the rising sun washed the stone floor with a yellow-orange color.

Hawk noticed the young man who had sat outside

Hai-lon's door during his conversation with the lama. The monk stood out from among the others, looking a good deal younger. Hawk chewed on his cigar and stared at the boy. The monk glanced uneasily back at him several times. The yellow-orange glow of the floor reflected up beneath Hawk's helmet, causing a shiny, inhuman effect. When the service was over, the boy hurried quickly outside to the fields.

"Hmm." Hawk grunted. That guy knows something.

Dreisen came down the stairs in a huff, as if he had been ready for hours, and was only waiting for the others. He immediately announced that he would be leading the patrol.

"Morgan, you couldn't find your ass with both hands. I *have* to go along," he said. "Time is of the essence." Holley was left behind with one of the radios, to relay messages.

"How do you like this?" Joe Canlon asked Hawk.

"I don't know. I guess he's better than Morgan. Ain't seen hide nor hair of the pilot in days, and now we go off on a tear. I don't expect much. It'll be a lot longer haul than he's planning on. Don't worry, he won't last long."

"Beats fighting," said Joe. "Can you believe this? A colonel? This Jap guy must be pretty damn big."

"Yeah. I guess that's the whole thing. He's big in Japan. Like Clark Gable, or something."

"Clark Gable is big in Japan?"

"Shit."

Hai-lon led them to the mouth of the designated trail, which looked more like a tunnel into the undergrowth. He explained which branches would take them to the land of Jarok. Dreisen held his map out at arm's length and marked it with a pencil. Without a word of thanks, or any word at all to Hai-lon, he led the Marines into the jungle. Hawk lagged behind. Hai-lon looked fearful, almost terror-stricken. He sensed the betrayal. He had trained himself for years to expect the best of men, but now he knew there was treachery.

"I ain't got it, sir," Hawk said.

"You lied, then?"

"Well. Sort of. We got this job to do, see? We couldn't get you to understand about that. There's men back on the beach fighting and dying to buy us time to do this. I didn't want it to come to this. The colonel is real high up in the pecking order, see. You can't mess with him. You gotta do what he says. I'll come back and I'll find that thing for you. All right? You got my word on that, if you'll take it, after all this."

Hai-lon hung his head. "I forgive you for what you have done. Nothing may replace the relic. Many will lose their faith. It is you who do not understand. Someday, you may, and it will trouble you. Remember in those days that you have been forgiven, and need not suffer any sorrow."

"Yessir. Thanks for being a sport about it."

"I will tell you more. It may help you, and it serves no good to conceal it now. I will show that my forgiveness is sincere. Two women and three men accompanied the Japanese soldiers. These were high-ranking prisoners. One of the women was an American nurse captured on Verhangen, they kept the other woman masked. One man was a governor of a British colony. The other two men were Americans—one an officer and one a pilot, not with the military."

Holy crap, Hawk thought. This was a lot of information. He squinted at Hai-lon. "All them people went down the same trail as Zanji?"

"No, they did not. The trails in the Jarok are not like the trails in other places. It is a land of demons. No one lives there. You will find an ancient lighthouse there, look there first. All of the prisoners were to meet there. A very capable Japanese *hancho* landed here to lead them. He has a powerful presence. You must beware of this man. You are following dangerous and dedicated men. They are very experienced, from the days of the China war. They do not smile or jest like your men. The countenance of Zanji alone would frighten the spirit of Genghis Khan."

Hawk smiled and put his hand on the monk's shoulder. "We got a cure for ugliness. They'll have to come up with something better than that. See you in a few days, old timer. And don't worry about the bone thing. It's still around here somewhere. You might even find it before I get back."

Hawk turned onto the trail and ducked under the overhanging foliage. Hai-lon watched the Marine's shadow disappear in the drowning leaves. He pondered the lengths that men will go to for purposeless evil. It only made him sadder to know that after everything that had happened, Hawk was as ruthless as his prey.

5

HELL WITHOUT A NET

HAWK FOLLOWED AT THE REAR OF THE PATROL. HE LET
the men ahead of him get out of sight, a practice seldom
followed. Never is the need for closeness greater than at
war in the jungle. Hawk was a loner, even under these
circumstances. His angry soul felt more of a kinship
with the beauty of the deadly rain forest. The uniquely
exotic setting nearby made him pause on the lonely
road.

A marvelous swamp spread behind the screening
leaves at the roadside. It was different from the others
he had seen in Asia, or in his own Gulf coast. Those
were rough bogs, suitable for the spawning of
dinosaurs, with most of their beauty originating from
their forbidding gloom. It was the pure green hue here
that first caught his attention. The water was the
glowing green of a traffic light at night. The inky, bottle
green vegetation hung lavishly over the water. It grew to
the sky and only patches of blue disturbed its green
perfection. There were no browns, no grays. Though

many sorts of large and small trees, shrubs and vines spilled layer upon blanketing layer across one another, they were all the same shade of green. The water scintillated, as if it were running swiftly, and yet it went nowhere. A refreshing coolness, with little humidity, breathed from its surface. The color of the water may have been supplied by some form of algae, providing its own light source. The surrounding plant-life seemed uniformly painted green by some form of fungus. In places, huge stumps hovered beneath the glassy surface of the water, while never breaking it. No animals could be seen within the dreamscape recesses. The scene extended forever, the dark green of the plants and the light green of the water creating a magical eternity, mocking the commonplace road upon which Hawk stood.

Hawk took out his chewing tobacco. "I've seen green before," he said to the swamp, "but now, *that's* green." He spat, and took up his lonely march on the hot road, thinking his dark thoughts.

* * *

TANIGUCHI LED his party down the steep and narrow trail along the mountainside. Below him, the vast open expanse of a gorge dominated his vision. Dense brush grew to its banks. The walls of the canyon were a hard gray, with swirls of orange running throughout. At the bottom of the chasm, a string of white water could be seen and heard. On the other side of the massive crevice, the *hancho* saw men. He studied them intently, without breaking his stride. He knew that they were

Japanese. He looked over his shoulder and told the others. They began to talk. Zanji remained silent. The pilot was a relatively tall man, with a mustache and the beginnings of a beard on his chin. His face was rock hard, with unrefined features, and his skin dark. A permanent frown was his only expression. Tanaguchi had never liked the looks of such men.

They reached the bridge that spanned the gorge, and a man was selected to lead in the crossing. His name was Kirishima, and he was one of Taniguchi's most vicious scouts. His face was red and purple with some riotous facial infection. A pipeline crossed the gorge, and the enterprising residents of Cokoni had fastened planks over it, and swung handrails over the planking. This transformed the long out-of-use pipeline into one of the most important bridges on Cokoni. For though no one lived in the Jarok region, it was often necessary to cross it, and one wanted to do so as quickly as possible.

When the *hancho* Taniguchi got to the other side of the bridge, he suggested to the officer stationed there that the bridge be destroyed. Many American Marines were on the island, but none had crossed to this side of the gorge. The officer assured Taniguchi that his suggestion would be followed. But after the esteemed party left, the officer decided that total destruction would be too difficult. Instead, he settled for destroying the planking and pulling down the handrail. He left the rusty pipe, its buttresses, and a few wooden braces here and there, which he reasoned would benefit the Cokonian rebuilders, after the war. He had no qualms about the half-completed demolition. It would take an adventurous soul to tightrope the naked pipe across a yawning, windblown chasm. Knowing that in the distant past, a Cokonian must have at some point done just that, and that adventure lives in the hearts of men, the officer put a machine gun emplacement on his side of the gorge. This made doubly sure that no one could cross.

The officer watched contentedly from high above, along the bank of the gorge, as in the distance, Tanaguchi wound his party deeper into the stronghold recesses of the Jarok. *Better him than me*, he thought. The wind pounded constantly at the eardrums along the wall of the wild gorge, the raw isolation promising the guardian merely routine duty, and comforting safety.

* * *

SERGEANT HAWK LOOKED down the mountainside, to the canyon below. The pipe looked like a thin black line from this vantage point. The sergeant saw it clearly, however, and he knew what it meant. He pulled the buttonholes on his canteen flap from over the studs on the holder. Why was there a pipeline in an uninhabited area? He slid the little silver bottle out and took a drink. The bottom half of the cotton holder was saturated with moisture from the sweating bottle. Black fuzz stuck to the bottom of the canteen. Hawk wondered what the dangling boards on the sides and the top of the pipe signified. He took another drink, rammed the steel vessel back into its case, and snapped one flap. The whole thing just had a bad look to it.

Dreisen strutted among the resting men, an elbow

folded behind his back, as if someone had an invisible hammerlock on him. If he was having second thoughts about this undertaking, he did not show it. Hawk knew that the colonel would not stop now. That expectation was gone. This was the nature of officers. They all had an arrested development, around the age of a boy scout, looking for the next merit badge. They had gotten all the merit badges so far, and they knew they could get more. And your ass better not be in the way of the merit badge. Hawk had a longing to be in command, to be free of Dreisen, Morgan, and Repler. But he was not; he had not taken his merit badges seriously enough. If he were in command, would they even be doing this? There must be a better way to do it. Fortunately, Hawk needed no reasons to go through with the task. The open air, an enemy, a Thompson submachine gun, and youth, were all he needed for motivation. He raised his eyebrows and looked into the distance, the distance that would be his tomorrow, and beyond.

Other mountains stretched their necks higher, behind the gorge, that Hawk might have the seer's look at them. The air was cool and still. The sky was slate gray, and closer to the earth, it grew pink, as if an early sunset approached. Hawk spat a mouthful of water onto the stone of the mountain.

"It's gonna rain," he told Joe Canlon. Joe looked reflexively upward, like some barnyard fowl.

Dreisen pushed them down the steep ledges to the approach to the gorge. They could see that a makeshift bridge of some age had been recently dismantled to a great extent.

"Looks good. Looks good," said the colonel, "proves

there's something here besides rock and buzzards." No one else saw anything good about it.

Hawk waded into the thick neck-high brush that ringed the gorge. He looked over at the mirror image of the choking brush on the other side. The sky grew darker, and he let his head fall back for a long look at it. He clenched the weight of the Thompson in his hand. Carrying ten pounds of steel around would annoy most men. To Hawk, it was no more burdensome than would be a locket with the photo of his sainted mother. If he had had a sainted mother. Joe Canlon stepped beside him, leaning over to see the trickle of water so far below them.

"What do you think he'll do about this?" Joe asked.

Hawk snorted. "Walk that goddam pipe." Maybe it was his accent, or maybe some dark emotion he put into it, but everything Hawk said seemed more bitter, angrier, and truer, than what other men said.

"You'll do something, though, won't you?"

"Yeah. I'll walk it. It's a colonel. Did you notice that?"

Joe's eyes twitched as they confronted the immensity of the drop. "Listen, Hawk, we're talking about staying alive here. You've screwed with these assholes before. Don't get carried away with this colonel shit. It's us and him out here. He'll listen to you, and if he won't, there are plenty that will."

"What the hell are you talking about?"

Dreisen took out his binoculars and scanned the shrubbery on the other side. "Looks good. Looks good. Clear as a bell. Bet my life on it. Who's going first?" The colonel threw his chest out. "Why, if I was ten years younger, I would do it myself." He laughed.

"Yeah, me, too," Joe mumbled to Hawk.

"You were playing hopscotch ten years ago," Dreisen shouted at Joe. Joe turned stop sign red and looked up nervously. "I don't want a man that runs like a goddam monkey out on that thing. Get the rope. We need a good man to string us a safety line. Who's going over? Come on, come on, let's have a volunteer. It ain't Niagara Falls, for god sakes." It was a coincidence that the colonel said that, as Joe had just been thinking of tightrope walkers and Niagara Falls. You didn't just wake up one morning and decide to do something like that.

A man named Edwards volunteered. Slender and of medium height, he alleged having a good sense of balance, having done some construction work on skyscrapers. Because no one stepped forward to contest the privilege, he was the man ordered to string the rope. He casually slung the line over his shoulder and walked jauntily onto the pipe. He took four steps, looking like he intended to stroll across, like it was a sidewalk. On the fifth step, however, his common sense seemed to kick into gear, and he bent down and touched the pipe with his hands. From there, he gingerly lowered himself until he was astride the thick cylinder. It had a wide diameter, a circus performer could have walked it with ease. Edwards was not a circus performer, he was just an average man, the kind of man impressed into fighting wars.

Edwards scooted across, lifting his weight with his hands and sliding his butt along the top of the rusted tube. Dreisen supervised approvingly with occasional shouts of encouragement. He asked Koichi what the pipe was doing here. The guide told him how some rich entrepreneurs from Hong Kong had expected to strike oil in the Jarok. No one told them to strike oil first and build a pipeline second. This lack of foresight creeped into other aspects of their endeavor; the rich entrepreneurs became rich no more, and the project sadly came to nothing. The Cokonians ended up with a nice bridge in the bargain. They deserved it, of course, having built the pipeline for little or nothing in the way of wages, and losing a few native sons along the way.

"Gittin' dark," Hawk observed. Joe took a deep breath.

"I can hardly wait to get out on that son of a bitch," Joe said. "Spooky out here. Rainy, dark, and that old, rusted thing." Edward's' back was arched with maximum tension as he scooted along.

"Yeah," Hawk said, out of the corner of his mouth, "they're watching us. This is where they hit us."

Joe snapped his head around. "You see them? How do you know?"

"No. I don't see nothing yet."

"Just a feeling?"

"More like a fact. You don't pass up a trap like this. They didn't just tear the bridge up and waltz on down the road. They're here all right. Right here. Waitin' and a-grinnin'."

"Glad you told me. Wish you were on our side. We'd be hell."

Edwards reached the end of the pipe and pulled the rope over his head, making a little ducking gesture as he did so. He whipped a bowline around a green sapling leaning whimsically over the endless drop. Having done that, he pivoted nicely on his belly, turning to come back. Everyone could see his face now, and became somehow less concerned for him. He had the features of a man in a shirt advertisement. He got along well with

Repler, and had always been reliable. He tried to let the rope uncoil from his shoulder on the trip back, but it was not working out well. He had to laboriously uncoil it one loop at a time, stopping to do so. The return trip was much slower and precarious. His complexion turned a dough-white before he got halfway back. He looked intensely at the pipe, at the place where he would next place his hands. The pressing perils of merciless outer space were closing in on him. Edwards whipped the rope around the three jutting braces of the erstwhile bridge, the three yet remaining attached to the pipe. He did the job well, although he looked appropriately frightened.

"Guy's got guts," said Joe. "I couldn't do that." Hawk said nothing. *You're going to be doing a hell of a lot more than that,* he thought. He watched Dreisen and the other side of the gorge. He had no reason to watch Edwards. He deduced that the enemy would not attack one man and give away their concealment. The line was finally strung, and the man on the pipe safely made it back. Repler and Sprack made an elaborate show of lashing the rope to their side of the gorge. It was the sort of thing bystanders do, so people would include them in recounting the tale of the grand task. Edwards sat on the ground with his eyes closed, exhausted and relieved. He enjoyed the simple pleasure of having his eyes closed, on solid ground.

"Good work, son," Dreisen stood over him. "How was it out there?"

"Made me a little dizzy, sir. There is just...nothing around you."

"Know what you mean. Know exactly what you mean," Dreisen agreed. "Let's get going, men. Strike while the iron is hot. Safe as hell, now. We can cut some safety ropes for each man to tie to the main line there."

Sergeant Kreski suddenly objected. He contended that having the men tied together like that would cause problems if someone fell. The balance would be too delicate. Hawk watched the argument. Kreski was tall and young, and claimed to have done some mountain climbing in Colorado. Dreisen was short, old, by all indications of low intellect—and a colonel. If Kreski got away with this, Hawk decided that he might try something himself. He did not like the idea of crossing the pipe. Something was out there. He did not expect Kreski to win the argument. Low intellect people in authority never let you win arguments.

Kreski did win his argument. But Hawk lost his.

"We have them on the run, and you want to waste time, going all the way to the bottom of this canyon and climb all the way up the other side? That's...that's tactical foolishness. *Foolishness*. What's the matter, Hawk? Scared of heights?"

"Not as much as bullets, sir," Hawk answered. "Japs might have been sitting there forever waiting for us to try this. If you were going to guard the pilot's escape, this would be the place to do it."

Dreisen made a disgusted expression. "Here, take the binoculars. Look for yourself. Check it out all you want. If you're afraid to go forward, you can be the rear guard. I never forced a man to do something he wasn't up to."

Dreisen was disappointed in his platoon sergeant.

Hawk could tell Dreisen was angry. Two challenges to his orders in five minutes was pushing it. He should have been first. Hawk did not press it. Maybe they could pull it off. Like Dreisen, he saw nothing in the brush on the other side, which meant very little. War was all luck any way. Men could stroll around in front of the enemy guns for weeks unscathed, and then get picked off at the battalion CP. He could think of many specific examples.

"Tell you what," Dreisen said, "we'll take the cautious route. Let's get about five men to go over and scout out the other side. When we get the all clear, everybody goes." Hawk clenched his teeth. That didn't sound very cautious. He considered offering to go over alone. Joe stood prominently in front of the colonel, to remind him how clumsy and inadequate he was. Joe was anything but clumsy, but sometimes one can put the perceptions of others to good use. "Let's see, Edwards you been over there once, you'll want to go. Hawk, you want to go, don't you? If it's all that damn dangerous, you don't want someone else taking your place, do you?"

"No, sir." Hawk looked up, his mean eyes narrowing. "Yeah, I'll go." Dreisen proceeded to pick Kreski, and two others of the more daring men. Hawk flinched. He saw the logic now. Challenge the colonel, and get the deadly duty. Kreski was paying for the suggestion about the safety ropes.

"Sergeant Kreski should not go," said Hawk. "We don't want to lose two non-coms." Dreisen could tell Hawk was pissed off. He let Kreski drop out. Another man, named Ames, volunteered in his place. Ames said he had flounced about on thinner spans than this working construction in New Jersey. He did not mention that they were flat surfaces, and not of this great height. He was thinking it, however. Edwards had sense enough to ask to be left out, stating that he was beat. This left an opening for the best friend of Ames, a man named Lloyd. He boasted of no particular qualifications, other than a willingness to do it.

Because of his purported skills, Ames led the way. Lloyd followed. Their boots moved in time to one another. They walked it without crouching. One hand was held out for balance, and one hand slid along the handrail of rope. Their rifles were slung across their backs. Ames could not slow down, or Lloyd would hit him from behind. They both walked swiftly and confidently, by all outward appearances. What went on in their heads was a matter of conjecture. Hawk was the third man in line. Two men, named Cappelletti and Price followed. Price wanted to hug the pipe, in spite of the safety rope. He moved sideways, half crouching, edging behind Cappelletti. This did not look good.

"You're gonna fall, young fella," Dreisen encouraged. "Do it right, or you'll fall. Let somebody else go if you don't have any more sense than that!" Price whispered an obscenity at the colonel. "Ames! Buckle that strap! If you drop it, you are out of a helmet!" Now Ames muttered an obscenity at Dreisen, loud enough for Lloyd to hear. He did not attempt to buckle the helmet strap.

Hawk's impatience with Dreisen grew. The folksy needling of the officer was not as amusing out here in the thin deadly air. Darkness swept the canyon briskly, in typical tropical fashion. A fine mist swooped in from above, peppering Hawk's face with moisture. The whole atmosphere was one of incredible danger. His hand was tight on the rope. His boots moved like magnets on the metal surface of the pipe. He knew the longer he was out here, the more slippery it would get. The footsteps were loud to him, louder than the wind smothering his hearing. He was fastened to the planet earth only by his sense of balance, twitching muscles counterplaying against one another, and a gyrating rope. He had the sensation of riding this unsteady object in a wild surf. He was not dizzy, and he did not watch his feet or the riotous river below. He watched the far bank and waited, because that was where it would come from. The danger that so preoccupied everyone else was as nothing to him, it was the danger on the other side that he thought about mostly. He did not expect to make it across. He did not think he would fall, but he did not think he would make it. He was rather cold about it, and told himself that he did not care. After all, he knew this day would come. Here it was. His Thompson dangled from his shoulder, its muzzle pointed at the vastness beneath him. The only thing that kept him going was the only thing that had always kept him going: *Maybe I'll make it.* Same odds as not making it. They'll play hell if they think I'll help them get me. This defiant philosophy had worked for him so far.

The dusk was cold and pure out on the pipe. The land mass grew darker. The open eternity between the two banks of the canyon simmered with its own waning purple light. Hawk was refreshed by the drops of rain on his lips. It did not seem that they were getting any closer to the other side.

The patient machine gunner on the other side watched the five Americans through screening leaves of something like water hemlock. "This is how the spider must be when his web is full," he whispered to the officer standing near him. The officer smiled grimly. He was looking ahead. He knew that these men would be killed easily. It was what would follow that vexed him. But he had to eliminate them. He could not have five of the enemy on this side of the bridge, in his lap. He could let one or two pass, but not all of these. The canyon air blew the smell of the freshly turned earth, leaves, and the well-oiled machine into their faces. The wait was exhilarating.

The men on the pipe did not breathe. It was only step, step, step. Every step had to be perfect, the kind of perfection you never think about, until you need it. The scene below was a fantastic blur of beauty and horror. It peeked at them from either side of the pipe. The magnetic power of the bottomless depths tugged at them. One calculated step followed another, and the calculations had to be done more quickly than they preferred, because of the men behind them.

Hawk's thoughts ran unexpectedly to a condemnation of Dreisen. You're a little late for that, he told himself. The time for any confrontation was long past now. The almighty power of colonels did not seem so almighty out here on this thing. If they made it, the maneuver would be brilliant. If they didn't, the results would be tragic. Hawk had little sympathy for this dilemma that plagued all leaders.

They saw the muzzle flash first. It looked like a hard object, a gaslit jewel burst through the striped stems of the foliage. The bullets hit the pipe with the loud ringing of a hammerhead. Hawk's gullet shrank into itself. Expecting it did not help in the least. A crimson acid came from nowhere and filled his stomach. The banging and the clanging reverberated along the vertical cliff walls. The two men in front took the brunt of that first burst.

Ames was killed instantly. His perforated body somersaulted to the right, colliding with the wall of the gorge twice on the way down. Lloyd had time to cry out in terror. A helmet, dripping with blood, flew from his head. The cloth cover was instantly saturated a black color. He let go of the rope and put both hands to his face. He stood there a moment, somehow balanced and absorbing the shock of the onrushing lead, until he plummeted off to the left with a prolonged and ululating shriek. His arms and legs fought the inevitable flight all the way to the sharp earth below. The chain of bullets cut the rope between Hawk and the far bank. It dropped and dangled under the pipe. The sergeant now found himself facing the unopposed vaporous white spray of an automatic gun barrel.

James Hawk had an amazing instinct for fighting back. Anything attacking him, soon regretted it. He found his abilities neutralized this time. He felt nothing, but a sudden, immediate, and concrete hopelessness. Men, and other animals, usually freeze when they experience this futility of resistance. But his instinct to keep moving could not be overcome. Keep moving, and maybe something will work. This forced him to go to one knee and then to his belly. His helmet toppled from his head, banged on the pipe, and spun out of sight below. It felt as if a monster was wagging a chainsaw just above his head, the metal crackling in the wet air. The firing continued, he could see it, and he could hear it, and still it failed to connect with his flesh. The rope hung slack in his hand. He heard Cappelletti grunt heavily behind him. Price, closer to the American side of the gorge than any of the others, crawled back along the wet surface of the metal tube. He had the best chance of making it back. The Japanese gunner jumped to his feet in his excitement, waving the pounding muzzle back and forth at Price. Shells clanged between his boots and then in front of him. Hands reached out to him from the bushes. Breaux's BAR returned the enemy fire. Price half stood, then stumbled. Out of the greenery stepped Dreisen, catching Price and slinging him back to solid ground. The colonel ducked and retreated to cover, under fire.

The Japanese gun fell silent. The Americans poured everything they had into the concealing brush on the other side of the gorge, in the hopes of keeping the weapon silent. The roar of the rifles was sharp in tone, and unending. The echoes coming back to them from a distance did not sound like their own weapons, but seemed to reflect a distant battle by two other engaged forces.

Hawk knew that he could not let the noise of the automatic and semiautomatic explosions paralyze his thinking.

"Cappelletti! Are you hit?" Hawk called.

"Yeah. Yeah, I got hold of a board here," Cappelletti gasped. He was holding onto one of the wooden braces that had not been removed. He let himself slip over the side of the pipe, that he might present a smaller target. His bleeding legs hung out into the eager vacuum. His arms were folded tightly around the brace. The curve of the pipe gave some support to his torso. His head and shoulders remained visible above the glistening pipe. Upset by the added weight, the rotting brace rocked threateningly toward Cappelletti.

The machine gun spat lead again. Enemy voices engaged one another hysterically. Hawk smashed his face flat into the steel pipe. It smelled like hot dust, freshly wet. But the gun was engaging the Americans on the other side of the gorge this time. There was no hurry to finish off the two harmless men trapped on the curved span. The Marines fired back, some screaming at the Japanese. Hawk could hear the Japanese returning the invective. Caught between the two sides, Hawk learned the meaning of fury. He was helpless in the face of the slashing bloodthirstiness. He let a leg fall onto either side of the pipe and tried to inch backwards. The Thompson slid rapidly down his arm, and he caught it in the crook of his elbow. He could smell and taste something like vomit behind his nose.

"The board is slipping," Cappelletti groaned. "Grab it and balance me!" The brace was shaped like half a square, with two cross braces on its lower beam. Slowly, it leaned more toward the clinging Cappelletti, giving every indication that it would spin over the pipe and tumble into thin air, taking its added human weight with it.

"Shit." Hawk growled. "Is this rope tied to anything?" he yelled at Cappelletti. He still held the slack safety rope in his hand. Cappelletti turned his bobbing head. The rope had been severed between him and the American side of the gorge.

"No! Only to these boards I'm holding onto." The firing rose and fell, intensifying after every lull. Hawk went to work, in spite of it. It would only be noise, until it hit him. He pulled a length of the rope up and threw it around the pipe. Catching it with his boot, he wrapped another length of it over the cylinder, lashing it tighter.

As he pulled up yet another length, to wrap it again, the Japanese officer noticed all of the sergeant's industrious movement. He tapped the machine gunner on the shoulder, calling his attention to Hawk. The flash guard lowered toward the sergeant.

Hawk saw the shells ringing along the pipe toward him. They left big asterisks on the metal where they hit, as might a welding torch, and blew water vapor and dust from the surface. He knew that he had a split second to move, and yet he did so cautiously. He stuck his hand under the lashing and eased over the side of the pipe. He kept the other hand atop the pipe, clutching at the rope wrapped there. The bullets played angrily between his outstretched arms, spewing bits of rope that fell down into his eyes, before moving on down the span. The slugs splattered into the wooden brace and Cappelletti bowed his head under the unanswerable rage. Splintered wood showered his folded arms.

The Marines drew blood at last. While the Japanese gunner concentrated on the pipe, a thirty caliber BAR burst collided with a Japanese soldier hiding in the brush. The man fell through the pliable stalks and lay hanging over the side of the cliff. His helmet dropped over the precipice. The machine gun raised its sights, to once again engage the men on the far side of the canyon.

* * *

JOE CANLON CRAWLED behind the firing Marines and latched onto the only rifle grenade that they had. He fastened it onto the adapter and then onto his M1. The M1 looked ferociously pregnant. The grenade was two hand lengths long and three or four inches thick, looking like a bloated cigar with a seam down the middle.

Hawk hung onto the side of the pipe, his legs swinging freely over the chasm. His body pressed hard against the curve of the metal, trying desperately to cooperate with his center of gravity. He glanced back at Cappelletti. He was just out of reach. Cappelletti looked at Hawk. The rain had soaked them both. Hawk's hay colored hair had turned black. Somehow, Cappelletti still wore his helmet. His legs were solid red, in spite of the rain and the wet.

Cappelletti had recognized Hawk as his sergeant, his mentor, his safety net, his protector and his experienced authority, an authority even greater than the empty authority of the officers. And now all of that reassurance hung helplessly out over empty space the same as did he.

"Hang...hang on," Hawk said.

The machine gun bullets again raced down the pipe and stopped attentively at Hawk. The gunner tried to skewer the clinging man's hands atop the pipe. The sergeant sensed tiny pieces of the mighty ricochets on the fingers of both hands. The fingers were purple with strain. It felt as if someone were popping his fingers with rubber bands. A second Japanese soldier was hit as the fire concentrated on Hawk. Learning his lesson this time, the gunner abandoned the men on the pipe, and poured fire into the jungle on the other side.

Hawk pulled his free arm off the top of the pipe. The left hand remained lashed under the rope. It strained under the great pull of the weight. He groped for another handhold under the pipe. If he could hang off the side, he would have a fair amount of cover. The machine gun was positioned more to one side than the other. He wedged his right hand under the rope, with a new and reassuring grip, and tried to free his almost paralyzed left hand. It took a layer of skin, but he managed. He slid lower along the side of the pipe. Then came the unexpected surprise. Instead of gently sliding, as all of his planning had anticipated, he suddenly dropped. The fall was for only a foot or so before the rope caught him, though it took a while for his stomach to process the brevity of the fall. The modest relief was short-lived. The rope was slowly unwrapping itself.

The Japanese officer stubbornly ordered the gun trained back on Hawk. The gunner tried to lower the muzzle, but he could see only the edges of the Marine's struggling body beneath the protection of the pipeline. The gun chugged urgently. Most of the shells collided with the cylinder over Hawk's head. The others sailed out into the chasm. Hawk could hear them, a thwacking noise, like wind rushing through rotors. The enraged Japanese officer ordered a soldier with an Arisaka rifle to crawl out on the bank of the gorge and snipe Hawk in the back from that angle.

"Our men are clear," Dreisen shouted. "Get some grenades on that position. Come on, men, you've got the arms for it!" It did not look possible.

Hawk's rope slid lower. The quick and poorly done wrapping could not long support his weight. "You're falling!" Cappelletti screamed. Hawk swung to and fro on the lengthening cord. The machine gunner could almost see, and hit him now, waving the muzzle back and forth, out of sync with the live pendulum.

Hawk threw out an arm to catch the rope on the other side of the pipeline. If he could hold both ends of the rope, it would cease to unwrap itself. He could not reach it, the pipe was too wide. The farther down he slipped, the better target he made. He thought a slug tapped the tip of his boot.

"Grab my legs!" Cappelletti groaned on a deep breath of air. Hawk looked over, and realized that he could almost reach the legs.

"Can you hold me?"

"Yes!" said Cappelletti. "What goddam difference does it make?" He whispered to himself. He was thick-bodied and strong, but he was badly hurt. He braced himself for Hawk's weight.

Hawk first caught the blood-soaked trouser with two fingertips and then pulling it closer, latched a hand onto the injured leg. "Hang on!" he yelled as he let go of the slipping rope. Cappelletti held. The brace turned on its side with a screech, rotating a quarter of the way around the pipe. It refused to break loose. Maybe that is why it was still there. The pull was unbearable, and Cappelletti screamed.

Hawk considered climbing up the horribly stretched body of his comrade, but it seemed impossible. The added movement would no doubt dislodge the other man's grip.

American grenades fell harmlessly into the gorge. A few exploded on the bank of the Japanese side, but too far down to have much impact. The explosions lit the dark and terrible abyss below. Joe Canlon walked boldly out onto the pipe, and threw his rifle to his shoulder. The tubular rifle grenade jutted from the muzzle. He squeezed the trigger, and the propellant swished the bomb across the intervening open space.

The Americans heard the direct hit. The machine

gun was knocked off its tripod with a clatter and there was a roar. The enemy soldiers burst apart from one another in the quick explosion. The burst looked like orange fire behind celluloid. Silhouettes of leaves and branches flashed like the taking of an old photograph.

The ordeal was far from over for the two men on the pipe. The sergeant heard a single shot crack from the enemy side of the gorge. It was dangerously close. The bullet struck Cappelletti's knee, about an inch from Hawk's head. It hit with a splat and a puff of smoke. Hawk heard the bone crunch and the leg lengthened. Still, the man above clung to the brace. Hawk marveled at the superhuman strength.

Hawk worked his Thompson submachine gun into one hand, and tried to return the fire. The last snapping fibers in his departing soul hoped to kill the bastard, but he would settle for scaring the sniper off. The kick of the machine pistol and resulting gyrations made both he and Cappelletti swing dangerously back and forth. The lightning bolt from the gun muzzle stabbed upwards, slinging bullets into the wall of the gorge below the sniper. The aim was awkward and hopeless. The sniper fired again from the safety of solid ground. The one shot was loud, and it echoed forever. Hawk could not close his mouth now over his clenched teeth, as he held back the trigger of the submachine gun. The other Americans could see where he was aiming this time. The barrage of .45 slugs fell low again.

"I'm...falling," Cappelletti squealed. Hawk let the Thompson strap slide down his arm toward his shoulder. More pressing duties called. He latched onto the other man's belt and hauled himself upward. The brace cracked and Cappelletti seemed to be stretching like some malleable substance. Hawk looked up and saw that his companion had his arms lashed to the brace with the rope. Cappelletti, his strength spent, had not been holding them at all: the rope alone held his arms in place. His body sagged and continued to stretch. Hawk grabbed the back of the other's collar and pulled up higher. The sniper on the bank fired again. His bullet struck the pipe and the Marines' return fire poured toward his direction. One of Cappelletti's restrained arms slipped from beneath the rope. The rope tore at his sleeves and then his flesh, bloodying his arms. He slipped more. Flesh flew asunder.

Hawk grabbed the brace frantically, in the last instant as the wounded man fell. Every ounce of his great strength surged into his hands and bolted him to the splintered wood of the brace. Cappelletti had no strength, but still had the instinct to claw weakly at Hawk. The sergeant could not reach back for him and hold onto the brace at the same time. His legs managed to scissor the almost dead man, who slid downward, flailing to break his fall. The ancient vines that strapped the brace together began to loosen, and Hawk could see at least an inch of space between the joined timbers.

The Japanese sniper ducked back under the heavy fire. The gun crew was dead. He was one man against an army now, and yet unfazed. He lay on his stomach as the bullets sliced over his head. He crawled back to the former machine gun position. The gun was but a twisted piece of metal, the crew a conglomeration of bleeding corpses. The earth was still warm from the explosion. The soldier searched his belt for ammunition. It was spent. His hands fumbled along the dark ground, searching for someone else's bandolier, but the blind fingers found only writhing flesh. The American fire raged over his head, slashing at the leaves.

He bit his lip and drew his knife. He held it up, to a better lighting, and shook the blade with determination at the sky. He jumped to his feet in the withering fire and ran from under cover, onto the pipe, as a man might run on solid and level ground. He cried out horrible threats, understood by no one still living, other than by their tone. Hawk watched him through measuring eyes as the lone survivor drew near to the brace. Six feet from Hawk, the man threw up the knife hand, holding the weapon in a blade under position. The Marine sergeant stared into the oncoming face, distorted by both hate and terror. A lone shot snapped through the night, and the attacker fell forward on the pipe, his arm outstretched. The knife crashed down, missing Hawk by about a foot. The point of the blade struck squarely in the middle of the pipe and the force shattered it in two. The dead enemy soldier lay astride the cylinder, the knife handle clenched tightly in his fist.

Joe Canlon was the first man to run out onto the pipe. He put a hand on the stubborn wooden brace and looked over the side. The rain was falling heavily now, and he saw Hawk below in a flash of lightning. The rain poured off his helmet and down onto the sergeant. Hawk could see only the white branches of lightning in the black sky.

"You hit?" Joe asked.

"No. Hurry up."

Joe hung over the side, one hand holding onto the flimsy brace, the other encircling Hawk with a rope. He could have easily gone over with the other two into the bottom of the gorge.

"Cappelletti!" Joe called.

"I can't hold him much longer!" Hawk said.

"He's dead, Hawk. Let him go."

"No, he's not."

"Yes, he is. Let him go. You're going to pull us all over." Joe stared down into the darkness. Hawk's legs held a little longer. Then his boots slipped from the locked position they had been holding. Cappelletti shot soundlessly into the void, in a vertical position, and with incredible speed.

"You got me tied off yet?" Hawk felt weaker instead of stronger after releasing the great weight.

"Yeah. You're okay." Joe said, then looking over his shoulder to the others, he screamed, "Hey, how about a hand? What the hell?" The others still had their weapons trained on the smoking forest beyond the gorge. Dreisen walked out onto the pipe.

"Here," said the colonel, "tie this line to that one, and we'll swing him toward the bank." He handed Joe another rope. Within minutes, they slid Hawk down the pipe, and slung him into the canyon wall. He scrambled up a few feet, clawing at the stone. Several men seized his arms and pulled him up onto the level ground above.

It was not long before Hawk found himself sitting alone on the edge of the rocky gorge, drinking from a canteen, and looking out at the little white asterisk bullet marks on the pipe. They glowed in the dark. His sense of balance swirled with unfamiliar sensations. His head went far back under the canteen and water ran down his neck. After a minute, his eyes, and his brain, were on an even keel again. There lay the pipe, once more, just a solid object. *Had Cappelletti really been dead?*

"All right men, we'll camp on the other side tonight," the voice of the colonel boomed. "We won this crossing, and we'll hold it. There won't be any more traps here."

The men looked quietly at the water dripping from the pipe. It seemed quite possible that another machine gun could be hiding fifty yards farther along the trail. Lloyd, Ames, and Cappelletti were gone. There did not seem to be any great reasons for celebration. Dreisen nevertheless went around slapping backs, inevitably coming to Hawk.

"Great job, Sergeant," said Dreisen. Hawk looked up at the talking fat head, and then looked vacantly at the dead Japanese soldier draped across the pipe.

"I didn't do nothing but hang on," said Hawk. He had hung onto a flying dragon and lived. "Always been lucky."

"More than luck, more than luck. You were fighting back out there. Never seen a man do such a thing. You did a fine job. This will cut two days off the trip. We'll get that bastard now. We never would have caught him without this bridge. You can be pretty proud of that."

"Yessir." Hawk could not restrain himself this time. "And three men got a faceful of copper jackets."

"Hate it. Hate it like hell. Sad state of affairs. But you know what the job is, and what it takes. That's why we are the U. S. Marine Corps."

The words seemed like more than a platitude this time. They struck home. Hawk saw something of himself in the stupid, uncaring eyes of the colonel. God forgive them, the colonel had spoken the truth.

"Yessir." There was some word for this strange sort of callousness, but he didn't know what it was. The people who made up words had never experienced this. He and Dreisen could communicate it to one another, but not with words. Get the job done. The job was killing. That was fine. But ignoring the killing of your own was a big part of it. That was not as fine. He reflected upon the fact that the three men so far below at the bottom of the gorge, or at the bottom of the eternal universe by now, had suffered a fate only centimeters away from his own. Would they have cared, if it had been him, instead of them? Yes, probably, but they would have understood. They would have understood this thing that had no word to identify it. And for now, it was his turn to understand. Duty would have to suffice as the word for now. But it wasn't quite right.

"Sergeant Kreski," Dreisen called, "take another rope across. Come on men, hot grub and a night's sleep on the other side." The colonel reached down and hit Hawk on the back. "Come on, son."

"With your permission, I'll get my night's sleep on this side, sir," Hawk said evenly. Dreisen frowned, looked down and walked away. Hawk watched the men walk across the abyss, with an ease that had been denied him. He took a block of chewing tobacco out of his shirt. He held it for a moment. *Had Cappelletti been dead, or had he just fainted?*

Dreisen decided that leaving Hawk over there was a good idea. It all fit the plan. He needed a rear guard. He did not want his patrol trapped on either side. The colonel ordered Joe Canlon to stay with him. Hawk remained sitting there throughout the migration, like a mule who refused to march. Dreisen realized he had been too chummy with him. Now the sergeant was taking advantage of him, and getting sassy. *Same old story*, Dreisen thought. He had let it happen a hundred times. He got too buddy buddy with his men after they did some little insignificant thing. You had to especially watch those old non-coms. An entitled bunch.

"Just an old softie," the colonel muttered as he prepared to sleep on the scorched soil of the machine gun position. The ants and insects worked feverishly on the spilled blood. Dreisen scratched. "Just too soft. Wouldn't have been that way ten years ago." His sensitivity became less and less intrusive, however, as he fell asleep in twenty seconds.

On the other side of the gorge, two other normally insensitive men remained awake, deep thoughts troubling their usually shallow psyches. Hawk sat on the edge of the gorge, feeling the majesty of the wind playing along the vast drop, and across his face. Joe sat near him, but a little farther back, smoking a cigarette. They each propped a foot on opposite sides of the pipe. A man on watch across the gorge shouted at Joe to extinguish his cigarette. Joe shouted back a humorous obscenity. The orange glow lit the dead black night.

"I guess they could have left a Jap running loose on this side," said Hawk.

"If they did, he can go to hell," said Joe. Hawk nodded. If they did, he would certainly like to get his hands on him right now.

"This Dreisen is dangerous," said Joe. "He's shoving us down the Japs' throat."

"Oh, I'll give you that. It's aggravating," Hawk admitted. He spat, and seemed to pause in his thinking. "I'll tell you something. It's something that's been bothering me. You'll need to keep it to yourself." Joe listened attentively. If something was bothering James Hawk, it had to be good. But only silence followed.

"Well, what?"

"That *swanee*, back there. He told me something. He said the Japs had some prisoners. Important people. Some kind of English governor, and a couple women, and somebody else, like a pilot."

"Yeah?" Joe took a drag on the cigarette. He thought Hawk was going to tell him something good. He lost interest. He thought of New York. It would be nice this time of year. He couldn't talk about New York to Hawk. Hawk would go into an insulting diatribe about New Yorkers, probably first mouthed by some redneck drill instructor fifty years ago. "So what?" Joe asked at last, vaguely remembering what Hawk had last said. He looked with a new fascination at the unblinking stars over the glass-colored mountains.

"So...Dreisen would really be pushing our ass if he knew all that shit. He'd get somebody else killed without a second thought." Hawk turned and looked over at Joe, who still did not seem that interested. "Like maybe you."

"Hmmph."

"He's a full bird now," Hawk continued. He'll make general for sure off this deal. I just don't want to tell the son of a bitch. This just don't strike me as all that important. Like Guadalcanal, that was important. We were stopping the whole Jap Army and Navy. Now, that Jap pilot may never get off this island, no matter what we do. And even if he did, he may never fly again. He's just a man. A lot of shit happens to a man out here. Like... like that kid that fell in the river today. He saved my ass. I don't even know if he was dead."

"He was dead. I can tell you that one. You don't have to worry your pretty little head about that. He was dead. Nice guy, too."

'I don't know. Then, I got to thinking of those two women. You know? Caught by a bunch of Japs. That's pretty rough."

"Ah," Joe waved his cigarette. Women. Phooey. What were they, angels or something? He remembered going up to Canada in the summer, getting out of the dirty city, taking canoe rides and camping out. "I wouldn't tell anybody *shit*. Like you said, just more shit for us."

"Yeah. I guess. It's all just talk anyway. I don't know, though, that old *swanee* was pretty reliable. That's a lot of wild shit to just be making up. I mean, he was giving me details." Hawk shook his head. Then he said something that suddenly got Joe's attention, and changed the whole tenor of the harmless conversation. Joe realized that he had as much at stake in this idle chit chat as did Hawk. "The old guy said that one of those women had been on Verhangen."

Joe's casual posture stiffened. Hawk could not see the ashen expression on his face in the dark. Joe no longer had thoughts of New York. His mind snapped back to the bloodbath of Verhangen, only months earlier. He remembered getting shot. And he remembered the Navy nurse, Ivania Broeder.

Thunder rumbled in the distance. It rolled on the ground, closer, through the mountains and up the high walls of the canyon, loud and echoing. At the same time, it was growling far out at sea. A crack sounded high and nearby.

"I didn't know they had any nurses on there," Hawk's voice was getting lower, as he ventured into one of those areas he never expected to speak of, or think of again, "except for them two that was with us." The words slid out like a glacier. Hawk had personally seen one of the nurses slain: his friend, Belva Cook. He presumed that the other one, Ivania Broeder, was killed by the Japanese as well. He had known the two women and spoken with them often. While Belva had an interest in him, his interest was in Ivania; but she was a bit arrogant, with the arrogance that only an exceptional beauty can have. She was dating a captain at the time, for what she could get out of him; and what she wanted out of him most, was off the island, before disaster struck. Hawk had done what he could. He saw her face her executioners bravely, without asking for mercy.

"That...that Ivania. She reminded me of Veronica Lake in that picture. Remember that? When she blew herself up at the end, to kill all them Japs?"

Joe shifted nervously. Great movie. Just Hawk's kind of woman all right.

Joe rocked with increasing anxiety. He now had a few stories of his own to tell. Should he? "Uh...listen, you know how you said you was afraid to tell Dreisen about those prisoners?"

"Yeah." Hawk rubbed his dirty, hairy chest, still smiling as he thought of Veronica Lake blowing herself up at the end of the movie. Got those bastards. What was the name of that movie? Something about the flag? Veronica Lake.

"Well. Keep that in mind. You know how you and me were the only two men left on that island?"

"The only two *Americans*," Hawk snorted. "Got outa that one."

Lightning flashed over the camp across the gorge,

silhouetting several helmets. The lightning bolts were long and traversed the entire sky.

"Yeah...yeah." Joe now had second thoughts. He shut up. But a little too late. It looked a bit too obvious.

"Were you gonna say something?"

"Oh. Yeah. Yeah. I was."

"Well, what? Goddamnit."

Joe took a deep breath. "We weren't exactly the *only* two Americans on the whole thing, you know. We were the only two men. I had seen her. I seen her alive. The Japs had her."

Hawk held the tip of his nose for a moment. He finally pulled down on it, and spat between his knees. Slowly, he put a name to "her". Hawk had seen Belva killed.

"Ivania Broeder? You *saw* Ivania Broeder alive?"

"Yeah. I was in a hell of a shape though, you remember? I was scared to tell you. There was no way in hell we could get to her, but I knew you would go all overboard and try."

There was a threatening pause. What would Hawk do? Beat the shit out of him? He never had before.

"That was pretty chickenshit," Hawk finally said.

"We both got out alive, didn't we? I was in the hospital for weeks. We wouldn't be sitting here if I had told you, you would have gotten us both, and probably her, killed, too. Now, she's alive, too. Nothing lost." Joe turned toward him and held a hand out with the palm open. "You're doing the same thing to Dreisen, ain't you? Not telling him? People got to make some hard choices sometimes."

Hawk spat. "That means the Jap prisoner has to be her. She's here, on this very rock." While the presence of the great Isamu Zanji had done little to impress Hawk, the nearness of this newest celebrity was a different matter. All of this stupidity made sense.

"That's right," Joe said with reluctance, and with regret for ever bringing it up. "I knew it when you mentioned a nurse. It must be her." He could see Hawk's brain kicking into gear. Just exactly like it would have done on Verhangen.

"Now, ain't that some shit?"

"Yeah. It is. So...will you tell Dreisen now?"

Hawk sat back a little, staring at the sky. "Probably. Yeah. I guess so. Yeah. I don't know."

"I think that would be stupid. You said yourself, he will be like a bloodhound on the trail. I wouldn't do it." As soon as he said it, Joe knew he had made a mistake. Hawk was seeing all of this differently. Dreisen would be a bloodhound all right: Hawk's bloodhound, now.

Anger rose quickly in Hawk's throat. Something in Joe's character rubbed him wrong. He was quiet for a while, and took into account that Joe left Verhangen in a plastic bag. He had been protecting Hawk, more than himself, by withholding the information. It was all in the past. They had been through a lot of shit together, including this very day. Joe was out there on that pipe while everybody else was in the bushes. That entitled the guy to a few passes. His anger subsided.

"It don't matter," said Hawk. "You not telling me, I mean. Kind of chickenshit. But, yeah, I got to tell the colonel now." Hawk faced him. "See this is what I was talking about. If that woman wasn't Ivania Broeder, she still would have been somebody else, with a different name. You can't just leave people like that."

Joe nodded. *Whatever*, he thought. He was relieved

that Hawk was not mad at him. It had been bothering him the whole time he was in the hospital. It was a two-part regret: first, leaving the nurse, and second, not telling Hawk. Now that the heaviness had left his conscience, a little anger replaced the regret. He had just blown the cover on two secrets that were bound to set off the two craziest bastards in the Marine Corps.

"That old *swanee* was right, you know," said Hawk, waxing philosophical. "About the truth and all that shit."

"Mm hmm," Joe replied to this preposterous wisdom. All of a sudden Hawk was Mr. Truth. "You ain't never been nothing but a dumb plow jockey, Hawk. That woman never gave a shit about you. You oughta use your thick head, and keep your mouth shut. Five minutes ago, the truth didn't mean shit to you. Now all of a sudden you're goddam Buddha."

"Keep quiet, like you done? Caused everybody else some grief and saved your own ass?"

This provoked Joe from a little angry to extremely angry. He was butting heads with Hawk's cornball Mississippi chivalry. He probably would have hit anyone else. Hitting Hawk, however, would be kind of like hitting the Devil. He wanted to throw something. But he needed everything that was within his reach too much to throw it away. And he didn't want to start anything else with Hawk, after just getting back on his good side. He still felt a little guilty about the whole matter. But just a little, now. He didn't owe Ivania Broeder anything. She was a Navy officer and all that great stuff. She wasn't getting her ass shot at twenty-four hours a day. He dropped his cigarette down into the gorge and walked away. There would be no sharing of good night wishes. Against all protocol and common sense, the two hardened, experienced, and exhausted warriors would cavalierly post no guard.

Joe lay down under a bush, flat on his back, his eyes still open. Hawk was lying down as well, now. Joe called out to him, just loud enough to be heard: "Dumb ass."

"Shitball."

6

LIKE A MUTINY

A LITTLE BEFORE DAWN, THEY WERE BOTH STILL ASLEEP. Hawk's nerves awakened him. His system was already strung taut, and a stealthy noise caused his eyes to open. He was accustomed to waking up in bizarre and unhealthy places, and so he was instantly alert. Another morning in hell. He lay still and listened. His subconscious had been waiting for the sound of a lone infiltrator, but the rocks above grated under the movement of many feet. The trickle of the pebbles came to his ears, which were still ringing from the firefight. His hand tightened around the pistol grip of the Thompson. He rolled over twice and slapped Joe's helmet onto his own head.

"Joe!" Joe snored louder. Hawk crawled over to him on his elbows. "Get up, dog shit!"

"Huh?"

"Something's coming. We gotta get outa here."

"Huh?" Joe sat up with half closed eyes and reached for his shotgun. "Uh...where's my hat?"

"Come on, step on it."

"Where we going?"

The pipe was the only safe direction. Hawk had an aversion to the avenue of his trauma the night before. Intruders were on the mountain above them. The two of them would have little time before the unseen men were upon them.

"Shit. The pipe, I guess."

The dark morning remained moonless. Starlight and open space contrasted the pipe with the utter blackness on either side of the gorge. Joe grabbed Hawk's arm.

"Hey. Wait a second. We could get drilled out there, Hawk. It's wide open."

"Goddam right. We can get drilled here, too." Hawk didn't wait for Joe to decide. He didn't want to go running off in another direction along the edge of the canyon. The approaching noise did not sound like a couple of kids out berry picking. As well as escaping, they needed to alert the men on the other side. He stepped out onto the pipe. He crouched, moving slowly, even considering scooting across as Edwards had done. He walked farther and groped for the newly strung safety line. The rough fuzz of the hemp met his palm. The makeshift handrail felt weak and dangerous in his grip. A violent jerk on it informed him that Joe was right behind him.

Hawk stepped quickly, lifting his feet only millimeters above the now familiar curve of the metal bridge. The rope jerked again, this time more forcefully. Hawk sensed the muscles on the right side of his body contract to maintain his balance. *Dreisen had been right*, he thought, *Joe was an oaf*. Canlon pulled on the rope like he was in a tug of war. Joe was one of those people that slam doors too hard, bang glasses down too hard, and even sit down too hard. This was not the kind of place you wanted to share with a person like that. Hawk let go of the rope. It was either that, or let Joe tip him into the gorge. He nevertheless continued on at a fast pace, ever conscious of the swimming darkness breathing beneath him. He waited for shots to explode from the rear. He could already see himself dangling off the pipe again. It was galling to know that Dreisen was right, and that he should have made this crossing last night. But the two of them made it over, and clawed their way noisily into the leaves on the other side.

Hawk heard the bolt of an MI click.

"It's me, Hawk! And Canlon."

"What the hell are you doing?" A voice came from behind the place where the heavy click had come from. The voice sounded like Price's.

"We heard Japs coming up behind us on the other side."

Price awakened Dreisen with the information, who quickly awakened Kreski. Kreski made the rounds, rousing the others. The men formed a line on the cliff. Breaux, with the BAR, took up the position formerly held by the Japanese machine gun. They could see nothing in the mysterious and threatening night on the other side.

"Put up a flare," Dreisen ordered. It popped overhead, and blew about in the high-altitude winds. It swung a quicksilver light back and forth under its little parachute, like the lantern on a ship. The illumination of the utter darkness immediately solved part of the heart-stopping mystery.

Many stocky men were gathered on the far side of

the canyon. They squinted upward. Only one had a foot on the pipeline. The first impression was that they were Japanese. Being awakened suddenly in the night had a lot to do with that impression. They were all shirtless, and some wore short pants, while others wore tucked loin cloths.

"Hold your fire," Hawk spoke up boldly. "Looks like locals." He recognized the ordinary attire of the Cokonian fisherman, who were usually found near the sea. Of course, he could be wrong. People can wear whatever they want, including Japanese soldiers. He was not wrong about the main thing, however: they did not have firearms, and that was not characteristic of the servants of the Emperor. Several carried long knives. Men without firearms were meaningless to Hawk. They may as well have been children. Whatever your other physical, mental, social, or economic powers might have been, if you had no firearm, you were nothing.

"Koichi!" Dreisen shouted, "ask those damn fools what they're doing? Good way to get your ass shot off."

The guide did as instructed. Upon hearing his voice, the Cokonians broke their own silence with angry voices and brandished their knives and sticks. The foremost one on the pipe began to cross it.

"What the hell is that all about?" Dreisen demanded of his guide.

"Not sure," Koichi answered, "very angry."

"That's too damned bad," said Dreisen, unsnapping his 1911 .45 automatic pistol. "Tell them to halt or we'll cut down every one of them." Koichi did as he was told. The shouting died down considerably and the man on the pipe stopped his forward progress. "That's more like it," said Dreisen. "See, this is the kind of shit you get when you try to be nice to these people. Find out what the hell the dumb s.o.b.s want."

Koichi again questioned the fishermen as to their intentions. The man on the pipe responded for them in angry tones. He never really finished his speaking, as the words degenerated into a tirade, and the screaming continued throughout the translation. The gorge reverberated with his outrage.

"This man," Koichi pointed at the speaker, "says that you have stolen the sacred relic of the martyr. They want it back and must chop off the head of each man who touched it. Must have the head of leader, too. You, sir," Koichi pointed at Dreisen, with a polite bow.

"Sounds fair to me," Hawk growled to Canlon.

"Yeah. These guys are making sense."

The Marines watched the drama with more curiosity than concern. Dreisen looked thoughtfully at the ground. He had forgotten about the relic. Actually, he never gave it a thought. He had to think a minute to recall it at all. He looked up.

"Did any of you men take their goddam thing?" Dreisen shouted. He was willing to give it back, if he had it. No one answered him. Someone mumbled something and laughed.

"Tell them we don't have it, and to shove off." the colonel instructed Koichi. The guide did as he was told. His tone was more conciliatory than that of the colonel. After all, he had to live here. Such is the fate of interpreters. The fisherman did not like the response, or Koichi. The shouting began again. The man on the pipe resumed the trip across. Others charged onto the structure behind him, slipping and sliding quite recklessly. Some swung on the buttresses, on the underside of the first section of pipe. The Marines tightened the grips on their rifles a bit. The flare drifted to the height of the pipe, and then below it. The illumination came from below the mass of moving islanders. It was an odd static light with peculiar shadows.

"Hold your fire, men!" Dreisen ordered. "It's against the Articles of War to shoot innocent civilians." His mind ran through several ramifications. This was part of the home islands, so maybe these men were classified as Japanese. But, they were still civilians, so that was no good. You could kill a hundred thousand civilians in a bombing raid, but shooting one with a rifle was unsporting.

Dreisen raised his .45 pistol and squeezed the trigger. The muzzle blazed and the round glanced off the pipe in front of the foremost man. It startled the Cokonian so much that he dove headlong into the chasm, finally beginning a scream forty feet down, after realizing what he had done.

"They're entitled to a warning shot," Dreisen explained. The warning was sufficient. The others retreated from the half-demolished bridge. "You got to be careful with civilians," Dreisen told the men around him. "Be diplomatic."

"Did he shoot that guy?" Joe asked.

"Uh...I don't think so. Maybe." Said Hawk.

The flare had become a lesser and fallen star, floating down to the bottom of the gorge. Quiet reigned for a few minutes, until the Cokonians again began shouting from the concealment of the wooded area on the other side. They now had the grievance of the relic, as well as that of the murder of their friend, relative and compatriot. Dreisen did not care for the sound of the harassment. Someone who hates your guts can never really be considered totally harmless. The colonel called for the radio.

"Better get hold of the monastery back there," the colonel said. "Who was that fellow?"

"Holley, sir," Lieutenant Morgan answered.

"Get Holley. Looks like some shit brewing here." Sprack propped the radio up in front of the two officers.

Hawk rummaged through his shirt pockets with a thoughtful expression. His hand closed on something, and he rejected it, until he at last found what he was looking for. He pulled out a half-burned cigar. He walked closer to the radio operator that he might hear and understand what was transpiring.

"I have Holley," Sprack announced.

Dreisen sat down several feet from the radio. He saw the sergeant. "Come here, Hawk. Talk to this bastard. See what's happening back there. Something has set these loons off."

Hawk took off what was now *his* helmet and put on the headset.

"Hey, you at the monastery, can you hear me? Over." The sergeant listened carefully. "Yeah. Yeah, I know. They just got here, too, and affirmative, they're still pissed off. Over."

Dreisen put his chin in his hand and stared at Hawk from about a foot away.

"No shit? Maybe you should get out of there. Wait one." Hawk pulled up one of the earphones. "Holley says the native guys came to the monastery looking for us, with their bowels all in an uproar. Hai-lon had to hide him from them. They want to chop our heads off. He said they burned a tank down by the beach. It's all about the bone. Two clans of them are even fighting each other about it, for some reason. He's not sure what that is about. He wants to know if he should go back to the beach."

"Hell, no! We need that radio to relay messages. We're well out of the range of the beach now. We might need the radio to call in an air strike, or a pickup, or who knows what, if we find this pilot. Tell him that is a negative," Dreisen insisted. The very idea so rattled him, he fell to explaining himself. "Tell that s.o.b. absolutely not, and that's an order! Keep his ass right where it is. Those slick heads will look out for him. No, ma'am."

"Yessir." Hawk dropped the earphone in place and relayed the order to Holley. "The colonel says no dice on that. Hey, listen, we just crossed over…"

"That's enough of that, Hawk," the colonel interrupted him. "Don't go broadcasting our position all over the goddam Pacific Ocean."

"Yessir. Well…that's it then, Holley. Unless you got something to say? Over." They waited as Hawk listened. "Oh, yeah. Okay, roger that. Over and out." Hawk took off the headset. "He said to keep in touch more. He's kind of scared of what might happen."

"Oh, bullshit," was Dreisen's reply to that. The colonel paced to and fro in the dark. "This is another wrinkle. We'll have to post a guard here to keep the silly s.o.b.s off our rear. They could ruin the whole operation. Didn't plan on all of this. We're just lucky we hit on this bottleneck here."

Ames, Lloyd, and Cappelletti weren't so lucky, Hawk thought.

"Who wants to volunteer for a detail like that? Easy

duty. No more marching. One man can hold them off here without a problem."

A boy named Dussair volunteered. Shooting Cokonians off a pipe had some degree of clarity about it. Following men like Dreisen, Morgan, Hawk, and the glowering Repler into nowhere was not quite as inviting. The best thing that could happen to the madmen would be a bloody showdown with crack enemy paratroopers. Dreisen questioned Hawk about Dussair's youth. Hawk insisted the kid could handle the job. He liked the idea of getting the boy out of whatever was about to happen. Dussair had parents waiting for him at home, with no concept of the danger he was in. They imagined experienced older Marines watching out for the welfare of their beloved son. They did not envision or include any Colonel Dreisens, or James Hawks, in their evening prayers.

"Can't go getting all sentimental if they start coming across that s.o.b.," Dreisen told the boy. "They'll overrun you and then us, if you do. You shoot to kill. You are a United States Marine."

"Aye, aye. I understand, Colonel," said Dussair.

Daylight arrived and the men prepared for another day's march. Some were getting near the end of their rations. They had prepared for crossing an island, not a continent. Koichi had the day's objective circled on the map for the colonel's scrutiny. Dreisen wanted to reach the fabled Lighthouse of Jarok. He reasoned that as the only structure in this entire wild region, it might attract the ace. Shelter, especially if it could be fortified, was always a valuable commodity. He pondered the ultimate goal of the Japanese. What were they up to? From Dreisen's perspective, they seemed to be lessening their chances of escape as they plunged deeper into this nothingness.

* * *

TANAGUCHI SAT COMFORTABLY against the stucco covered wall of the lighthouse. The sun arose beautifully this morning. Pink clouds were emblazoned with orange shafts of light, radiating from the auburn sun. Zanji sat beside him, holding a bowl of rice and a pair of chopsticks. They might have been looking at a Japanese naval flag that God had painted for their enjoyment across the dawn sky. An omen? Zanji pushed the mass of rice into his mouth. Taniguchi's mood was broken. The presence of Zanji reminded him of his mission, and of death.

"The American Marines are very close," Zanji observed in his quiet, dangerous sounding drawl.

"Yes. If they crossed the bridge last night, it is possible that they could reach the lighthouse today, Lieutenant," Taniguchi admitted.

"It sounded to my untrained ears as if they did," said the pilot.

"Yes," Taniguchi nodded. "Or if they did not, they will." Taniguchi and Zanji were experienced fighters. They had no need to delude one another about the invincibility of their troops. The Americans overpowered them as a matter of course. They were driving them across the Pacific and back to the homeland. The numbers of the Americans were superior, they had moved their entire nation by ship into the South Pacific. Their weaponry had thirty years advantage on that of the Japanese.

Zanji placed his chopsticks beside the bowl. His cruel eyes glared at the sunrise. Zanji was fearless in the air, regardless of the enemy's technological superiority. Today, however, he was concerned. He was not in the air. He had heard the stories of the American Marines: the dregs of prisons and mental institutions, inbred rural hill dwellers, and refugees from gangster organizations. He disliked being on the ground and dealing with them on their own terms. Pilots, even American pilots, had a greater code of honor.

"I shall end like Nishizawa," the ace said prophetically. "Unable to strike a blow in my own defense. The eagle at the mercy of the jackals."

Tanaguchi rubbed his nose and said nothing. He did not like men singing their own praises, or whining about their fate. How was he supposed to answer such dramatic claptrap?

"Would that I had a plane, Sergeant Tanaguchi."

"The plane was supposed to be here yesterday, honorable Lieutenant. The Shiden Kai was supposed to land in the field here. It will either land here today, or lie buried in the ocean." Taniguchi shook his head. "We are so fortunate to have found this natural airfield. I doubt there is another place so perfect on Cokoni."

Zanji looked at the bright sky. His eyes were closed by outward appearances. But they saw. The eyes of Zanji were like those of no other man. They were a delicate instrument of war. Like the eagle's, they saw everything. His reflexes were those of a jungle animal. He was without a doubt a superior being in the air. He saw it all, he knew what to do, and he had unmatched experience. He had shot down four times the number of planes of his nearest American competitor. He had the reflexes to make the machinery do exactly what it had been designed to do, at the exact moment that it had to do it. He was a man born with unique hand-eye skill, who also happened to be inhumanly brave. This morning, he was the samurai without his sword; watching the sky, waiting for that sword to descend.

"You are a fine soldier, Tanaguchi. I have great confidence in you. You do not need to call my rank every time you speak. You remind me of my best wingman at the beginning of the glorious war. Tell me, if this should fail, do you think we can reach the shore and put in place our alternate plan?"

Tanaguchi shook his head with a sigh. "I would prefer not to. The hardship would be great. The chances of success would be less. I would like to give your Navy pilots every opportunity to deliver the Shiden. Sometimes these things take a few days. Things become confused. The steps occur out of sequence. Yes, the Marines are coming. They will come swiftly. I predict, however, that there will be but a few of them able to reach this place, and those will be greatly overextended. When our numbers are evenly matched, they are not quite the fearsome opponent of report. All of their victories have been when we were badly outnumbered."

Zanji nodded. He liked confidence. "You will engage these Marines then, Taniguchi?"

"I will not avoid it. If we can prevent the necessity of taking you to the submarine, it will certainly be worth it. For there would be many engagements, if we have to go to the northern beach. Many engagements between here and there. Even one engagement is very dangerous. And then you still must overcome their Navy. But...I am ever subject to your counsel, honorable Zanji."

"No. No. You must do only what you think must be done," Zanji sighed. "Never interfere with a man who knows his trade. This is your theater. And I admit, I prefer to meet them in the sky."

* * *

DREISEN LOWERED HIS BINOCULARS. "There it is," he told Hawk. Hawk had seen the top of the lighthouse a mile back.

"Any Japs, sir?"

Dreisen looked though the field glasses again. "Don't see any. Want to take a look?"

"Yessir." Hawk took the glasses and the lighthouse of Jarok leapt into a tubular blurry view. Perched on a lofty promontory, it was a thin white shaft topped by a pagoda roof. Long columns supported the roof. The columns, of great age, looked gracefully delicate. The tall open chamber formed by these columns served as the tower's lamp room.

The structure was several hundred years old, though it had been refurbished many times since the original construction. The upkeep had been done more to preserve its historical value than to ensure the safety of any passing ships, for the lighthouse stood many miles from the sea. Once it had protected ships from the rocky shores of northern Cokoni. Almost three hundred years before, however, the bottom of the ocean had arisen during an earthquake and doubled the size of Cokoni. Most of the residents had been killed by the tidal wave. Now the lighthouse was high and dry, and invisible to the far away ships. It leaned over a cliff overseeing a jungle, that once was the ocean bottom. Its tall chamber had once been lit with wood-fueled fires in metal baskets. It had saved the lives of many sailors in the days of motorless crafts.

Hawk did not know any of the curious story at the time. He didn't care about any of that. It never crossed his mind that a lighthouse should be located on the seashore. He was like the businessman who frequently travels to other cities and never sees anything of interest but his work. The damned thing was just there. He learned the history of the building later, in conversations with Koichi. What Hawk did notice, with the aid of the glasses, quite easily, was that half a dozen figures were moving around the base of the tower. He took the glasses from his eyes.

Dreisen had said there was no one there. He recalled Dreisen saying there were no Japanese at the gorge as well. That was right before Hawk found himself chewing on a 7.7 mm machine gun barrel at high altitude. There seemed to be some sort of eyesight problem here. A dangerous one.

"I believe...I see some folks milling around down there, sir. You don't reckon them's Japs?"

Dreisen snatched the glasses away from him. "Can't tell. Can't tell. Islands full of people, you know."

Hawk could tell one thing. Dreisen still didn't see the people down there. He wondered for a moment what it would be like to watch your faculties deteriorate. He supposed it would be all right if you were Aunt Matilda in your rocking chair, feeding the cat chicken parts, when you meant to give it tuna. Here, they found themselves in a different set of circumstances. What was Dreisen doing here?

In the grand scheme of things, Dreisen was not that

old, after all. He had merely chosen to play out the greatest drama of his life amidst the largest assemblage of vicious young men in the history of the world, and was suffering by comparison. But a lot of people make a similar mistake, climbing back into the ring one too many times. What else does one do? Give up? Isn't it better to be beaten? Hawk or Zanji would have great difficulty comprehending this.

"But it's a possibility," Dreisen finally admitted. "Our boy might be there. Not too many other places he could be. We have to check this out. This may be it."

Joe Canlon walked up to Hawk, after he saw that Dreisen was a safe distance away. "Did you tell him?"

"Not yet." Hawk looked back at the lighthouse. "Didn't come up." He had the urge to be in charge again. Or at least, to be free of Dreisen. "I don't know about the fella. I'm getting tired of shittin' like a sawmill hand every time the straw boss walks by."

"What do you mean? You're the guy always saying, 'he's a *colonel*, he's a *colonel*; oh, no, everybody, look, he's a goddam *colonel*'." Joe mocked.

"Yeah, well. It takes a long time to get to be a colonel. Maybe too goddam long. I'm gonna wait a while before telling him any funny stories. He might not be as sharp as I thought."

Joe was relieved. "That's what I think. That's what I tried to tell you. He does all this ramrodding to cover up for being a dumb ass. What kind of officer goes jumpin' off into the boondocks to do some shit like this? He could go any place in the world, and sip his scotch and push people around. Comes out here with us, where the shit hits the fan every minute." Joe shook his head. "There's just something funny about this whole thing. And it ain't just because of the flier out there."

"Well," Hawk began, a little dejectedly, "it won't matter. If the prisoners are there when we nab the pilot, so much the better."

Joe's eyes narrowed. "And if they ain't there?"

Hawk smiled and shrugged.

"I'll be god... you're going after them, aren't you? Deal me out. No more of that shit for me. Joe Canlon gets his guts blown out, so Ivania Broeder can live happily ever after with the president of General Motors, or better yet, with some *officer*?"

"All right. Crap. Keep your pants on. Nobody asked *you* to do *shit*."

"What if..." Joe stopped suddenly. He realized that not every thought should be spoken.

"What if what?"

What the hell, Joe thought. "What if they just kill *all those people* down there? Maybe accidentally. What if somebody makes this high level decision that Dreisen can't get the pilot alive, but they can still knock him off? Blow him up."

"That would take some thinking," said Hawk. "Might have to speak up then."

"You might be speaking up a little late, you know. MacArthur has been known to make a few moves without clearing it first with you."

The patrol climbed higher into a jungled plateau. The plateau continued gradually upward. It was so gradual that they did not notice it until the backs of their legs were tightening up. Hawk saw Dreisen having a discussion with Morgan and the guide over the map. Lieutenant Repler walked up to them. They looked at

Repler and stopped talking. The climb resumed. There was evidently some sort of difference of opinion on the route to take. Hawk decided to stay out of it. Whether he was right or wrong in his opinion, with three officers involved, somebody would hate him. He had the whole Japanese Army taking care of that job, and did not need to expand the work force.

The forest grew denser, with strange high elevation plant life sprouting in profusion. Some of the trees were shedding their bark, giving them a mottled, reptilian appearance. The air became cooler, and Hawk rolled his sleeves down.

Dreisen called a halt. He sat on a reddish-gray rock, breathing heavily. The rock was so colorful, it looked artificial. Hawk noticed how beautiful the woods were. He had rarely been in a cool jungle. *This is damn nice,* he thought.

"Damned altitude. Let the damned altitude get away from me," Dreisen wheezed. Hawk, healthy as a young horse, wasn't sure exactly what that meant. "We won't get there before dark at this rate."

Hawk stood with Morgan and Repler, the three of them respectfully staring at the top of Dreisen's red, sparsely covered, graying head. "Open out that damned map again," the colonel gasped, as he noticed himself becoming a curio. "Give it to Repler." It sounded like Repler and Dreisen had agreed upon something in the argument that Hawk had observed from afar. Which also meant that Koichi disagreed with them, which was not good.

The colonel waved Koichi over. The guide knelt at the colonel's feet by the map.

"I'm not what I used to be," said the colonel. "Helluva time to find that out, eh? Koichi, show me again where we're headed. I just can't get it into my mind how this will get us to the lighthouse. Hell, we can't even see the s.o.b. anymore."

Koichi pointed to their position, and then slid a finger across the page to the lighthouse. He then returned his finger to their position and directed it into a circuitous path to the lighthouse. "We go this way."

"Why, hell. That's a long way. We'd be better off going back to the beach and starting over. Why don't we just go straight? Look, here's that damn river going that way. All we have to do is follow it. Straight as an arrow, not even half the distance."

Koichi shook his head. "River comes out of gorge." He had just explained this thirty minutes earlier, from the perspective of the earlier location. Not much had changed. "Then river goes underground, two, three kilometers. It is easy to draw a picture of a river on a paper. But river is not there. It goes under the tall mountains. We cannot follow this river, and it would be much climbing to go over these mountains. You go where I show you. You go this way. All go this way." He ran his finger the way he had indicated several times before.

"Well, hell. We can follow the course of the river, can't we? We're climbing right now, ain't we?" Dreisen leaned close to the guide. The sudden and aggressive leaning was Koichi's instruction on how to answer. Koichi looked at Repler and Morgan, hoping for some intervention. Evidently, they had heard all of this before. They looked away. Without support, Koichi nodded reluctantly.

"All right. Finally. We're getting somewhere," Dreisen said. "We gotta improve our communication here. You know, I ain't no mountain goat. We'll rest ten minutes and cut a trail that way." Dreisen pointed off to the left, toward a stand of trees and jungle that a bulldozer could not get through. "Find that damned river, and walk right up to those Jap s.o.b.'s in no time."

Koichi nodded again. He stood and walked off. His face betrayed no expression. Hawk followed him.

"Hey...uh...wait up a second." Hawk stopped him. "Listen, podnuh, can we do this, or are you just trying to be agreeable?"

"It has been done."

"Then why did we come this-a-way in the first place?"

"This is the usual way."

"Oh, yeah? Then there must be a pretty damn good reason for it. If you don't like this new way, you better tell him. He don't know nothing about these mountains, or anything else. You just have to tell him. Ain't no disrespect in that."

"He is the colonel," Koichi answered simply. His expression was dark and troubled. Hawk nodded. He knew all about that.

"Okay, kid." Hawk slapped his shoulder. He hoped he had at least established a rapport with the young man. He had a feeling Koichi would be needing a friend with whom to confide in the very near future.

Hawk went from this disaster in the making, to sit with Canlon, so that further disasters could be contemplated. The air was invigorating. This was no time for a break. He knew Dreisen wasn't taking one because he wanted to. He had to.

"You know what?" Joe looked serious. This was not going to be good. Had he told Dreisen something?

"No. Now what?" Hawk replied angrily. He knew that was going to be it.

"I ain't shit since I got on this island. Must be the climate. How long can you go without shittin'? I might explode or some goddam thing." He shook his head. "You can get all kind of stuff by not shittin'. I ain't eatin' right or something."

"Well, hell, you ain't eatin' nothin', what do you expect?"

"Maybe so. A man's got to shit, though. You get locked bowels, your kidneys go, you get dry heaves."

"Is this gonna be the topic of conversation from now on or what?"

"No, I'm serious. This is serious business, Hawk."

"Listen, it's serious business if you're hanging around in New York and got nothing else to do but go to some quack. You're in the middle of some real serious business now, so you can forget that kind of shit."

Joe did not especially appreciate this consolation. Hawk would make a very poor medical doctor.

"Okay," Hawk shook his head. "It's serious. We'll be back at the beach in a couple days. You can make it that long." He stared at the uncompromising forest all around them. "Maybe they'll have one of them movies with all the men dancing around and singing. That'd make anybody shit."

They passed the forest and came to an area of sparse vegetation, meeting the narrow river that tumbled from the gorge. It ran furiously in its slender rock channel.

Blue water spewed gray and white between the reddish, papier-mâché-looking rock. Unused to mountainous regions, Hawk found that the terrain often appeared unreal. Following the course of the river proved to be untrying. Several men complained of the effect of walking on stone upon their feet. This inconvenience soon became forgotten when they reached the point where the river turned into an underground waterway. The rushing water ended in a monstrous cataract that spilled its contents over a cliff and into a hole in the earth. The great funnel was cone-shaped, and though it was rocky, tender-leafed plants grew all the way to its floor. At least a hundred feet down, the stone walls of the pit tapered to catch the water in a blue pool. The pool drained into a cavern at one side. Through this cavern, the river continued to run its course under the sharp mountains. The men gathered around the waterfall. The roar that arose with the boiling water vapor was intimidating. This was the route that they were to follow.

"Damn!" Edwards was the first to react to the sight. "What do we do now?"

"Men," Dreisen stepped up to the edge, to show that command was always in control. "Get those short ropes strung together. Let's get a few men down there. Get the lay of the land. The rest will cut timber for rafts. Lieutenant Morgan will assign the teams." If Dreisen was surprised at what he had led the patrol into, he gave no outward indication. Hawk had to admit, *he* was a trifle surprised.

Edwards and Price looked at Hawk. Joe walked over to the sergeant.

"Don't you think it's time you stepped in?" said Joe.

"Stepped in?" Hawk took off Joe's former helmet. "Stepped in what?"

"I think we need a mutiny. You need to talk to him

before he takes us into that drain hole," said Joe. Edwards and Price nodded agreement.

"Is that right? A mutiny? Then why don't you be the leader, Clark Gable? Take us all to Tahiti with you."

"Me, hell, I'm just a corporal."

"And I'm just a sergeant. There's a lot of daylight between me and that colonel."

"So, we all drown, Sergeant?" Edwards said. "You know this is all because he didn't want to climb that little hill anymore. Another fifteen minutes and we would have been there. We had to come all the way back to...this." Hawk listened impatiently. Mutinies occurred at sea, after months of abuse. The time element just was not there. The motive was weak: stupidity? That was not exactly a change of conditions.

Lieutenant Morgan walked over to the little discussion. He had a worried expression. "You two are in the team going down. You can be in charge of it, Hawk." Edwards stepped back a few inches, lest he be included.

"Aye, aye, Lieutenant." Hawk shot a glance at Canlon. Morgan looked distant. The officer stood silently for a moment. Maybe he was waiting for a comment from Hawk about the project. He did not have one of his own. He finally turned around and walked back to Repler.

"Well, that was taking a stand, all right," Joe said to Hawk. He wiped the sweat from his hair. Joe never liked wearing helmets, they were heavy and awkward, but now that Hawk was wearing his, it looked a lot better. "A man could damn sure bust his ass if he fell into that thing."

"Reckon? Then don't fall." Hawk bent over and tied two ropes together.

The sergeant seemed resigned to go along with the scheme. Joe became frightened. If Hawk went along with this, everyone would. Hawk knew what all the men were thinking. He did not see how they could expect him to do anything. *But men aren't always rational in such situations*, Hawk thought quietly. So far, all they had to do was climb down a rope, for crap sakes. Koichi said that it had been done. There was no need to panic. Then he noticed something. He nodded. "Let's just watch Morgan," Hawk said to Joe.

"Why?"

"Just watch him. He's scared shitless."

"I wonder why," said Joe.

"No, watch him. He's gonna do something crazy."

Joe turned and looked self-consciously at the Lieutenant. Morgan was talking excitedly to Repler. He was gesturing wildly, in spite of being a somewhat reserved individual, who never spoke with his hands.

"Yeah, you're right, they're up to something," Joe observed hopefully. He never expected much of anything from the two young officers. That's why the military preferred youth: they did what they were told. But this looked like it had possibilities.

Morgan and Repler faced away from each other, and toward Dreisen. The colonel was directing the felling of the slim trees that grew nearby. The whole idea of the raft project added to the anxiety. Evidently, the general idea was to raft miles through a black, unexplored, underground river. Morgan took a few long strides toward the colonel. He watched his boots and worked his lips with what looked like determination.

Hawk smiled. "Come on. I don't want to miss this shit."

About the time Hawk and Canlon caught up with Morgan, the others noticed that something was amiss. Rebellion was in the air. The men continued their duties at a safe distance, but still maneuvered closer to the action. Hawk noticed the others in his peripheral vision, a grim smile on his lips. Contrarian that he was, he was thinking of backing dumb old Dreisen, since he didn't like Morgan much.

"Colonel Dreisen," Morgan began in his deepest voice.

"What is it, Lieutenant?" A pause followed. "Get busy, Morgan, and quit fartin' around," the colonel snapped distractedly.

"Colonel Dreisen, there comes a time when an officer must do what he thinks has to be done. Sometimes circumstances..."

"Morgan, I'm not going to tell you again. Get your ass over there and get those men down that rope. We are under time constraints here, man. That Jap does not plan on summering at that lighthouse."

"I'm taking over command, sir. I can't let you take the men down there. I'm not accusing you of incompetence, sir. It's just that...and you will be treated with respect...and will not be put under arrest, as long as you cooperate, sir." Morgan's words scared himself more than they did Dreisen. Dreisen had been playing this military game a long time. The wild setting, of course, was a little disconcerting for him, as it would have been for anyone.

The colonel looked around at the crowd. He saw Hawk's half smirking face.

"Hawk, is this your idea?" Rank and protocol fell by

the wayside. They were a gang of men under pressure. Dreisen knew that Hawk was the only man there capable of leading, leading in a fashion, that is, that Dreisen would call leading. He also knew that Hawk was Marine Corps. Morgan was a boy. The colonel found it difficult to believe that Morgan would have the nerve to dream this up on his own. Rank was serious business.

"No, sir," Hawk answered, in a low voice that all nevertheless heard. The smell of water vapor was in the air. Dreisen looked both surprised and relieved. As far as he was concerned, the only vote necessary had been counted. Even colonels relied on the vicious presence of James Hawk.

"Okay, you men get back to work. This ain't a sideshow. Morgan, you come with me, son." The colonel waved at Morgan dismissively.

"I'm sorry about this, sir," Morgan said without moving. He preferred to remain on center stage for his performance. He kept his voice appropriately deep. Dreisen looked disgustedly at the ground and strode over to the lieutenant. He thrust his face to within an inch of Morgan's.

"You want me to slap your jaws, boy?"

"We cannot go down into that thing, sir. If you're not going to listen to reason and cooperate, I will have no choice but to arrest you."

"Hey, pretty good," Joe said, nudging Hawk in the ribs. He was impressed by Morgan's formal performance. He had forgotten that Hawk had been similarly arrested, not so long ago.

"Yes, you *can* let me, a colonel in the USMC, do whatever I damn well please, Lieutenant. But I'll do this,

I'll let you tell us what the alternative is, before I knock the ever-loving shit out of you."

"Sir, we've spotted the Japs at the lighthouse. That was the extent of our job. We have found the enemy pilot. You can call in an airstrike on that position and we can return to the beach and rejoin our unit. There is no necessity to throw away the lives of any more of these men."

Three or four of the men nodded to each other. The others listened attentively. Morgan's words made sense to them. They had never heard anyone speak in such a manner before, especially to a commanding officer. Such nerve was usually beaten out of you in boot camp. Most of them had taken it for granted that they had already thrown their lives away. Of course, making sense has no relevance to the military.

"I don't know why you are doing this, sir," Morgan continued, "or handling this patrol in this reckless manner, but some of us think you are doing it to make a name for yourself. It is not worth the loss of another life." Morgan had probably gone a little too far with this accusation, but he was young. He had attacked both Dreisen's competency and his character. Most of the others were young, too, so it all struck a harmonious chord.

Hawk's half smile faded. He didn't like the tone of that last crack. The whole thing was getting serious. Dreisen was not bluffing as well as Hawk had thought he would. Morgan did not back down as Hawk thought he would. A little traction was taking hold. The lieutenant was one of those rich kids that had some kind of feeling of entitlement that the sergeant could not conceive of, and it ran deeply into his personality and gave him confidence. Morgan actually thought he could get away with this. Hawk felt a little sorry for both of them. They were both jerks on stage. The sergeant did not like the sound of Morgan's plan for bombing the lighthouse, due to the likelihood of Allied prisoners being held there, but then he did not like the idea of being swallowed by an earthen gullet, either.

The embarrassing argument continued. "We've spotted Japs earlier, Morgan, how do you know our objective is there with this bunch?" Dreisen shouted angrily. The worst thing he could do now was to get angry. He had already engaged the kid, which was far below his station. It made Morgan look more credible. "Our job is to get the pilot, not radio some damned airplanes. It won't prove a thing to bomb the lighthouse. A bunch of disconnected arms and legs all over the ground is no evidence of anything. There is a lot about this you do not understand, boy. And you are showing it."

"The fliers will tend to reconnaissance. The bodies can be checked at our leisure," Morgan countered. The lieutenant knew he was winning. Dreisen was actually arguing with him. The colonel's face looked deflated, and his eyes were concerned. Joe thought Dreisen looked sick. The outcome seemed unbelievable to most of the onlookers. They had been for Morgan at the outset, but now many had second thoughts. They had not expected him to get this far.

The men mumbled among themselves. Something was about to give. Order was breaking down. Hawk stepped forward. You do not let such men get to thinking for themselves. Some were young, but only a few of them were fresh from their mother's arms, as so many magazine articles portrayed. Because most of the retread unit consisted of the Old Breed, there were a lot of more mature men here as well. A lot were Depression era street people, and generally rough customers. They could drink, hate, and kill with the worst of them. The younger ones, for all of their youth, were no saints, either. Order would now be preserved in the manner it had been preserved on old pirate ships, when mutiny threatened. The men became quiet again, parting as Hawk moved forward, a slinking new presence, winding his way into the debate. The menacing presence of the sergeant meant more to them in the wild and deadly isolation of Cokoni than did the tarnished bars and eagles of the officers. Morgan and Dreisen fell silent, for the first time, also pausing to look at Hawk. This only added to his importance. He looked down in what appeared to be humble deference to the two officers, though everyone knew better, and knew why he had stepped forward.

"I just remembered something, sir," Hawk spoke to Dreisen. He spoke in a low voice, taking advantage of all of the attention directed at him. "All of this business jogged my memory some, with the talk of an airstrike. The *swanee* back at the temple told me that there were American prisoners with the Japs. A bunch of important prisoners, like governors, and things. An airstrike would be dangerous, sir, for all those important folks. Some of them were real fancy, even like from England."

Hawk turned around and walked back toward the waterfall. Turning a little to the side, toward the men, he looked at them meaningfully from beneath his brows. It had the feel of an audible message. They shuffled about and fell into a disorganized mass behind him. Before long, Dreisen and Morgan were alone and glaring at one another without their audience. The pause was awkward, but the experienced Dreisen knew how to take advantage of the opportunity Hawk had given him.

"A man has to do what he thinks is right," Dreisen said at last. "That's what you think you did, Lieutenant. Good initiative. No hard feelings, kid. You do it again, and I'll have you court martialed—or kill you. That is a promise. Now get to work, and you won't be scared any more. Idle hands...and all of that."

Morgan stood his ground for only another thirty seconds. Repler alone still watched the contest. With an expression that showed no defeat, but without continuing his takeover, Morgan turned and joined the men chopping trees.

7

STRANDED IN THE RIVER STYX

TANAGUCHI WATCHED THE SKY ANXIOUSLY. THE SHIDEN Kai was long overdue. The *hancho* realized that the American Marines could be upon him before morning. It would take them that long to cross the mountains. He did not think that they would be daring enough to try the underground river as he had done. And if they did, he had left a few surprises for them. Nevertheless, the murderous pursuers troubled him.

He lit a bitter cigarette. He glanced up as his scout, Kirishima, marched the prisoners from the lighthouse. He studied the blonde American woman. Many American women were quite beautiful, in contrast to their male counterparts. The prisoners climbed down the ledge that the lighthouse rested upon, and sat on the grass as their keeper stood watch with a rifle. Taniguchi looked at the clouds again. It would be hard on the women and elderly to continue this march. And hard for Tanaguchi to win any races with the athletic enemy, because of the prisoners. He would wait a bit longer for the fighter plane before leaving, making his odds even worse. He walked over to Ivania Broeder and looked down at her. He smiled and held out his package of cigarettes.

"I do not speak Japanese," she said.

Taniguchi nodded. It was all that she ever said. Her lovely blue eyes were filled with a permanent terror. She sat with her arms folded across her chest, and refused to look at him. He was touched. He feared that she had lost her mind. He knew that she had experienced some terrible things during the fall of Verhangen, as had he. She had also had to survive a time of incarceration. Taniguchi was aware that prison camps were not always pleasant. He went to one knee.

"We will not harm you," Taniguchi said in English. "You need not fear us." Ivania Broeder shrank from him and repeated her sentence. Taniguchi smiled sympathetically. He did not think his English was that bad.

"Leave her alone, you filthy pig," the English governor shouted. He sat nearby watching the encounter play out. Taniguchi looked up at him suddenly. The governor's hands were bound. Kirishima took a step forward and reared back with his rifle butt. Taniguchi raised a restraining hand and shook his head.

Taniguchi took out his knife, stood and walked over to the governor. "Do not act foolish and you will not be harmed," he admonished the prisoner. He bent down and cut the bonds. Without another word, he sheathed his knife and walked away.

* * *

EDWARDS AND JOE CANLON worked together on the ropes. "Well. The boss shut that shit down," laughed Edwards.

"Yeah," Joe answered, "did you see their faces, when he walked up to them? Hussshhhh." He brayed like a donkey, and just as loud. "He's got them all buffaloed," said Edwards. Lieutenant Morgan looked over at them angrily, from the other side of the gathering.

"You, men! Shut that up! Do you realize we are in a combat situation?" Morgan castigated them. His shout was much louder than the laugh had been. But then, the falling water was louder than both.

This actually made it harder for Joe to keep from laughing. But he didn't laugh out loud.

"No, I didn't know *that*, you goddam son of a bitch," Edwards whispered. Tears ran down Joe's face.

"Got that rope tied off?" Hawk yelled.

"Yeah!" Joe replied. He coughed loudly to hide an irrepressible laugh that had escaped.

Hawk threw the coiled length over the cliff. Knots had been tied into the rope to aid in the descent. Dreisen looked down into the depths.

"I can get down," the colonel said, "but I damn sure can't get back up."

Hawk did not look at him, and continued to move about, swirling the rope away from outcroppings below. He craned his neck to look at the pool at the bottom of the rock enclosure. Dreisen was pushing himself harder than he was pushing the others. He would have to, if he was going to stay with this. The sergeant finally said, "Oh, we can pull you out, if we got to, sir."

The colonel looked up at the cruel, confident eyes of

Sergeant Hawk. "It's hell to get old, Hawk, don't ever let it happen to you."

"I'm doing my goddamnedest, sir." Hawk did not look at him. He knew Dreisen would be counting on him now. He did not like that. People always did that. Life would be simpler if everyone just looked out for themselves. Dreisen had not thanked Hawk for saving his command. That was fine. He probably thought he had done it all himself. Hawk had the double duty of looking out for the officer, and pretending that he was not doing it.

Baker walked back and forth, close along the perilous edge of the drop, chewing gum madly and looking down. Hawk glanced at him and shook his head. Baker didn't have all his marbles in the best of circumstances. He craned his unusually long neck farther and farther over the edge.

"Baker. You see something down there, Baker?" Hawk asked. Baker stopped pacing and looked at him with a vacant expression, though still chewing his gum frantically.

"Uh, no, Sergeant."

"Well, shit. Then do something," Hawk said quietly. Baker flinched, like a marionette whose puppeteer had suddenly jerked his strings, and walked away from the edge of the abyss.

Sgt. Kreski was the first man to try the descent. His long arms and legs clambered down without any difficulty. Dreisen watched solemnly. Perhaps he was concerned, or perhaps he envied Kreski. It was an odd envy, since Dreisen had at one time been quite good at this. But this was not one time, it was this time. It was the envy of the boxing coach, or the football coach, for their protégé, with the slight difference that Dreisen was still in the ring. The colonel thought of the pilot, Zanji, and wondered whether the ace would ever pass his prime. He supposed that wars did not last long enough for that to happen. The true heroes stayed forever young in blazing combat.

The slope was steep, but it afforded many places to stop and rest. No one, including Dreisen, had any trouble negotiating the trip down. Hawk descended last, after the colonel. He looked at the men gathered below, standing around on the ledge that bordered the pool. For one glorious minute, he was detached and above this madness. Morgan had ordered everyone down, including the team cutting the trees. It occurred to Hawk, that they would be extremely vulnerable after he went down. He looked around at the furious and beautiful rocks surrounding him. There were a lot of hiding places. Others, besides the usual demons of the wilderness, could be watching him. He sniffed. You have to take a chance every now and then. Any finished product always had that ugly seam of imperfection. He grabbed a knot and stepped casually over the side. He looked relaxed, even as he climbed down the worst of it. Each physical challenge fell easily before the hard outdoorsman, and he seemed to only increase in skill as the challenges arose.

His clothing soaked with spray from the waterfall, and his hands grew raw from the wet rope. Hawk reached the bottom in a matter of seconds. He noticed Sergeant Kreski watching him. He glanced back at Kreski, to see if he wanted something. Kreski looked away. *What the hell was that?* Hawk thought. Bastard.

Hawk crossed the ledge cut by the falling water and

eyed the cavern that eternally swallowed the river. It descended into the core of the earth at a slight angle. Its mouth spat and snarled at the travelers. It looked like something out of ancient Greek mythology. Dreisen had already launched the patrol's three rafts into the pool. They bobbed rhythmically, as if eager motors were running. The cavern's ceiling left only a couple of feet of headroom above the water. It was, however, wide enough at this point to accommodate the log rafts.

"See how deep the water is," Hawk spat in his angry accent, which always managed to get a response. The order was directed at no one in particular. Of all people, Kreski, closest in rank, waded into the stone floored pond. The water came to his thighs. He waded across the pool to the cavern and the water rose to his waist. He stepped into the entranceway and the level reached up to his chest.

"Can we get through the son of a bitch?" Hawk shouted over the noise. Jets of water sprayed between the two men from above.

"Yeah." Kreski's tone was ironic.

Hawk did not like the idea of going into this thing on general principle. Seeing Kreski standing there brought it all home. They were really going to do it. He did not like water in the first place, and secondly he did not like tight places. This had it all. It was kind of insane.

"Waiting for the order, sir," Hawk rumbled with resignation. Dreisen looked at him and back at the cave.

"It's gonna get dark in there, quick," Joe Canlon said above the roar of the waterfall. "Like black as hell—can't see nothing—dark. No light." His New York accent was loud and pronounced.

"Launch those rafts! Hold onto the sides of them. Get moving, men. Sergeant Kreski will lead the way," said the colonel. He slapped Joe on the back. "Don't worry, son. We got a flashlight and a carbide lantern." Dreisen stepped into the water and waded through the arc of ripples created by the plunging cataract. "Whoa! Icy on the old clappers!" he called back to Canlon.

When Dreisen was out of earshot, Joe looked at Edwards and said, "Carbide lantern, my ass."

The tunnel was every bit as dark as Joe had expected. He put a hand on one of the ropes and lowered himself to his knees. The cold water rushed about him. His head bumped the stone above, which snatched a handful of hair from his scalp. The half bending of his neck, together with walking on his knees, was excruciating.

"Hey, Hawk, give me my helmet back," Joe's voice echoed oddly in the stone tomb.

"Shit, no. I need it. I'm taller than you."

The level of the water rose as they descended deeper into the close chamber. Hawk found his breathing to be more difficult. The thick black air was filled with water vapor and a rocky mineral smell. No one spoke. The common hope was that the tunnel would become too narrow for them to go any farther. But the rock walls tantalized them, always leaving just enough room for their heads, and for the width of the rafts. The rough bottom of the stream cut the knees out of their pants. After a while the river deepened, giving them more headroom, though not enough to stand upright. Higher water accompanied this convenience. It slithered heavily around their necks. Finally, it rose to their noses, and they had to stand, half floating, on their toes.

The ceiling was not tall enough for this to be done comfortably. They inched along with their backs painfully bent, trying to protect the weapons, most of which floated safely on the rafts. The river pushing through the dark stone made a boring, constant sound that seemed neither loud nor soft.

On either side, Joe could feel the walls of the underground river's tunneling course. "Shit on this goddam shit," Joe whispered. At least nothing but a sightless crustacean could live in the unwelcome environment. "Where is that light?"

"I don't know," Hawk answered. But a damn good question. "Where is Colonel Dreisen?" This was intended to get a response from the colonel. No answer.

"Hell," Joe growled, "where am I?

The tight quarters made Hawk sweat, in spite of the icy water. His claustrophobia was acting up. A man would have a hard time finding a worse place than this in the known universe. The feeling was below his throat, and spreading through his chest, making him a little lightheaded. He kept moving, because it was his only alternative.

He dealt with the feeling in the way he dealt with everything else, by denying it. He thought better of the tunnel when the ceiling graciously leapt high above them. The men stood and the relief was immense. Dreisen lit his lantern, which hissed and gave off a bluish white flame. The water now bubbled waist deep around them. Overhead, hung an ominous pattern of jagged stone and shadows. Scintillating blue specks dotted it. The specks looked like crushed sapphires that had been blown up there. The river spread wider. Hawk waded up toward the colonel. Now that he could see him, he wanted to be close to the decision-making process.

"Ain't this something?" Dreisen asked, playing the light along the high roof. They were in a clammy grotto. The river ran into another narrow hole as it exited the cave.

"Damn sure is," Hawk answered in a distant tone. "We going ahead, sir? Think we can get through that?"

"Hell, yes. Why not? I'm dousing the light, men. Proceed, Sergeant Kreski." Kreski's face showed misgivings as the light died. As the result of a permanent crease between his eyes, he always looked worried. This time, he really was worried. The men splashed in the dark, going toward the spot where they last remembered seeing Kreski standing. They clumsily groped their way into the narrow crevice of the wall exit. The rafts scraped both sides of the opening, threatening at any moment to refuse to go farther. No one wanted to leave the rafts. If deep water presented itself, they would become lifesavers. The river could plunge off a ledge at any turn. The logs made hollow noises against the uncompromising stone.

"It's opening out again," Kreski called back. Then there was a splash, and a muffled call for help. Kreski was having trouble.

"Deep water," Hawk told Canlon. "Go get him." Joe was an excellent swimmer. He mumbled an obscenity and waded quickly ahead of the others. They stood still as he bumped by them. Dreisen lit the lantern again. Joe saw Kreski as a pitiable shadow, flailing about in the water of another high grotto.

Joe stepped off into the deep water. The bottom disappeared under him. He swam a couple of easy strokes, latched onto Kreski's long hair, and pulled him back. Kreski coughed as Joe held him up out of the water. Dreisen helped Joe pull the half-drowned man onto the foremost raft.

"You panicked, son!" Dreisen chided. "What the hell were you doing? Hold onto the rafts, men, we'll float across this deep part. The current is with us. It's no problem. Don't get scared until you have a reason to be scared."

Kreski, looking a bit worse for the experience, rode a raft, while the others clung to the sides of them. The men gamely launched themselves into the bottomless liquid. Hawk felt the ethereal chill of nothingness beneath his boots. When they had navigated the width of the grotto, the bottom returned. A strong undertow seemed to draw them to the far bank. The men crossed the dangerous space without breathing. "Hawk, take the point." Dreisen ordered when everyone was safely across.

"Aye, sir." Hawk waded ahead of the others to perform this unwelcome duty. Swimming was not his strong point, especially under these conditions. He had no desire to plunge into a watery crypt. The channel remained narrow. Hawk could hear Repler volunteering to take the point next. He considered abdicating his position early, and letting the officer have it. Repler was trying valiantly to prove himself. It was probably all for Dreisen's benefit. The officer did not want it to look like he had been part of the mutiny—although if anyone had been a part of it, it was Repler. It was always a good idea to take advantage of guilty volunteers, such as Repler, when they are around. They usually aren't around for long.

The stone had been smooth, but now it became rough. Clawing formations of rock reached out from the walls to bite into tender flesh. Hawk kept a hand on the wall, feeling the changing pattern there. For some reason, unknown even to himself, he stopped. "Pass up a light," he said. The old brass, right angle headed flashlight was pressed into his hand. Dreisen had had that baby for a while.

He flipped the L-shaped light on and looked around the ceiling. The water ahead of him gurgled downward, in the general direction of the lower depths of hell. The water was at his knees now. Searching all around, he finally looked down. No more than three inches in front of him, and an inch above the water, a wet cotton string extended across the tunnel. It was slack. Sweat shot down Hawk's straight and narrow nose. He took a step back from the string.

"What is it?" Dreisen shouted. "Hurry it up, Hawk."

Hawk's eyes followed the course of the string. "Somebody done put out a trotline, sir," he said quietly. The string ended in a hole, carved by nature out of the side of the rock. The sergeant's subconscious had informed him that the change in the feel of the rock meant a change in terrain, and at the same time, it suggested a good spot for a trap. Hawk had a sensitivity to traps. Had Kreski stayed at the point, they might all be dead. The string was attached to the spoon of an American grenade. The grenade was wired to a box that had been fashioned out of limbs. Inside the box were several sticks of dynamite. He looked deeper into the hole. Another bundle of dynamite lay behind the box. Among all of the misty shadows, he could not distinguish a detonator. He did not know if such a crude rigging would work, but he would take the word of whomever left it there, that it just might. It looked like enough explosives to turn the mountain they were under into a crater.

"Y'all stay put," Hawk said in a voice approaching a whisper. "And hang onto them goddam rafts. Don't let them break loose. Got a tripwire here." He picked the string up gingerly and made a slight loop in it. The grenade sat quite still, like a merry little troll, observing all of the action patiently. Hawk drew his knife, thrust it through the loop and severed the cord. It floated snake-like to either side of the tunnel. Dreisen, breathing heavily, came to the sergeant's side. He shined his lamp on the explosives.

"The damn Japs have been here," said the colonel, as if to convince himself. How could anyone have been in *here*? It was like finding footprints on the moon. Hawk said nothing. He picked up the pieces of the loose ends of the string, still attached to the grenade, and draped them over the little bomb, lest one of the rafts snag the string. "Watch your step, Hawk." Dreisen inspected the crude set up.

"Yes sir." *You bet your ass*, he thought.

"Are you going to slip a pin in it? Dreisen asked, like the interested neighbor boy at the garage workbench.

"Nah, shit." Dreisen did not like this, but he kept his mouth shut.

Hawk held onto the flashlight. He didn't want to waste the batteries, but traveling blind had suddenly become a bit out of the question. He waded a few feet and blinked the light on and off. After several hundred yards of this, Hawk stopped again. The trip was exhausting. The tension was incredible. The muscles in his neck waited for something deadly to happen. He tried to see everything in the brief flashes of light.

"Koichi," Hawk called from the front, "how much farther you think we got? Of...this?"

The guide did not answer for a moment. "We should be there by now. Almost through mountain." That sounded encouraging.

"I bet we're lost." Hawk recognized the optimistic barking of Joe Canlon. He could really sound like a fool sometimes. Joe was toward the end of the column. Being lost in this place was a nightmarish prospect. Just the suggestion would be sufficient for a few years of nightmares. Hawk took up the trek again. Every loose pebble under his boot was a mine. Every time he switched the light off, the vision of a string appeared in the darkness. Was that the pulling of the current, or the pulling of a wire? He breathed with his mouth open. The cave was hot despite the cool, swift-running stream. The narrow tunnel widened into yet another grotto.

Hawk shined the light across this new room. The circle of illumination exposed another surprise. On the far side of the grotto, where the river again disappeared into yet another channel, a large trapezoidal net hung covering the course of the stream, and barring further passage. It resembled a landing net in configuration. Hawk could tell by the way the light glinted off its inter-woven strands, that it was made of steel cables. The men stopped and looked across the grotto at it.

"That's a sub net, ain't it?" Dreisen said, leaning forward to see better.

"I guess," said Hawk. "It's a goddam net."

"Jap sub net," Dreisen nodded, and agreed with himself. "Canlon, go over there and see if you can move

the s.o.b. Are there any other good swimmers here!"
Price volunteered meekly. "You, too, son, get over there."

Joe and Price waded out into the grotto. They did
not have to swim. Halfway across, Price screamed and
dove, or fell, into the water. Joe crouched in horror,
looking around, for he knew not what. Price's head
broke the water.

"What are you doing?" Joe asked breathlessly.

"I thought I hit a trip wire. I know I hit a trip wire,"
Price answered. He stood and looked around himself in
the water, and along the edges of the cave. He looked
puzzled and a little embarrassed. From somewhere, or
coming from the very stale air all around them, they
could hear the chugging of a motor.

"What is that? That's new." Hawk asked the colonel.

"That sounds to me like a boat motor," said Dreisen.
"The man probably hit a warning device. They may
have a boat right here outside the mountain. They must
be running." Dreisen waded toward the net. "Come on,
they are right here!" The colonel called with excitement.
The men waded cautiously toward the net. They were
not quite as enthused about rushing to greet the waiting
Japanese troopers, as was the colonel. Dreisen pulled at
the net. He might as well have been pulling on the Eiffel
Tower. It did not budge.

He reached down under the water. He found a U-
shaped rod securing it to the rock floor. The rods had
either been driven into the stone or concreted there.
Nothing short of a cutting torch would sever them. The
men were effectively caged inside the mountain. Hawk
wondered what a grenade would do to the underwater
rods. He also wondered what it would do to the interior
of the mountain.

"Price, climb up there and see what's holding this thing at the top," Dreisen ordered. The barrier had to have a weakness. He looked up at the dark and eerie recesses near the top of the grotto.

Price dutifully climbed the rungs of the net. Three quarters of the way up the cables, he could see that the net was suspended from hooks driven into the rock.

"Hooks?" Can you lift the damn thing off of them?" The colonel asked, adding, "there's some slack in this thing."

Hawk snorted. The complex of cables had to weigh a few thousand pounds. Price would not be lifting it off the hooks, or at all. As they watched Price struggle above them, there was a buzzing, thunderous crack. The net blazed a phosphorescent blue. The smell of burnt flesh filled the grotto. Price hung tangled in the cables, his clothing aflame. Zig-zag strips of white fire ran up and down the cables that held him. A powerful vibrating force ran through Hawk, and then he was knocked into the water. Numbed, he crawled onto a raft. Several seconds later, he saw others doing the same. They looked dazed, and dazed as to why they were dazed. Fiery thick strands of electricity continued to slap at Price's wedged body. No one recalled his crying out.

"There's a current running through that thing," Dreisen said. All of the men had taken a few volts. The water was a conductor. Only Price had been seriously injured, and he was unquestionably dead. The crackling finally stopped. The motor, however, could still be heard, running somewhere close by.

"The electric current must have turned off," Hawk

told Canlon. "It looks like it goes off and on. It's shorting out or something."

"We can't get by that. Are we going back?" Joe asked.

"Why don't you ask Dreisen?" Hawk growled. "He likes questions like that."

Joe nodded knowingly. They were not going back. He looked at Price's charred corpse hanging melted into the cables above them. "Then how are we getting through that?"

"I don't know. Maybe we can blow it." Hawk tried to understand the puzzling mechanism imprisoning them.

"I don't know about that. I don't think so."

"No. Me neither." The sergeant admitted. Hand grenades worked wonders on human flesh. Steel cables were another matter. There was the dynamite, still lying behind them, deep within the mountain. But he would need a detonator.

"The current is off, men," Dreisen shouted. "Who wants to go up there and unhook that net." Hawk shook his head: *he's still stuck on the "unhooking" idea.*

There were a few obscenities and one anonymous voice asked, "Why don't you do it?" The cable started to glow again, lighting the chamber softly with an ultraviolet sheen. Price's body sizzled. After a minute, the glow and the sound gently subsided.

"Come on, men, show some spunk, we can get up there before the current starts again. Who's going?"

"We?" asked the same anonymous voice.

Repler looked at the reluctant men. His lips were thin and white. He thought that he would have enough time. "I'll do it," said the Lieutenant.

"Wait a minute, Lieutenant," Hawk attempted to stop him. He did not believe that the current disconnected for an interval long enough to allow for any more acrobatics. And no one was ever going to lift that net.

Repler jumped from the raft and latched onto the net. He climbed it swiftly. The heavy cables swayed only slightly. The lieutenant maneuvered around what had been Price. Black flesh sloughed off one of the dead man's arms, like it was a glove. It smacked into the water below. The bones of his arm were clearly visible. Repler reached the top, but his race against time was not over. He pulled at the hooks supporting the net. The chugging of the motor droned on. Hawk thought now that the sound was coming from above them.

"Shit, I can't bend these hooks," Repler called. "Maybe I could beat them loose with a hammer." He strained some more on them. "That motor is up here somewhere. It's a lot louder up here." Repler looked at the rock above himself. "There's a little tunnel up here." He went back to pulling on the hooks, but they were too stout. The lieutenant knew that his time was up. He could either drop to the water below, or climb up into the tunnel he had found. He would do neither, for when your time is up, your time is up.

The air exploded. Blinding light filled the chamber. Repler fizzled like an electric sign in the rain. He fell crackling down the net and splashed smoking into the water.

Hawk watched stoically. Beside him he noticed the small length of pipe that the extra rope had been wrapped around. It would make a good cheater pipe. He unspooled the remaining rope, and took the pipe in his hand. He got off the raft as the cables stopped glowing. He waded over to the net and took off his shirt. No sense in burning up a perfectly reusable shirt. He ran up the hot square rungs of the net, and latched onto a hook at the top. He slipped the pipe over it. He pulled down mightily on the end of the pipe, making maximum use of the leverage. The great muscles that lay coiled along the backs of his arms and shoulders knotted. He looked more like steel than the steel he clung to. The hook surrendered all at once, screeching and straightening out into a spike-like object. The weight of the net pulled down on it, pointing it farther downward.

The sweat in his eyes clouded Hawks vision. He felt his heart pounding a warning. Every beat told him to prepare for a final hot surge of voltage.

He swung with amazing agility and speed to the next hook, as if he had been training for this since childhood. He slipped the pipe deftly over the top of the large rusty hook. It gave more quickly than did the first one. He swung to the next one and repeated the procedure. This hook broke completely off, and one side of the net sagged violently. Hawk hung onto the gyrating spider web.

"That's good!" Canlon shouted anxiously. "There's a big gap now. We can crawl through. Get the hell down!"

Hawk looked into the tunnel above him. He shined the light inside. He could see at least two generators and a transformer.

"Get off it!" Canlon shouted again.

"Jump, Hawk!" Dreisen screamed. "Time's up!"

Hawk continued his inspection. This was where the motor noise was coming from. How did this work? Feeling that he had used up his enormous quantity of luck, and time, he released the net and dropped like a rock into the shallow water below.

"Good job!" Dreisen shook his clenched fists. "We can get through there, if we just leave the rafts."

Hawk waded breathlessly back to the colonel. "The net is wired to some generators. I guess it is shorting out every once in a while. The current is probably supposed to be on all the time. Price must've turned the generators on when he hit a tripwire coming in," the sergeant said. Dreisen was not interested. That aspect of the problem was over. Hawk could save the details for his diary as far as Dreisen was concerned. Moving on was the important thing. The colonel only wanted to slip the men through the narrow opening and get out of the mountain. To Hawk, however, the man to whom all these insurmountable problems had been assigned, what was past, was prologue.

"Do you think we ought to grenade the generators, sir?" Hawk put on his shirt. He was no engineer, and it baffled him that a trip wire had turned the generators on. Had a weight fallen on a floor starter pedal, like those used in a truck? Or was there a simpler explanation? A human explanation. He suspiciously eyed the dark tunnel above them.

"No. Let's go. The s.o.b.s will run out of fuel."

Still, it bothered Hawk. This was a little too sophisticated for ordinary soldiers, or even a pilot to set up. Now—an aircraft mechanic—could tinker around with something like that. What would an aircraft mechanic be doing on this side of purgatory? How about working on an aircraft? *Damn*, Hawk thought. They have a whole crew here. *What are we walking into?*

Within another hundred yards they saw the painful silver glare of the bright outside world. Their eyes grew accustomed to it as they got closer. The pinpoint of light grew to be a hole a little over ten feet high. The river spilled out of the mountain and into another little waterfall. Joe Canlon was the first to run out into the welcome daylight. He stood in the rushing water and took a deep breath of the brisk mountain air. It was cool outside. But it was not cold, and Joe was surprised to see tiny snowflakes falling down. They melted upon contact with the earth. Joe looked up at them, and noticed with some alarm, that he was almost within shouting distance of the lighthouse. It dominated an immense valley on its farther side, and men walked aimlessly about the curious old building. If they had been in the tower of the lighthouse, they would have spotted Joe easily. He could tell for certain that they were Japanese. The inside of the dark mountain seemed much more inviting now than it had five minutes ago.

Hawk came up behind him from the inside of the tunnel. He squinted as he saw a man appear from around the rock and leap on Joe's back, knocking him into the water. Hawk restrained a laugh as he watched Joe scrambling to his hands and knees with the nearly naked little brown man on his back.

"Ahhh. Shiiit! Help!" Joe screamed. Hawk's knees bent with amusement.

Hawk unslung his Thompson and walked calmly toward them. The attacker lashed an arm around Joe's neck from behind. Joe clawed at the arm, bucked like a horse and collapsed gasping in the water. A small chuckle burst from Hawk's lips this time. This was funny stuff. "Help!" Joe repeated.

A short-bladed karambit flashed over the heads of the two men fighting in the sunlight beneath the water. Hawk's smile faded. "Uh oh," he said.

Hawk touched the trigger of his submachine gun. The report had the rhythm of someone knocking rapidly twice on a door. A lightning bolt erupted from the muzzle, seemed to pass under Joe's arm, and pierced the attacker. The little man flipped out of sight, over the cataract. Hawk pulled Joe up by the arm. They looked down. The knife-wielding stranger had tumbled over the waterfall and lay bleeding in the river below them. It was one of the Cokonian men who had been following them, and he was dead. His arms and legs were positioned as if he were running on a horizontal canvas. Hawk looked above and behind them, and over at the place from which the man had approached. He saw no others. He thought he heard the sound of bare feet running away, but the noise of the waterfall made it difficult to distinguish with accuracy. He shook his head as he looked down.

"Wonder what the Articles of War's got to say about that," Hawk commented.

The men in the lighthouse had no trouble hearing the brief report of the Thompson. Taniguchi lifted his binoculars in time to see the patrol blundering out of the tunnel. To the right, he could see the northernmost reaches of the green swamp of Jarok.

"The Cokonians must not have set the traps as you instructed," Zanji told the *hancho*. "We have wasted some good equipment."

"Yes," said Taniguchi, "I do not suspect treachery, only incompetence. The Americans have shot one of them. They are upset about the Marines stealing their talisman. It is fortunate for us that the Marines did so. These islanders were at best lukewarm subjects of the Emperor. I am afraid they were cooperating with the enemy, until this fortunate turn of events." He put down his binoculars. "You can rely on Americans for that. Now, we must leave here immediately. I did not fully expect them to choose that route. They can reach us in an hour, if they are sure of the way. We are very vulnerable here."

"But my Shiden Kai will not find me, if we leave. If it ever arrives." Every muscle in Zanji's face was tightened.

Taniguchi shook his head and again looked through the field glasses. What could he say? "Yes, *if*. We have done all that could be done, honorable Zanji." Taniguchi looked at the Marine who had shot the Cokonian. His lips parted. No, it could not be. It was only wishful thinking. The bearded thugs all looked similar beneath their camouflage helmets. If only it could be. The man looked too slender. He remembered a trim, but heavily muscled man. Taniguchi did not realize it quite yet, but he was looking at the murderer of Keizo, the same man who had brought him to Cokoni. He had not noticed that he himself was growing rather slender under the spell of exotic Cokoni.

* * *

DREISEN LOOKED at the Japanese through his glasses. "That's our Japs! We got 'em now! Get me the map. It'll take 'em a long time to get down out of there."

Hawk looked at the flat plain behind the pinnacle upon which the base of the lighthouse stood. "See any prisoners, sir?"

"No. That was probably just talk. Come on. We can chew the fat on the march," said the colonel.

"Can't we have about ten minutes, sir?" Joe asked.

He was sitting in the shallow waterfall hanging his legs over the edge. He had a cut on his forehead. Joe had not taken the Cokonian attack as lightly as had Hawk and Dreisen.

"You can rest all you like, young fella," Dreisen answered. "You'll just have to run twice as fast to catch up with us, and protect yourself while you're doing it. I hope you can run better than you did the other day."

Joe shifted his mouth to one side and looked at Hawk. Hawk winked. Joe turned away. *Hawk was all tickled*, Joe thought, because they were going to find Ivania Broeder. Joe was fearful of Dreisen. They were about to have a violent clash with the Japanese, and the colonel had proven again that he was not one to grieve over casualties.

The men vaulted over the waterfall, descending into the river below. They all had to pass Joe. Joe watched for a minute, looking around. This was a damned beautiful island, he could not help but notice. If only you didn't have to walk every square inch of it.

Hawk was the only one who paused by the still seated Canlon. "Coming? Or what?" Hawk looked around on all sides, waiting for a response. "Shit!" he added.

Joe looked up, looking a little pathetic, with the red streak across his head. "When I get goddam good and ready. You better shave, Hawk, if you're gonna be seeing that babe. You look like crap. Not that you still won't look like crap."

Hawk snorted.

"That's why you're going along with all of this bull-shit, isn't it? You're gonna end up getting shot, and getting everybody else shot, for no reason."

"Come on, get up. I'm going along because I'm in the Corps. When they start letting you do whatever the hell you want, I'll join your army."

"Yeah. Ain't it funny, they always end up doing just what you want them to do?" Joe stood with a sigh. "You're a dumb ass."

"Well. You're a shitball."

8

DUEL ON A MOUNTAIN LEDGE

TANIGUCHI HERDED THE PRISONERS DOWN FROM THE upper stories of the lighthouse. The guards escorted them at a trot down the crag of rock upon which the lighthouse rested. Access to the plains required a gradual descent of a dozen feet below. The *hancho* felt distress now, as there was an increasing likelihood of being overtaken. The Marines were not moving like the Americans usually moved. They were coming after him with determination. The prisoners sensed the stress as well. While they wanted freedom, they had no particular desire to be in the middle of a pitched battle. Their best hope was to be abandoned. They were nervous about their fates *after* the projected rescue of Zanji. Their enemies often fretted about the fate of Zanji, but refrained from any mention of concern for them.

To the south of Taniguchi, beyond the plains, was the waterfall and the strange green swamp. To the west was a drop of several hundred feet, and the jungle valley below, where the Pacific Ocean once lay. To the east and north, beyond the plains were woods and mountains, with the woods predominating on the north and the mountains on the east.

Taniguchi led the fleeing party eastward, toward the nearest range of difficult peaks. If he could reach these mountains, he was confident that he could lose the Americans. He was not yet ready to completely abandon the lighthouse and strike out for the beach. The prospect of the Shiden Kai landing on the plains, and ending all of his problems, was too inviting to merely forget about. The party of Americans looked small, but larger than his own. Taniguchi was not one to shrink from a fight, especially if it had a purpose. Eliminating these Marines would be advantageous. For the time being, they were his only tormentors. First, he had to get Zanji to some kind of immediate safety.

It was only a short while later that Hawk swaggered up the gravelly soil toward the door of the lighthouse of Jarok. The others climbed in a single file below him, at a respectable distance. His eyes shifted from the earth, where they searched for mines, to the lamp room above him, where they expected a diehard, suicidal sniper. He flattened along the curved wall and edged toward the open door. Hearing nothing, he looked inside. Seeing nothing, he stepped inside. The other men remained on the ground a few feet below, their weapons trained on the door, the windows, and the lamp room. Morgan kept his rifle pointed at Hawk's back.

Hawk found a spiral stairway leading upwards. A large table and a few rickety chairs were placed behind the stairway. Cast off Japanese Army gear lay against the walls.

Dreisen scoured the eastern hills for a glimpse of

the enemy. He raised two fingers and motioned Kreski and Sprack toward the building.

"Nobody home," Hawk told them, when they entered. "Down here." He mounted the stairs. His boots fell softly on the ancient steps. He glanced in each room along the way. They were empty save for blankets, bowls, and other useless paraphernalia. There were three high ceilinged floors, not including the top room. When he reached the top of the stairs, he stuck his head cautiously into the open air of the lamp room. He saw that it was vacant of life-threatening humanity, and he stepped up into it.

A breathtaking view confronted him on all sides. The wall of the room was only four feet tall, but the ceiling was over ten feet from the floor. He could see the whole island from this open platform. He walked to the western wall and looked out. The earth dropped away for almost a thousand feet in front of him. Close, sweating jungles crouched under green canopies of trees on the floor of the valley at the bottom of the cliff. Behind him, to the east were the purple, blue and orange-swirled mountains. He immediately saw Taniguchi's party, struggling up a lesser slope. The lighthouse enjoyed an elevation that rivaled the highest peak on Cokoni. Hawk could see the dim, gray haze of the ocean in the far distant north.

"Pretty nice." He nodded.

A 13.2 mm machine gun, and its accompanying crates of banana clips were the room's only occupants. Hawk studied the powerful mounted weapon. The bullets it used were slightly larger than the American 50 caliber gun. It was a heavy weapon, the gun without its pedestal probably weighing around ninety pounds.

Such guns were used routinely for anti-aircraft defense. Hawk had rarely seen the enemy in possession of such a magnificent piece. The Japanese Navy used them as double mounted guns on their ships, complete with seats and cranks, all carefully ensconced behind a turret. *Who put this here, and why?* So much for the reports of an uninhabited wild region. Unless, the squirrels had sent away for this by mail order.

Hawk glanced at the flat plains, and then he looked at the sky. The Japanese must have thought that it would be necessary to defend themselves from an air attack. He looked back at the well lubricated weapon. Either that, or they thought it would be necessary to provide air cover for a plane or two of their own. That thought made him turn, and once again watch Taniguchi fighting his way up the nearest mountain-side. Zanji had to be with him all right. There did not appear to be as many of them, as he had suspected. Maybe they were having the same difficulties staying alive as the Americans.

He rested his hand on the ring-coiled barrel of the weapon. It probably had a ground range of over a couple of miles. He swung the double pistol grips around and sighted them in on Taniguchi. The gun would scarcely aim that low. But Taniguchi was climbing higher. The gun pivoted easily, and with a barely audible oily squeak. He set the point of the knife blade foresight into the little peephole on the hindsight. Crosshairs radiated from the peephole, so that a gunner could track a rapidly moving airborne target. He put the knife blade on Taniguchi's head and followed him up the mountain. His mouth drooped into a cold smile as he fingered the trigger. He longed for that feeling of well-being that he got when a well-directed shot smacked hard and clean into a hated object. It was a difficult feeling to describe. The feeling of perfection. That was war's compensation, for ridding you of your mental and physical health.

"Bust your rotten brains all over them goddam rocks," Hawk growled at Taniguchi.

Taniguchi disappeared behind one of the white columns that supported the upturned corners of the lamp room's pagoda roof.

"Good gun," Hawk whispered. He released a deep breath. He let the grips go, and the weight of the gun caused the barrel to point upwards. He walked down the steps. He met Dreisen at the ground-level door.

"The Japs are getting away, sir," he said, pointing to the eastern mountains.

"I saw them. We'll catch them. Damn soon, too."

"They got a heavy machine gun up there...nice one. We could probably drill them from here with it."

"Probably doesn't count. Mr. Probably is probably booby-trapped, too," Dreisen said. Hawk swallowed. He had forgotten about that. He had been spinning it like a toddler with a merry-go-round. It wasn't like him to overlook such things. One mistake like that and you were out of mistakes. He was a killer, and he had been enthralled by the glamorous killing tool that he had found. Such was the allure of booby-traps. Every man had his bait. Well, he had not fired it. "Could you see the prisoners?" Dreisen asked.

"No, sir." Maybe you can, with the glasses." Dreisen went to the top floor and tried, and of course, could see nothing definite. Dreisen glanced at the weapon. "That's an old Hotchkiss. Damned, if it isn't. Helluva place for something like that."

Dreisen ordered the men into a hot pursuit. They were given ten minutes to rest while he inspected the lighthouse grounds. Some of the Marines were getting angry. They had not eaten today. This was the sort of thing that would make you mad. The colonel paused long enough to radio Holley. He told him to ask for a ration drop on the lighthouse.

"Send jackets, nippy up here. And ammo and grenades, too," the colonel instructed. "Tell them we will get Zanji today. In a matter of hours. Got him in sight." Dreisen had yet to try his back and his legs on the rough eastern mountains.

Holley relayed news of what was going on at the beach. The Marines were firing over the heads of marauding Cokonians, firing into the heads of marauding Japanese, and burying tons of surplus equipment with bulldozers, that had been arriving by ship daily. The men on the beach were under the mistaken impression that large numbers of patrols were searching the island for Isamu Zanji. The Americans were also growing increasingly unsympathetic toward the indigenous outrage over the theft of the relic of Hai-tai.

Locally, however, the chase began in earnest. Dreisen closed the gap between the pursuers and the pursued. He told the men to hold their fire until fired upon. This was a policy strictly out of character with other Pacific campaigns. The frequent and tantalizing glimpses of the enemy above them would have allowed for a few good sniping shots. Most of the men wanted to take advantage of the opportunities. The Japanese, in a most irritating way, refused to fire on them first.

Hawk had to admit, all things considered, Dreisen was accomplishing his objective in style. If he could just keep up the pace, which Hawk secretly doubted.

Taniguchi could see the Marines below him, in the wide panoramic view from above. He was shocked by the ease with which they were gaining on him. They would catch him. The women and the elderly prisoners were slow, by design, or otherwise. The *hancho* considered leaving them behind now, in order to save Zanji. The pilot was the priority. The beleaguered public on the home front had never heard of Ivania Broeder or the others. It was Zanji, however, who insisted that abandoning them be postponed until absolutely necessary. This was the first time the ace had interfered with Taniguchi's authority. The *hancho* had to concede. It seemed the pilot, by doing this, was making an almost certain choice of a fight over the flight. His high value of the prisoners would soon change, after he saw what a fight was going to involve.

The British governor fell behind. The guards stopped trying to stay behind with him. The Marines were close now. Contact was imminent. Ivania Broeder lagged behind as well. The other woman was much hardier. Taniguchi suspected that Ivania might have been a little hardier than she seemed. Taniguchi took Ivania's hand and pulled her up the slope. Bringing these unwilling people was a mistake. Had Zanji believed that hostages would deter their pursuers? He did not know the enemy on the ground as well as did Taniguchi. When the shooting began, they would care nothing for innocent bystanders. The *hancho* was tired, and all that awaited him when he reached the mountaintop was the trip down, with the Marines above him, instead of below. He decided that he did not make a good fugitive. He would make up for these shortcomings when the time came to engage the Americans.

The exhausted governor, well past his prime, fell on the incline and slid down a few feet. The Japanese stopped. The governor made no outcry or attempt to get up. An angry guard went back to get him. The brutal scout, Kirishima, went back also. Taniguchi went with them to make sure that there would be no abuse, or at least, killing. There was no time for such foolishness. That sort of conduct was a luxury for noncombatants. When the sergeant reached the Briton, he realized that the prisoner was dead. White hair was plastered to his red face. It had probably been a heart attack, or some other ailment, common to the unfit. Taniguchi was not interested in the pathology of it. He could hear American voices below. He ran back to Ivania Broeder, and pulled her forcefully up the slope. She was the slowest now. The others passed him.

"They're almost to the top, sir," Hawk observed from the head of the American column.

"We got 'em! Got 'em now!" Dreisen replied excitedly. It looked like he did.

"Gonna be some shootin', sir," Hawk warned calmly, thinking that perhaps Dreisen might be forgetting himself, and the gravity of the situation. This was not exactly the hunt for an unarmed fox. It was not even a police action, where an armed force pursued a greatly inferior force. This was a contest where the pursuer and the pursued could quickly change roles, and a role change like that could become quite stunning.

"Fine. Fine." Dreisen wheezed.

The first of the Japanese soldiers reached the summit. Without pausing to enjoy the view or the accomplishment, he dove down the other side. Their pace quickened as gravity aided in the descent. The Japanese knew, however, that any gain in speed was going to be outweighed by their visibility as the party below their pursuers.

Taniguchi fell farther behind with Ivania. She appeared to be trying to keep up with him, but was just unable to do so. She was easily fifteen years younger, but it did not seem to help. They negotiated a narrow ledge that led to the summit. The others had made it along the ledge without incident. Ivania was exceptionally agitated by the dizzying view of the rocks below. Long blond hair blew across her eyes. Taniguchi patiently edged along the uncomfortable footpath, his ears filled with the sounds of the approaching Marines. One place on the ledge, narrower than the rest, required him to hop across. He let go of her hand, and gestured at the opening in the ledge, that she might precede him. When she did, she fell, or more precisely, slid down, a few feet below the ledge. She clung to the root of a weed-like shrub that grew there, her legs swinging out over a two-hundred-foot drop. Her hair blew into a straight yellow line out over the fall.

"I can't....hold on," she said. She was not feigning that, Taniguchi decided.

Taniguchi heard angry boots bearing down on them. He looked down the curving ledge. The Americans would round the bend in the trail on the ledge, and be upon him at any minute. He knew that he should leave her there.

"I'm...falling."

The *hancho* turned and reached down, taking hold of one of her arms with both hands. Taniguchi was a strong man, and she was under even her normally light weight. He pulled her up easily. Once back on the ledge, he had difficulty in balancing the both of them. If he fell, no one would be pulling *him* up. After a tense fifteen seconds, he had reestablished their equilibrium. He was dangerously far behind the others now.

"Your own people will take care of you now," he told her, and leaping the narrow portion of the ledge, he disappeared behind the outcropping rocks. Ivania raised a hand and started to call to him. She did not want him to leave her here. She made a weak movement to follow him. The routine of running was still in her mindless reflexes.

The very moment that Taniguchi disappeared around the leaning rocks, the grim and merciless figure of Sergeant Hawk stepped onto the ledge. Had he been a second sooner, Taniguchi's fate would have been much different, and of much briefer duration. Hawk blinked quickly at the sight of the woman and lowered the muzzle of the Thompson. He eyed the ledge for a trap. She knelt against the mountainside and looked up at the tall, terrible, and unkempt man before her.

"I don't speak Japanese," she said to him.

Hawk looked into her haunted eyes. She only remotely resembled the haughty Ivania Broeder he had known on Rechnung and Verhangen. She huddled there and refused to look at him again. Did she recognize him?

"Neither do I," he said, looking up the ledge. His vicious eyes burned. He clicked the safety off the

Thompson. He had a cast-off prisoner and a gap in the ledge that he would have to jump. It was a perfect trap. He was not slowed by tender mercies, after finding this woman he had thought so much of, for so long. No, he felt something else, more pressing. By the grace of God, most men with such feelings are safely locked away in secure places.

He went quickly around her and hopped over the open space. An ugly fate awaited the first Japanese soldier he could find. He outdistanced the other Marines, and raced Taniguchi to the summit.

Hawk and Taniguchi were both separated from their comrades, one for being too slow, the other for being too quick. The *hancho* knew that he could not get away. He stopped at the summit and unslung his Solothurn submachine gun. He stood in the open without cover. When the first American reached the last leg of the trail, he would bowl him over, and gain precious time, as the others took cover, and approached more cautiously.

Sergeant Hawk had other ideas. He knew an ambush when he saw one. He had two hand grenades. He unbuttoned one from where the safety lever was thrust through a buttonhole. Tiny, salt-like snowflakes, or ice crystals, began to fall from the late afternoon sky. They hardly paused at all before melting on his whiskers and helmet. He pulled the ring of the grenade and let the spoon fling itself over the side of the ledge. He lobbed the heavy little pineapple up toward the summit. Hawk advanced through the smoke and dust following the short, businesslike crack of the grenade. He could still hear ghostly echoes of the blast passing through the recesses of the neighboring peaks.

Reaching the top, he saw no one. A submachine gun rattled beneath him, and he threw himself down. A handful of bullets meowed over and about him. He heard boots skidding down the other side of the mountain. Slowly, he got to one knee for a look around. *How did that sorry bastard avoid getting blown to bits?*

Immediately below him was a wide table of rock, jutting from the mountainside. It was littered with boulders and heavy outcroppings, as if it had been the dumping ground for debris during the construction of the peaks. Across the table, and through the debris scampered a powerfully built Japanese soldier. Hawk jumped to his feet and slid down the hard slope. He ran swiftly after the enemy trooper. They both dodged frantically in and out of the scattered boulders. Hawk stopped, threw his stock to his shoulder and fired a burst. Taniguchi hit the ground and crawled through the mad ricochets for cover. Safely behind a sharp-edged stone, the *hancho* thrust his Solothurn up and over, to return the fire.

Hawk ducked. Chips of stone spat over his head. Taniguchi sat back down, breathing heavily. He was nearly forty now, and this kind of activity taxed him. The running and climbing had no effect. Getting shot at is a different type of calisthenic. He held his weapon by its perforated fore piece that encased the barrel. It was hot. He slid another thirty-two-round clip of the 9 mm shells into place, and flicked the lock under the magazine housing. The *hancho* knew that this was more than just life and death. He *had* to get away. Without Taniguchi, Zanji had no hope of escaping these jackals. And more importantly, if Taniguchi did not win, he would never find the coward who killed Keizo. He could not waste his life battling with this rash fool pursuing him.

Hawk crawled toward the last position the Japanese had occupied. No one fired at him. "Gonna play it cool, Jap?" He whispered. The snow blew thicker, looking less like specks of ice and more like flakes. The air was cold, but Hawk's shirt was open, and he sweated profusely. The sergeant stood in a cautious crouch. He aimed his Thompson toward the enemy's suspected position. He waited with the murderous patience of a hunter for the Japanese to bounce up again. And emerge he did. But Taniguchi had crawled twenty feet to the right. The Solothurn bellowed loudly from the unexpected position. The startling death hammer made Hawk feel as if needles had been stabbed into every pore of his body. Fountains of erupting steel danced before his fluttering eyes. He dropped as quickly as his shattered nerves would allow, and the shells continued playing just above his helmet. Hawk breathed deeply. His skin was clammy and cold. It was a miracle, yet another miracle, that he had not been hit.

This was a game for which Hawk was uniquely qualified, and yet he was far from winning. He gained new respect for his adversary. This was a bad guy. "Well, that's okay," he said quietly. He noticed the snow now. He scowled, turned over, and crawled again toward the enemy soldier. He was going to close the distance, although to whose advantage that was, he had yet to decide. The two of them could crawl about forever in these massive stones and crevices, without ever seeing one another. It would be pure luck, like any other wartime engagement, large or small. One of them would bounce up at the wrong moment, and eventually tag the other. Someone would stand when he should be sitting. And still, if you remained under cover, the opponent would sneak up on you. There could be no disengagement, because they were both confined to this table of rock. Anyone running from it, and trying to escape back along the trail, would be within clear view, on an open carnival shooting gallery stage, well-lit and well above his executioner. Hawk reflected not at all on any of this. He knew it intuitively. He did not hesitate.

Taniguchi, as well, was unafraid. He had outwitted many an American Marine. He only wondered how it would come to pass that he would finally kill this one. It was taking too long. He had so many things to do. He peered over the rock. He saw nothing. He ducked down and ran his sleeve across his deeply wrinkled forehead. Where was the American? Had he run?

Hawk raised his eyes above the rock. Nothing. He crawled forward on his hands and knees. He reached for his last grenade and fingered it reassuringly. It hung heavily on his herringbone twill fatigue jacket, weighting down the roughly treated material of the shirt. He could hear movement ahead of him, behind a low slab of rock. Hawk's hands tightened on his Thompson. The slab was only two feet high. If Hawk jumped up on the rock that he now hid behind, he could see behind the other slab, and riddle the enemy soldier. That was the plan. He put his lower lip under his teeth. *Okay, I'll do it,* he thought. Ultimately, the bolder force would win the field. The only question was when. He chose now.

He jumped into open view, standing full upon the rock, his legs spread and his chest heaving. It seemed a mistake, until he saw the grayish-green uniform cringing behind the other slab. It was all as expected. The Thompson exploded in rage, belching spent casings from its breechblock that trickled across the mountainside. The slab disappeared behind a .45 caliber curtain of vaporized lead.

Hawk finally released the trigger. Immediately, a human head and a Solothurn whipped from behind the low covering stone, with the quickness of a cobra. Hawk dove beneath a well-aimed line of fire. Taniguchi jumped to the pursuit, for his turn at the slaughter. Hawk heard him coming. He feared the Thompson clip was nearly dry. He crawled a devious route quickly through the stones, hoping that he could put enough distance between himself and the Japanese that they would again be lost to one another, allowing time to reload and rethink this encounter. He came abruptly to a slope that fell steeply downward. Didn't see that coming. "Crap!" He drew back just in time. He could slide down it, all right, but the man above him would have a clear shot for hundreds of feet. Hawk pivoted. Now he was the cornered rat. He exposed himself again, this time out of desperation. He saw the Japanese running boldly toward him. The two of them fired simultaneously, frantically trying to destroy each other. They both missed, striking only the air. They both scrambled for cover.

That stopped his ass, anyway, Hawk thought. He rammed another clip in, and snapped it against the trigger guard. He figured he might have left one or two rounds in the last clip. He ripped the bolt back. He did not like having his back to the slope. He had exhausted his room to maneuver. The Japanese soldier could go anywhere, but Hawk was effectively pinned on this strip of stone that lay adjacent to the fall.

Taniguchi caught his breath. Slowly, it came to him. He had been able to glance at his opponent's face on several occasions. The brow, the violent tiger eyes, the well-sculpted nose—yes, it was him! It was not just wishful thinking. The brutal face was unforgettable. The *hancho's* wariness evaporated. Hate fired his gullet. He ripped out his magazine and inserted a new one. He now had an advantage denied to Hawk: personal hatred. He knew this was the man! He had waited for this for so long. It seemed impossible, but true.

Hawk lay crouched there, content to rest and think of all these life-altering, and permanently sleep disturbing events, for the time being. He had no regrets about getting into this. He was puzzled for the time being as to how he was going to eventually win this contest, however. It was troubling. This guy was truly a bastard. Then he heard the Solothurn banging above him, as if its operator were holding the trigger down and blowing an entire clip. The ricochets chewed into the rock above his helmet. He did not dare return the fire. He did not dare move, for the Japanese could vault the rock and shoot him in the back. What was the guy doing? He was going to run out of ammunition and be helpless. But Taniguchi charged Hawk's position, refusing to let go of the trigger.

Hawk smiled only mentally, as the insane fire drew closer. He reached for his grenade. Instead, he found a rotted and torn buttonhole. His eyes darkened. He cradled the Thompson. The enemy gun would either overheat or run dry any second, and then he would kill the unwise tormentor. Of course, if neither of those things happened, he would have nothing to worry about, where he was going.

The clip of Taniguchi finally exhausted itself, but not until he had reached Hawk's covering rock. Ammunition or not, the *hancho* was not finished with his enemy yet. He jumped on the rock in full running charge and reared back with his submachine gun, using it for a club. Hawk looked up in belated shock at the absolute audacity of the madman. The stock of the weapon came crashing down into his face with enormous force. Before it did, it caught the brim of his helmet and knocked it over his eyes. The steel pot took the brunt of the blow, before the heavy force made the Marine fall backwards, to the edge of the slope. Taniguchi jumped onto Hawk's stomach with both feet, and reared back again, as if the Solothurn were an ax. This time he hacked the stock into Hawk's squirming ribs. The American forced the helmet from over his face with the heel of one hand, just in time to catch a third, more awkward blow against the side of his head. Taniguchi screamed out the depth of his passion, as he bludgeoned this hated vermin. Hawk's desperate hand reached out for his fallen Thompson. Taniguchi's boot ground down on the thick American hand. The *hancho* swung the Solothurn strap over his shoulder, lurched down, and snatched the Tommy Gun from the reaching fingers of its owner.

Though his head sang with an echoing numbness, Hawk realized that he was catching the worst of this. He threw his hips over the edge and rolled down the slope. He recognized the loose, clanking rattle of the breech-block of his traitorous Thompson. He aided the momentum gravity provided him by tumbling to the left and right. He heard the bullets striking, but he was too dizzy to know where. Avoiding them would be strictly random.

This was the scene that Dreisen and Kreski came upon, after following the sound of the furious gun battle. Dreisen aimed his .45 at Taniguchi's broad back. Had anyone else in the United States Marine Corps fired the shot, Taniguchi would have been dead. Instead, he was only warned. Kreski raised his rifle as Taniguchi threw the Thompson at Dreisen, and dodged into the labyrinth of boulders.

Hawk tried to dig his heels into the rock and stop falling. He had the dim, faraway knowledge that Taniguchi had stopped firing. His brain was lost in a morass of dizziness. He was not aware of plunging over a ten-foot drop and landing on his back. He sat up, uninjured, and too disoriented to think of the fall. His tightly bound tendons, ligaments, bones and muscles absorbed the impact well. He only knew that he had stopped rolling. Nausea overwhelmed him. His empty stomach wretched, but nothing came up. He lay back with his eyes closed. A few minutes later, Joe Canlon found him.

"You hit? Hey, you hit?"

"Shit. I don't think so. Am I?"

"I don't think so. Yeah, that Jap was after you. What happened?"

"I ran outa ammo. Clubbed me over the head with his gun. He was probably doped up. Tell you what, I'm gonna get that son of a bitch."

"Hit you on the head, huh? That was a mistake. Broke his rifle, I guess. Hey, I need my helmet back." Hawk was in no mood for Joe's needling.

Joe helped him to his feet. "You'll get your chance at the guy. Dreisen is on his trail. He ain't lettin' go. I think he's going the wrong way, though. We better catch up with him and set him straight."

"You know, that Jap looked familiar." Hawk was far from in any hurry.

"They all do."

"No, something about this one. I've seen that face. Kind of ugly looking."

"The others look sweet?"

"I tell you, I've seen that shitass. He's kind of dried up...and all."

"Yeah. Well. Okay, Hawk. That's good. Maybe he left his phone number with the guys. You two can have a beer. Come, on. Can you walk all right?"

"Yeah. Whoa. Yeah, probably. Or, maybe not." Hawk tried to focus on the mountains whirling around him.

"Yeah, this is turning into some real shit, ain't it," said Joe.

"From where I been it has."

"At first, I thought this might be okay. You know, no artillery and rockets, and all that aerial shit. But this getting shot at stuff isn't much better."

"You know, I don't feel so hot."

"Yeah, but come on. Dreisen'll be blowing blue exhaust if we don't get back there."

Night caught Dreisen's patrol on the mountainside. The colonel was angry, but he was also sad. He knew that the Japanese would run through the night. It would be hard to get a productive chase going tomorrow after the defeating ordeals of today. His Achilles had been conquered in the only contact with the enemy. Three men were selected to go back to the lighthouse for the ration drop. They were told to be back before morning, so that the men could eat before setting out again. Nevertheless, all of this was going to take time. He knew the Japanese would not be sitting around breakfasting like his own men. Hawk found it difficult to sleep on the rocky ground, for more than one reason.

Hunger was starting to bother the sergeant. His body was an hourglass, with the grains of sand running out of it. The glass walls of the empty hourglass were rubbing together in his stomach. There was no excess fat to burn for fuel. Everything he ate went straight to his metal-hard muscles. Had he been left to remain stationary, he could have gone much longer without hunger pangs, for he seldom thought of food as anything more than a necessity. If you needed something, the Marine Corps would issue it. His appetite was a tool to maintain his strength, and his taste was an underdeveloped sense. But the day had been arduous. The lack of food was turning into something more than discomfort.

The pure mountain air, likely the purest in the world, thinned with a cold breeze. A little heavier snow began to fall. Hawk lay watching it. He had seldom seen snow. He smelled fresh mountain evergreens, growing incongruously among the jungle plants. The snow still failed to stick to the ground. It reminded him of a trip he had made as a swamper on a truck run up to West Virginia. He smiled. The snow stuck there. Yeah, West Virginia. He smiled again. But pleasant memories were few for James Hawk. From out of nowhere, he next remembered setting three Japanese on fire about a year ago. He heard the sounds and smelled the smells. He remembered today. Then he began to remember his own men, whom he had lost. And the memories were not of smiling obituary photos. He growled and sat up.

"Goddam." He was sweating in the snow. His shirt-sleeves were rolled up, but he pulled up his collar. He was cold in one place, and hot in another. *Probably catching something*, he thought. *That's how shit like that got started.* Men were snoring with exhaustion. He rummaged around the odd objects in his shirt, and pulled out a damp cigar. With some difficulty, he lit it.

Sergeant Kreski walked over to him. "Better put that out. The Japs can see it for miles," said the man on watch. Hawk looked up at him. Hawk saw only a silhouette in front of ten thousand brilliantly shining stars. He did not answer. Kreski finally turned and walked away. Hawk shook his head.

They were always assigning supernatural powers to the Japanese. Ridiculous powers. *That character today, though*, Hawk thought, *that guy was tricky. Real tricky.* Hawk had never seen anything quite like that. *He damn near killed me*, he thought. All of that running, feinting, and hiding was like nothing he had ever encountered. The enemy soldier had looked kind of old. Those old guys are full of tricks. Hawk stood and stretched.

Damn, I have to move around, he thought. I'm going to start thinking about shit, if I don't move around. He recalled one thing that he had been thinking about a lot over the last few months. And tonight, there she was, across the encampment, also awake and sitting up. He walked over to her. She didn't seem to notice.

"Getting cold, ain't it, Lieutenant?" he said.

"I don't speak Japanese." Her old defense mechanism kicked in at the sudden start.

"Me, neither. Well, a word here and there. You

cold?" She turned her luminous face with its perfect features toward him. She didn't answer, but she appeared to be studying him carefully. *Probably going to scream, or run, or something*, he thought. Great.

"You remember me, ma'am? James Hawk. I took you, you and Belva Cook, over to Verhangen." She looked at him with a puzzled expression, but this time, not completely blank. Perhaps it was the voice: the horrible, unforgettable bass voice. It sounded an octave lower than any human pitch, and as if the volume came from the chest of a lion.

"I know I ain't house broke, but I'm actually harmless," he said, which may have been just about the biggest lie spoken by humankind, or otherwise, since the one by the serpent in the Garden of Eden. She still said nothing. Ordinarily, he would have thought this was just her normal aloof and rude self. It did not seem at all out of character. But now...maybe she was also traumatized. He decided to hit a little closer to home.

"You remember ol' Captain Jordan?" He had a feeling, that this just might get through the fog.

"Clinton?" she responded. There it was. She had a new word in her vocabulary.

He hung his head and nodded. "Yeah. Yep. That's right. Got killed on Verhangen. Remember me, now?" He knocked the ashes off the cigar. Fire fell from his hand to the ground. Ivania flinched, her eyebrows came together in fear. "I, uh...ain't gonna hurt you, ma'am. You're okay, here with us, now."

"Where is Taniguchi? I told you I do not speak Japanese. Send Taniguchi," she said.

"Sure enough," he said. He didn't know what a Taniguchi was. "Listen, the Japs is long gone. You ain't gotta be afraid of them no more. I just wanted you to know something. I didn't know about you being left on Verhangen. I never would have let that happen. I never would have left you there. There was this goof that knew about it. But he didn't tell me." He looked into her eyes, but could see no understanding. "Well," he said at last, "you rest. Hard to sleep. I know." He turned to go.

"James Hawk," she said, staring at nothing. The name did not seem to offer her any sort of consolation.

"Yes, ma'am."

"I remember."

Hawk nodded. He looked around and rubbed his empty stomach. Maybe remembering him was not the best restorative in the world. If you asked ten different people what they remembered about James Hawk, it would likely involve ten different killings.

"Well, you rest."

Hawk went back to his lonely part of the universe. A flaming meteor swam across the clear sky above him, and he never saw it. He lay down to sleep again. As his head struck the ground, he remembered his brain rattling around inside his skull during a bombardment on his last island excursion, his vision unfocused for days, and his hearing almost gone. His dizziness today seemed to reproduce all of that. He sat up again and sighed. He looked at the endless stars above his current far-flung, claustrophobic, war-island prison, and shook his head.

He dreaded any more recollections. "Well, God, got anything else in the old family album we need to go over?" But God would not answer. He sent no further memories, however, and that was enough for Hawk to fall asleep, to try to forget his hunger.

It was perhaps a sad portrait of a tortured and exhausted soul, worthy of sympathy, worthy of esteem, maybe even worthy of reward somewhere, for all of the terrible things he had seen and done. Except for one unredeeming factor: he wanted nothing more than to wake up tomorrow and do it all again.

* * *

TANIGUCHI CRAWLED on the cold stone. The dark leaves shielded him. He looked around the American camp. Several of the tall enemy Marines walked about. Where was his? Perhaps, he had killed him. Taniguchi had to be sure. It did not have to be a glorious kill. A shot in the back would do fine. Kreski walked toward the Japanese observer. The watcher shrank into the foliage. They were no more than ten feet apart. Kreski stopped and stood over him. After a while, the American turned and walked away.

Taniguchi decided to leave. He would know one way or the other if Hawk lived, tomorrow. When the chase began, Hawk would be there, if he lived. Taniguchi had learned something else of importance to his mission: the Americans were quite easy to infiltrate. His scout, Kirishima, was even more stealthy than Taniguchi, and he could make good use of this knowledge.

At daylight, Joe Canlon found Hawk cooking in his helmet.

"What's that?"

"Poke salad and toadstools."

"Yum. Are you out of your mind?"

"No, hungry."

"We're getting rations today."

"Nope. They're already back from the lighthouse. No rations, shit-for-brains. They did drop us thirty-eight field jackets, though." Hawk turned sideways, displaying his new jacket. "Sharp, hunh?"

"Field jackets? Where is the stuff to eat?"

"A fighter plane ran them off. One of our planes made it through. He was the one with the jackets."

"The goddam Japs. They got ten planes left in the world and have to send one of them here to stop our ration drop." Joe sat down and cracked his knuckles. "What is this shit? Is it any good?"

"Damn right."

"Ain't toadstools poisonous?"

"Some is. Some ain't. That's just the seasoning."

"How do you know which is and which ain't?"

"You eat 'em."

Joe rubbed his big nose. Insects flew around Hawk's face. He swooped a hand at them, caught some, and threw them into the smoking helmet. "These dog-ass gnats are out even in the dead of winter."

Joe took an anguished look around the camp. "All right, shit. I gotta eat something. It don't smell bad. My mother used to make something like that. Cabbage or some goddam thing." Joe pulled out his spoon and reached for the greenish soup.

"Hey! Don't put your nasty spoon in my pot."

"What do you mean? You had it on your nasty head all day. My spoon ain't no dirtier than your head. And by the way, that's my damn helmet."

Hawk looked thoughtful. "Well, it ain't sanitary, but I guess you can have some. Better than you sitting here bitching like a bastard all day."

"Sanitary. Shit. Thank you, General MacArthur." Joe

dipped his spoon in and pulled out a boiled weed. He sneered and lowered it into his mouth. "Hot," he said, as he tucked it through his reaching lips. The hot part was good. He munched slowly and then spat it out. "Godamighty!"

"Shit, you didn't even taste it."

"Godamighty." Joe spat again. "Tastes like grass...or something. Some kind of chemical is in it."

"Good, huh?"

"Not too bad. I guess cabbage tastes like shit, too. Let me go get my mess kit. I think I'll try some more."

Thirty minutes later, Dreisen was getting the men into motion. It was already warming up.

"We have field jackets here men. Plenty of them. Warmest coat you ever wore. Hurry up, now. Get the lead out." Most of the men did not bother to get a coat. It would be 90°, and fairly soon, once they got off the mountain. They did not like to carry excess baggage.

Hawk sat with Joe against a tree. They watched solemnly as the patrol prepared to leave. Joe belched a plant-tasting gas. He leaned over quickly to vomit, but managed to prevent himself at the last notch of his esophagus. His eyes were half closed and his eyebrows high on his forehead.

"Wasn't bad, was it?"

"Hope it don't kill me," Joe said. His face was a boiled green. He retched again. "Godamighty. Hope it don't kill me."

"Once you get it down, it feels better. Gets stuck up in your guzzler there. It'll keep your stomach from hitting your backbone."

Joe looked over at Hawk's muscle knotted abdomen. "Yeah, you still got a good two inches to go there." Joe looked over at Dreisen strutting around. "Look at that dumb ass. I am really dreading this," he said. He sighed. "You know, I think them was the wrong kind of toad stools you used."

Hawk shook his head, looking down thoughtfully. "Hard to say."

9

KNIVES AND THE NIGHT

TANIGUCHI HAD BEEN ON THE RUN SINCE 0300 HRS. HE had another surprise for the Marines. He had decided that they were not going to chase him into the wilderness. After endless consideration of the problem, he had no intentions of leaving the vicinity of the lighthouse. He led his men along a route that encircled the ancient structure. The fighter plane could yet arrive at any moment. If it did not show today, it would come tomorrow, and if it did not come tomorrow, it would come when the Japanese high command realized that Zanji would not be making the trip to the beach. Taniguchi would personally put Zanji in the Shiden Kai. He would fight the Americans, if he had to. He would not allow them to force him to fight their war. If they drove him to the beach, thousands more of the Marines awaited him. Out here, the odds were much better. The *hancho's* surveillance told him that he had nearly as many men as did the American patrol. Perhaps a dozen or so men chased a dozen others. For now, that would be acceptable. His mission did not encourage contact. His duty was to protect Zanji. Taniguchi was a wise and practical man. He knew that the overly cautious Americans always preferred overwhelming odds before engaging in battle. He could stand and fight, and win, and their pursuit would cease. But when would Taniguchi stand and fight? Should he keep running until only a single American chased his party? He would be able to study this problem at great length, for he intended to whittle a bit more at the odds as he retreated.

* * *

KOICHI POINTED TOWARD THE NORTHEAST. Lieutenant Morgan stood at his side. "Soldiers go this way. Leave three or four hours ago," said the guide.

"Damn," Morgan said, "they are just as far ahead of us today as they were yesterday."

"They do not rest like American"," said the guide. "They do not eat. They do not talk."

"Yeah." *They're great*, Morgan thought. He was tired and hungry. He did not see how he could rest any less. They had been on the trail less than two hours, and weakness already claimed him. "We should have bombed them when we had the chance."

"Then kill pretty American lady. Very beautiful. Looks like girl in pictures."

"Repler and Price would be alive. And no telling who else. Repler didn't think he would ever get it." Morgan suddenly remembered who he was talking to, and shut up.

Koichi looked at Morgan's drawn face. It had changed considerably since this began, in some indefinable way. Something behind the face had changed, and changed the outer light of the face as well. Morgan no longer looked like the young lieutenant learning his trade. The eyes had a reckless, far away glaze. The mouth had a dry, dead look. His whole body had a slouched, tired-of-living appearance. Koichi decided to stay away from the officer that day. Morgan had *the look*.

Hawk walked beside Ivania. She seemed less exhausted today, and even less exhausted than the men. She had been on the trail longer, but she had the benefit of the skills of Taniguchi. Taniguchi did not run his men into the ground, the way Dreisen did. Taniguchi rested often, and yet stayed ahead of his pursuers. Hawk noticed that she was more alert than before. Her eyes stared at fixed objects now, and they shifted less. Her bearing was again erect, and proud. Perhaps not arrogant, yet.

"Feel like talking?"

"No. Why?"

"You remember me yet?"

"I told you that I did. I'm surprised you're alive. I guess I'm not too surprised. I remember the way you walked into Verhangen, like it was nothing. A lot like you're doing now. Staying alive is your specialty. It's a pity that it isn't contagious. How many others got out of Verhangen alive?"

"Joe. Joe Canlon. And you."

They walked on. He did not go away. She wished that he would. He was everything that was wrong with the world, with the war, and with mankind in general. What did he want? A thank you? For what? She had told him that she did not want to talk. She knew that she would have to get rid of him, or go mad.

"I don't know what you are after. I don't know what you want to know about any of it. I was taken away during the battle. I was kept in a camp for women for several months. We chopped trees and loaded gondola cars, just like the men. Then the Australians liberated the camp. Most of the women were Australians. But the Japanese moved me here. I was going to Japan. Is there anything else that you could possibly want to know?" Ivania hoped that the reunion would formally end now. All of the celebrations and speeches were over.

"I'm sorry you got left there, see? You wanted to come with me, you remember? I told you it would be..."

"Yes, I wanted to come with you. You told me so, right? Is that what this about? Yes, yes, yes. You are wonderful. I was insane for having anything to do with you. I admit it. You need not feel guilty. You certainly knew yourself better than I did."

"Well, I guess really, you were the one that was right. To leave with me, I mean. The place you left did not end up any better. If you'd stayed behind, you would be dead now. But, you aren't. I mean, none of it was good. But you lived through it, this way."

She seemed surprised. "I did not know that. I don't know which is worse. Not to change this fascinating subject, but I am wondering if you can tell me something? You seem to know everything, and everyone seems to cower to you. Am I to go along with this march, forever? If you don't mind my saying, I know that wherever you are going is extremely dangerous, for other people, not you, of course. And I know that you will never catch Taniguchi. I don't see that I have a part in this."

"I haven't heard what the plan is on that score. I'll go

see." Hawk left to talk with Dreisen. The conversation with Ivania had not been satisfying. She still seemed to have a grudge against him. This was worsened by the fact that he thought the grudge was justified. That damned Joe Canlon had made him leave her there in the middle of hell.

Kreski killed a rabbit and cooked it. He gave Joe Canlon a piece of the meat. Joe had a belly full of weeds and could not face it. He found himself walking beside Ivania Broeder after Hawk left, and offered her the rabbit.

"Thank you," she said. She took it greedily, and ate it as she walked. "I remember you, too. From the island," she told Joe Canlon.

"Yeah, I was there." Joe looked away quickly and returned to his place in line. He had no interest in Ivania Broeder, or memory lane. Or anything else about Verhangen.

Hawk and Dreisen discussed Ivania. The sergeant proposed setting up a base camp with two or three men at the lighthouse. She could stay there with them. The colonel did not buy it.

"Let's see how she does today, Hawk," Dreisen snapped. "I don't want to give up all the ground that we've gained. She's safer here."

Hawk nodded. He did not see how any of it had anything to do with losing ground. As to safety, while they spoke, an explosion lit the head of the column. Someone screamed fitfully for five seconds afterward. Then all was quiet. *Shit*, Hawk thought. *Who was at the point?* He had not assigned the man. The men lay flattened in the rocky forest.

Morgan knew that he should not have taken the

point. Officers did not do such things. But things were getting informal, and he was a Marine officer, not an army officer. Everyone else had done it, and more than once. Sergeant Kreski had done it, and of course—the bastard, Hawk. He felt obligated. As he walked at a brisk pace, he saw something ahead of him. It was not threatening, it was some sort of small animal.

It came closer, and he recognized it for what it was, a beautiful white dog. Something about the dog made him feel good, and he smiled. A dog, way out here. When he took another step, he felt something like a red-hot steel door slam into the entire front of his body at once. Just as quickly, the ground slammed into the entirety of his back. The feelings were sudden and intense, but he experienced them, somewhat slower than they actually happened. He did not remember hearing anything. All was quiet. He felt dirt trickling down on him from the sky. He lay still for a moment and then threw a hand across his chest. Something large and slick was moving along the outside of his opened chest cavity. He knew that it was his heart, and that he could not hold his heart and live. Something told him that dying was a practical thing, a natural blessing to escape the horror of life. He agreed with the sentiment, but screamed anyway, and then he lost the strength to scream, and everything else.

As everyone lay expectantly under cover, Sergeant Kreski was the man who went forward to see what had happened. Morgan lay across the trail with his lungs torn out. The internal organs continued to twitch for a moment, and then stopped. The man who had been nearest to Morgan, Koichi, was unhurt. Kreski and Koichi stood over the corpse. Kreski's eyes narrowed and he shook his head. Koichi looked over at him, as if to say, didn't you know this is how all of this ends?

"Grenade, booby trap," Kreski choked. "They had it stuck in a tin can nailed on the tree there." He picked up a thin little wire tangled around Morgan's leg. He thrust his chin out angrily. Hawk came up behind him. "Morgan's dead," Kreski said, as if Hawk were deaf and blind.

"Okay. Let's get him buried. Dreisen won't be wanting to take much time." Hawk looked at the tin can nailed to the tree. It was about chest high. He pulled it loose, with a powerful one-handed grip, tearing the bottom out of the can. Kreski still stared at the bloody shreds of flesh in Morgan's once powerful chest. They were braided into the herringbone twill.

"Just like that?" Kreski asked. Bury him? What good did that do? Hawk acted like that meant something. The dust from the explosion still swirled in the stagnant air. To the others, watching from cover, the cloud made it look like some biblical scene, containing three celestial creatures come down to carry off a dead prophet.

"Yeah," said Hawk. He looked up the trail. "Come on, man." Hawk knew he had to get Morgan under the ground in a hurry, before Dreisen could object with some lame excuse. He managed to get it done.

The trek became worse after that. It had always been boring, irksome, and possibly pointless. Now it was deadly. These men that they chased, weren't going peacefully. By afternoon, it was getting obvious that the Japanese were going back to the lighthouse. The chase was no longer just *possibly* pointless. They had gone in a circle. They could have just stayed where they were this morning and been closer to the enemy. The enemy wanted the lighthouse. Everyone realized at once that they were chasing their tail. Rebellion was in the air yet again, but there was no Morgan to lead the rebellion. Morgan had risked his career for them, and lost, and now he had lost his life. Had they listened, he would be alive. Hawk was now the man under Dreisen, in the chain of command. Hawk would not abandon an objective. There would be no mutiny. This did not create any warm and fuzzy feelings for the sergeant.

No one missed Morgan on a personal level. Repler had been his only close friend. And yet, no one wanted to see him die on the trail. He was not a bad man, not a bad Marine, and he stood up to Dreisen, for them.

Hawk quickly recognized the politics of the situation. One couldn't be a sergeant without thinking about that. He wondered if the men would attach themselves to Kreski now. Hawk gave no thought to going against Dreisen. The Marine Corps was his home. He had never had a home before. He played by the rules, when they let him.

Koichi and Hawk tracked the Japanese across the difficult terrain, though they could see the obvious destination. Sergeant Kreski took lessons from them, without their knowing it. Kreski was able and cool, in spite of the permanently concerned crease between his eyes. He would be ready to take command when his turn came. He did not perform well for the purpose of taking charge. He hoped his turn never came. There are those who long for power and those who do not. But anything was possible. Both Hawk and Dreisen were the types of men who could disappear in a blinding flash as suddenly as had Morgan. They both took unnecessary risks as a matter of course.

Hawk was aware of some sort of ambition on the

part of Kreski, although he kept the awareness to himself. He was always a little skeptical of those with ambition, because in his line of work, it often involved death, and specifically, the death of someone else. For his own part, Hawk did not seek power, but he also did not like the idea of someone having power over him. The fewer of those guys, the better.

The man with all the power, the colonel, slowed down. He urged the men to greater speed, all the while lagging at the rear of the column. They never came close to the Japanese that day. There were no shortcuts this time. Tough ground separated the two parties. The terrain kept coming, and it kept getting tougher.

Dreisen stopped them in the midafternoon. He looked beaten. The mood was in stark contrast to the day before. Today it seemed hopeless. Taniguchi was proving himself the master. The colonel surprised everyone when he quit for the day, and let them strike a camp. The chase was over, until tomorrow morning. Some held out the hope that the lack of enthusiasm would prove permanent.

"Did it for the woman," Dreisen confided in Hawk. The colonel fell asleep, and did not stir until the next day.

'The woman', Ivania Broeder, was of better fiber than Dreisen. Decades younger, she had been chopping trees for the past few months, an invigorating form of exercise. The Navy lieutenant was lean and strong. She sat around the fire with the others until an hour after dark. Hawk grew stronger, too, with the unexpected rest. He was looking forward to beginning the chase again. He still had no great interest in a Japanese pilot, other than making the colonel happy. His greater interest was in killing that son of a bitch that he had fought the day before. Of course, anyone else would do nicely, too.

The weather remained fairly cool, though at the lower elevation, there would be no snow fall. Hawk stopped to report to Ivania before she went to sleep. He had been avoiding her, for the most part, because his news was not good, and there was always the chance that it could change.

"I talked to Dreisen," he said. "He won't let me set up a base camp at the lighthouse yet. Probably a good idea. Looks like the Japs are going back to the lighthouse again. They act like they like that place. You would end up back with them. The Colonel is accidentally right a lot, you know. I guess he does this by habit. We're slowing up, though, if you can hang on, I really believe he'll give this up." Hawk had an absent look in his eyes. It didn't much matter what her reaction was.

She looked at him with something resembling contempt. "So, he's like a broken clock, right twice a day?" Ivania said. Hawk understood her tone, more than the gist of her comment. Joe Canlon came over with a jacket and a blanket. Chivalry was not the prime mover in this courtesy, as he was the corporal in charge of such matters.

"You might need an extra cover," Joe said, handing it to her. She smiled. Joe smiled.

"Yes, thank you. I certainly appreciate that. I nearly froze to death last night."

"Sure," said Joe. He turned and walked away. Hawk looked up at him from beneath his eyebrows.

"Isn't he nice?"

"Yeah. A saint." Hawk stood to go. "If you want

anything, just ask. I mean, if you're cold, say so. We're kinda used to taking care of ourselves."

"Very well. I will."

Hawk pulled at his nose. "Well, night."

"Good night."

Hawk slouched over to where Joe Canlon lay. He eased himself onto the ground, knocking a few of the larger stones out of the way. Joe raised up on an elbow.

"You know what?" Joe asked. "I finally shit."

"Congratulations."

"Owe it to you, I guess. That stuff you fixed would make a buffalo shit."

"Vegetables. Balanced diet."

"Yeah. If you cook breakfast tomorrow, don't wake me up, till it's over."

"Don't worry."

"She sure is something, ain't she?" Joe said. "I mean, the eyes, the teeth, the hair. The girl's got it all. You don't see women like that every day. And here she is, here, with us. You were right, she reminds me of Veronica Lake, too."

Hawk raised his head. "Yeah. She thinks you're nice, too. I ain't told her why you're so goddam shittin' nice. I'll save that for you."

Joe frowned. He looked over at Ivania, and then lay back down. She was busily pretending that she did not know half of the men in the camp were watching her. In a few minutes Joe was snoring. Hawk stared at a large sliver of moon overhead.

The fire went out early in the morning. Kreski sat up suddenly. Dawn was breaking. Kreski reached for his canteen. He washed away a dry mouth and a nightmare with some warm water. He looked over at the radioman,

Sprack, beside him. Sprack's mouth was wide open. A bulge was under his blanket.

Kreski shook the other man. "Sprack. Hey, Sprack?" He ripped the blanket back. A long Japanese bayonet protruded from Sprack's midsection. It was driven right through him and into the ground. Kreski jumped to his knees.

"Sprack!" Kreski clutched at his knees and looked around. The camp was still asleep. Unless, all of the others had been slaughtered as well. Kreski went cold. He shivered. He heard someone stir on the other side of the camp. At least, he was not alone. He seized his rifle. He thought of Waterland. Waterland was supposed to be the man on the last watch.

"I'll kill him," Kreski whispered. "I'll kill that son of a bitch!" He leapt to his feet. His bewhiskered lip trembled. "Waterland!" he screamed

Heads rose from the blankets. Men cursed Kreski. Hawk sat up and slid his submachine gun to his knees. He pulled the bolt back.

Kreski found Waterland before the others could get up. The sentry was propped against a tree on the outskirts of the camp. His pants had been cut open. He had been crudely castrated, the mutilation extending up past his navel. His bloody genitalia were stuffed into his mouth. Kreski dropped his rifle, and caught it by the strap. His knees weakened. He went back to the dead Sprack and sat down. Hawk walked past him.

Hawk looked at Waterland and then at the surrounding jungle. Joe Canlon walked sleepily behind him. "My God," Joe's eyes snapped open.

"Old Jap trick," Hawk rasped.

"Yeah."

Dreisen appeared shaken when he found out about the infiltration. "Count noses," he said.

"Two dead, sir," Hawk immediately reported. "Japs crawled in. I couldn't get that bayonet outa Sprack... uh...neat. But it's got that old style loop on it. It was a Jap."

The men paced about the clearing. There was something worse about tragedy at dawn. The night is full of unreal, half-dreamt horrors, but the day brings hard and kind reality. This day brought more of the unreal horror. Two of the men started digging holes. The others paced and clutched their rifles. Kreski remained kneeling next to Sprack until they carried the body away. Then he got up and slammed his helmet on his head.

Dreisen was already studying his map. Kreski walked up to him abruptly. "Sir, I think we should call a halt to this, sir. With all due respect."

"What? Why is that, Sergeant?" Dreisen acted as if nothing had happened.

"I think we need more men, sir. They probably outnumber us now. It may not have been the Japs. It could have been the natives. They're nothing but Japs themselves. There could be hundreds of them. I don't think what we're trying to do is a practical thing, sir, with these few men. I do not believe we can accomplish our objective."

"I have noted your objections, Sergeant. I understand your feelings. You were lying right next to one of the casualties. I assure you that I hate it like hell. But we cannot stop now. This is just too important. I have tried to stress that, but you men still are not understanding."

"Yes sir. I agree, sir. I don't question that. But we cannot do anything without more men."

"Good point. Listen, son," Dreisen put a hand on his shoulder. "I came out here to be with you men because you were the nearest to this Zanji. I came for another reason, too. You're some of the toughest riflemen in the Corps. By God, I never thought I'd run into all this foot dragging and crying. Now, you lost half your company back there on the beach. You've seen men die. You're hurt now and you're not thinking right. What good did any of these men die for, if we give up? They died doing a job. We are obligated to them to finish that job. I've noted your objections. Now get the men ready. We will catch them today, and wrap this up." Dreisen slapped Kreski on the shoulder and turned away.

Kreski watched the fuzzy, hated, graying head move away. The old 'dead versus the living' speech. Kreski clenched his fist. Hawk put a hand on his shoulder. He knew Kreski had a tough morning.

"Tough duty, huh? Come on, kid, got a lot of walking to do."

Kreski knocked his hand away. "Two more dead. It doesn't mean anything to you, does it, Hawk? They won't get you, will they?"

"Sure...it does."

"No, it doesn't. You don't have any insides, Hawk. There was a time when I wanted to be like you. But you ain't nothing. There ain't nothing to be like. You're just a shell walking around. You don't feel nothing, you don't..."

"For crap sakes, take it easy. What the hell did I do?"

"Take it easy? Let it all slide. That's all there is to it, then?"

"Look, I didn't care much about this deal in the first place," said Hawk. "Now we have a reason to catch the bastards. I want to kill every one of them and chop their goddam heads off. We have to keep going now, we have to kill them. Sprack and Waterland are dead, but the Japs that killed them are still out there. The Corps doesn't fold their tent when somebody gets killed, they even the score."

"Kill them? That's not the Corps, *that's you*. Isn't it? They kill us. We kill them. Kill, kill. Then everything is okay. Everybody is happy as goose shit. Sprack comes back from the grave because the almighty Hawk kills a few worthless Japs. Killing is the answer to everything."

"Well, it ain't a bad place to start. Take it easy, it's tough, but you can't go losing your goddam mind over it. That's why they did all that shit. That's what they want. That was the whole point. The men are dead, it don't matter how. You got to fight back." Hawk looked down. "You got to. You gonna leave the son of a bitches laughing their asses off, eating their fish heads and rice?"

"Fight back..." Kreski sputtered and turned away. "I'll fight back." He stalked off.

Hawk bit off a plug of chewing tobacco. "Damn right, you will." He held his head a little higher than usual. It seemed like a lot of people were laying the underlying causes of World War II on his doorstep lately. These were the people he knew, and put his life on the line for. And they hated him. The girls sunning themselves on the beaches back in California, who didn't know he existed, must really hate him.

Hawk watched them lower Waterland into a hole. He assumed that graves registration would someday have to retrace the untraceable footsteps of the patrol. Kreski had been wrong about Hawk. He had feelings, and he was motivated. Oh, they weren't good feelings. He waited for things like this to unleash his feelings. He already felt a sort of freedom coming over him. A freedom of expression. He still had to be careful where he directed all of this freedom.

The men prepared themselves quietly. Hawk glanced at their enigmatic faces. He watched Joe pack Ivania's blanket for her. He spat. Was the guy serious? What was he doing? Dreisen shouted as he always did, but the orders floated above the angry helmets without landing. The men were fighting themselves to get moving. They moved mechanically, thinking of other things. They thought of the next time they would wake up, or not wake up.

The loud and usually joking Cajun, named Breaux, took the point. His eyes burned with hatred. He found no reason for joy today. It was hard to get down to that level in most men: the serious, mean level; because most men are optimists at heart. Here were the good men gone bad. Hawk had seen it all happen before. It had even happened to him, long ago. He could not have been born this way. The Marine Corps tried, but it could not make you that way. The war had to do it. Slap a little brutality on a man, and he'll slap you right back with it.

Kreski lapsed out of his shock, and into a more logical anger. He was not ready to forget this, to blame it all on the Empire of Japan. As Breaux took up the march for yet another grueling day, and the others followed, Kreski paused in front of Hawk.

"Why don't you stop this?" he asked in an almost pleading tone.

"Me?" Hawk half smiled. Now, he was not only responsible for starting World War II, but he was also the one keeping the damn thing going. But, Kreski seemed more sensible now. Might as well humor him. "How can I stop it? It ain't my war."

Somehow that rubbed Sergeant Kreski wrong. Somehow it was Hawk's war. The insanity of it all was personified by the calm, grim, business-as-usual face of Sergeant Hawk. Perhaps Kreski finally realized he had been mistaken in choosing his branch of the military, and that he did not belong here. He was a strong man. His body was like that of a running back, and he was almost three inches taller than Hawk. He doubled his fist and struck Hawk a ferocious blow on the chin. Unblinking, Hawk staggered back a step. He spat. They stared at one another. Hawk controlled his violent temper, an element comprising almost ninety-nine per cent of his soul, with the remaining one per cent of his psyche. He waited for what would happen next. Kreski kept his fist doubled. Dreisen saw it all from the beginning, and watched without comment from a safe distance. He was glad it was Hawk facing the massive fists. Everyone held their breath as they waited for some horrible, unimaginable thing to happen to Sergeant Kreski. After a full minute, nothing did happen. Kreski unslung his rifle. He stepped into the line and proceeded down the trail. Hawk spat and ran a finger along his lower gumline. The men were very quiet. The march continued.

Joe took up a place in line behind Hawk. "Why didn't you hit him back?" Joe asked.

Hawk thought for a moment. "I don't know. I guess he was right."

"What if he hits you again? Will he still be right?"

"Maybe not as much."

"Yeah? And when he goes to beating on you all day?"

"That ain't what happened. What would you do?"

"I probably would have hit him back. Even if he was right. I don't want nobody beating on me. Course, then he'd whip my ass."

Hawk shrugged. "I don't want a hurt man out here on the trail. I was willing to leave it at that, if he did." Hawk spat.

Joe nodded. That sounded more like Hawk. The real explanation came out. He knew fear or kindness could not have been involved in the odd occurrence. There had to be some military consideration. Kreski had to be handled like equipment: a grenade, or a canteen. "He'll be trouble now," said Joe.

"Nah. He's a good kid. He's wound a little tight. Just high strung. Been a lot going on, you know. This kinda shit ain't for everybody."

"It's unprofessional," said Joe.

"Unprofessional? Where do you get all that shit? *Unprofessional.*" Hawk spat. He didn't see any blood.

They followed the trail of the Japanese into the jungles of the valley below the lighthouse. High overhead, the great monument of the Jarok always watched over them. Once again, they were gaining on the enemy. Ivania Broeder was trapped into staying with them now, a situation that she had found herself in since leaving the United States. She was a prisoner of the Navy, of the Marine Corps, of the Japanese, and now of a rough contingent of abandoned and desperate men, who called themselves Marines, on their better days. They did not have the manpower to leave her at a stationary camp, nor to send her back. But she felt a little different about it now. She suddenly had some affection for her crude rescuers. That strange tribal instinct that has forged nations for centuries rose in her. She was among Americans again.

She liked the clean-cut Sgt. Kreski. She was thrilled when he struck Hawk. She feared for him when Hawk did not fall. She admired a man who could stand up to such a vicious hoodlum. Like everyone else, she had expected the worst. But Hawk was a madman, and madmen are totally unpredictable. He likely would shoot Kreski in the back, or something worse. She also liked Joe Canlon. He was a thoughtful and decent human being. One cannot fake such qualities. Her admiration for these two spilled over onto the others, with the possible exception of the career-obsessed Dreisen; she was proud of them, and she felt safe with them. Hawk was, of course, the underside found in any sort of society. The best one could hope for was to avoid it.

Though one could not fake thoughtfulness and decency, circumstances could enhance these qualities. Joe carried a good deal of guilt about leaving Ivania on Verhangen. He knew that eventually he would have to tell her what he had done, as he had told Hawk. It would be easier to forgive a thoughtful and considerate Joe, than it would be to forgive an anonymous Marine who had stabbed her in the back.

Joe helped her down the sharp drop that led from the promontory upon which the lighthouse sat, and into the rain forest below. His thick arms made her descent easy. Today, Hawk was in no mood for entertaining Romeo and Juliet.

"Let her climb on her own," he shouted at the lagging couple. "She ain't no goddam invalid!" Hawk could envision a sniper picking them off. People lolly-gagging around at the end of a column were extremely vulnerable. Joe was the rear guard, not Sir Walter Raleigh.

"All right!" Joe shouted back. He was not afraid of Hawk like the others, but then again, he usually did what Hawk said. "Asshole."

Ivania joined in, with enthusiasm. "That has to be the most evil man I have ever known," she said, continuing to cling to Joe. She had known some truly evil individuals, one of whom, she suspected of the murders of Waterland and Sprack.

"Hawk? He just looks mean. Kind of ugly." Joe laughed.

"Oh, he looks all right. That's what happened to Belva Cook. She was madly in love with him. He was so handsome, and so strong, dah dee dah dah...it was disgusting. I realize she was middle class, but there is a lot more to a man than what he looks like."

"Uh...I remember her," said Joe. He didn't care for stories about old times. Especially stories about Belva Cook. That one had a really bad ending. And it brought to mind another story or two.

"He's just evil. That's the only way to describe him. Everything he does, everything he says, he is just dangerous. He belongs in a cage. He just does horrible things without thinking. He has a twisted mind. This is what happens to the military in war time, when you have to take in everyone. Do you remember him on Verhangen?"

"Hawk?" Joe felt somewhat obligated to defend his friend. "Nah, he just sounds tough. That's the way those crackers are. From Tobacco Road. Kicked around. Don't have nothing. You should've known this drill instructor I had on Parris Island." Joe laughed, trying to keep his donkey bray to a cool level.

"I'm not talking about drill instructors or coaches or training children, I'm talking about a cold-blooded monster. Look at him. He's just a murder looking for a place to happen. He loves this. He is why we are still on this patrol. He simply wants to kill somebody. I don't think he is particular about whom, either. The way he looks at people, the way he moves." She feigned a shudder. "Have you ever seen another man *move* like that? Slinking around like that...he's reptilian. Waiting to strike out at something, and poison it."

Joe cleared his throat. Man, she was really down on the guy. Hawk was a little rough around the edges, but shit. He was Joe's best friend, and had saved his life on more than one occasion. He tried to turn the tide, but just a little.

"Well, he ain't so bad. I mean, he ain't no Laurence Olivier, but he ain't as bad as you think. Why are you against him so?" Joe asked. He did not recall Hawk slighting her in any way. Did it have something to do with Belva Cook? Should he tell her that Hawk had always liked her more than Belva Cook? Best to stay away from that. Joe did not know much about paranoia or how it may have affected her. Whenever he became terrified, which was often enough, it never affected him for long. He came close to reminding her of how Hawk was responsible for her being here, but he was still a long way from telling her that Hawk would have died trying to get her off Verhangen. That would have involved the part about Joe's not being so willing.

"I don't know. He just scares me. Everyone flocks around him like he is the King of Siam. Everything has to have his stamp of approval. Nobody moves without seeing if it is okay with him. They are all afraid of him, Joe. Don't you see that?"

"Well, not really. That's not really how it is. I been with him a long time. These guys here ain't afraid of that much. He is the platoon sergeant and all, he knows more about stuff. I mean, it's more like respect. You know, that guy can field strip just about any Jap gun you can find laying around? He's got...mechanical instincts. If he tells you something, you probably better listen. It's for your own good."

She quickly followed up on that theory. "If he told Dreisen to turn around right now, he would have to do it. Do you deny that? He's not doing that, is he? Why are you all so fascinated by him? I mean, I guess he is brave, but that's only because he enjoys hurting people. He enjoys...*this*." She waved her hand angrily at the world around them. "*This!*"

Joe was quiet for a moment. "Well, yeah, he's got guts. There's that."

"Guts," she repeated contemptuously. "He's got a mean streak a mile wide and just wants to hurt things, and he's too stupid to know that he can get hurt back. Guts aren't everything. This is real life Joe, he's not some drill instructor calling you funny names. This is life and death. This is getting thrown into a hole in pieces, covered up, and forgotten. It takes more than guts to make a man. If we were back home, Hawk would be in a prison, or a bum on skid row. This is the only life he is good for." She clung tightly to Joe. "Look at you. You've gone through just as much as he has. You're still a human being."

Joe groaned as he flexed tired leg muscles and negotiated a step. He smiled to himself. He felt pretty good. "Yeah," he said. He was getting even further from telling her about his inglorious deeds on Verhangen. As the subject became more distant, it become more guilt-inducing.

Breaux, Kreski, and Hawk led the chase. Fresh tracks abounded. They expected to be fired upon as every new patch of vegetation was brushed aside. Yet when darkness came, no enemy troops had been sighted. It was one of those days that seemed half as long as other days. The Japanese trail led in an arc, back to the slope, and toward the lighthouse. Though they had suspected this all day, now it was a certainty that they were being led in a circle.

Hawk and Dreisen discussed holding the lighthouse and abandoning the chase. Hawk suspected that there was something about the crumbling old lighthouse drawing the enemy there. Holding it should be the Americans' new objective. Dreisen refused to do it.

"Coincidence. It's just an easy route to run. Could go off anywhere," Dreisen said.

* * *

TANIGUCHI STRUGGLED on the slope above them. He would time his run around the invisible oval race track, so that he was the one sleeping at the lighthouse that night.

Joe Canlon lay near Ivania. Hawk and Kreski did not sleep. They sat at opposite ends of the camp, staring at one another in the dark. They could not see each other's eyes. Kreski considered telling Hawk that he was sorry for hitting him. But that might make it look like Kreski thought that he had won a fight or something. It was only a sucker punch. And Hawk was pretending to be gallant, or some dumb thing. He was a foxy old non-com. Kreski knew that he might do it again, if Hawk said something callous, the next time someone was killed. So, no need to complicate things.

Hawk thought of nothing. The infiltrators made no appearance and he got tired of waiting. He went to sleep a couple of hours before dawn, and left the remainder of the watch to Kreski. They did not speak to one other to arrange this. Hawk slept soundly until dawn, waking up feeling like he was plastered under the polar ice cap. Through groggy eyes, he saw that Kreski had main-tained his vigil.

Dreisen pushed the men as steadily as ever. He even led the way, for a while, up the slope. Going up was not as easy as the trip down. The men tired quickly. They were sick of this. After his surge of energy, Dreisen dropped behind a little at a time. Joe fell behind, too, until he was climbing beside Hawk near the end of the column.

"Hey, Hawk, you didn't tell her nothing, did you?"

"What? About what? Verhangen? No." Hawk was taking deep breaths and grabbing at limbs and shrubs to pull himself along.

Joe nodded. "Do you want to?"

"What? No, shit, no. Why would I do that? That's your place to tell her, if you want the story told. You're her sweetie-poo. I already told her that I didn't know we left her there. That was just the facts. I don't think she gave a shit what I told her, to tell you the truth. You're all worried about nothing. As usual." Hawk looked over at him with a scowl. "You know, you smell like a duck wallow?"

"Yeah, I got this mildew growing all over me. Plus, I think I mighta slept in something." Joe looked about himself with an investigative seriousness.

Hawk shook his head disapprovingly. "The ladies don't like all that."

"Yeah, but what I was getting at is, why don't you tell her, tell her that I *did* know that we left her there?"

"Me? *Me*, tell her? Aw, I get it. You want to make me out to be a big pile of shit, right?"

"Yeah. Sort of."

"Make it look like I'm trying to make you look bad?"

"Yeah. Kind of. It would sound better coming from you. She really don't like you. She hates you."

"Is that right?" This came as no surprise. Hawk climbed slowly. He was getting tired as hell. He needed those few hours of sleep he had passed up. Joe fell behind him, lost in thought

"Come on, big nose, you're not the rearguard. Keep up. If you don't keep up, a Jap will stick your nuts down your throat."

"What's this big nose stuff?" Joe asked, looking over his shoulder nervously and climbing faster.

"You got a big nose."

"Yeah? I get it. So? You're better looking than me, huh? You can forget being jealous. Ain't nothing—ever

—happening with you and her. She talks about you like my grandma used to bitch about Hitler." Joe laughed like a half-wit. He pictured his grandmother, bundled in a smock and bent over the kitchen table in her tenement on the East River, ranting about the evils of Hitler. From there, Joe imagined Hawk and Hitler standing together. It was so funny to him, he had to repeat it, even louder. *"Like my grandma bitched about Hitler!"* And he brayed, even louder.

"Hey, *shit!* Keep it down. Are you nuts?"

Joe composed himself. "Well, will you do it?"

Hawk clenched his teeth and strained to pull upward with the aid of a root. The lighthouse could be seen peering over the cliff, above his head. It was in their every scene, all day long, like a bad moon. "Yeah," Hawk grunted. "If you want." The pestering had gone on long enough. He didn't see the point, but what the hell was it to him?

"Really? You'll do it?"

"Yeah. If, you want. Shit. I think you ought to do it, though. Or, better yet, keep your big old fat trap shut. It ain't exactly your best story. She seems kind of funny. You give her a reason to hate you, she just might take you up on it. She'll go off on you, like she does on me."

"Hell, I can't. It's kind of...awful. Yeah, you just do it. Kind of work it in the conversation, though. Don't just walk up to her, and start reading a speech to her, or something. She'll know something is up. But like, the way she hates you, I figure she'll hate the whole story."

"Okay, man." Hawk pulled his helmet back and looked at the rocks above him. "I'll tell you one thing. Climbing up and down this shit pile is getting pretty old. Like digging a hole and filling it in."

Dreisen ordered a ten-minute break on the slope. When the time was up, he called for the men to get moving, in his usual half cheerful, and half abrupt way. No one moved. Dreisen had a sinking feeling.

"Let's go, men," Dreisen insisted. He started climbing alone. No one moved. He looked over his shoulder. They would not look at him. He continued on. Hawk got up. He wondered if Dreisen would go on alone. Apparently so. Hawk leaned his head back and looked up. The irregularity of the cliff had temporarily made the lighthouse invisible. The sun swathed his face in silver fire. He pushed back his helmet and looked around. The men, clad in dirty and torn remnants of utilities, stared painfully back at him.

"Git up," Hawk said. It was not friendly or considerate. It was far from pleading. Joe Canlon stood. The others rose slowly. Kreski was the last to stand. What was so hard about this? How long had they been doing this? Not that long. If only there was a point. Actually, that wasn't it, either. It was the death. They dragged themselves skyward, with Hawk the foremost, other than Dreisen.

Sergeant Hawk passed Dreisen, as if it were the natural thing to do. They did not speak to one another. Dreisen sensed that Hawk's support was wearing thin. He knew that it was only bloodlust, and not Zanji or the flag, that kept him on the trail. The heat, the cold, the futility, the hunger, the years of war, and even the Joe and Ivania thing, were all taking their toll on that lust. But the lust ran deep.

Hawk thought of the Japanese gloating over dead Americans. He seethed. He was not objective about the enemy. He thought of them as predators. Zanji was just one of them. Hatred had become Hawk's civic duty. The propaganda of the time tried its best to convince Americans that the Japanese were inhuman: in movies, magazines, posters, and cartoons, with exaggerated facial features and speech. Here, where the savage combatants met face to face, Hawk did not need cartoons. Funny voices and cartoon noses didn't mean shit to him. He remembered Waterland. The latest memory. To him, that had not been the work of one man. It was all of them. The enemy.

Kreski watched Hawk's swaggering back. He had developed a hatred of his own. The Japanese were too intangible. You could almost have sympathy for unseen men going through the same hardships as yourself. Hawk was visible and in your face. The Japanese were like a natural disaster that a man should have enough sense to avoid. Kreski did not take them personally. He could not hate them, if he did not know them. Oh, he could be scared of them. Kreski was still young and immature, and his hate was as the young hate. Hawk was the athlete, who was always statistically a little better than Kreski. Hawk was the bully down the street who was always a little stronger, no matter how hard Kreski worked out. Hawk was his abusive father. Hawk was an unmet challenge. And now, Hawk was the abandonment of reason.

"Pick up the pace," the platoon sergeant called down the slope, as if to fuel the hatred. Kreski looked up at the heavy growth of blond stubble on Hawk's beastly face. His hand still hurt from striking that rock-hard skull. His finger tightened on the trigger of his M1. The young sergeant still had one shortcoming. He was a decent man. That worried him. How could he deal with this problem and remain decent? How did one interact with James Hawk and have any decency left? The trigger tightened more, until he thought for certain it was going to go off. But it didn't. How could he justify this? If he only became another James Hawk, he would have accomplished little, other than achieving eternal damnation. He would have to rid himself of Hawk in a just way, or not at all. Hawk would at some point go too far, and reason would demand that he be dealt with. That was the problem. Hawk had not gone too far, yet. He came across as unconcerned and disinterested, but the bastard was crafty. It was obvious now, however, that he would go too far. He was running out of rational options. Hawk was a madman, and would eventually act like one.

Hawk climbed steadily, unaware and uninterested in the animosity brewing below him. The sweat made his quickly growing facial bristles itch. Damn nasty thing, he swore to himself. What the hell was the purpose of a beard? He touched the loose gravel to steady himself, but the gravel was no longer loose. He froze. He pumped his arm, and the column froze. A drop of sweat fell down his straight, narrow nose.

He dusted the soil away from where his hand had landed. His square fingertips uncovered the edge of a metallic, disc-shaped object. An inch or two from the exposed corner of the mine, gravel dropped away from the winged plunger. He breathed deeply. Holding his boots firmly in place, he twisted his body to look behind himself, and then looked up. This was going to be it. The Japanese were going to poke a battery of Arisaka rifles over the edge of the cliff. He watched the edge above and the blue sky behind it. Cotton bundles of clouds sailed peacefully across his line of sight. A sea bird called with urgency in the distance. Quiet reigned ominously on the ridge top. Maybe the Japanese were waiting for something to blow, before showing themselves. There was the tornado watch quiet of a battlefield yet to be. He aimed his machine pistol upwards. Grasses twisted one way, and then the other in the wind, enjoying their peaceful morning dance.

After a full minute, nothing had happened. One enemy grenade could trigger the mines, and wipe out the patrol. Hawk signaled for the men to remain in place. He concluded that the Japanese had missed their chance, although he was not fully convinced. The enemy had become more accustomed to running, rather than trying for a clean sweep. This little set up could have afforded them the opportunity very easily. He would have to pay them back for the oversight, and the time they let him borrow. He climbed on, much more slowly. Ivania watched Joe watching Hawk. She had to admit this time, that she was glad it was Hawk up there. She did not know it yet, but she had contracted the germ of what Joe Canlon called "respect" for Hawk. Whatever awful thing that he was doing, it was probably being done in the best way it could be done.

Hawk touched the incline slightly with his hand as he climbed. He brushed another solid object. His stomach turned to blue ice. It could easily be one of the spring steel plungers. He dusted carefully around the edge. It was only a flat rock. A foot above it, however, lay obviously disturbed gravel. He planted a stunted twig beside it. He could see other disturbed spots to the left. Those had been placed less skillfully, which did not serve to make them any less horrifying. Whoever planted them, probably got tired of doing it. Hawk climbed on, and paused only for a moment before thrusting his helmet over the cliff. The lighthouse looked as vacant as ever. No gun muzzles met his fiery, questioning eyes. The grassy plains behind and beside the lighthouse blew in synchronized waves in the wind; alternating shiny rolling waves with cool dark waves. The gust whipped across the ground on a level with his head, and puffed under the brim of his helmet. It felt good.

His eyes looked down the hard, level ground, that ran a good distance beyond the lighthouse, as if he were sighting down a gun barrel. The distance was long and smooth, long enough and smooth enough for a runway.

"All right. Mines," he shouted down to the others, "y'all back down some and come up this-a-way." He slung a straight arm behind himself and pointed at the path with two fingers. "One at a time. This way," he pointed at the way that he had come. After a while, they had all safely made the ascent.

"Japs are asking for it," Hawk told Dreisen. The colonel was quiet. Hawk could see that the chief was losing his blustery confidence. This trail was going to take more than bluster. This was the road to Calvary. You didn't just air drop in and out of this baby. It was a commitment. For all of their finger wagging and words of wisdom, the old can never match the young at brutal hardship.

Dreisen made them cross the plains and ultimately reach the mountain, where they had first found Ivania. The colonel allowed a camp to be struck long before dark. They had seen nothing of the enemy but footprints and broken vegetation.

"He's fixin' to give up," Hawk told Canlon. It was Hawk seeking Joe's company now, instead of the other way around. Others avoided talking to Hawk. He needed someone upon which to bounce an idea off, on occasion. "I guess losing them boys hurt him."

"Shee-iit. Don't nothing hurt him but his feet and his ass. It was a dumb idea in the first place. He should have planes flying over this place, and a couple of battalions of men sweeping it back and forth. One to drive them and one to catch them. It would be easy. Hell, there's just a few of them. This is bull shit. He just wanted to be a big hero and catch that famous Jap all by himself. Big shit." Joe lit a cigarette. "The Nips know we are right behind them. Right in their footsteps. All they have to do is leave shit behind for us to fall into. This ain't nothing to play with, trying to get your damn name in the newspaper." Joe had the Marine's perfect insight on what his commanders should have done.

"Well, he thought we were close, at first," Hawk defended the colonel. Although he knew it sounded ridiculous, he added: "Things got complicated." It invited fifty more criticisms.

"Yeah, and *we were* close, until this genius took over," said Joe. He found no redeeming values in Dreisen.

"Jap son of a bitches. It's time they got a dose of their own medicine," said Hawk.

"Are you talking about going after them?"

"Goddam right. They ain't the only ones that can play Santy Claus."

"Why, man? Dreisen's gonna give up. You said so yourself. Why stick your neck out?" Joe did not like the sound of the idea. Hawk was suggesting nighttime infiltration. Alone. It was the most dangerous thing a man could do. Joe could think of no one else there who had even done such a thing, other than Hawk.

"Because they need it. You forget Waterland?"

"I'd like to."

"Well, I ain't, and I don't want to. And grabbing hold of that landmine made me remember a lot of other things." Hawk took out his knife and whetstone. "I don't like shit like that." Joe watched as he scraped the blade back and forth. Hawk had a trance-like expression, as if killing were his religion. "Give me them two grenades you been carrying. You ain't gonna use them. Tits on a boar."

Joe handed them over. "I don't get it. The Japs are just doing what Japs do. What are you doing this for? Just for that goofy Dreisen?"

"Maybe."

"Why? Man, you don't owe that crazy bastard anything." Joe thought of Hawk crawling behind the enemy lines, into their very camp. A shiver ran through him. What kind of a son of a bitch could do something like that? The kind that was sitting right beside him.

"Everybody gets old."

"Yeah? Well, we ain't. Listen, can you imagine what them men went through, and knowing they was gonna die? I mean, I'm sick of this Hawk. I don't mind a fight, but there's no point to this. Can't you see that? Morgan, Repler, Kreski, do you think everybody is wrong but you? You ever notice it's you and Dreisen against everybody? Nobody likes it."

Hawk nodded. He looked with approval at the point of the blade. "Still want me to talk to her?"

Joe sighed a ragged breath as he shifted his mental gears. "Yeah. Later."

"I'm going up the mountain tonight. I reckon if I'm gonna tell anybody anything, it ought to be now. Otherwise, it might be left up to you."

Joe put a filthy thumb in one eye and a forefinger in the other. "Okay." He nodded. "I was thinking, though. Take it kind of easy on me. You know, none of that: 'the dirty chickenshit bastard', kind of stuff. It wasn't like that, really."

"I will." He pointed the knife at Joe. "Easy does it. She's got a short fuse anyway."

Dusk floated down upon them early in the shadow of the mountains. They could see the sunlight on the higher slopes and on the upper third of the lighthouse. The base was white, and the top was yellow. It seemed safe in the clean, fresh-smelling open area at the foot of the mountain. Plenty of space surrounded them. Infiltrators did not prefer such open spaces. Hawk walked over to Ivania. She was talking to Dreisen. *That conversation ought to be good*, he thought. Hawk stood over them, watching. They stopped talking. Only she looked at him.

"Like to talk to you," Hawk said to her. "If you don't mind, sir?"

"Go right ahead," Dreisen said. The two of them walked a few paces away from the colonel, as if Hawk had just stolen his dance partner.

"Sit down," he said. She sat. For all of her complaining and mocking, she followed his orders just like everyone else did. He stood for a moment, took out his knife and whetstone, and sat beside her. He began sharpening it again, focusing less on the point and more on the blade.

"Did you call me over to watch you do that?"

"Nah-uh." He spat. "Listen. I'm going up a-ways and see if I can kill me some Japs. This is all getting on everybody's nerves, and things will be a lot better after that. Try to...try to get this show on the road, see? One thing is, though, there's something you ought to know about Joe Canlon. About the Verhangen bidness."

"Why are you telling me this?" He ignored the interruption. He just wanted to get this over with.

"Joe knew that you was alive back there. He seen you, he seen that the Japs had you, and he didn't tell me about it. On purpose. He knew that I would've tried to get you away from them, and probably got all three of us killed. He was right, I guess. He played it smart, and we're all still alive." Hawk dragged the blade across the pale gray stone without looking at her.

She stared at him. "And why did *you* think that I ought to know any of that?"

"I don't know. Y'all are gettin' pretty cozy. It's better something like that comes out now." He glanced up quickly. "Ain't it?"

"I don't see why."

Hawk nodded. "Well, good." He shifted. "I mean, it don't matter much. It don't take much for you to get cozy. Like with Captain Jordan and all."

She suppressed a gasp. He was, without a doubt, a charmer.

The scraping was getting on her nerves. "Must you keep doing that? How sharp does that damn thing have to be?"

"Never know."

"So, you are not quitting, are you?" She sighed. "I want a bath and some clean clothes. You're doing this because of that feather-brained colonel, aren't you?"

"You been talking to Joe?"

"No, he's been talking to me."

That made sense. That's where that dumb ass got all of his whiny ideas. Hawk studied the light gray edge of the black blade. "Maybe you forgot about them prisoners," he said. "Clean clothes and a bath ain't all there is to this, you know." He blew at the blade and rubbed the stone on his pants. Ivania shuddered. She knew that this was no act, and that he would soon be hacking the thing into the flesh of some unsuspecting human being. Perhaps, someone she knew. He began scraping again. "Wasn't one of them prisoners with you a woman?"

"Yes. I didn't know the others, though. They kept us apart. They kept a rice bag over her face. Someone said that she was a pilot. She was American. Maybe she was a WASP. I have trouble remembering much of it. I was confused...during most of it. You probably can't understand that, having few sensibilities, and no mind whatsoever. I do wish you would stop doing that!"

He stopped. "No. I ain't real sensitive. But getting them people back means more to me than a bath and clean clothes." He cocked his head arrogantly at her and jammed the knife into its scabbard. He pocketed the wet stone. It clunked against something already in his pocket. "Kind of like I would've got you back, when you were a prisoner. And...kind of like I did." He stood. "I expect, I'm just uncouth. I ain't like you." He half turned. "Sleep tight."

His mocking sneer did not pass unnoticed in the waning light. "There are other ways of doing things. You and Dreisen don't have a monopoly on the war. You are just doing it for him," she said as he walked away. "You want to be his little flunky when he makes general."

Hawk looked over his shoulder. "Didn't know I was so easy to see through. You know...it's easy to say shit like that when you're sittin' all comfortable on the American side of the fence."

Two minutes later, Hawk was kneeling in front of Dreisen. He was still thinking of Ivania. She filled his visual and auditory memory storage to capacity. She really hadn't changed any since he first met her. His infatuation with her was practically dead. The only way she could maintain any infatuation, he decided, was if she were to be suddenly struck mute. A man can like a woman for her looks alone, but there are time limits on even that. He didn't know that she had made the same assessment of him, long ago.

"What is it?" Dreisen demanded weakly.

"Gonna do a little scoutin', sir. I figure it's time we show the Japs that they ain't the only ones with a bag of tricks. I was kind of curious as to whether you wanted this pilot fella dead or alive, sir. See, alive might be a pain in the ass. Dead, I might be able to take care of pretty quick."

"Oh." The colonel stared at the ground. "Hawk, I've radioed for help. I asked for two companies. We're finished here, my boy."

"Yeah, well. Maybe not. That's gonna take a while. Dead or alive, sir?"

"I wanted him alive, bigger splash and all. Now, it doesn't matter. But if he's dead, I have to know he's dead. That it *is* him."

"How about his head? Will that do, sir?"

Dreisen looked up. "I... well...I don't know. If he doesn't have any papers on him..."

"Well, sir, if we had caught up with them, how were you going to know which one was him?"

"I was going to catch all of them. He's with them. We know that. They wouldn't be running, if he wasn't with them, and they would've scattered, if they weren't protecting him." Dreisen rubbed his face. He looked into Hawk's eyes. The powerful young man was trying to help him. Trying to...salvage...something.

"Yeah. A head will be fine. Intelligence has a photo of him."

Hawk nodded. "See y'all in the morning."

10

CAPTURED

TANIGUCHI PUT OUT HIS LOW FIRE. HIS SCOUTS WOULD rest tonight. The *hancho* had no way of knowing how much psychological damage their harassment of the Marines had caused. He knew some of the Marines had been killed. His running days were almost over. He decided that in the near future, he would stand, fight, and hold the lighthouse. He outnumbered the Americans now, if only slightly. Winning was a little more complicated for him, than it was for the Americans. He had to do more than have the last man on the field. He had to get Zanji out of here. He had no interest in that on a personal level. He did not especially like Isamu Zanji. The ace had lately been pressing for the execution of the three prisoners, a virtual reversal of his earlier sentiments. Taniguchi killed soldiers in battle without batting an eye. Prisoners were another matter. He also didn't like differences of opinion with people whose opinions changed so rapidly.

Taniguchi, Zanji, a guard, and two other men who were cleaning their rifles, remained awake in the early evening. Zanji came over to sit with Taniguchi in the darkness. Without any prefatory comment, as was his direct way, the flier said: "This woman is a legend in America, Taniguchi. Her picture has been in the newspapers for years. They think she died at sea. Our government has denied knowing her whereabouts. If these Marines should accidentally get her, just as they did the other woman, there will be repercussions in Tokyo. No good will come of this. She and her pilot friend should disappear, immediately, to protect yourself, Taniguchi, if no one else."

"Repercussions? A war, perhaps?" Taniguchi asked, and opened his round canteen to take a drink. "No. Absolutely not."

"I am your superior."

"You are a lot of things. But first, you are my charge. I control this patrol, and you are its subject. I am the captain, and this is my ship. I respect your name and I respect your rank, but this I cannot order."

"I will do it myself, and you will have no say in the matter." Zanji stood. "Unless you kill me." Taniguchi took another drink. He watched Zanji walk back to his own blanket. Could things get any better?

A few very dark feet away, from out of a black hell, orange firelight simmered in cold blue eyes. Hawk scratched his bristly neck, as he watched the pilot lie down. He had no idea that it was Zanji. Because of Zanji's height, Hawk did not suspect that he was a pilot, and was not even sure that he was Japanese. There was nothing of a celebrity about the man. Taniguchi lay down soon after. The watcher could not see Taniguchi well, but he could tell that he wielded some sort of authority; a map was open on a pile of rucksacks next to him. Everyone had settled for the night. The other two soldiers had finished with their rifles.

One guard paced the clearing. Hawk noticed that the sentry stayed closer to one side of the camp than the other. Hawk crawled over to that side. The damp leaves made no sound. He slid his long sharp knife from its leather scabbard and knelt. Snores drifted over the haphazardly strewn blankets. An hour passed. Death is patient, it is inevitable, and it is forever. The guard looked over the camp, and then sat down and rubbed his eyes. He was too far from the jungle to be attacked.

A sleeping man lay closer to Hawk than was the guard. A dangling clump of leaves swung only a few feet away from him. Another half hour went by. The guard got up and unbuttoned his fly. He looked around, and then apparently, as a courtesy to the others, or fear of censure, strolled to the edge of the woods.

Hawk came off one knee as the guard approached. *Banzai, baby.* He was beside him. Perhaps the only emotion lacking in the American was fear. He was intoxicated with the feeling of superiority reserved for unseen killers and banshees. The guard began to urinate. The crook of the American's arm flew under his chin, numbing his Adam's apple and bending his small body backward. The flow of urine stopped. The guard was strong. He struggled, lifting both feet off the ground. But the encircling arm was a vice. The unknown attacker was a rigid structure of iron that allowed no escape and little movement. The point of the knife hesitated as it met the solid flesh over the guard's kidney. Whether this was the intended target or not, it drove inward with all of the Marine's merciless strength. Cloth ripped and flesh sucked. Warm blood erupted over Hawk's pants leg. He eased the body down. The sleepers did not stir. He felt satisfaction as he thought of them saying: *"I never heard a thing,"* in the morning. Like the Artful Dodger, he slipped the wallet from the falling corpse's pocket, with three flashing fingers. Another man lay sleeping ten feet away. He did not move.

Poor fella's tuckered out from all that damn running, Hawk thought. Crouching, taking quiet but quick steps, Hawk reached the man's side. He put a knee firmly and precisely on the side of the soldier's head. He raised the knife high over the man's neck. The victim squirmed weakly, in a confused manner. Perhaps he thought someone was playing a joke on him. The American's expression never changed. He glanced up at the sleeping camp. Again and again, he rammed the blade down, until the head was almost severed. He watched the rest of the camp, perhaps more than he watched what he was doing. The razor-edged knife scratched the back of his hand. Eliminating this victim had been a little noisier, and he had to be careful now.

His eyes glistening in the starlight, he surveyed the other potential victims. He had to have more. It was a mathematical fact. The body count was the key as to who pursued whom. The others lay closer together, however, in little clumps. It would be difficult. And it was dark as hell. *No pilots, tonight*, he thought. He dashed back to the cover of the forest for some planning. He was the rat who had had his nibble, and waited patiently for another. His red and sticky sleeves stuck to his wrists. He sheathed the bloody knife and unslung his Thompson. His heart pounded with exertion and emotion. The exhilaration was boundless. So boundless, that it is one of the reasons it is very difficult for soldiers to go back to selling shoes in Peoria after front line action. When asked why soldiers did such things, this part of the explanation was always withheld.

Hawk decided that he could get at least one bunch of the sleepers in a burst, before the others knew what was going on. A grenade would probably do better. He might even be able to disable them all. But the fire was almost out, and the darkness was very irritating, and becoming disorienting, almost dizzying. He could not tell where the prisoners lay. He had seen the two men cleaning their rifles, before Zanji went to sleep. He knew that they were soldiers by the tasks that they performed, and he knew exactly where they lay. They were bedding closely beside two other men, who were therefore, more than likely, soldiers as well. More than likely was a sufficient burden of proof for Sergeant Hawk. His finger tightened a slight degree at a time on the Thompson's trigger, until the spring reached its breaking point. He continued thinking and observing, until the point was reached. The night erupted in a blazing thunderbolt. He waved the muzzle back and forth across the four shuddering bodies and a flying carpet bundle of blankets that lifted above them. Then he turned and ran. The quantity and stopping power of the slugs guaranteed him four sure kills.

The Japanese were up and running in an instant. Taniguchi had even seen the muzzle flash. He fired his Solothurn into the undergrowth in that direction, as he shouted orders. He motioned for his men to spread out. They could hear the leaves lashing against running legs.

"Kirishima! Seiji!" Taniguchi shouted for help. In a prearranged manner, two of Taniguchi's most able men threw themselves over Zanji's outstretched body, and the *hancho* knelt behind them. The other troopers charged into the forbidding jungle. The sound of an American submachine gun clacked nearby, and a scream followed. Taniguchi tensely moved the muzzle of his own submachine gun from one side of the clearing to the next, waiting for an attacker to burst from the cover of the black verdure. He was convinced that there was only one attacker. But that attacker was obviously emboldened by madness, and anything could happen. Zanji managed to maintain his considerable dignity, as he lay flat and helpless beneath the weight of his two protectors.

Hawk hopped the entangling vines and woody obstacles as he flew the scene of the massacre. After a while, he stopped and went to one knee. Men were clawing at the dark jungle on all sides of him. Without the sound of his running, they had no frame of reference as to where he had turned. A concealed evasion seemed preferable to headlong flight. He slipped a grenade from his pocket and set it on the ground. The sounds of the pursuers proceeded deeper into the jungle. They had passed him. He picked up the grenade.

Sergeant Hawk was not a detailed planner. His philosophy was that brute strength and raw courage usually undid the best of any plans. He wished that he had improvised a bit less this time, however, and given it more thought. He realized that a little reconnaissance probably would have nailed down the location of the hostages. His lack of foresight created a dilemma. He could easily circle back, and grenade the remaining men in the camp. But the prisoners had to be among them. On the other hand, if he did not assault the camp, he would not get the pilot, Zanji. Amidst the noise and confusion in the darkness, he tried to estimate the odds against him. It sounded like a healthy portion of the enemy had survived his efforts, so far.

He rolled the grenade about in his hand. A course of action eluded him, causing another of his shortcomings to immediately come into play, the conviction that any action was better than none. He put the grenade in his pocket and crouching over his Thompson, followed the men who had passed him by. He was sure of what to do with them, since the prisoners would not be among them. The fewer of them the better.

Success was not immediate. The night, the jungle, the passage of time, and the hundreds of unidentifiable sounds finally cooled his ardor. Perhaps he should go back down the mountain. He had had his revenge. Zanji remained a fugitive, but the protectors of the pilot were fewer now. Hawk was ready to escape with a claim of victory. The hand was stale, it was time for a new deal. His promise of a head to Dreisen had become too ambitious in the unfolding chaos.

He paused and listened. He could not hear the pursuers anymore. He knelt. He would not be the one making the noise. They could not approach him without giving away their positions. He turned his head to look about. Only the shiny-topped leaves and the hulking shadows of layer upon layer of shrubbery met his eyes. He inhaled a soundless breath. Insects ticked at one another and hummed like machinery. He waited for a sound, not knowing if it would be a blast or the rustle of leaves. It was neither. Japanese voices barked in the distance. They were far ahead of him and returning to their camp. He glanced at a riotous fern, growing up to the foot of a rain tree. The voices sounded suddenly closer. He crawled into the blue-green fern and braced his back against the tree, facing the direction from which the enemy would have to approach.

Two obviously enraged troopers came slashing through the jungle. They moved energetically, and Hawk realized, in comparison, how tired he was. He had been climbing and walking all day, and now, for most of the night. Nothing called attention to exhaustion more quickly than vibrant armed men bent on dismembering you. The American leveled the gas compensator of the Thompson on the chest of one of the men. The two of them looked down occasionally, spending most of their time in efforts to avoid a slap in the face by one of the myriads of branches confronting every step. They split and went around the rain tree. Hawk held his breath as they passed, one at each of his elbows. Still, he smelled them. He heard other voices off in the distance, to the right. He decided that it was over. If he could get out of here alive, he would. And that would not be easy. He still had the grueling trip back to Dreisen ahead of him.

Hawk took out his chewing tobacco and bit off a small piece. He sat there in the dark for about an hour, seldom spitting, and swallowing most of the tobacco. He was elated, with the elation moderately subdued by the necessity for escape, and by growing exhaustion. *Damn, I'm tired*, he thought. It was comfortable here. Before he knew it, he had blacked out. The deadly and dangerous night hours flew by as he slept.

Taniguchi did not sleep. He left his resting men to search for the bold infiltrator. He knew that the killer had to be near and that his men had probably passed him in the darkness. Taniguchi was a gentleman. He could, however, match wits or brutality with the worst of these Americans. He had no knowledge of the atrocities that his scout, Kirishima, had perpetrated upon the Marines. He would not have approved of the mutilation, but he would have approved of the deaths. A certain amount of hatred is necessary to win a war, but it cannot blind you.

Taniguchi left some rather hardened soldiers with his prisoners, Kirishima among them. His greatest error, however, was leaving Zanji alone with the soldiers, and by sheer power of rank, in charge of them. When the *hancho* returned from his inevitably fruitless search of the leafy darkness, the prisoners lay on the earth like so many livestock, with their throats neatly cut. If the infiltrator had hoped to rescue them, he had achieved the opposite result.

Although stunned, the *hancho* looked at this without comment. *Of course*, he thought. He said nothing to Zanji. He saw to it that the innocents were skillfully buried. Taniguchi was now torn between two intense emotions. He no longer cared if the Americans caught Zanji, the man. In fact, he would have liked that. On the other hand, he hated the Americans, even more than before. He hated the murderer of Keizo, more than any of them. Duty meant a great deal to the *hancho*. It was interwoven into his personality. His career was so much a part of him, that he sometimes did not know who Taniguchi was and who the *hancho* was. He spent another restless night, balancing these hatreds, and by daylight had decided that he would get the pilot off Cokoni. That was his obligation, not only to the Emperor, but to Keizo, and to the honored grandfathers and grandmothers of Japan. For as despicable as he was, Zanji could wreak untold damage on the enemy. The good people in Japan, who had sacrificed so much, loved the invincible ace. For them, Taniguchi would succeed. He would see the pilot placed in a fighter plane. After that, justice would be dealt to the ace on his own terms—for the new American pilots were as many as the stars in the sky. The Hellcats and Mustangs that they flew were far advanced over the planes that Zanji had made his reputation on.

Emotions aside, Taniguchi was still a soldier, and able to weigh all of the factors involved. He had to admit that getting rid of the prisoners meant that he could travel much faster.

The sun struck Hawk's closed eyes. The orange glow under his lids turned to white, and caused them to suddenly open. He leaned forward and reached for his Thompson. He sat back with a sigh. His neck ached from the way he had been lying on it. He tried to calculate how many hours had disappeared from his life. Dreisen would be moving again, if he had the heart for it, and if anyone would follow. Hawk wondered if he should wait here for the others to catch up. They might go in another direction. He was rested and capable of more of the endless walking. As a physical creature, he looked forward to it to a certain extent. The pain in his stomach, however, was like two saw blades rasping against one another. He decided to hunt game, and as part of this design, to drift toward Dreisen. It would not do to fire shots here, in the vicinity of the enemy.

He kept to an unhurried pace, moving quietly and hoping for the chance appearance of some meat. He threw away his new jacket and unbuttoned his stiff, faded utility shirt. Cokoni was no sportsman's paradise. He saw why the natives had turned to the sea for sustenance. After an hour, he had seen no sign of Dreisen coming his way. After almost another hour, he became concerned. He kept walking, all the while, with an uncomfortable feeling causing his pace to quicken.

He reached the Marine camp of the night before. Something had happened. A large number of men had been here. He saw no sign of bloodshed, and he temporarily forgot his hunger. Who were the visitors? The rocky earth did not surrender very many footprints. He saw the toes of bare feet. These could be the Cokonian bearers for the two companies Dreisen had ordered. They might have already arrived. It did not seem likely. *Well, they weren't worried about me*, Hawk thought. It looks like they went in the direction of the lighthouse. He took up the march again. He was troubled by the thought that something, he did not know what, had happened. It was also aggravating that no advantage was being taken of the damage he had done to Isamu Zanji's patrol. Of course, that is what war is all about: superhuman effort for naught.

In a few minutes, he came down the well-traveled route to the plains before the lighthouse. The structure could be seen clearly from this vantage point. He went quickly to one knee on general principle. At least seven hundred to a thousand men were gathered below him. He studied the scene carefully, almost paralyzed by the unexpected sight. The Cokonian islanders made up the vast majority of the roaming crowd.

He sat on the rocky slope, propping his gun on its butt plate beside him. He closed one eye and put the lighthouse in the hook of his vision. He could see the windblown robes of the monks of Hai-tai amidst the fluid crowd. At the center of the great assemblage, sitting against the lighthouse, were the members of his patrol. One of the standing Marines, shorter and wider than the rest, had to be Dreisen. Hawk did not see Ivania Broeder. He shook his head. What in the stomped-up hell was this? Did the men, U. S. Marines, let themselves be taken prisoner? Did the islanders cross that bridge, and kill Dussair? Even at fifty to one odds, such things did not happen. This had to have something to do with the relic. *The damn thing's gonna screw up everything.* He felt a little guilty.

Hawk got up with a disgusted groan and proceeded down the slope. "The goddam bastards." His thumb kicked the safety off the machine pistol. He carried the weapon loosely in one hand. He looked over his shoulder frequently now, until he stepped onto the plain. Who knew what the shit was behind him? He was becoming more and more furious as he saw his men lounging around behind the crowd, with apparent acceptance of whatever had occurred. That was when the Cokonians saw him. Angry shouts arose over the crowd. It sounded like an excited portion of a sporting event. He continued walking toward them, ignoring the din, his lazy gait never missing a step. His face was aimed downward, but if he were marching into the *Place de la Revolution*, he gave no indication that he knew about it.

Dozens of knives leapt from sheaths, and men charged toward him. *So that's how it is*, he thought. Incredible as it seemed, the Marines were prisoners. How could this have happened? However it had happened, it was about to stop happening. He put the fore stock of the Thompson into his left hand and stopped. The Cokonians swung their knives bloodthirstily, and bore down on the lone, slouched figure on the plain.

Hawk touched the trigger. A line of heavy shells erupted in front of the advancing horde. The echo of the blast skipped along the mountain tops. The Cokonians stopped, and it became eerily quiet.

"Ease off, shitbags," he rumbled at them. The dark eyes of the islanders simmered with only temporary frustration. They had a few such weapons of their own now, although lying in a harmless pile. They shouted to one another, and a single man started moving toward Hawk. He moved cautiously. Hawk slid a grenade from his pocket. He let it hang from the little finger of his hand, while gripping the fore stock with the others.

"What the goddam hell is going on here?" he demanded.

No one gave him an answer. More of the islanders crowded behind those facing him. They spread out in an arc in front of him. The arc grew unwieldy in size until he found himself at the center of a wavering semi-circle. He took a careful backward step, swaying the muzzle, slowly and easily across the mass of faces closing in on him. He had every intention of taking as many of them with him as the laws of physics, and a Charles Fischer Spring Company, Brooklyn, N.Y., ammo clip would allow. His cold mind had settled, and it troubled him with no indecision. The blue eyes burned with calm and assured murder. "I'll show you son of a bitches the U. S. Marine Corps." The natives watched the defiant eyes as they approached. Some in the front decided to change places. Hawk hoped that the discharge of the first clip would stun them enough to allow him to replace it with a second. And, there was the grenade. They might have thought that the contest was a certain win, but he had far different plans for quite a few of them. A weak cry came from the rear of the crowd, and seconds later, Hai-lon elbowed his way to the front. The people bowed respectfully as they recognized him. An assistant accompanied the lama, but he lagged farther and farther behind as they approached Hawk.

Hai-lon and Hawk stared at one another for a moment.

"How are you, sir?" Hawk asked politely, eyeing the crowd arrayed before him, shoulder to shoulder, from his right elbow to his left. Men were beginning to break off from the mass, and trickle stealthily behind him. Hawk's eyes shifted anxiously. "You best move, sir. There is trouble and I cain't go to picking my targets too scientific."

"Ah, but there will be no trouble, honorable Hawk. We are all peaceful men. Do not point your weapon at these poor unfortunate laborers."

"Yessir. They don't look all that neighborly from here." He lowered the muzzle, only slightly. "Looks like I missed something. Why do you have my men?"

Hai-lon stepped from the concourse, and walked toward the American. Hawk's swaying muzzle stopped and gaped ominously at the monk's thin chest. "You're gonna get yourself killed, Mr. Hai-lon." Hawk's eyes still watched the crowd. They could leap at him at any second. "I won't be taken prisoner." He glanced quickly over his shoulder. A half dozen men were behind him now.

"You better get on outa the way now, I mean it."

Hai-lon swept his robes around, turned and faced

the crowd. "This man will not harm you," the monk told them. "This man is not one of those you seek. This is a good man." Hawk understood none of this. The Islanders looked skeptically at the bearded, hate-filled face of the weapons-laden beast by Hai-lon's side. They were simple folk, but they had eyes. Hawk looked back at them, with even greater skepticism. He had to judge a thousand, they had to judge only one. But after a minute, the crowd at the rear began to dwindle.

"Leave us now," Hai-lon commanded them, with renewed sureness. "I must talk with this man of the things that trouble us. He has much to tell."

Hawk watched them walk away. He lowered his muzzle before half had left. Of course, a rock bouncing off his head would still have been no surprise. He stuck the spoon of his grenade over the top of his pocket. "Thank you, sir. I don't think them boys meant well."

"And you, honorable Hawk? You meant them no harm?"

Hawk bit off a well-deserved plug of tobacco. "Well, you don't see me chasing after them none. I think that was what you might call, self-defense."

"Is it still self-defense when the loss is a certainty? Would such injury have served any purpose? This could not be self-defense."

"No, sir. I guess not. But it's something."

"You would gain nothing by harming a few of them. You have much to learn, young seeker. You would die and you would cause others to die needlessly. You are a good man, in your heart, but we need to do more to bring that goodness to your actions. So that you may reach it quickly, when you need it, instead of this other thing that you reach for."

Hawk nodded agreeably. "Yes, sir. No, shit. So, what is going on here? Is this about that bone thing?"

"I am sad to say that it is. We have not recovered the relic of the martyr. It is not a patient thing, this matter. The island is in turmoil. Everyone is of a belief that your party has taken the relic. I, of course, do not know whether you did or not."

"Well, you know, a lot of men that were over there on the day that this all started, are dead, sir. You got two strikes against ever finding it, even if one of them did take it." Hawk spat. "Why don't you let the colonel go, and y'all can get on with your rat-killing."

"You are the one killing the rats, young seeker. We are on a mission of peace."

"It didn't look so peaceful."

"Emotions run high. If you tell me what you know, then you may leave. The others, I am sorry, must stay. They are not as trustworthy as you. Did your leader, this rude and tormented colonel, did he ever mention the possibility of committing this sacrilege?"

Hawk looked down. This was turning into some real shit. He finally looked up and met the monk's pure chestnut-colored eyes. "Yeah." Hawk suspected Hai-lon knew the answer to that one, so no need to lie.

"Ah, the truth. Is it not beautiful? You speak it well, as I knew you would. Now that you have told the truth, you must tell all of it."

Hawk spat. "Ain't much to relate on the subject. He said that we ought to take it."

"And—forgive my persistence—that he would return it, when you had the information that you were seeking?"

Hawk thought for a moment. "No, sir. Not exactly. He said something about throwing it into the ocean."

Hai-lon looked as if he had been physically hurt. "The truth is not always beautiful." He sighed dejectedly. "But it is always true. It is always good. Thank you for this, my friend."

"You're welcome. Now let them loose."

"If you mean, with their weapons, this I cannot do."

"You got to. We're in the middle of something here. We almost got that fella we came for."

"It seems that our matters of importance conflict. All the more reason not to release your friends. Bloodshed is not a thing to seek, nor to help others in seeking. Perhaps our two matters of importance will come together in peace and result in goodness."

Hawk fingered the trigger of his submachine gun. Neither of them would have been surprised if he used it. Hawk spoke aloud of their thoughts. "I don't think so. I can make you let them go."

"You could. But you will not. I understand you, young seeker, you have forgotten. You know that these men are safe here. You see as much. They know it as well. You are free to pursue this evil goal to your heart's content. And, unlike them, you will find the truth in it, for that is all that you are after."

"Well, if they think they're safe here they're a bunch of stupid son of a bitches. The Japs ain't that far away."

"But the Japanese will not come here because of our presence. We are many." Hai-lon turned and walked away.

"Mm hm," Hawk muttered. Like the Japanese give a *shit* about your presence or anything else. He looked around. The islanders were generally ignoring him. Some glanced curiously, and suspiciously, in his direction, and just as quickly turned away. Hawk noticed his own shadow on the ground. He nibbled at the inside of his lip and walked unchallenged over to the colonel. It was like picnic day at the State Prison, and Hawk was the invited guest.

"Good to see you, good to see you. Give me that Tommy Gun," the colonel ordered. Hawk took a step back.

"Whoa. Wait a minute, Colonel Dreisen. I can walk out of here right now, but you'll kind of mess things up, if you go to waving my gun around. There ain't no way you can shoot your way out of this, sir, not with a 20-round clip." Of course, Hawk was not thinking along those lines ten minutes ago.

Dreisen looked at the sullen faces of the Cokonians. They watched him, hoping that he would take the weapon. Of all the Americans, they would most like to kill him. Though they had reluctantly accepted the amnesty extended to Hawk, it by no means extended to Dreisen. Even Hai-lon would probably have difficulty finding a kind thought about the colonel. If any individual was a suspect in the sacrilege, it was Dreisen.

Dreisen cleared his throat. "You know, help is on the way," he said in a low voice. "It might take a while. But this is not as bad as it looks. But if you don't do something now, Zanji gets away."

Hawk pushed his lower lip over the upper. "Fact is," he said, "I got about half of them last night. Probably get the rest tonight. And, I guess I shouldn't be saying it, but I should have done it a long time ago. Your way didn't seem to be working." Hawk shook his head and looked up into the sky over the plain. He shook his head again and looked down. "I reckon...I reckon bringing in more men, just means traipsing around a lot longer. More men getting killed." Hawk did not see the pursuit as a manpower issue, as had Kreski, he saw it as a conceptual issue.

"I'll tell you what," Hawk spoke slowly, as he was thinking. "You sit tight. This being captured...or whatever it is, won't hurt a thing. The reinforcements won't change nothing. I'll get the pilot for you. I was a guest in his camp last night. It'll still be your patrol. Just like you wanted." Hawk winked. "It'll end up like you wanted. You can buy me a beer sometime."

Dreisen stared at him, trying to process this. Hawk was saying that he was going to wave a magic wand and make all of this go away. Dreisen did not know how to feel, because...Hawk...always did what he said he would do. For once in his life, Dreisen could say nothing.

Hawk did not wait for an answer. He knew the effect he had on people. He started to turn away, and then turned back. "What about Dussair?"

"They said they escorted him to the shore," said the colonel. "He didn't hurt anybody. They didn't hurt him."

Hawk nodded. "Oh, and, you ain't got these folks' bone thing, have you, sir?"

Dreisen's stunned, empty face became angry. "No, I don't have their goddam thing, what the hell do I want with that? I want Zanji, and I want out of here."

"Okay. I guess I better talk to the *swanee* one more time then. But I gotta be hitting the trail. The Japs got a good jump on me. They'll be expecting me, I imagine. They're gonna shit when they see this carnival at their lighthouse. It's gonna be a turd in their punchbowl. I don't know if they got buried treasure here or what, but they sure want this place."

Dreisen tried to look betrayed and angry. He only succeeded in looking pathetic. Hawk turned away and walked into the lighthouse to find Hai-lon. One of the monks directed him to the stairway. Hawk found the lama in the airy lamp room, contemplating the vastness of the beautiful vista. A consciousness of time and space struck Hawk as he stepped into the open-walled tower.

"Sir? Can I talk to you?"

"Yes, honorable Hawk."

Hawk glanced at the antiaircraft gun. He walked over to it. He remembered Dreisen's reference to a booby-trap. He looked down the barrel. Something that looked like newspaper was inside it. He pinched the edge of it, and slid it out. The paper was wrapped tightly around an explosive powder, and twisted at both ends. As Ivania Broeder had said, Dreisen was right twice a day. Hawk held the thin stick of explosive for Hai-lon to see.

"Me and the Japs are always exchanging gifts. Good thing I didn't fire this, like I wanted to." Actually, he doubted if anything would have happened; but he wouldn't have left it in there regardless.

Hai-lon nodded. "You see the advantage in being a peaceful man? There was never the slightest danger to me. The machine has only been my quiet companion."

Hawk smiled and considered the truth of the statement, as he sat down. The old bastard. The wicked machine gun loomed over them, and cast a huge shadow across their eyes. It looked as if they wore dark masks.

"Mr. Hai-lon, when we talked about this... relic thing

of yours, before...you said it was a gimmick. Like a magic trick or something? To hoodwink the yokels, right? To keep the collection plate full or something?"

"Not exactly, young seeker. There is much imprecision in your interpretation of the role of the moonstone."

"Yes sir. I don't doubt that. I'm kind of thickheaded. I get everything wrong. But now, I do know, you said that when the time comes, this relic will disappear. Now, all the same, you did say *that*, didn't you?"

"Yes."

"Well. It looks to me like the time done came and went, don't it? I mean, looks like somebody missed the Second Coming here. Why don't you just explain that to these people, and cool them down some? Let them get onto the next step in this religion thing. Going to the ancestors, or whatever the plan is."

"Because I cannot lie. The time has *not* come. They are not ready. They would not understand. When I said that the relic would vanish, I used words that the people would use. In reality, the lama would dispose of it in a purely physical manner. Someone other than the lama has done this thing. An incomplete man has intervened. You see, my friend, the people do not have the faith and goodness to stand alone at this time, along their path to truth. Do you not see their discord? Their hatred? You who have faced it? The man who did this terrible thing, lacked the faith in goodness and the knowledge that this is not how things were meant to be. The time is, and was not right. Such a man could never know when the time is right."

"Unless maybe it's you that ain't got the time right, or the faith in these people, sir?" Hawk lit a cigar, thinking of how broken clocks can be right. He stared at Hai-lon. Hawk's expression was stern and unflinching. The monk closed his eyes. Who was this man, to say such things to him? He must not let himself be intimidated. His confidence was clearly shaken. "You need these people's support, don't you, sir?"

Hai-lon kept his own eyes closed, to avoid the hypnotic effect of Hawk's eyes blazing through the shadow on his face. "Confucius teaches us order. Order comes from those who can teach us. They learn from me. They need the lama if peace is to reign."

"Yeah, but when it comes to teaching, what if those doing the teaching are wrong"?

"Goodness cannot be wrong. I understand your words. Though you are unlearned in philosophy, your mind has been formed by Western ideas. You speak in words and not in concepts. Did not your own Socrates, or your own Christ, refuse to write down their concepts? This was so that words, much like those that you speak, could not be twisted by others, in misusing their concepts. Only when others later wrote the words down, were they misused. Man is capable of more than words. I know that you understand this. I know that you are a man who does not trust words, but trusts in himself."

"Awright. Fine. But you see my point, don't you? You and me been pretty straight with one another. I know you don't lie. You don't like lyin'. I *know* you see my point."

"I understand your words."

"I'm thinking that maybe not everybody thinks your ideas are so good. Maybe even one of your own people?

Maybe that relic is a lot closer than you think. It could be one of your monks that took it."

Hai-lon opened eyes and looked at Hawk for a moment, and finally shook his head. "Such a thing could not come to pass. If you understood our order, you would know that such a thing is not possible."

"One thing's for sure, one of us is wrong about all this."

"Certainty is rare."

Hawk drew on his cigar. Crap.

"Okay. You give me your word you want let anything happen to my men?"

"You have my word. That has been known since the beginning of time. I harm no one."

"And the woman?" Hawk did not recall having seen Ivania.

"She has left us. I believe she thought she was escaping captivity. I would not allow a pursuit. This is not a captivity. She has suffered enough. I know that she is innocent. Another soldier escaped with her. I believe that to be her lover. I do not suspect him of any wrong-doing with regard to the relic. Lovers are innocent people, while they are in love. Is it not so?"

"Yeah, I guess." Hawk's lips tightened.

"They are interested only in one another, during that brief time."

Hawk stared at the floor with some unknown and additional agitation. He stood. "I guess I better go then." He walked to the stairway. "I'll be back. You and me will have to wrap this subject up somehow. I don't think we really got to the answer yet."

"I joyfully await your safe return, and wish you still

no success," Hai-lon smiled. "Remember, young seeker, your journey will take you to the truth. Prepare yourself well for it. It is not always beautiful, but it is always true."

Hawk looked out over the vividly blue sky behind the 13.2 mm gun. The tips of the mountains were visible in the distance. "I stay prepared," he said grimly. He padded down the steps.

The first American that Hawk encountered at the bottom of the landing was Joe Canlon. This surprised him, because of what Hai-lon had said. He thought that it had been Joe who had left with Ivania. He looked around and quickly deduced that it was in fact, Sergeant Kreski, who was missing.

"Hey, Joe. How you getting along with all this business?"

"Damn good. This is all right with me. I can sit here forever. Beats walkin', or getting' your ass blown off."

"Yeah, till the goddam Japs come back here and blow your goddam peanut brains out. What happened? They snuck up on you? Got the drop on you?"

"Sort of, we seen them, but you know, what the hell you gonna do with that many of them surrounding you?" Joe laughed. "It was quick. Dreisen was asleep and Kreski wouldn't shoot them, so they just sort of lifted our rifles out of our hands. Kind of glad you and Dreisen were out of it. Might not have gone as well."

"Is that right? That's just about the stupidest thing I ever heard of in my whole goddam life. You call yourself a Marine? Did they teach you in boot camp to hand your rifle to the first silly son of a bitch that asks for it?"

"Well, yeah. I figured that would be your take on it. I guess that's easy to say. But this all happened in about two seconds. The whole thing was Kreski's fault. He could have killed the old guy. Anyway, the old guy said we could leave whenever we want. He just didn't want us carrying rifles around and shooting people. Which is what you would've done." Joe scratched his head. "They say we aren't prisoners, but, if you *do* try to leave, one of these guys grabs you. I guess if you ran like hell, like Kreski did, they'll let you go. Sort of a difference of opinion going on, I guess. Or maybe, the old guy just lied."

"Reckon? You mean to tell me Breaux just turned over his BAR to these characters?" Hawk remained incredulous.

"No, no. He didn't have a weapon, the BAR was on the ground with the rest of our shit. You got the wrong idea. This took no time, I'm telling you. They were everywhere. For shit sakes, you're gonna have us all up before a firing squad, if you don't shut that shit up. We didn't turn over nothing to nobody."

"Okay, okay. Shit. So where is Kreski? Did he join up with the Japs or something?" Hawk turned his anger to the sergeant in charge.

"No, he just took off. He was lucky, they didn't chase him, or anything. I think these people are pretty easy going, they're just pissed off about their church thing. Hell, you know how people get about that stuff. I remember..." Joe was about to digress into a disgruntled churchgoers story from his childhood, when Hawk stopped him with an open hand.

"What about the woman?"

Joe looked solemn. "She's the one that took off first. She just ran through the woods, just ran right away. I never had a chance to stop her. See, you're seeing all this after it happened. I'm telling you, it all was over in one second. Then Kreski followed her, when he saw how easy it was. It was kind of like a lot happening at once. Dreisen woke up and then, whoa, baby, the shit hit the fan. There was all kind of yelling, and then the people weren't quite as nice about all this. He pisses everybody off. I tell you. I was surprised by it all. Looking back, I guess if we had hung onto our rifles, they would've let us go. The only bad thing is, I hope Ivania is okay. You know, out there, by herself."

"Right. That's your problem. You just worry too much about other people. You need to start thinking about old Joe more. Which way did they go?"

"You know where we was camped? She went out toward the south. I think that's where she was going. I don't see why. Dreisen checked the map, and he said that she would run into that swamp. It kind of hooks around the mountains over that way."

"You saw the map?"

"Yeah. You've seen the map. I thought about making a break for it. But I would have had to leave without my rifle, I think. Kreski was cuckoo to do that. What's he gonna do out there without a weapon? I guess she will be okay."

"Left without his rifle? You mean, without a goddam rifle, like you are right now? If you ain't the goddam dumbest son of a...Why the hell will she be okay? If the Japs keep following that route they been going, they will pass that way tonight. Ain't that right?" Hawk asked.

Joe looked a little guilty. "Yeah. Maybe. You never know what they're doing. I don't think they know what they're doing."

"Maybe, shit. Maybe I can just catch up with everybody," Hawk said. He relit his dead cigar. "I'm getting kinda worried that them goddam Japs are gonna scatter all over hell and half of Georgia. Then I won't be able to find anybody."

"Dreisen figures they're sticking close to this lighthouse for a pretty good reason. He says they're going around and around here waiting for an airplane."

Hawk nodded. "Makes sense. Hope so." He winked. "I need those son of a bitches on a regular schedule." He stepped around Joe and out the door. "I figure if they are, they won't be back here for a while." He did not speculate on the alternative.

"Hey," Joe called.

"What? Shit. What?"

"Be careful," Joe said. Then he realized, it sounded funny. "About Ivania, I mean. Those are some rough Japs, you know, cutting people into pieces and all that stuff."

"Yeah. I know about Japs." Hawk looked down with a serious expression. "Are you scared I'll get hurt?" Hawk looked up at him, unable to suppress a smile. They both laughed at once, like the maniacs that they were.

"Yeah."

"Stupid asshole."

Hawk shook his head and turned away. He waved toward Dreisen as he walked out onto the plain. He didn't want to screw with him again.

"Hey!" Dreisen shouted. "Where the hell do you think you are going?" Hawk pointed toward the mountains. "Hey! Come back!"

Hawk steered himself toward a jungle strip that lay between two of the slopes. "Cain't! Got to get a move on." He waved again.

Joe watched as Hawk brushed off the colonel. Baker came and stood beside him, with his cockeyed, ever present smile. He had seen the departure as well. "There he goes," said Baker with a laugh. "Walks in here. Walks out. Does whatever he wants. Nobody can say shit. Look at Dreisen."

"Yeah," said Joe. "Pretty much."

"So, what did hep cat have to say about us getting caught?" Baker laughed again. He chewed his gum furiously.

"Nothing good. He was pissed. Even for him."

Joe Canlon had a chill as he watched Hawk's rolling shoulders disappear. Hawk would be safe. But anyone near him would not be. Maybe he thought he was a rescuing knight. He had forgotten that knights fought with swords. When you use bullets and explosives, a little more discretion about your surroundings is required. Hawk was the bad side of nature. He was careless, brutal destruction. And he didn't even know it. He thought he was a tornado with good intentions, instead of just another dumbass tornado.

"Crazy bastard," Joe whispered.

11

BEAUTY AND THE BEAST

SGT. KRESKI SAT AGAINST A ROCK. BEFORE HIM SPREAD the northern edge of the great swamp of Jarok. The emerald beauty of the place was lost upon him. He saw only an obstacle to further flight. Ivania Broeder stood beside him, looking in the opposite direction. She was thinking that perhaps she had made a mistake.

"We'll rest here a while," Kreski said. "I don't think they're following us. We should be able to get back to the shoreline somehow."

"Aren't those Japanese paratroopers between us and the beach?" she asked.

Kreski pushed back his helmet. "I don't know. To tell you the truth, I'm not real sure where we are, much less them. I didn't think we would run into this marsh right here. We'll have to skirt it and find that canyon with the pipe across it. I believe that we are past the Japs already. I think we can go back the way we came, past that monastery and all."

"Oh." Ivania sat down. "Thank God. I'd rather die than go back to them, Sergeant Kreski. I ran when those

other people surrounded us. I'm allergic to being a prisoner again. I would just rather be dead."

"Call me Fred." He smiled. She smiled. She didn't
tell him that she was a lieutenant; and not a mere
Marine Corps lieutenant, a Navy lieutenant.

"Fred." She took a deep breath. "I was so glad to get
away from the Japanese. Now, I think I'm happier to be
away from Dreisen. There was a very polite, sensible
man at the head of the Japanese patrol. I think Dreisen
was being unreasonable about that pilot, don't you?"

"Hell, yes. When I saw a chance to make a break and
maybe get my ruptured duck all at the same time, I took
it. Yeah, Dreisen," Kreski shook his head, "and that
damned Hawk. I just want to be back with normal
people."

"Yes. Hawk," her lips trembled with the word. "Yes,
I'm glad we're here." She smiled. She felt a tired, happy
glow. She knew that the feeling was freedom. Freedom
from confinement and freedom from madmen. She
leaned back and nearly touched Kreski's broad shoulder. Their clothing touched. "Joe Canlon was the only
thing that kept me going. I liked Joe. He's such a nice
person. In all of this, a truly nice human being, it's hard
to believe. Don't you like him?"

"Joe? Yeah, he's all right. Too thick with Hawk,
though, in my book. Don't tell Canlon anything you
don't want Hawk to know. That's how Canlon made
corporal, and he's going to ride that pony to the round-
up. The whole platoon was like that before it got
chewed up at the beach. Hawk could do no wrong with
those guys. I think they must have all been his illegiti-
mate kids or something. Personally, I'm glad to be away
from the bastard."

"Well, I don't know why it is," she said, "but men in a group of men always seem to be drawn to the crudest fellow around. I guess they think that is manly or something. They get quite irrational away from women. You probably disagree. But women are a better judge of character, and can see these things. You don't find someone like that getting any respect in a mixed society. Only where there are a bunch of men. Even in the Navy, it was different. There is much more refinement and, and a code of conduct, in the Navy. You probably disagree, but I've noticed these things."

Kreski didn't say anything. He sensed that it was better not to criticize Joe Canlon, for whom he had absolutely no respect. Or the Navy. At the same time, he was relieved that Hawk was fair game. He had nothing good to say about *him*, and could not even fake it. Ivania locked her fingers around one knee.

"I'm going home, whatever it takes. I'll do it. I'll never leave America again. Maybe Joe will meet me when the war is over. They told us in the Navy that when you step off that ship, you are no longer in the United States. And brother, they were not kidding." She closed her eyes. "I'm afraid I got a little too patriotic there, when I joined the Navy. I didn't expect to go overseas. Maybe I'll see Joe Canlon again, back home, when all of this...ends."

"You like Joe that much, huh? Too bad he's not here. He stayed put back there, when we had the chance to make a break."

"Well. I like him. But, I mean, I think I would rather you were here. Joe doesn't belong here, and neither do I."

"Joe is too nice? It's okay for me, though?" They

laughed. "I got a little too patriotic, too," he said. "This Marine Corps thing is for people like Hawk. I learned what cannon fodder means." Kreski studied her perfect features. He glanced at the curve of her hip. "Well. Joe is lucky you feel that way about him." Kreski was not exactly sure how he felt about her, other than, if they were at the Red Cross sock hop, she would be his first choice for a partner. He took out his canteen and felt quite lonely there with her beside him in the jungle. "How serious is this? Marriage?" Kreski was remembering Joe Canlon. Not exactly Cary Grant. Not even Cary Grant with a broken nose.

"Oh. I don't think so. That would be a long way off. You see, I don't think I am the marrying kind. But, I could do worse. He's very well off. His family is in business. In industry."

Kreski swallowed hard and the gush of water hurt his throat. "Canlon?" He took another drink. "He worked...sometimes...in a factory in upstate New York. They laid him off every three months or so, and he'd go into the City and sell bananas down on the wharf or something. He's got some relatives that are immigrants, and they push fruit carts around down there." Kreski laughed. "That's the only business he's got. His industry was a homemade wheelbarrow, and a stick to chase the rats off." Kreski laughed a low bitter chuckle.

Ivania's widely spaced eyebrows came together in a frown. "Immigrants?" Kreski laughed again. After her lecture to him about women's judgment of character, this was pretty funny. She thought that moron, Joe Canlon, was wealthy.

Kreski stared out at the mysterious swamp, ignoring the effects that his efforts, fully intentional, had wrought upon the budding romance. He wondered if it would be possible to cross the swamp and avoid the gorge and the pipe altogether. The islanders could have the pipe blocked. "Yeah, that's right. Immigrants." He glanced at her face. What perfection.

Ivania's large and slightly tilted eyes slanted farther above her high cheekbones. "Joe might have a little problem with the truth, sometimes." After a moment of silence, she leaned against Kreski. Her straight, long hair draped across his arm. Oh, well, she had crossed no bridges with Joe Canlon. Her eyes closed. "Can't we rest here for a while? I'm so tired." Coolness emanated from the swamp.

Kreski looked over his shoulder. He would've liked sitting there with her forever. "No. I don't think it's such a good idea. Not yet."

* * *

TANIGUCHI CROUCHED over the bent stems that he had found. The party had crossed over his path. One was a large man, obviously a United States Marine. The other was smaller, perhaps a Cokonian. The *hancho* never considered Ivania. He thought that perhaps the Marine in question was the one who had attacked him last night. The tracks led toward the swamp to the south. The *hancho* wanted desperately to trail the man who had halved the size of his patrol. He likely had help from an indigenous guide, who accompanied him. But Taniguchi could not lose focus. He had to keep moving, keep circling the lighthouse until the Shiden Kai, or some of the other generously promised, and poorly delivered, help appeared. He told his scout, Kirishima, to go after these two outliers, whose tracks he had found. Kirishima had attacked the Marines in the night and was a capable man, who would be able to catch up with them. Taniguchi had no doubt that the order meant that the Marine and his companion would be dead before dark. The scout disappeared into the jungle like the stalker that he was. And Taniguchi proceeded over the mountains, with his increasingly burdensome albatross, Zanji.

* * *

KRESKI FOLLOWED the edge of the marsh. He and Ivania paused frequently to stare into the intricately woven green loveliness. The depths of the morass seemed a little too forbidding to attempt. The man behind them, Kirishima, never stopped. His eyes, the color of diluted coffee, glanced down at their tracks and then up in the direction of his prey. He was especially furious at the Cokonian guide for associating with the Marine. He often touched the handle of his knife. Kirishima had a disfiguring skin condition, and he was not a pretty sight. Today he looked particularly horrible beneath the flashing green shadows of the jungle.

* * *

COLONEL HEITO POUNDED the map on the conference table. "They are moving more of the Marines into the interior! Sergeant Taniguchi will be overwhelmed," the officer told his staff. A dignified officer from the Naval Air Force looked at Heito with a superior expression.

"We can get the Shiden Kai to the lighthouse of

Jarok at any time," said the Naval officer. "I have often told you this. All you have to do is give the order."

Heito looked angrily at the calm face of the officer. "Very well, you have it! You know that I have been awaiting the paratroopers." Heito turned to one of the members of his staff. "Get a unit on that plain," he sputtered. "Immediately!" He turned to the Naval officer. "And get the Shiden in there! I want Zanji out by tomorrow!"

The officers all bowed quietly and left the room, their ears ringing.

* * *

SERGEANT HAWK WAS SOMEWHAT confused by the manner in which the trails divided. He knelt over the moist soil. It slowly came to him. Zanji was keeping to his old, circular route, but one of the Japanese troopers had broken off, and was following Kreski. Hawk glanced at the sun. He stood. "You're in for a surprise, old buddy," he growled in a low voice. He abandoned Taniguchi's trail and went after Kreski and Ivania. Kreski was unarmed, as far as Hawk knew. Maybe he had a knife. Zanji's trail had become so routine, that Hawk could predict to within a few hundred yards, exactly where the pilot would be at any given time of the day. Zanji was nothing more than the hand on a giant sundial. Away from his superiors, Hawk was a patient and confident predator. Instead of following the hands of Zanji's clock, the sergeant could cross the diameter of its face, and intercept the ace. But it would have to be after he got this lone stalker off Kreski's trail. Hawk had the maddening desire to do two things at once. At least, he limited it to two.

Sergeant Kreski stopped. "Did you hear something?" he asked Ivania. She shook her head. "Come on, then." Kreski looked over his shoulder. His ever-present worried expression truly reflected his feelings. They walked a bit farther. The barely audible sound of stealthy movement came to him. It moved when he moved, stopped when he stopped. This made it difficult to detect. Was it his imagination? No. "Something is following us," Kreski whispered.

A starburst of paralyzing white adrenaline exploded in Ivania's breast. She looked up into Kreski's widening eyes. He looked boyish and good, and she lost some of her confidence in him. "What?" Ivania whispered. She knew there was only one answer to that.

"Come on." Kreski took her arm, and they moved faster. Their breath became labored. Ivania stifled a sob with every quick breath, and Kreski's breathing began to sound like that of an overworked horse. They ran back into the rocky-floored jungle, away from the open spaces on the edge of the swamp, running, running like the chase in a nightmare, and going nowhere. She tore her clothes on the sharp undergrowth.

Behind them, invisible, with only a gentle hiss of accompanying sound, Kirishima glided in their wake; not so much running, as covering the ground like a spirit. His finger tightened against the trigger of his rifle. He knew that they could not escape. Kirishima could run for miles. He had been a scout since the beginning of the war. He was tireless, soundless, and fearless. He did not gloat, however, for he was also emotionless.

Patience was Kirishima. It was only a question of a little time. The outcome had been determined.

Kreski came to realize this also. He knew that they could not shake this thing, whatever it was. Maybe alone, he could. He stopped and crouched. He pulled Ivania beside him.

"I'm going to lead him away. You stay here," he whispered. The sound from within the jungle stopped. Inquisitive birds cocked their heads and held their tongues as they watched this age-old drama. Kirishima watched the Americans from thirty feet away. He glared at Kreski, and raised his rifle swiftly. He flicked the tall, hinged hindsight up and tried to set the foresight within it. The Marine stood, and dashed into the jungle. Kirishima brought the rifle down to his side. He would have to come back for the woman. He had to kill the man. He saw no weapon, but the man could pick up a rock or a stick, get out of his sight, and become dangerous again. Especially this man, an especially large Marine. The scout took a path around Ivania, and sliding like an arrow through the foliage, kept doggedly on the trail of Kreski.

From her vantage point, Ivania could hear both of them now, running madly in a death race, through the forest. She shuddered. She pulled the remains of her clothes tightly around herself. *Kreski will kill him*, she thought. He was six feet three and built like a Roman statue. He had stood up to James Hawk. How could anything harm a man like that? But she remembered the look of horror in Kreski's eyes. She remembered the pieces of the big men that she had to pick up from the deck of the hospital ship. And she also remembered the not so big, fearless men, who had held her prisoner for months.

The noise always seemed to revolve around her, the slashing leaves, the stumbling boots, sounded closer and closer, spiraling in on her. "Kill him," she cried to herself. "For God's sake, kill him!" There was no other solution, no other wish. There were no considerations, no compromises. "Kill him!" *Why was Kreski running?* Kreski, of course, could have answered that. He did not have a rifle, and Kirishima did.

Then the leaves in front of her suddenly parted with an angry slap. It was not Kreski. It was a hideous enemy soldier. Nearly six feet tall, with a chest like a tombstone, the soldier had strange looking growths on both sides of his head, face, and neck. It appeared as if knobs had been welded into his skin. She well remembered him from her time with Taniguchi. She had never had any dealings with him, but she had always feared the possibility. With Taniguchi there, he meant nothing to her, other than something to look away from. His black eyes had always been upon her. Looking just like they did now. They were narrowed and expressed no intent. A reunion of old friends. She stifled a scream and cringed against a tree. In all of her time with the enemy, none of the captors had ever done anything life-threatening. That meant little now.

Kirishima pointed his rifle at her. He did it only for pleasure. She was not going anywhere. He had no concern over the conduct of a woman. He still had to kill the Marine. He would return for this one. He knew her well, the way that she ignored him, tilting her head up and away. He would have his way with her. Kirishima hated women. Only the waterfront prostitutes granted him a second glance, and then only with a shudder. Yes, he would kill her in a special way. This made him rather elated, and determined to vigorously dispose of Kreski as soon as possible. He strode past her in large, affected steps.

She muffled a squeal, even though she saw that he was only going to pass her by. She could smell a dirty, diseased odor as he passed and plunged into the jungle.

Kreski heard her weak scream. The worried crease between his eyes deepened. He stopped and turned around. He was tired, and unarmed, but he had to save her. He deduced that the stalker had not followed him after all. He ran toward the cry and found her there, right where he had left her.

"Fred!"

"What happened?" He reached down for her. For a brief moment, she felt safe again. The shot split the air between them, with an electric crack. Kirishima's shoulder jolted under his Arisaka's heavy kick. He folded down the hindsight. The bullet pierced Kreski's stomach and blew blood and pink tissue out his back. Even experts miss their mark, when the mark is human. But it was good enough. The American fell with his face up and his eyes open. He saw clouds twirling wildly above him. He was paralyzed. He was conscious only that something was wrong.

Kirishima stepped into the clearing. He looked at Ivania and allowed himself one small, gloating smile. She scrambled into the jungle on her hands and knees, with childlike cries, the obstructing limbs latching onto her every second. The scout frowned and looked down at his victim's elongated frame. He pulled out his knife with an overly dramatic gesture. He knelt and in one motion cut open the sergeant's fly. The buttons ticked off. But then Kirishima decided to rank his priorities. This would take time, and it could wait. First, the woman. He did not want to spend another hour tracking her in the maze of greenery. She moved too fast. Kreski could see the frightening visage above him, whirring along the edges of his darkening sight. Kirishima stood with shoulders hunched and went into the leaves after Ivania. She was noisy, and would be easy to catch.

Ivania rose from her knees. Her lungs burned. She was so tired. He was close behind her. She raced at the greatest speed that she could manage in the undergrowth. Why of all the monsters in all the world did it have to be him? He moved steadily, unhurriedly, and he was gaining.

"I don't speak Japanese," she said. "Joe!" The steps behind her grew louder. *"Fred!"* she screamed hysterically. She fell roughly onto her face. She felt the cold dirt all over her bare skin. She could barely rise, she could not go on. The end had finally arrived. All of the crushing evil of the world had finally overpowered her. She admitted that she was no match for it. She saw Kreski lying there in the dirt. She saw the mutilated and dying men on the hospital ships. They were boys for the most part, although some were men, and they were the worst, because they died screaming, like boys. They died knowing that they were no match for the unrelenting evil in the world. There was no escaping it. She remembered their screams for their mothers. But it was not really their mothers that they were calling for, it was only a concept, a concept of something that could protect them from the merciless, pursuing evil.

Kirishima walked out of the forest. She looked boldly at the horrid countenance of evil now. From somewhere, far back in her subconscious, a word crept forward, not a word, but a concept.

She shrieked, "Hawk!"

Kirishima threw his rifle down. He pulled out his knife and grunted angrily. He walked over and put a hand on her head. He took a handful of the silky blonde hair and knelt beside her. His odor was like that of a gangrenous limb. But she had smelled gangrenous limbs before. The horror would get much worse than that. Ivania refused to faint. But she could not bring herself to scratch him, she could not bear to touch him. He tore at her blouse.

"*He-aww*, Jap!" It was a deep, guttural sound, the kind that rough men used to herd large animals.

Kirishima wheeled around. The cry had made him urinate on himself. He saw a filthy, slouched Marine with tattered and rotting clothing hanging off his slender frame, pointing a submachine gun at him. He knew the power of such guns well, and he urinated again.

Hawk took a step forward. His shoulders were cocked and menacing. "Looks like you done dropped your rifle, podnuh," he snarled in his Delta accent. The words meant nothing to Kirishima, but the voice was heavy and frightening. In his imagination, it made the air shake between them. The infernal scarecrow kept coming. The scout stood in a crouch, stretching his knife arm toward Ivania's forehead. The other hand reached and stretched for his rifle.

"Too far?" Hawk asked sympathetically. He took another forward step, lifting his knee high over some intervening debris. He was a mass of shadows: the helmet, the whiskers, the flapping and torn utilities. His face was underfed, and his eyes were horrible. But the Thompson stood out clearly and real in the haze of the demonic vision, it was like a detailed photograph in the middle of a misty impressionist painting. Kirishima grunted, and shook the knife viciously at the woman's head. The two men's eyes locked onto one another, the rest of the world swimming in a blur around them. Kirishima suddenly shuffled his feet in a feinting maneuver. Hawk stood still, watching the performance. The man who could outmaneuver a Thompson submachine gun had not been born. Kirishima, too, stood still at last. He was able to move ever so slightly closer to Ivania with the knife point, thereby abandoning the rifle, forever. Still, the two men did not take their eyes off one another.

At last, Hawk decided that he could make the shot. A .45 doesn't leave a man with much after it hits. Hawk was concerned that the Japanese would stab her without warning. The Marine was convinced that the bullets could travel the few feet to Kirishima, before the knifepoint could cover the few inches to Ivania.

Without prelude, he snapped the trigger back. The bullets hit in a diamond pattern in Kirishima's chest and abdomen, none of them striking more than two inches from one another. It was the work of a steady hand. Both of the scout's feet left the ground, he spun and fell on his face with his arms tangled under him. A shrill hissing noise exploded from his throat, as the evil soul left his body. The knife was lost in the smoke and dust.

Hawk took several more casual steps, and touched the trigger again. The corpse shuddered under the impact. The dead inner organs groaned as life, tension, and air fled them. Hawk stood over the quaggy mass of ripped flesh. The skirted helmet of the scout had been knocked off, lying upturned with his ration of rice in it. Gnarled growths covered his shaved head.

"Looks like a alligator," Hawk commented.

Ivania's eyes were opened as wide as they had ever been in her life. She could not close her mouth. Her voice was high, strained, and strange. "Is he dead?" She had prayed for it. She stared at the limp and baggy uniform of Kirishima, the dirt of it streaked with the cleanliness of bright red blood.

"Sure enough dead." Hawk spat down onto the knobbed head. "Come on, let's go," he said, without looking at her. She put her forehead into her hand. She was trembling all over. "But could I... Could we rest for just a moment?" She shook her head. "That was..." She trailed off and shook her head again. "Just a moment, maybe?"

Hawk looked suspiciously at the jungle around them. The shots had announced his presence and his location. "Where is Kreski?"

"He...they shot him. *He* shot him. I think he's dead. He's back there." She pointed an unsure finger. Hawk turned toward her.

"Come on," he said. This time she stood. He did not offer her his hand.

A minute later, Hawk was standing over Sergeant Kreski. Kreski stared at the sky with sightless eyes. A stanchless flow of blood widened the red pool under him.

"Kreski?" Hawk searched for a pulse. "You're gonna

be okay, kid." Hawk knew that there was nothing he could do. "Kreski?"

Ivania leaned over only from the hips, as if afraid to get too close. Apparently, none of her medical training was kicking in. "Fred?"

Kreski's lips trembled. "Immigrants," he whispered.

"*Immagrunts*?" Hawk asked. The eyes continued to look into the mystery of the sky above, but Kreski was gone. Hawk stood. "Good kid," he nodded. "Damn sure was." He sighed. *Was everybody in the world going to have to die before this was over?* Ivania turned away from them. The medical profession had hardened her, but not entirely. This was something else.

Hawk decided that he did not have time to dig a hole with his fingers. He dragged two heavy rocks to the edge of the swamp, edged the body into the cold, green water, and pinned it under the stones. He picked up his Thompson and slung it over his shoulder.

"Should we...say something?" she asked. His startling blue eyes looked back toward hers through several fathoms of ruthlessness. He shook his head.

"Ain't nobody nowhere wanting no prayers from the likes of me, missy." He shuffled through Kreski's tags and a couple of bloody letters, jamming them roughly into various pockets.

He looked back down at Ivania, who had been watching him intently. "I'll get the Jap's rifle and papers," he said. "You can rest a minute. But then we gotta move on. We will have to go."

She looked up at his face. She saw nothing warm or kind.

12

LOVE'S LABOUR'S LOST

DREISEN LOOKED WITH DISMAY AT THE SKY ABOVE HIM. A twin engine Dinah, and a Saiun carrier reconnaissance plane circled the edge of the flatlands behind the lighthouse. There was no one to take a pot shot at the aircraft. Zanji was not only going to get away, the colonel was going to have to watch it happen. It would have been easier for Dreisen if the ace had disappeared into the forested mountains, and then the colonel had heard the report later, about the pilot having been evacuated by submarine. Watching this unfold was the ultimate failure. The Japanese were going to do just what they had threatened to do all along, the one thing that Dreisen could have prevented. They would fly him out. Mercifully, Dreisen did not even consider his biggest problem. He could well end up a prisoner of war. Hai-lon stood beside the colonel, shading his eyes with outstretched fingers, and watching the metal birds.

"Well, slick, looks like your side won," Dreisen told him. "This one, anyway."

Hai-lon shook his head. "My side? Warriors have

sides, I am a man of peace. Men who refuse centuries of wisdom have sides." Hai-lon stood on his toes. "This looks strange. The Japanese were to land a fighter plane, that Zanji would be able to use his unmatched skills in evading your planes, and escaping Cokoni. These poor craft are not fighter planes. We will not get to see him fly."

Dreisen looked over at the monk. "You know a lot about planes for a peaceful man, with centuries of wisdom."

Hai-lon nodded. "Yes. I like aircraft. I would like someday to ride in one. Since boyhood, I have envied the bird." He smiled as he watched the planes. "A vanity, perhaps?"

* * *

HAWK SLIPPED Kirishima's bloody wallet into his pocket and ripped the scout's insignia off his uniform. He walked back to the edge of the swamp where Ivania remained sitting. He knelt over the shiny water and splashed it into his face. As the ripples disappeared, he saw the apparition below him. *Crap!* he thought. The bones of his face stood out, even under the whiskers. He glanced at Ivania. She was watching him. Embarrassed, he splashed another handful of water on his face.

"Are you injured?"

"Nah. Looks like it, don't it? Quite a sight."

"Don't worry. I remember what you looked like. You should have been in the movies." Hawk stood and walked back to the shade of a tree to sit down. Maybe he did need just a minute's respite, put to good use, of course. He emptied his pockets of partially used clips and began forcing the spring-loaded bullets out of them. He thrust the rounds into another magazine, in order to fill it. He had never carried the bulky Thompson bandolier, and his pockets were heavy with the used clips. "So, did you decide to rest on my account?"

"I guess," he answered distractedly. "Probably not. I gotta get these clips straightened out. Cain't get caught short in a shoot-out, you know. You gotta watch your ass out here."

"I don't want to slow down your war."

"Not my war. Just passing through. Gotta start thinking about demobilization. Had enough of this."

"Yes. I believe that. Another harmless draftee, longing for mom, apple pie and a Yankee's game."

"Come on," he said, standing. "Sounds like you're back to walking speed. You're pretty damn snappy again. If I can find a shortcut across the swamp, I can catch that flier at the lighthouse. Dreisen is waiting on something to happen. It would be nice if I could sit around like everybody else and wait for shit to happen, but I can't."

Ivania stood. She tried her old smirk, but her facial muscles could not manage it. "Yes, now that sounds more like the James Hawk that I know." She pushed her yellow hair out of her eyes.

They started walking. Her legs felt heavy and shaky. The events of the last couple of hours played murkily through her head. She remembered the amazing moment when she called out for James Hawk. And— there he was! Do such things happen? She wondered if he had heard her. She had never experienced such terror in her life. She realized that the man walking beside her was security. Rough, crude, and brutal, he was equal to any force that he encountered. He was not sporting, he was not fair, he was not nice, he was only there to get the job done, and he was equal to any job he encountered. As she watched him put the helmet over the wild hair, and sling his Thompson, she knew that today she would be safe. Hawk stopped and looked out into the swamp.

Tears ran down her face, but he did not see them. She wiped her eyes, over and over. God, it had been awful. God, he had been wonderful. Everything she knew about him or felt about him, now came together in the memory of that moment when he stepped into the clearing and called out to Kirishima. A primitive urge stirred her. She realized what Belva Cook had gone through. Only the lowest classes, or the youngest of women loved a man for sheer physical prowess. Even Belva had admired him for his looks, whereas Ivania was not even considering that. It was not love, she knew, for she was neither immature nor impractical. But she felt something. With death all around her, she was overwhelmed with a new emotion for the man beside her. He was incredible security, an incredible...man. Where had he even come from? Do such things happen?

He, obviously, did not share any of these emotions. The insults and abuse that she had heaped upon him, had taken care of any fondness he once had for her. She knew she had to forget him. They were not meant for one another, and it was her fault. Perhaps voicing a simple and honest thank you to him, would help to calm her nerves, and set something right between them. She was easily able to fight the emotions, and cover up the feelings. A part of her was repulsed, not by him this time, but by herself.

She could not keep her glance away from the careless shoulders, the mocking grim face, and the flashing eyes. She knew that he saw her looking at him. She wanted to fall into his arms, and tell him that she had been wrong, that she had never known anyone like him, and had not known how to judge such a person. She was afraid he would laugh in her face. She had enough of her old feelings to know that he was a mean son of a bitch. These old feelings also told her that if she were to show the slightest interest in him, the result would have been like falling into the gorilla pen at the zoo, for he was nothing but a lower animal. But now she had found that there were worse things than James Hawk, and that pen at the zoo. Maybe a lot more.

"Hell," Hawk growled. All of this bubbling emotion was lost on him. He had a limited range of emotion. The sergeant was calculating his route. He had to innovate. He had to speed this up. He looked with dejection at the swamp. Going around it would take *forever*. "We might as well get our feet wet." He stepped into the alien bog. "You can stay here a minute. I've got to see how this goes."

She watched him wade through the water. If Joe or Kreski had gone out there, she would have been worried, terrified, for their safety. She knew that Hawk would come back. Nothing would happen to him. Before, that would have infuriated her. Now, she liked having that knowledge, and that feeling.

Hawk waded farther into the two-colored swamp. The dark green of the plants and the glowing green of the shimmering water had a hypnotic effect on him.

The water was icy. It licked at his knees and then at his waist. The bottom of the swamp rolled about like a loose marl underfoot. The scenery dazzled, and calmed him. He saw no reason to distrust this mystical place. It was pure and clean, and he could save a lot of time by wading through it. The stumps that lay beneath the surface were scattered within a few feet of each other, like some ancient benevolent force had left stepping-stones for him.

He waded back to her. "This ain't too bad, at all. No snakes, not even a turtle." He was definitely not in Mississippi anymore. He waved her to him. Ivania entered the water. She shivered as the coldness collided with her warm body. "Oh, my!"

"Yeah, a little nippy."

Hawk kept to what he thought was a due westerly direction. The sun was high, and he may have misjudged it a little. The water remained shallow and cold. They wound deeper into the marsh, around scattered islets covered with vegetation. It was quiet, except for the singing of the gentle water, moving, and yet going nowhere. They did not speak. She felt uncomfortable as they left the sight of the solid ground, and were swallowed by the watery sanctuary. By nothingness. But Hawk waded on, without hesitating, as if he lived here in this boundless space, and she grew unafraid.

Ahead of them, they could see a bright patch of white among the spongy leaves. It glided serenely on the phosphorescent green water. As they drew closer, it became identifiable as a flock of waterfowl. The long-legged birds watched disinterestedly as the intruders approached. They turned their little round heads and aimed quizzical pink eyes at Hawk. They had never seen a human interloper amidst this beauty. The sergeant pictured one of them roasting over a spit. The two of them walked up to the creatures without startling them. Ivania stretched out her hand and petted the downy feathers on the back of one of them. It was almost as tall as her. The fowl stepped rather indignantly away. He did not appear frightened, however, only annoyed, or perhaps inconvenienced. He raised his wings and spread them out at her as he retreated, like Dracula opening his cape. Ivania looked back at Hawk and laughed weakly. For the first time in a long while, he noticed how beautiful she was. He knew that had no relevance to him, and that was just fine.

"Grab that son of a bitch," he said. "We can eat his crazy ass," Hawk urged.

She looked shocked. "No, we can*not*. Look how sweet they are."

"That's some horseshit." Hawk waded past her, and toward the flock. The beady little eyes of the birds doubled in size as he neared them. They were not quite as sure of him as they had been of Ivania. He was moving a little too fast. They stepped high and thrust their crooked necks rhythmically in and out as they moved away from him.

"Hold up. Look, here," Ivania said to his back. He turned. She pointed into the clear emerald water. "Fish by the thousands. You can catch one of those with your hands, and leave the birds alone. My God, how disgusting can you get? Eating a stork! They probably have parasites in them."

Hawk slung his Thompson. He did not want to offend any tender sensibilities, or violate any rules of medical science, but he had to have something to eat.

For a man who had been eating weeds for the last few days, the birds looked pretty good. She waded in among the fish and reached down quickly. With evidently the best of beginner's luck, she scooped up a large gray fish out of the water. It flipped wildly in the air, and she trapped it against her breast. She pinched its tail with her fingers and held it securely. It threw itself about, trying to escape.

"There's your fish," she said. "Easy as pie."

Hawk stared at it for a moment, hoping that she would drop it. It looked too much like an alligator gar to him. Too tricky to fix, and not very tasty. But, there it was. "Well, all right. Let's cook the bastard, I guess."

One of the bolder birds stepped toward Ivania with an interested expression. He turned his head on one side and eyed the fish. The bird opened his long orange beak and picked at her elbow. She almost dropped their dinner.

"Ow! Get your own! They're everywhere, you ignorant bird!"

"That long legged son of a bitch," Hawk kicked the bird in his feathery hindquarters. The creature squawked with displeasure and with a slapping explosion of wings, the entire flock burst skyward. Hawk and Ivania were saturated by the water that the innumerable wings threw on them.

"I didn't know they would do that. He was stealing our dinner."

Her hair hung heavy and straight down, though still yellow. She couldn't open her eyes. "God, that was stupid!"

Hawk had to agree. A huge flock of birds would be a prime signal to anyone tracking them. But then, who would track them here, and how? He decided that the place was remote enough, even after all this, to start a fire.

They waded a little farther, until they found an island less marshy and overgrown. A clear grassy area bordered the water. Behind the grass grew the green trunked trees, festooned with green moss. Hawk gathered a few sticks. He ran his hand along one of them, and the encasing rubbery green fungus that gave the swamp its color, floated to the ground. He propped the sticks together and took out a match with a wax covered head. In a short while, he had the fish filleted and over the fire.

Ivania tried to catch another one, but failed. She took the rifle with the bayonet of Kirishima and tried to spear one, with even less success. She became queasy about handling the rifle, as she remembered its owner. She came and sat by the fire.

"Is it ready? When do we eat?" she asked.

"You eat when you catch a fish."

"What? I caught that one."

"That was for me, so I wouldn't cook a bird."

"What the hell? I couldn't catch another one. I tried."

He picked up the rifle with the bayonet on it. He tried to stab a fish as well. They were slippery bastards. He noticed his hands rubbing up and down the wooden stock and remembered Kirishima's skin condition. "Shit, I don't want any of that shit rubbing off on me." He grabbed his helmet and quickly scooped up a fish. As they cooked the second fish, the birds returned, one by one, with graceful landings in the fertile waters. They pranced about, stretching their necks and pointing curious eyes at the fire. The color must have intrigued them. Odd colors usually meant a tasty morsel. They refused to come close to the people this time.

Hawk took off his wet shirt. He leaned back on his elbows and checked the height of the sun. Afternoon was deepening and he was no closer to the pilot. He was not worried. He was certain that he could cut the Japanese off, with time to spare.

Ivania poked at the fire. She lay on her side across from him. "Your arms are big for your body," she said. "Did you ever notice that?"

"No. I imagine everything is too big for it, since it ain't had nothing to eat."

"Why did you do that?" she asked.

"What?" He followed her eyes. "The tattoo? That's my serial number. If I get my head blowed off, might lose my dog tags. They'll still know who I was. A lot of these kids got families and stuff, and I don't want them to stick my carcass in somebody else's body bag. That stuff is important to some people."

"But not to you."

He squinted at her. She was kind of irritating. On purpose. All of the time. "I got the tattoo, didn't I?"

"Sort of low class."

"You're big on that class shit. It serves its purpose."

"Everything serves a purpose, right?"

"No, not everything." For some reason he thought of Joe Canlon's hand grenades. Tits on a boar, he had said. He smiled. Misinterpreting this, she hesitated, and smiled back at him.

"Well, I reckon that's enough resting for the day. You ready to get back in the saddle?"

"If we have to. Where am I going? Back to the lighthouse?"

"Well. Where else do you have to go? You know what I have to do. Lot going on here."

"Yes."

They stood. He gathered the rifle, the helmet and the Thompson awkwardly in one hand, by the straps.

"Did you find them last night? The Japanese?" she asked.

"Yeah."

"Did you see any prisoners, or the pilot?"

"No. Not that I know of. It was damn dark. I got some of them, bunch of them. But the pilot probably got away. Can't be sure for a while, I guess. Gotta fix all that."

"One man against their whole camp? How could you possibly do it?" She walked closer. He looked down into her eyes.

"Kill 'em? Stabbed 'em. Shot 'em." He said it rapidly; like a litany of his life.

She looked down and shook her head. Before he realized it, she stepped against him and put her arms around him. Her face rested beneath his neck.

"It's so dangerous. Everything you do. You're...unnatural."

"Nah. Not when you're careful." His eyebrows drew together. *What the hell was this?* "I kind of know what I can get away with." She tilted her head back and looked up at him. He did not know what to think, so he kept talking. He thought that maybe she had *completely* lost her mind. This time. He did *not* want to deal with that. "It's just what I do...a lot of. You know, practice."

He did not hold her. All of the gear that he was

trying to hold in his one hand bumped against her. "Well," he said, and backed away, pulling the weapons and helmet from around her. "I'll secure this stuff." Secure was a Marine word, used when you didn't know what else to say.

"You don't like me much, do you?" she asked.

"Not like a whole lot. Why?"

She laughed, and laughed again. "An honest man. Very rare."

"Listen, lady, you and me know where we stand."

"Things change, you know. That's what life is, change."

"Oh, yeah?" he said. "You and me don't change. How did anything change? You change partners pretty easy, that's the only change I noticed."

"Slow down, mister. Don't get ugly. I'm a woman in a world with five million men. If I want to have a conversation once in a while with someone, I will."

"Sister, you can be the Queen of the May Pole for all I care, and have conversations all day long."

She recovered her temper. "I'll tell you how it changed." Her face was beet red now. He was such a bastard. And not likely to let you forget it. "To start with, by saving my life. By giving up your precious airplane pilot and your precious colonel, and coming after me. And if you hadn't, I would be dead. Here in nowhere. And no one else on earth would have done such a thing. No one else *could* have done such a thing. Shall I go on?"

"Oh, yeah. That. Well, I came after the kid, too. You're right. Yeah, I could, so I did. You know...so."

"If it had been just him, would you have come?" She asked.

"Probably not. I would have figured he could take

care of himself. Nobody told him to go running off like a striped-ass ape. Sorry about what happened to him, though. He was a good kid. Punched me in the face once. He had nerve. Too much probably."

"Therefore, I repeat, you came after *me*. Not him."

"You're a woman. You don't act like one, but you are. That was just something that had to be done. If I only helped people that liked me, I wouldn't have a whole lot of shit to do. I didn't give up nothing. I'm going back there and do just what I goddam said I would do."

She stepped forward. His hands were free this time. She moved quickly to him, touched her lips to his, and embraced him. His arms, having no place to go, encircled her small body. She pushed hard against him and moaned. He was not kissing her back. She pulled her face away and rested her head against his chest. Then suddenly she pushed him away. She brushed the golden hair out of her eyes, turning away.

She spun around. "Not everything has a purpose, right? Always in control, right?" The tone of her breathy voice was angry. She looked defiantly at him, but still felt that old fear, the fear that everyone had of him.

"No. Not always." He stepped toward her this time, and taking her into his arms, bent her head back with a fiery kiss. Her fingers dug into his back. He was powerful, and it was like she had latched onto a portion of the war itself, the reason for wars, and there was no letting go. "I can't stand it," she said. An irresistible fury engulfed her, as he pulled her to the grass. By sheer persistence, she had fallen into the pen.

* * *

TANIGUCHI PULLED IMPATIENTLY at the rifle strap digging into his shoulder. The numbed flesh enjoyed the moment of relief. The swivel grommet of the strap broke and the rifle, held by only one side, teetered to the ground. Taniguchi bent over wearily and picked it up. There was no pointless cursing, as might have occurred if this had happened to his American counterpart, Sergeant Hawk. The grommet had rusted through. A serious look was on the *hancho's* face, as he tied the strap below the Solothurn's U-shaped sight protectors. He was tired. He had done all that he could. He was a mature man, who knew that men had limits. Men do sometimes give up. He had neither the youth nor the madness of Sergeant Hawk. The Americans would get Zanji, in spite of his own superior skills. His command had played it too close to the wire, and for no reason that he could tell. By now, the Americans had noticed that he was only revolving expectantly around the lighthouse.

The *hancho* stared at the white shaft on the plains, surrounded by Cokonians. He smiled sadly. So, what if they get Zanji? Was Taniguchi's being a successful soldier and being himself the same thing?

Out of this unwelcome daydream simmered the sound of aircraft. Taniguchi watched the specks until he identified them as Japanese. They flew in from behind him. A flying boat circled back there. In the distance, he could see parachutes. Taniguchi's lips parted with a dry click. Zanji stepped beside him.

"So!" the ace growled triumphantly. "We get support. Soon, *my* plane will land." Then he stepped away from the *hancho* and looked at the lighthouse. "You have done well, Sergeant Taniguchi. You are without question a great soldier. Men such as you seldom receive praise or thanksgiving, but I give you mine." Zanji watched the sky, the sky that meant freedom and invincibility for him once more. He knew that he was the greatest man to ever fly an airplane in modern warfare.

Taniguchi looked quietly at the white clouds in the blueness over the lighthouse. He was not quite sure how to take all of this.

* * *

IVANIA SAT in the softening light of the afternoon, the light that made her face the most beautiful, as she had often been told. She now saw other colors in the swamp. In the bright light, the marsh looked like a picture colored by a child with only two crayons. Under this kinder afternoon illumination, one could see the colors made by the shadows in the arrangement of the leaves; the dark secret shadows near the tops of the trees, and the lesser ones below. She saw yellow lights flickering on the tips of the little waves on the water's surface. She felt calm and happy.

Hawk sat with her. He only saw the sun going down. This damned day was gone. He ran his fingers through his sandy hair.

"You might as well sleep," he said. "We'll have to move all night to get anything done."

She nodded dreamily and lay down on the grass. She sighed, looking up through the treetops. Hawk clenched his teeth as he sensed the minutes ticking by. His breath was short, his fists closed.

"It's nice to have someone to stand by you," she said.

"To know that you are not alone in the world." It seemed like a perfectly logical thing to say to her.

Hawk said nothing. Was she talking about him? He could recall a day or so ago, when by all accounts, he was not of a great deal of value.

"Do you believe in God?" she said to his tensed back.

"Uh...yeah," he nodded. *She is really off the wall*, he thought.

"A lot of people don't, you know? But *you*, of all people, in all of this, do believe in God? Isn't that something?"

"A lot of people believe a lot of crazy shit. Ain't nothing to me." The relic of Hai-tai occurred to him.

"They say there is no evidence of God. I don't know about that, but there is a lot of evidence of the devil," she said.

"No, shit," he laughed abruptly.

"If not for God, we would be consumed by all this evil. Something has to keep it away from us. You must be very fortunate to have a life where you don't ever see that; where the evil is so far from you, you don't need anything to keep it away. You see, that's where I was raised. You could pay for evil to go away. But that's not here. Here, you can see it, feel it, taste it. It doesn't care who or what you are. It's not going away. Evil is a blackness all around you and closing in. We're...we're barely here at all, it's crowding in on us so. We couldn't stop that by ourselves. Don't you think?"

"Probably not." He was so tired, he blacked out instantly in sleep, while still sitting there, bent over, every muscle tensed, and speaking. He had no intention of doing so, and never would have willed it. It just could not be stopped. Blackness had suddenly closed around him.

When the sergeant awoke, a quarter moon was high overhead. The swamp was quiet. He heard no frogs or insects, there was only a haunting silence. Far in the distance, deep within the scattered islands, he occasionally heard a loud splash. He suspected it to be a variety of local crocodile. He had not heard them bellowing, and the splashing noise bothered him. He had heard alligators before in his lifetime, and he had heard crocodiles, but here there were neither. The splash sounded like a large boulder being tossed into the water. Hawk supposed that might be exactly what it was, considering the rocky terrain. He watched the moon's corona glide across the feathery skein of treetops for a while. The water was cool, and it made the entire swamp cool. He could tell that as the night progressed, the marsh would grow cold. The water probably came from some high-altitude source. He awakened Ivania. After a few minutes, they were on the march. The shimmering liquid, white in the moonlight, was ice water now, and Ivania trembled.

Even in the places where it was motionless, the water glowed under the vivid tropic starlight. Their legs moved through it with swallowing noises. All otherwise remained quiet, giving their human presence an exaggerated feeling of importance that it did not have elsewhere on the earth. In the black distance, echoing like a crash in the remote room of a rambling mansion, came the heavy splashing. Probably rotten tree limbs falling in the water, Hawk finally decided. He did not think about it for long. Ivania had noticed the sounds, and they also concerned her. Neither of them mentioned the splashes. The swamp seemed supernatural, and her mind conjured up supernatural causes for the ghostly sounds. Hawk had no such imagination.

Hawk bit off a chunk of wet and dried, and then wet again, chewing tobacco. It was swollen and flavorless, even more so than government issue generally was. He was satisfied. They were making good time, moving across a shorter space of territory than their quarry. By daylight, or maybe before, he would catch them. He smiled a little and spat.

"That's disgusting," Ivania whispered. He laughed, and then she laughed, and they both felt a little better in the dark cold. She tried to remember if she had ever seen him laugh. He seemed to have developed an extra set of dimples. She put her arms around his waist. She perceived, however, a distance between them. He was not closing it.

They rested once, and took up the trip again. Time passed quickly and the sleepy sun finally poured a diluted solution of gray into the night sky. Dawn edged slowly through the swamp. Hawk had an odd feeling about it. *This will be an unusual day*, he thought. Maybe it was only the strange light in the even stranger swamp.

Before long, they stood upon a lengthy peninsula that jutted into the swamp, and led out onto the plains. They had completely crossed the neck of marsh on the swamp of Jarok's northern extremity. Perhaps no one had ever dared such a thing before. The plains stretched before them. In the gray light, however, what they saw tempered any feeling of jubilation. Far out on the flatlands, stocky men moved about three orange fires. Hawk could see bare calves under their pants, where they had not yet wrapped their puttees.

"Shit," he whispered. "My old buddies." Ivania stepped beside him. "Jap platoon," he muttered. "They're sizing up the lighthouse. The plane can't be too far off now."

"They will capture it, so they can land the plane there, won't they?" She asked. Her hand was on his shoulder.

"Yeah." Hawk pushed back his helmet. "I wonder if them natives will fight them. I have to figure that they won't." He spat angrily. "They'll get all religious and peace-loving all of a sudden, and back down. Hot lead will do that. They gave us a bunch of shit, of course." He knew that was the difference between American tolerance, and Japanese intolerance, but it was still infuriating. Hawk studied the enemy encampment. Forty of them at the most. That would be enough, though. His stubborn brain revolved in the search for a solution. How could he ruin a few lives and defeat the whole purpose of those men? He didn't reserve his own life from these plans for ruination. Still, it was discouraging. Last night there had been a possibility of killing all of them, when only a handful were left. That was over.

He heard something heavy dragging behind him. His subconscious dismissed it. The more engrossing problem lay in front. A muffled cry from Ivania forced him to spin around. "A dinosaur!" she cried.

Hawk looked at her perplexed expression and followed her line of sight. He saw a giant brown lizard, about eleven or twelve feet long, crawling toward them from out of the half-lit swamp.

"Son of a..." he exclaimed. The dry scales reflected the gray murkiness. Hawk unslung his Thompson. The great beast alternated swishing his head and tail in slow but large steps. Hawk's finger tightened on the trigger. But he dared not fire. The platoon out on the plains, leisurely carrying out their morning duties, must remain unaware of this hidden little drama.

"Give me that rifle," he snapped. She pulled the strap off her shoulder, and he took the Arisaka.

He thrust the rifle at the creature with a circular motion. What the hell was the son of bitch doing? "Git on! Git! Devil!" He spoke in a low but urgent voice at the approaching animal, in an effort to frighten it away. He couldn't afford to be loud. He motioned for Ivania to get back. The startled monitor, native to Cokoni, saw the human beings for the first time. It breathed a nasty hiss, sounding like an air brake. The disturbed lizard reared onto its hind legs standing over them and swishing its massive tail. It opened its reptilian maw, showing a row of teeth with which it could rip wild boars to shreds. Its feet were studded with long, sharp talons. Hawk could smell the odd, damply sour reptilian breath.

"Goddam bastard," Hawk cursed softly, glancing at the Japanese behind him. *If this kind of shit don't attract their attention, nothing will*, he thought. P. T. Barnum couldn't have put on a better show. He flipped the hinged bayonet out on the rifle. "Git...*out of here!* You *bastard!*" He thrust the weapon at the lizard and added a few blasphemous obscenities. The lashing tail swung around in the dim light, nearly tagging the man. Hawk jumped back quickly. The power of the leathery tail was comparable to that of an island crocodile's.

The tail came after him again on the backswing. Hawk leapt over the tip. When he did, the lizard jumped at him. They collided. The blunt and heavy head rested suddenly on Hawk's shoulder with back-

bone compressing force. The teeth crashed shut metalli-
cally in the man's ear. He found himself staring into the
oily ball of an eye that had all of the predatory meanness of an eagle, and none of the majesty.

Hawk kept his balance, pushed back, stayed on his
feet, and continued his efforts to back away. He dodged
an uncoordinated and wildly thrown swipe of the
deadly claws. The lizard swished determinedly after
him. The monitor was obviously not willing to let
bygones be bygones. Hawk reared back with the bayonet, drove his elbow forward and lunged, sinking the
knife into the tough hide between the neck and shoulder. The skin was strong, but beneath it, the lizard was
soft. The steel entered easily. The animal jerked in the
direction against Hawk's grip, pulling the rifle from his
hands. The bayonet hung in the neck for a moment,
until the lizard shook it loose. The creature hissed
horribly and backed away in an angry frenzy, slithering
into the water. It did not want to feel the wrath of this
single-toothed creature again.

They could see the brainless little head pivoting left
and right with the precision of a machine, as the lizard
negotiated his retreat through the shallow water. Hawk
breathed heavily, unable to understand how he had
avoided being either bitten, stabbed, or clubbed to
death.

"Are you okay?" Ivania gasped.

"Yeah." Hawk looked back at the Japanese. They
were still peacefully tending their breakfast fires. The
entire caveman-versus-carnivore affair had been less
noisy from their perspective, than it had been from
Hawk's.

"What in the hell was that?" she asked.

"Lizard."

"Lizard, hell."

"Yeah...no shit," Hawk said, catching his breath. "I mean, what the shit? The thing surprised the hell out of me." He suddenly laughed at the absurdity of it. "I mean, you're standing there, and out of nowhere, a goddam...thing...is all over you."

Ivania looked up at him. She saw only puzzled amusement in his face. She found herself smiling at him. Hawk laughed again, and tears rolled down his face. He kind of wished Joe Canlon had seen that. He was not easily entertained, but evidently, this had done the trick. She could not help but laugh now.

"What do we do now?" she finally asked. She did not find the lizard incident quite as amusing as he did.

"Aw shit, get around these Japs here and get back to the lighthouse. That'll take for goddam ever, naturally. I'll have to get my men back, one way or the other. We should be getting help ourselves here, pretty soon. Two companies. So they say. Been hearing that line of shit all my life. Believe it when I see it. If we can stir up a little shit and stall these son of a bitches, we might get ahold of that flier after all."

The monitor hissed loudly from the recesses of the swamp, like a departing locomotive. They heard a heavy splash.

"I didn't want to hurt the old fossil," Hawk said. "I imagine they're usually pretty harmless. But, shit. I bet them things can lay you up."

13

THE LIGHTHOUSE LOST

THE CAPTAIN IN CHARGE OF THE PARATROOPERS congratulated Taniguchi on his successful evasion of the enemy. They drank tea in the front of the morning cook fire.

"It is well for you," the captain told Zanji, "that Taniguchi does not hunt the skies." The three men laughed. "Then there would be a fierce competition in destroying the American airplanes."

"Yes. He has done well," Zanji admitted. Secretly, he did not like even jokes about competition with his greatness. "I would enjoy that kind of competition." The ace looked gratefully at Taniguchi. In keeping with his celebrity, Zanji had well-polished social skills, and no troubling sincerity.

Taniguchi looked away. His polite smile faded. "This has not yet ended," the cautious *hancho* told them.

"Always the optimist," the captain laughed again. "Is that the secret of your cunning?"

Zanji nodded knowingly. "Sergeant Taniguchi takes everything seriously," he said. "Much too seriously."

The captain looked across the plains toward the lighthouse. "We must frighten off these islanders. Otherwise, they might interrupt the escape operation. They have had sufficient time for their little religious pilgrimage, or whatever they are doing. We should disperse them with as little bloodshed as possible. They are simple, innocent people, who are subjects of the Emperor, as are we. Among these mobs, however, one must always watch for troublemakers."

Zanji said nothing. Taniguchi nodded his approval. The *hancho* was satisfied with the new officer in charge. He seemed a sensible man. Zanji was preoccupied. He looked at the sky.

* * *

DREISEN, Breaux, and Joe Canlon stood near the lighthouse door. Dreisen had seen the parachutes. He knew that something had to be done. A lone Islander guarded their weapons, stacked against the inside wall near the door. The colonel was confident that he could run the Cokonians off, if he could get to those weapons. The islanders had shunned the firearms for the most part, and were probably, to some extent, afraid of them. Dreisen had seen Hawk defy the Cokonians by himself, and took hope from this. He did not have Hawk's perspective on the incident, however. It had been a touchy situation from start to finish, to say the least.

Joe Canlon fidgeted nervously. He did not like Dreisen's plan for rushing the guard. He had been content to sit here, safe and sound. The sight of the enemy paratroopers had swayed him to go along with the scheme. Joe had no desire to end up in a Japanese

POW camp. He knew that reaching one alive was only the first and the least of a prisoner's problems. He needed his M1 and shotgun to have a fighting chance. He had seen one of the Cokonians carrying an American rifle, and he feared the weapons might soon end up scattered, and used as walking sticks and clubs.

Joe was secondarily motivated by the ridicule Hawk had heaped upon him. The recovery should go a long way in redeeming him for surrendering his weapons in the first place.

Dreisen put his hands in his pockets and sauntered in front of the open door, as he had done countless times before. Canlon and Breaux stood on either side of it, out of the guard's range of sight. The colonel stopped, looked at the sky, took a deep breath and dashed inside. The other two followed. Dreisen caught the guard by the neck and pushed him over a leg, neatly tripping him. The Cokonian, however, reacted with superhuman swiftness, ripping his knife from its sheath as he fell. Joe caught the knife arm and stood on the man's hand. The guard cried out and there were answering cries from outside. By then, Breaux had latched onto his BAR and went to one knee in the doorway. The approaching crowd was met with its muzzle. Dreisen stood behind Breaux, on the stairway, holding an M3 burp gun. They knew that Hai-lon was alone above them, in the lamp room. He couldn't do much. The rest of the building was unoccupied. Joe covered the prone guard with his shotgun. Part of the planning for this overthrow included the mutual assurance that they would shoot to kill, if the citizens attacked any one of them.

"Get inside!" Breaux shouted to the other Americans. They filed past him, being careful not to interfere with his line of fire. They seized their weapons. The islanders pressed toward the door, glaring angrily at the BAR muzzle. Breaux returned the glare, unsympathetically. From inside, Joe could see the milling and muttering Cokonians over the top of American helmets. He was glad that being an instigator of the recovery provided him with the privilege of being inside.

An explosion shook the ground. The Marines flinched. The islanders screamed in terror. Dreisen stepped down beside Breaux to see what was happening. A small gray column of smoke and dust faded into the wind out on the plains.

"Mortar. 81 mm," Dreisen said.

Breaux looked up. "That's a Jap rifle grenade, sir," Breaux said. They watched for the reaction of the Cokonians. Some began a fast trot toward the mountains. They knew that when the Japanese fired weapons, it was better to be somewhere else, regardless of any shared ancestry or motive. "They've got to be on the edge of the woods. We are way out of their range for a grenade," said Breaux.

"Not if it's a mortar," said Dreisen.

"No, sir. But it's a rifle grenade, sir."

Joe wondered if the old lighthouse had any historical or sentimental value for the Japanese. He hoped so, but he seriously doubted it. *It should have*, he thought. The disrespectful bastards.

The Japanese captain's face was hidden behind his large binoculars. "Very good," he said. "Let us try another. Careful not to hit too close to the fools." The Cokonians were evacuating as fast as a crowd of that size could, but the captain was of the opinion that some continued to drag their feet. Another of the sheet-steel grenades was carried up to the muzzle of the anti-tank rifle.

The gunner re-tightened the washer that held the adapter onto the gun, and a second man held the grenade against the muzzle. It was a large, bowl-shaped projectile, that he held with two hands. The gunner tightened a bolt that fastened the explosive bowl onto the adapter. Everyone stood aside. The gunner aimed for a few tense seconds, and fired. The loud report was followed by the whoosh of the propellant, and the bomb exploded far out onto the plain. They could see the shrapnel streak both up and outwards. The explosion was large and impressive.

"You telling me that's a rifle grenade?" Dreisen said.

"Yes sir, a big one." Breaux was unwavering. "I guess it doesn't matter what it is, sir. Where it is, is what worries me."

Hawk climbed over the edge of the cliff and reached down to pull Ivania up and beside him. He glanced over his shoulder at the swirling tornado of dust left by the grenade. She watched its proximity suspiciously. "Come on," he said. "Looks like we're just in time for the fireworks."

"They must have known you were coming. You attract attention. I'll give you that," she groaned as she climbed along the steep shelf.

They walked around the front of the lighthouse. Hawk shouted. "Hey, Breaux! Coming in!" Hawk called.

"It's Hawk, sir. Advance, Hawk!" Breaux replied. The word that Hawk had returned was well received by the men inside. Though generally met with dislike of late, Hawk had arrived at one of those rare times when he and his unique set of skills were appreciated. Ivania and

Hawk came through the door. He steered her forward, with a hand in the middle of her back. Joe Canlon noticed this little detail. It did not fit what he knew of Hawk, and it did not fit what he knew of her. The greetings were otherwise enthusiastic.

"It looks like y'all are in somebody's way, " Hawk returned the greetings.

"Good observation," the colonel answered coolly. He had not forgotten the way that Hawk had left him. "If we had some of our own rifle grenades, we'd give them a contest."

Hawk looked at him and nodded. If a frog had wings.

Hawk leaned on the doorjamb and eyed the plains behind the lighthouse. The woods on the edge of the plains were invisible due to a rise in the landscape. That was good, because it meant that the bottom of the lighthouse was similarly invisible to the woods. He looked up at the sky. That was where the climax to all of this would come from.

Breaux and Dreisen looked up, too. They were all infantrymen. They were uncomfortable about what unknown things were about to happen. What plans did the enemy have? What would fall out of the sky, and where? There was a general impression that a plane was landing, and that it needed the open and flat plain to do it. The details as to how that might happen, or be defended or opposed, were unclear.

"I don't like them rifle grenades," said Joe Canlon. "One time, I nearly got blinded by one. They spit back in your face when you fire 'em."

"That's because you gotta do it right," Hawk said absently, watching the outside.

Joe looked at Hawk's back. Ivania stood close to the sergeant. They had never been closer than screaming distance of each other in the whole time Joe had known the two of them. Hawk had been poison to her. What the hell was this? Like everyone else, Joe became his angriest at Hawk when Hawk least expected it. It was the sergeant's whole attitude that finally drove you mad. Ivania had not looked at Joe since coming through the door. He sensed that something had happened, and where he stood. It probably involved Hawk's telling a few more Verhangen stories than were necessary.

"Yeah. I can see me lying dead in some mudhole and Hawk standing over me saying, 'he should have read the instructions'," Joe said to the crowd. "If they're going to give a man something to fight with, it oughta be something simple enough to use without maiming himself."

"Shit, what would be simple enough for you to use? Brass knuckles?" Hawk still faced the plain, unaware of how Joe was taking all of this. They had roughly joked with one another all the time. This time, Joe was not taking it as well. Joe looked around and saw the Cokonian prisoner, who had been guarding the weapons. He kicked him. Everyone turned and looked at Joe for a moment. Without anyone speaking, the spotlight faded, and everyone turned away. The prisoner took the affair more to heart, and got up and ran. No one, including Joe, tried to stop him. He ran across the plain, his loin cloth flapping, and his bare feet having no difficulty flying over the ragged stone.

"No sense that asshole getting killed in here with the rest of us," Joe muttered.

"Reckon we ought to get out of this trap and set

some positions up out there, sir?" Hawk turned his head half toward Dreisen, without looking at him.

"I thought of it. But that anti-aircraft gun up there has to be held. If those s.o.b.'s land a plane here, we can get it with that thing. They damn sure can't take off and land without us getting it. If we just can hold it."

Hawk nodded. He thought it was entirely possible that the Japanese *could* take off and land just fine. No one had any extensive training with anti-aircraft gunnery. Especially with a crazy-ass Japanese gun, that to his knowledge, had never been fired. He also didn't like being confined here. But Dreisen was in charge. Things were back to normal. The snail was on the thorn, God was in his heaven, and all was right with the world.

* * *

"THEY ARE GONE," Taniguchi announced. "We should take up our positions in the lighthouse before the Americans arrive. If it has not been disabled, there is an excellent air defense gun in there, sir. We will be able to defend Lieutenant Zanji from any interceptors." Taniguchi was unaware of the lurking Trojan Horse that the Cokonians had left for the Japanese in the lighthouse.

Zanji smiled. "Have no fear of that, Sergeant Taniguchi. American planes will not trouble me, once I am in the cockpit of my own fighter."

"The pilot delivering your fighter may have trouble," Taniguchi answered. Taniguchi believed overconfidence had no place in war. Even the pilot delivering this advanced plane must have a great degree of skill, to merely be able to fly it.

"It is so," said the captain. "It is a good position under any circumstances, up there. Sergeant, prepare to advance to that position. We will dominate the airfield from there. I suspect we can even see the ocean."

"Yes, honorable captain."

Hawk watched the Japanese helmets bob over the rise. Faces followed. Some smiling, none concerned. The morning heat, rising from the rocky soil, distorted their features, turning them into wavy, vaporous spirits.

"Time to give 'em something for their trouble, ain't it, sir?" Hawk asked in a low voice. He put a hand on Ivania's shoulder and pushed her gently to the floor.

Dreisen swallowed anxiously. More of the faces bounced along the false horizon. Torsos appeared, moving rapidly toward them, as if on holiday. The two sides were no longer evenly matched. "Yes. Form a line...I mean..."

Hawk ignored this. There was no time for funny business. "Let's get a couple men in each window," the sergeant ordered. He was stuck with defending the building. "Breaux, you get in the second-floor window. I'm gonna see what it looks like from the top." He passed Joe. Joe looked away. "What's eating your ass anyway?" Joe did not answer.

Hawk climbed the steps. Hai-lon sat cross-legged on the lamp room floor.

"How are you, sir? What are you doing here? I think you might've fallen a little short on wisdom this morning. Maybe you should've stayed with your folks. Better get some cover down there with the lady. The Japs is coming on pretty fast down there, and there is a bunch of them."

"I will remain here," the monk replied. Hawk nodded and looked below. No time to shoot the shit with the guy. Hai-lon was hanging around, waiting for the relic to fall out of the sky, no doubt. The thing was going to get him killed. Hawk saw about forty heavily armed men approaching the door of the lighthouse. They looked much closer from up here. They moved without caution in a large group, rather than a skirmish line. Hawk smiled. Keep it cozy, Japs, he said to himself. He walked back to the 13.2 mm gun and swung it to its lowest elevation. It squeaked. The line of fire was interrupted by the lamp room wall. The gun had been emplaced strictly for antiaircraft purposes. It was cemented to the floor. The gun had changed hands several times. The conviction by both sides that they would ultimately be the ones using it, had allowed it to survive these changes unharmed.

Hawk could hear the men outside now. He well knew what the room, the lighthouse, and the world in general was about to look like. Flying steel from forty rifles was an intimidating prospect. But one he had faced many times.

Hawk returned to the wall in a crouch and deftly unslung his Thompson with one hand. *Might as well, he thought, might as well.* He slid the Cutt's compensator over the wall. His eyesight slid through the walls of the Lyman rear sight and laid the foresight on an officer's chest. *Too far, for this baby.* He held the officer there, moving the gun slightly to keep him sighted in. The wooden fore stock grated on the stone. An M1 barked below him. All M1's sound pretty much alike, but Hawk was pretty sure that this one was Joe Canlon's. Something was wrong with the guy, that was not like him. *Ah,* he thought. *The chick. That was it. The stupid ass.*

Joe fired with determination. The empty clip flew out of the top of his rifle with a ringing noise. He held the bolt open with the heel of one hand and forced a new clip down into the receiver with the side of his other hand, keeping his thumbs out of the snapping MI's maw. His first reloaded shot was true.

Hawk observed from above. An enemy soldier jumped backward with both feet spread wide. He landed on his back. The advancing Japanese crouched in surprise. Hawk opened up. The Thompson breech-block shuddered. The .45's fell short, and he lifted the muzzle higher, without releasing the trigger. He was throwing the bullets at them, instead of aiming. The arcing height boosted the range a bit. The enemy captain tried to outrun the trail of ricochets. One bit into his leg and he faltered. The other men, retreating behind him, quickly collided with him and climbed his back, roughly grounding him. The .45 caliber slugs climbed his leg. His body disappeared beneath a white cloud of rock dust. His arms slapped violently back and forth, piercing the dust, not by their own power, and the body stopped twitching.

Under his neck, Hawk tasted the coldness. There it was. That feeling of perfection. Physical skill and tortured emotion satisfying each other in one violent second of release. "One less murderin' son of a bitch," he growled.

The Marine rifles below exploded with a vibrating roar. The BAR was closer to Hawk, on the second floor, and it sounded louder. The heavy, rapid fire was comforting. The BAR was spitting shells at half the rate of the Thompson, but its range and accuracy was double that of Hawk's weapon.

Hawk ducked beneath the low wall, and looked over his shoulder at the monk. "There's one more for the Emperor, sir!" Hai-lon faced the valley on the other side of the conflict.

Hawk took another look at the battle. The vivid, smoky scene, criss-crossed by rocketing steel projectiles, that would have horrified anyone else, looked quite familiar to him. He decided to save his ammunition until the fight came closer to him. He could waste a whole clip on one man from this distance. He saw that the rifles had already thrown a half dozen of the enemy bleeding onto the ground. Not all were dead, but they were through fighting. The others crawled back to the defilade created by the rise in the ground. They would still be visible from the higher elevation of the lamp room. "Breaux! Bring the BAR up here!"

Breaux climbed quickly up the stairs, his eyes wide, gunpowder residue streaking his face. He threw the long barrel of the BAR and its swinging bipod over the wall, and pumped a jolting burst of fire across the backs of the crawling men. They had to retreat even farther down the slope of the rise to get out of his range. They left three more scattered and motionless bodies. The rifles below stopped firing. The men in the lamp room could still hear a grease gun roaring through the entirety of its clip.

"That's Dreisen," Breaux commented. "He thinks ammunition grows on trees."

"The little ladies make it every day in St. Louis," Hawk said. But he was anxious about the colonel's extravagance, as the grease gun used .45's, the same as did his Thompson.

The Japanese returned fire. Hawk and Breaux, at the top of the tower, were the only targets that they could see from their new position. The two Marines sat slumped, with their backs against the wall, to withstand the storm. Breaux stood his BAR up on its butt plate and leaned on it. Bullets rang off the columns and the roof of the lamp room. No place was safe, as the slugs played and replayed through the room, like steel fireflies. They could hear some of the bullets buzzing unopposed through the open chamber without striking anything. Breaux lifted his shoulder against his face, as if that somehow protected him. Hawk slid his helmet down over his eyes. The fury of the volley abated, and single shots continued to smack the outer wall. The lone shots sounded more threatening and precise. The two Marines were able to ponder the punctuated violence with which each single shot struck the limestone. Hawk pushed his helmet back. Hai-lon sat in a trance-like state in the middle of the floor. Hawk was impressed. The old man had to train more than his mind to ignore this, he must have been able to turn off his hearing, and his bowels, as well.

"This is a good place to get yourself shot," Breaux observed, nodding toward the monk. Hawk agreed. It was regrettable. But things were a little too tough all over to be worrying about individuals doing ill-advised things.

"Especially if one of those rifle grenades lands up here," Hawk answered. He must have subconsciously been thinking about that. They looked at one other with something approaching horror. They clambered simultaneously to their knees and crawled to the stairs. Hawk looked back at Hai-lon. *No more sense than God gave a baboon*, he thought. He went back and wrapped one arm around the monk and dragged him down with them. Hai-lon did not protest, or make any movement of his own, as he was carried with a hot Thompson muzzle pressing into his nose.

Out on the plains, a soldier aimed the antitank gun's ponderous grenade at the lamp room. Taniguchi laid a restraining hand on him, and shouted into his ear. "We must not damage the antiaircraft gun. Do not fire at the top. Save the larger grenades for later. Go and get one of the standard Arisaka ones for me." The antitank gun crew split into two directions, leaving the big weapon unattended.

Another soldier handed the *hancho* a rifle and a metal cylinder with a hole in it. Taniguchi slipped the cylinder over the rifle muzzle, letting the sight jut through the hole. He tightened it down with his hand by using an L-shaped wrench. The first soldier handed him the grenade and launcher. His steady hands went to work. He screwed the launcher onto the cylindrical adapter. The launcher contained the percussion and the propellant. Taniguchi then snapped the grenade onto the end of the entire discharger assembly. He slid the special blank cartridge into the rifle's chamber, and pushed the safety lever of the grenade under a piece of spring steel on the assembly. Upon launching, the lever would be shot from beneath the steel holder, and it would spring free. Taniguchi quickly pulled the grenade's pin and raised the rifle. The entire process was not for the nervous, the impatient, the imprecise, or the faint of heart.

The door of the lighthouse swam before the top-heavy muzzle of the *hancho's* rifle. Taniguchi pulled the trigger. The rifle leapt and the grenade fizzed out low to the ground and across the plain like a torpedo. It struck the doorjamb of the lighthouse, and the opening disappeared behind the orange and black bloom of the explosion. Taniguchi shook his head. Another three inches, and it would have gone inside, and he would have killed them all. Maybe he had at least hit someone exposed to the open door. It was a marvelous weapon, but lacking in accuracy.

The explosion numbed the Americans. The shrapnel blew through the door, tearing the side out of Edwards, the man who had been nearest the opening. He fell through the door to the ground below. He lay face up with a frown and his eyes closed.

Hawk and Breaux reached the ground floor about that time and pushed the heavy door closed. It was no easy task, as it had been open for years, and dragged along the floor. The two of them, with Joe's help, picked up the heavy table and put it on its end, leaning it against the door. The windows could not be closed, but it would take a greater degree of marksmanship to hit one of those, from this range, with a grenade.

Hawk and Breaux knelt by Dreisen, with smoke from the explosion still filling the room. "I think I got an idea," Hawk shouted. The blast, echoing and shaking the atmosphere within the small space, had left everyone half-deafened.

"About time," said Dreisen. "Let's hear it."

"Let's take it to them. We have all these automatic weapons. We got the firepower on them. If we can get within hand grenade range, we might be able to run them off. If that flier is with them, they may run to protect him. If we can keep them off the plains, they won't be able to fly him out, or shoot that damn shit at us." Hawk looked outside. "But if we stay holed up here, they've got a pretty good range on us with those rifle grenades. I believe we're in trouble. They can tag us with one eventually, and it's all over."

Dreisen and Breaux looked at one another. Whether their addled brains soaked up all of this or not was questionable. Mostly, they heard, 'Let's take it to them.' They were both aggressive men, but in the here and now, that sounded *aggressive*. "Not feasible," Dreisen said flatly. "We have eight men, and they have thirty."

"Aw, horseshit," Hawk shook his head. "You ain't gonna have nothing, if you sit here like a bump on a log in this chicken coop." Another explosion collided with the lighthouse's base, causing the entire structure to tremble, or perhaps even move an inch or two. A window went dark, and a man stumbled from beneath it with a dripping red arm. "I'm hit!" he shouted. He was quiet for a moment and then started screaming. Joe tried to get him to sit down and the screaming became louder. Ivania crawled over to him.

Hawk looked at Breaux and Dreisen. Breaux, by sheer fighting ability, had become a decision-maker in the chaos. Another grenade hit a few feet in front of the door, and the great wooden barrier bucked completely off its hinges, without falling. The massive table flew backward, as if made of cardboard, almost hitting Joe Canlon. Smoke filtered in around the edges of the door.

"All right," Dreisen conceded. "We have to abandon this position."

"Yeah," Breaux agreed. "What about her? Is she in on this charge? Or staying by herself in here? Or what?"

Hawk motioned her over. She was covered in the wounded man's blood. "She'll come out with us." Ivania, uninformed about the general plan, listened in terror. She knelt wide-eyed beside Hawk. "When we go out," the sergeant told her, "We're going toward the Japs. You go the other way, see, toward that cliff, the way we came in. Go down there, and stay there under the rim, until we come back for you. Don't go too far down because there's mines. Got it?" She looked skeptically at him. She opened her mouth to say something. But no one was going to want to hear it. They were talking to each other again in urgent tones.

"Listen up, goddam it," Hawk screamed at the remainder of the equally skeptical men, "they ain't gonna be expecting this, so let's make good use of that. After the next grenade," Hawk said, thinking *if we are still alive*, but leaving that part unsaid, "we're going right at the bastards. Right up the middle. We're gonna push them back off the plain. They got them old bolt action rifles, but these goddam grenades are gonna kill us. Maybe we can get them pinned down in the woods, or run them up the mountainside. We just can't stay in here anymore. This is the only way."

His projected goals sounded very optimistic, even to him. There was little time for argument, however, as a grenade exploded harmlessly a few feet in front of the lighthouse. It was a good omen. Everyone seemed to sense that they were fortunate that the bomb had spared them for a trial of one more idea. As soon as one of the Japanese grenadiers figured out that all he needed to do was crawl about six feet closer, they would be skewered.

When Hawk said, "Let's git 'em," there was no hesitating.

They plunged through the door one at a time. Joe Canlon's eyebrows were folded angrily, hanging three-fourths of the way over his eyes. Joe, a normally reasonable person, was thinking that he had to kill every one of the Japanese in order to survive, and therefore, that is what he would do. They ran through the grenade dust, tasting the sharp chemical smell of the explosives. Then crawling and crouching, covering the ground with vigorous speed, they closed in on the surprised enemy. The Japanese shuffled about in confusion, excitedly screaming to one another at the unexpected sight. It looked as if hand to hand grappling was imminent.

Taniguchi had been lying on his side, patiently attaching another grenade to his rifle, his hands automatically going through the lengthy process, when a half clip of bullets roared along the ground past his elbow. A startling paralysis prevented him from even flinching. It took him a moment to formulate the thought that he needed to duck. More accurate fire would have killed him. Two men dove over Zanji to protect him. Men fell dead on either side of the ace, some screaming beforehand, and some not having the opportunity. Taniguchi dropped the rifle grenade paraphernalia, and slid his Solothurn along the ground. He swung its strap, leveled it, and jerked the trigger back without aiming. The submachine gun's fury helped to balance the flow of the firepower. The American advance halted. Taniguchi knew that it would, after a little show of determination, and automatic firepower.

The Americans were not adept at these types of charges. This was more of a Japanese tactic. The Marines lay close to the ground in the middle of the barren plain, the element of surprise, and perhaps a lot of their fury, spent. In spite of their unenviable position, they poured out steady fire, forcing the Japanese to keep their heads down. The goal of making the Japanese withdraw was so far not happening.

They were now blasting at one another from half the range as before, when the Americans were in the lighthouse. It should have been easier to hit a target, but the opposite was true, as it was too difficult to raise one's head for a clear shot. That did not discourage anyone from shooting.

The Americans knew that steady fire was their only salvation. When the bullets stopped, the superior number of Japanese could easily overwhelm them. They fired their weapons passionately, with fierce and angry expressions, though they were horrified at the thought of what could happen when they stopped. Hawk crawled forward. He squeezed the trigger of the Thompson sparingly. His desperate charge had been stopped far sooner than he wanted. This did not look good. It was a shooting match with one side under cover and the other in the high grass. An enemy rifleman stood to get a clear shot at the advancing Hawk. Breaux steered a stream of spewing white fire across his upper body. It slammed him down and the Japanese fire slackened. Breaux stood and ran in a zig-zag pattern toward Hawk. Bullets hit between his boots at almost every step. He threw himself down and blew a good part of a clip toward the rise of ground hiding the Japanese. Beside him, he saw Hawk's hand flying upward. A grenade exploded short of the mark. They heard a Japanese rifle grenade whoosh somewhere to the right, and crack viciously. A man near the rear of the American attack had been killed by it. *They must have a hundred of those goddam son of a bitches,* Hawk thought.

Taniguchi looked over the battlefield. Things looked good to the untrained eye, but his eye was trained. If they got to Zanji, that was the end of this chess game. That must be what they are after, he reasoned. Their charge was insane. They could not possibly hope to dislodge the Japanese from this position, he thought, without cover and with fewer men. They know that they will kill a few of us, and they are hoping that Zanji will be among them. Quite bold, and quite suicidal. But their plan could indeed capture the king, and leave the Japanese with a pyrrhic victory. Taniguchi decided that Americans must not get any closer. His desire was to attack them, and eliminate them, and he was sure that he could. But that was not his mission. Zanji must come first. He told himself what he had been telling himself for twenty years: the hell with what I want.

"We shall take the lighthouse!" the *hancho* shouted. He had developed a plan certain to outwit the Americans. He ordered ten men to retreat to the right, in the direction of the woods. He could tell by the aggressive Marine tactics, who was likely in charge of the Americans. Taniguchi knew that he had mastered this brute before. This time, perhaps, he would be able to do more than just defeat him, perhaps he could avenge Keizo, and terminate this killer's war forever. The Americans would follow his ten man diversion, and the blunder would cost them the battle.

Taniguchi was not entirely wrong. But it fell to

Dreisen to actually make the blunder. When the colonel saw the ten men running for the woods, he was certain that the American attack had worked according to plan. Dreisen led all of his remaining men to the right, after the fleeing Japanese.

Breaux saw what appeared to be a successful charge by Dreisen and stood, cursing bloodthirsty oaths, before joining the colonel's attack on the fleeing decoy of Taniguchi. Unfortunately, this resulted in Hawk's being left alone on the left flank, and having to cover the center as well.

"Hey!" Hawk screamed. Had they all gone nuts? He might not be the best at strategy, but this did not look right. "Hey! Goddamnit!" It was too late. The BAR ripped off a burst as Breaux ran away from him. Almost immediately, Hawk turned around to see the arms and legs of twenty Japanese soldiers flying wildly in his direction. They were flanking the American position and taking the lighthouse. And there was only one man standing in their way.

Their fire was inaccurate and minimal as they charged. This was not consoling to the man lying in the path of the stampede. "Holy shit!" Hawk gasped in amazement. He looked over at the backs of the other Americans, charging blindly off the plain, after God knew what. The Japanese bore down on him, evidently intent on recovering the lighthouse.

"Well, you can have it, baby," he spoke aloud. He pulled the pin from a grenade by slipping the ring over his Thompson's foresight. The ring and cotter key flew aside like a piece of whittled wood from a knife. He let the spoon slip from beneath his fingers and rose on one arm to throw it into the faces of the enemy, now almost upon him. A moment before it detonated, he stood and ran toward the other Marines. Regardless of whether the others were heading into an ambush or not, he did not have a lot of choices on where to go. Hearing the grenade, and realizing what had happened, Breaux turned and ran back to meet Hawk and cover his retreat. Breaux knew that the larger force of the enemy could swing around and wipe out Dreisen from the rear. But would they? Instead, they seemed hell bent on the lighthouse.

Hawk's grenade fell short. The explosion covered him long enough to escape being trampled under the Japanese leather and steel. It also diverted the enemy flanking maneuver farther toward the left.

The Japanese overran the erstwhile Marine position and without pausing, continued on toward the lighthouse. They could have swung around and destroyed Dreisen with a rear attack. Taniguchi had preferred doing just that. But they absolutely had to have possession of the lighthouse, and now.

One of the enemy paratroopers lagged far behind the others bearing down on the lighthouse. Perhaps he expected Taniguchi would eventually come to his senses and attack Dreisen. The lone trooper had another burden, besides the one of indecision. He was the man assigned to carry the heavy antitank rifle. No one had taken into account the fact that it was difficult to charge a position with such a cumbersome weapon. The man carrying it was the lowest ranking member of the Japanese contingent. Likely at one point, he had an assistant, now dead, for it took a crew to move the great weight. Breaux, sensing low hanging fruit, went to a prone position, propped his BAR on an elbow and fired.

The trail of bullets chased the staggering straggler, and finally outdistanced him. He fell with what seemed to be more relief than agony. The antitank gun, its attached bowl rifle grenade and all, rattled to the ground under him.

Hawk and Breaux stood beside each other on the plain. They were between the two groups of men, who no longer seemed interested in fighting one another. Dreisen was failing to engage the Japanese that he had chased into the woods. The shooting had essentially stopped, although the chase was not over. Noticing the unique and cumbersome object beneath the dead Japanese trooper, Hawk walked over to the straggler Breaux had killed. He reached down, latched onto the shirt of the soldier, and lifted him off the antitank gun. His hand became slippery with blood, squirting on him from beneath the man's shirt collar. Blood shot all over the gun. Hawk looked up and squinted. "Shit." He shook his head, and looked down again.

"The no-good son of a bitch." Hawk looked down at the weapon, and the dome shaped grenade attached to its muzzle. It looked quite fearsome. "What the goddam hell's that?"

"That's what they started shooting at us with in the beginning," Breaux said. "That thing's a real son of a bitch. Dreisen thought it was a mortar."

"Yeah?" Hawk rifled through the pouches on the ammo belt of the weapon's carrier. He dug out an assortment of flimsy looking little tools and knelt beside the gun. He soon had the bipod, back leg, back plate, armor shield, magazine, handles, and several other unnecessary accessories taken off. "What are you doing?" Breaux finally asked.

"Getting rid of some of that weight."

Hawk lifted the gun and swung it across his shoulder. The damned thing was still heavy, but he handled it easier than its prior owner. Physically, Hawk was little more than an animal. He had done manual labor since childhood. He scoffed at strain. His hand dangled over the abbreviated half stock to keep the gun balanced on his shoulder.

"Can you shoot that thing?" Breaux asked.

"Shit, yeah," said Hawk. "I probably couldn't hook it up, but they already done that part. All I got to do is shoot it."

"You need them tools?" Breaux kicked the odd shaped pieces of bloody metal lying in the dirt.

"Nah. I'm like Daniel Boone. Only get one shot with this baby."

The two Marines looked at each other, and then at the smoking battlefield around them. They were tall and silhouetted by the sun. The Japanese under Taniguchi were crouching as they entered the lighthouse. Hawk eyed the cliff where Ivania lay hidden. She was dangerously close to the enemy, but they didn't know that. He could not do anything about her for the moment, except make sure that the others did not direct any fire over there. They heard the sound of firing, as Dreisen began to engage the decoy soldiers, far down the plains at the edge of the woods. *Well*, Hawk thought, *that shit won't be over any time soon.*

Hawk tossed his head toward the woods and his helmet straps swung. "Come on. Let's go see what the colonel is up to." One of the enemy at the lighthouse fired a shot at them and it kicked up the dust a few yards short. Hawk squinted in the direction of the sniper.

"That bastard." Breaux screamed obscenities across the open land, like a madman.

Breaux turned toward the woods with the sergeant, and they started walking across the empty field at an unhurried pace. "It looks to me like they outfoxed us," Breaux said.

"Yeah." Hawk looked over his shoulder. He did not like being outfoxed. "Maybe." He had not been climbing all over this terrain for the last week for nothing. They were out of sight of the lighthouse now. "Tell you what. You go on and help out the colonel. Tell him what happened, how they pulled the wool over his eyes. He'll probably say he planned it that way all along. Try to get through to him. I'll pick up with y'all later on. I don't like the idea of giving them that lighthouse, and that gun up there." Breaux nodded.

"Whatever you say, man. You gonna be lonesome."

"Nah," Hawk laughed. "I got my podnuhs to keep me company."

Hawk turned and walked back toward the cliff, several hundred yards to the right. The cliff ran beside and beneath the lighthouse, and he could follow its rim from below, and get close to the structure. He tried to stay under the range of sight of the lamp room. But he may have strayed too close, once or twice.

He let himself over the sharp edge and climbed along the steep slope, which always leaned at least forty-five degrees, and moved toward Taniguchi and his contingent in the building above him. While the slope was at this great angle, he was vertically straight up and down. His right hand bridged the angle, reaching and touching the rock to steady himself, as his ankles were bent almost sideways. The heavy weapon lay across his left shoulder.

His Thompson bounced muzzle down against his back. As he neared the lighthouse, he watched carefully for mines. He believed them to be farther down. His pace never slackened. He occasionally raised his eyes and wrinkled his forehead at the white shaft peering over the cliff at him. The lamp room appeared vacant. The sky flashed cobalt blue through the open columned chamber. Hawk cleared his throat of rock dust and watched his boots carefully again. The veins in his left wrist swelled as it hung over the heavy gun barrel. His fingers dangled long and lifelessly down, as the weapon see-sawed across his shoulders with each step.

Hawk saw a shape in the brush along the rim of the cliff that was directly adjacent to the lighthouse. He assumed that it was Ivania. He was prepared to drop the antitank gun, if it wasn't her. As he came closer, he confirmed that it was her. She certainly had not fled very far from the doorway that she had exited. She saw the man approaching, and recognized Hawk. She was looking at him. He motioned for her to go farther down the slope. She hesitated and he motioned more forcefully. He climbed higher, coming beneath the base of the tower. The gun grew heavier with each step up. He stuck his head up and looked over the ledge. A ground-floor window faced him. He saw a helmet pass across it, and he ducked quickly. He had noticed that the wounded Marine that Dreisen had left there had been executed and thrown out onto the plain. Hawk pulled his heavy prize of war alongside his body as he lay in the sharp and itchy grass. He would get them, if this thing worked. Couldn't blame Uncle Sam for this one. He hoped the little ladies in Tokyo were just as good at ordnance as their counterparts in St. Louis. At least this once.

Aircraft motors vibrated in the distance. Hawk turned on his back on the slope and faced the sky. He squinted in the glare. Two of them came from the north, the part of the island that he had not seen. He could make out wings. The propellers grew larger and louder. The air snapped. He heard excited talking above him in the lighthouse. There was laughing and cheering. Hawk's hand gripped the thin barrel of the antitank gun tighter. Now, he had a deadline. He had to do this before the planes got any closer. The planes were not cooperating, as they raced faster. He turned over and began crawling upward. They were moving faster than he expected, faster than he could move. They swooped low over the cliff and over the plain behind the lighthouse. Lightning-fast shadows ran beneath them on the grass and over Hawk. He could no longer hear the Japanese celebrating. Had they left? Were they out on the plain with the pilot? Would he be able to use this gigantic weapon on the plane, rather than the lighthouse? He looked over the edge of the cliff. He saw the planes banking. Then he realized why all had gone quiet. He recognized the long snouts and swollen air intake underbellies of the P-51 Mustangs, the deadliest American fighter plane to take to the skies. This was not what the Japanese wanted to see at any time, and especially not now.

Looks like we all get a chance to cheer, Hawk mused. The P-51's soared out over the valley and back toward the north. *They're looking for that bastard*, Hawk thought. "Here he is," he told them. But I'm going to save you the trouble. I might even be saving your asses, if that Jap is as good as they say he is.

Hawk glanced up at the lamp room wall. It remained unoccupied. He crawled over the ledge. *I'll just stand up and pump it in the window, and it'll all be over with.* A shout came from the lamp room. Someone was up there, maybe on the other side. Reflexively, Hawk hugged the ground.

Taniguchi had sent three men upstairs to serve as a crew on the antiaircraft gun. The gun emplacement could do little against the swift American planes, but at least the P-51's would find the skies challenged on their next sortie. One of the crewmen in the lamp room called out to Taniguchi. He had spotted yet another plane.

"That's it," Zanji said quietly. The relief was enormous. He looked at Taniguchi with glazed eyes. "The lone plane, it is symbolic. One great warrior against the world. Come, Taniguchi, we must go to meet it."

"Wait," Taniguchi said. He shouted up the stairs, "Does the lone plane look like a Shiden Kai?"

"I am not sure, Sergeant," said the soldier. Few had ever seen the newer version of the Shiden Kai. After a pause, came the word, "Yes. Yes, I'm certain that it is. It matches the silhouette in the picture," the crewman shouted from above. They had all been given a pamphlet containing the silhouettes of aircraft.

Taniguchi nodded. "Very well." He sighed. "Everyone stay inside. If the Mustangs return, there may be strafing. I alone will escort Zanji to his plane."

"You have earned that honor," Zanji said. Taniguchi hid his embarrassment. Or was it disgust.

The other soldiers acknowledged Taniguchi's order

with curt bows. The men muttered sincere encouragement to Zanji. The crewmen in the lamp room came down to wish their hero well. The *hancho* then made an uncharacteristic, but big mistake, warned against in basic training: the same mistake that Hawk had cursed Joe Canlon for; the *hancho* leaned his Solothurn against the wall, and walked outside unarmed. Zanji was at his side. They walked perhaps thirty yards from the building when the sound of a well-tuned engine made them turn and see the shiny new Shiden approaching the flatlands. Few had seen such a glorious sight. Green, with bright red rising suns decorating its wings and fuselage, it dropped gracefully for a landing, as if it had eyes, and was picking out the smoothest spot to rest its dainty feet.

Zanji knew immediately the triumph of technology that this plane represented. He knew the sacrifices required by his countrymen to get it here. He felt their confidence in him, and a tear ran down his cheek.

By contrast, a few feet away labored a man alien to warmth and warm feelings of any sort. No one appreciated anything about him for very long. Hawk stood and stepped closer to the old and crumbling window. Sweat poured from beneath his hot helmet. His eyes were fixed with an unshakable determination on the window. He smelled the now familiar moldy odor of the interior of the building exhaling out the opening. Nothing could have stopped him. A bullet in his back would have been meaningless now. He raised his left arm high in front of the window, and he raised his right arm still higher. The rifle and its grenade, looking like an overhead barbell, rested across his upraised hands. His thumb thrust backwards through the guard, he awkwardly snapped the trigger. The tremendous and unexpected recoil knocked the massive gun from his tenuous grip, and it went pinwheeling down the slope, into thin air, over the jungle, and out of the twentieth century. But in spite of all the off balance awkwardness, the grenade had been fired from far too close of a range for it to miss. The window belched sparkling red streaks outwardly, across the blue sky over the valley. A hot cushion of air pushed Hawk to his knees on the rocky slope. He bowed his head as flaming embers rained down on him, cascading over him in two lashing waves. The enormous explosion gave no one within the lighthouse an opportunity to cry out. They were all killed, and killed instantly, by the tremendous, confined force, which made several of them one with the buckling walls.

Taniguchi and Zanji jerked around in startled horror as the ground floor of the tower erupted behind them. The light from the massive blast reflected across their faces, and heat whipped their hair. The Shiden touched down with a tire-thudding bump, but they were watching the lighthouse, and missed the long-awaited moment. Taniguchi finally came to his senses, and pulled Zanji toward the plane. He was not sure what had happened, but his wily instincts told him to forget that, and carry through with his purpose. Before they could get halfway to the plane, they saw that the Shiden had attracted other birds of prey. The P-51's streaked into view from over the valley.

Taniguchi's blood ran cold. He was not accustomed to confronting such power and speed on an open field. The great American machines were hurtling battle-ships. The *hancho* was sure that they would both be killed. Still, he pushed the confused Zanji toward his

Shiden. He had vowed to put the pilot into it, and he was going to do just that. The other Japanese fighter pilot, the man delivering the Shiden Kai, jumped out of the cockpit, as Taniguchi and Zanji reached the cover of the plane's wing. The engine was running, the propellers spun, and the plane tried to turn itself in a circle. The other pilot shouted something to them, but they could not hear it. The man appeared to be frightened out of his wits, and for good reason. The P-51's manifested themselves from nowhere and nothing, like aerial demons. As Zanji and Taniguchi cringed under the moving wing, the pilot decided to run toward the recently stricken lighthouse, which still blew gray and fuzzy puffs of smoke from its ground floor apertures.

The American fliers dropped dangerously close to the earth, buzzing within inches of the solid walls of the lighthouse. They were both wild kids, trained quickly and thrown into the air war in the Pacific. For some reason, a reason that only a person under the age of twenty-two could explain, they both wanted to nail the scrambling pilot as he ran for the lighthouse. They probably thought that the Shiden would remain stranded there forever, to be a target at their leisure. They did not consider the fact that the pilot would have to stay there forever, too, without his airplane. They also forgot that the man climbing into the plane was Isamu Zanji, although they probably could not have understood what that meant, until they saw it with their own eyes. The P-51s opened up with .50 caliber bullets on the running man.

Machine gun bullets exploded in four churning furrows that blazed across the field faster than any man could run. The innumerable explosions leapt ten feet off the ground, dwarfing the man. The pilot, in his quilted and fur-lined suit, was knocked well into the air and did a somersault as the slugs hit him, held him there above the earth, shaking him, and hitting him again, all faster than the eye could track. The P-51's soared out over the woods and banked, more than likely arguing about who had shot the target.

The two American pilots had made the gravest error of their young lives. They had allowed Lieutenant Zanji of the Japanese Naval Air Force to climb into a fighter plane.

Still half-dazed, Hawk edged cautiously around the curved wall of the lighthouse to see all of the deadly excitement. He was amazed when he saw the Shiden Kai begin to move down the makeshift runway.

"There it is! And the son of a bitch is in it!" he said aloud in disbelief, to his almost deaf ears. It was reflexive to talk to himself, when he lost his hearing. He had not seen the plane land, or heard anything. This had all happened as if by magic. He looked inside the door of the lighthouse. He winced slightly at the incredible carnage. It was worse than he had expected. And yet, the main target had not been in there. *Why? How?* The pilot must have escaped the holocaust by inches. Hawk reached behind his back and grabbed the stock of his Thompson, pulling it off in one motion. He ran out onto the field toward the plane. He wondered how in the hell the two P-51's had missed the sitting duck, and what, if anything could be done about it.

14

SETTLING ON RIGHT AND WRONG

ZANJI SALUTED TANIGUCHI. THE *HANCHO* LOOKED UP AT him, and returned the salute, unable to restrain a burst of pride in his accomplishment, despite all of the misgivings about the entire affair. The magnificent fighter plane roared down the field, paying little attention to the small irregularities of the earth. Moments later, Zanji felt his first sensation of lift in weeks. He was free and invincible.

Now there were two bystanders, and one was not wishing the pilot a bon voyage. Ignoring Taniguchi, Hawk raised his Thompson and fired at the plane. He tried for the cockpit. It was futile, the bouncing craft moved swiftly away from them. If the bullets struck home, there was no indication of it. The cockpit had bullet proof glass. At least, Thompson bullet proof glass. Had Taniguchi been armed, he could have easily killed the Marine standing beside him, who had chosen to pay no attention to him while firing at the Shiden. He considered leaping upon him, but decided that another of his Marine comrades must have Taniguchi covered from a distance, or this one would not be so boldly standing here.

Failing to stop the plane, Hawk reconsidered leaving himself unguarded, and swung the muzzle toward Taniguchi. The *hancho* stood there stiffly, his arms at his sides. His mission accomplished, he had no regrets about his vulnerability. *What is this crackpot doing?* Hawk wondered. Something made him hesitate to shoot the man. Perhaps it was his utter defenselessness. Taniguchi did not know that he was one of the few, if not the only man, to ever stand in front of that particular muzzle and live. Hawk took his eyes off the fool to watch the plane gliding away. The misery of complete failure weighted him down.

Hawk shook his head. And *here* was his consolation prize. He cautiously approached the prisoner. Marines were not fond of prisoners. They had learned that the captured Japanese produced grenades, pistols and knives by sleight of hand, once captors were within striking distance. The fact that the enemy stood there with his arms at his sides made Hawk seriously consider ending this potential problem immediately.

"Git your hands on your head, you worthless bastard!" Hawk touched the top of his helmet with one hand and shook the Thompson in the man's face with the other. Taniguchi complied. Ordinarily, he might not have, and as a result, been summarily shot. In just this moment, however, he was still feeling elation, and subconsciously had a desire to savor the experience for a few moments. But his expression remained defiant. He knew that he must not allow himself to follow any further instructions. He must die for his country. Except—as he stood there, he recognized the face of his captor. The dilemma was solved. He knew that this man was not taking him a prisoner. He realized he was only being maneuvered somewhere else to be shot. The expression on Taniguchi's face showed no fear, only hatred. Whatever it was, Hawk did not like it. Emotions roiled within Taniguchi. Now he must live, he must live to kill this man. He had one last mission on earth.

Hawk was overwhelmed with agitation. He had lost Zanji, men were still fighting over in the woods, Ivania was still hiding in the middle of a minefield, and here he was with this stupid asshole. His finger tightened dangerously on the trigger. "Git down!" he ordered. What was he going to do with this son of a bitch? He knew the man would not lie down. He knew that he probably wanted to be shot. If the idiot would just lunge at him and get it over with, he could go on about his failed day.

But Taniguchi did not lunge at him. He fought his pride, knelt, and lay on the ground. He did all of this because he must kill this man. He had to putter around with his captor, until the muzzle was not aimed at him, until an unguarded moment presented itself. He knew the Marine and knew him well; perhaps, better than anyone, for the two had met where life meets death too many times. Taniguchi knew that along with his madness and cruelty, this man was prone to making rash mistakes.

With Taniguchi safely lying face down, Hawk again looked at the departing Shiden. It banked over the valley at incredible speed. "What's he, putting on a show?" Hawk asked...Taniguchi...since there was no one else around. The P-51's were nowhere to be seen.

Where the hell did they go? Weren't they here to get the Japanese fighter plane?

He looked down at his captive and mumbled an obscenity. The jackass had been out there with Zanji, so maybe he was someone important. "I been walking in circles for a month, all for *you*, mister. You better hope you're Tojo's brother-in-law or something, or you're going to the happy ancestor hunting ground."

Taniguchi understood a good deal of English, even Hawk's version. The words were pretty much what he expected from the animal. He had no regrets about anything that he had done, even being captured. This was perhaps the greatest opportunity of all. Taniguchi did not come here for the purpose of rescuing Zanji, after all, he came first and foremost to kill this man. He had schemed for months to arrange this very meeting. He could not let himself get separated from him.

Hawk frisked him roughly, using his boots as much as his hands. "Probably get some Jap-assed disease from touching this pile of shit," he complained. "All right, get up, shit head." Taniguchi stood. He could possibly elbow the American's weapon aside and strangle the Marine. But the man looked strong, wiry, fast, and hyper-aware, and Taniguchi could not risk some awkward and inglorious failure.

Hawk stared into the flinty eyes. He knew the soldier wanted to kill him, he could *see* Taniguchi thinking. *I might just let you try,* Hawk thought. He paused there for a moment, he saw something familiar about the prisoner. He was a little older than your average soldier, and therefore was somewhat distinctive. But Hawk had felt that way before, felt that he had recognized individuals among the enemy, even recently, with the guy on the mountain; and he figured he had to be mistaken. It was probably some brain thing, the brain trying to create order out of nothing, like seeing faces in clouds. "Over there," he gestured toward the lighthouse. He wished there was someone to turn the captive over to. He had not been a prisoner nursemaid before. He never should have taken him prisoner, but the man was so docile, Hawk had been kind of tricked into it. As the soldier began walking, Hawk stopped. He stood still in bewilderment and watched as the enemy soldier continued moving toward the lighthouse. It was the walk that finally caused the recognition. This was the man who had nearly killed him on Verhangen, and it was the same man who had nearly killed him in the duel on the mountain. And now, the *same* bastard turned up putting that pilot into an airplane. This was no ordinary servant of the Emperor. Hawk decided that Taniguchi's sentence as a prisoner was going to be a very short one. He owed this gentleman *a lot*.

Hawk was somewhat relieved that he had not shot the man right off. He would have never known the identity of his prisoner, because he never would have given him another thought. He also felt a little better about having to deal with him.

Taniguchi stood against the wall of the lighthouse. Humiliation was his only emotion now. The *bushido* code called for self-destruction before surrender. Taniguchi was not a young man; he was not troubled by any doubts about his bravery. Had he been armed, he likely would have taken his life as surely as would have a young fanatic. To do otherwise, would be to abandon all that he had lived and fought for. A good soldier did not back away from it, and he was an excellent soldier.

His hope of killing Hawk was fading as he confronted the monster face to face. He had to decide quickly, if it was mere fantasy. He could not delude himself into believing that he could eliminate Hawk, just to prolong and preserve his own life.

Ivania Broeder climbed cautiously over the rim of the cliff. She had seen and heard approaching activity from below, and decided that it was time to relocate. She saw Hawk beside the lighthouse, sighed heavily, and knew there would be safety there again. Next to the Marine stood Taniguchi, whom she did not recognize immediately. She stopped a respectable distance away from the *hancho*.

"Dreisen is coming," Ivania called to Hawk. "They're coming along the cliffside. I heard firing. I think they are being chased." As she spoke, Ivania could tell that she had interrupted something.

Hawk glared at Taniguchi, never an enviable position to be in. "Ain't that nice?" Hawk commented. "This isn't over yet. That Jap squad might even wipe us out."

Taniguchi glared back at Hawk, unintimidated. Ivania now felt certain of what it was that she had interrupted. She recognized Taniguchi, but he exhibited no recognition of her.

Canlon, Dreisen, and Breaux appeared over the ledge soon afterward, looking the worse for wear. Firing could be heard at a distance, as the last of the others were making their way upward in a fighting retreat. Evidently, the Americans had been outfought or outsmarted by the tough paratroopers.

"We need to get a fixed position here," Dreisen said. He looked like hell. The colonel was old, sweaty, and red. "They're whipping our ass. Was that the Jap pilot in that plane?"

"Yessir," said Hawk. "It was." Dreisen made an angry grasping gesture with his fist. This added to the general atmosphere of despair. All four of the men looked at Taniguchi. There was no sympathy on their faces. They were not old school 'good sports' with backslapping compassion for their valiant and vanquished opponent. They remembered Waterland, Sprack, and Morgan. And a dozen others. "This is his buddy," Hawk said slowly, nodding at the simmering prisoner. "I blew up the ones in the lighthouse, but I don't know how those two got out in time. This one here put the pilot in a Jap fighter plane. The pilot was by himself. A couple of P-51s were flying around, so it might not be over. I don't know what happened to them. The pilot took off like it was Sunday morning. I'm kind of afraid he's long gone, sir. He probably outran those fighters back to the Jap fleet."

"We'll be lucky to get out of this alive," said Joe Canlon.

"No, no, lad. We're evenly matched. Buck up," Dreisen said, wiping his crimson forehead with a hand-kerchief. "We just never got our feet on the ground out there. That little handful of them can't take us."

Joe frowned at the colonel. He would have liked to punch him in his puffy red face. "They can't take a forti-fied position," the Colonel continued. "Kill this one, and let's get inside. Get set up for a scrape."

Hawk flipped the switch on his Thompson to single fire. "Yes, sir." Ivania's face went white.

"Whaat? Wait! What in the hell are you doing?" Ivania shouted. Hawk had taken an unchecked pose, demonstrating every intention to quickly carry out the order. Ivania looked from Hawk to Dreisen with her lips parted and her breath coming quickly. Her blood pressure was pounding as hard as the colonel's. "What is this, Colonel? Are you going to shoot this man? An unarmed prisoner?"

"Oh, yes, ma'am," Dreisen assured her.

"I remember this man. His name is Sergeant Taniguchi. He was always kind to me. He was in charge of the patrol. He is a decent person. You don't have any right to execute him. He saved my life. He is a prisoner of war. That is against the law."

"Save it for the chaplain, lady," Dreisen said.

"What law is that?" Hawk muttered. He was not asking for any specific statute. He was speaking generally, as would a godless man in a lawless world. His mood worsened. This woman sure got around. She even had buddies on her Japanese dance card.

"Well, what difference does that make? I don't know technically...the Geneva Convention, or the Articles for the Government of the Navy, or the Articles of War, or the U. S. Constitution—or the Ten Commandments! Or something!" she shouted and waved her arms at them. She was used to taking on men in the hospital, under tense circumstances. But she usually had rank on them, and the circumstances were not *quite* this tense. "Are you both insane? You cannot do this."

"Japs didn't sign the Geneva Convention," Dreisen tightened his lips and looked at his boots. The prosecution rested.

"What's the Geneva Convention say about women loading gondola cars?" Hawk asked, not mentioning the incident in the jungle, with Kirishima holding her up by her hair with one hand, and swinging a knife at her with the other hand.

"What's the Geneva Convention say about stuffing a man's privates down his throat?" Breaux growled at her. He had *no* patience with this kind of talk.

"You done forgot Kreski? You got no business here," Hawk said. The four men surrounded, and towered over her slender figure. She suddenly noticed, however, incredible as it seemed, that they were listening to her. She persisted.

"You are all talking about two different things. War and prisoners. Combatants and noncombatants. Apples and oranges," she said. She fought valiantly for Taniguchi's life. He could not have cared less.

"We ain't talking oranges," said Hawk, "we're talking Japs."

A strained moment of silence followed. Taniguchi eyed the grenade hanging on Hawk's chest. It did not matter that he was interrupting his advocate. He had already decided his own fate. All he knew was that the distraction of the shouting match was an opportunity. The *hancho's* hand lashed out and seized the pineapple. But it was firmly buttoned down on the pocket. Joe Canlon bashed the sharp edge of his M1 butt on the side of the prisoner's head. Taniguchi fell dazed to his knees.

"Well, I guess you didn't see *that* coming," Hawk said to Ivania, and pointed the submachine gun down at him. "That oughta settle it."

"That doesn't settle anything," Ivania shouted. They all ignored the swooning prisoner. "I guess you wouldn't do the same thing with four overgrown maniacs getting ready to shoot you down like a dog. Four overgrown *cowards!*" She shrieked the last word.

Hawk looked at Dreisen. He seemed tongue-tied, for once. Hawk was not. "Awright. I don't give a damn what y'all do with the worthless son of a bitch. I've run into him on every island I've been on. I'll blow his head off on the next island, if I have to. We'll see who else is missing the next time we have this little discussion. I don't give a *shit* what you do. The day will come for him and me." Breaux laid a cautious hand on Hawk's shoulder, encouraging him to ease off.

Hawk left them there. His outburst left them all a bit stunned. He went into the lighthouse. Besides his usual anger, he felt quite guilty. He knew that he should have shot the prisoner. It was the right thing to do. Now when Taniguchi killed someone—probably Ivania, if there were any justice—it would be Hawk's fault. Hawk took such matters seriously. A lost life was a serious thing. Taniguchi was not your average soldier. If he was not killed, he was going to kill someone else, of that there was no doubt. Hawk should've protected the naïve Ivania from her own squeamishness. But all of them— especially that dumb colonel—had let her shoot her mouth off. That's what the Marines were here for, to do a dirty job that no one else wanted to do.

Without Hawk, Dreisen seemed to wilt before Ivania's rather brilliantly waged defense. *No one had ever intervened in these prisoner matters before*, the colonel thought. He tried to stay insulated from the sordid affairs, but he certainly approved of them. Pretty soon, she would be quoting the Bible at him, or some other tear-jerking crap. He just didn't want to hear any more. She could cause trouble for him. She was an officer, and he had heard she was from a wealthy family. *Hawk should have dealt with this*, he thought. What did Hawk have to risk? His post-war job on a trash truck? Hawk should have taken care of this for him. That's what sergeants were for.

The colonel was perturbed. What was wrong with her? It's not like she was some dope, reading about the war in the Seattle Star. She had been here the whole time. She knew the Japanese and what they were capable of.

"Well," said the colonel, "he might know something about the pilot. Maybe we should keep him around a while, give him to intelligence. Get him up on his feet, and wire his hands and legs together. There's some old wire back in there. See that old, rusted wire? Untangle that shit. And tie him good, because you can bet he ain't gonna be sitting there worrying his pointed little head about the Geneva Convention." Breaux nodded reluctantly. He thought that this was a lot of hooey. A quick boot in the kidneys helped Taniguchi to his feet. Ivania decided not to object to the rough treatment. Breaux's face suggested that she might be next. She was glad to accept the victory, as is. They marched the prisoner inside. The distant firing was coming closer. Ivania followed the men, unprepared for the change that had occurred to the interior of the ground floor of the lighthouse. She stepped back in horror when she saw the mangled flesh festooned from floor to ceiling. Hospital operating rooms didn't prepare her for this.

"Here, go up to the second floor," Joe said, taking her arm. Joe came back down the stairs shortly. He and Hawk looked at one another without speaking. Torn corpses with spilled organs of various geometrical shapes littered the floor. Heads looked like they had fallen off wax dummies. Joe turned away from Hawk. *I ought to slap his silly face*, Hawk thought. They walked away from each other. Their boots were sticky with blood.

"Ahoy, the lighthouse!" A call rose from outside. Breaux was standing guard at the window.

"Come on, Baker!" he answered the call, having recognized the voice. "It's crazy Baker," Breaux shouted to the others. Four marines climbed over the top of the cliff. Two of them were grinning. One of them was Baker, who everyone thought had a screw loose.

"We finally lost them," said Baker, wiping his nose on his forearm. He grinned at his fellow travelers, like they were all in on some great joke. The other men were rather solemn, although one occasionally grinned back at him. "They're about ten minutes behind us," Baker said.

Dreisen looked at Hawk expectantly, cleared his throat, and looked back at Baker. Usually, people in authority have a second in command that they rely on to make all the decisions in the background, and then the person in charge takes credit for it. That step had been expedited of late. "How many do they have left now? Dreisen asked.

"I would guess seven, or eight," Baker grinned wider.

"That's not bad, good work" Dreisen said. He had an urge to grin, after looking at Baker. He looked quickly away from the grimy face.

"Hawk, I think we should get the woman out of here, while we have the chance. I'm sure we can hold that many of the bastards off without any trouble, but anything could happen. She is kind of a pain in the ass, anyway. Don't need the sermons. Be plenty of those when we get back home, right? Not the place for it. I'll send Koichi and another man with her. Maybe they can link up with the column that's on the way here."

Hawk nodded. "Yes sir," he said quietly. "Good idea."

"Go tell her."

Hawk exhaled loudly through his nose. He turned for the stairs. He had to step around Joe to get there. They avoided each other's eyes. Ivania was looking out the window, her arms folded, when he came to the second floor.

"The colonel says you can go. There's probably gonna be a little more shooting here. Shit, I don't know if it's ever gonna stop. You might accidentally get in the middle of it. No sense taking a chance. Things haven't been working out lately. They'll probably tag somebody else."

"*Taking a chance?* No. That would be something new, wouldn't it? You're going to murder that man as soon as I leave, aren't you?"

"No." He took a breath, controlling his anger. "Ain't nobody said nothing about that. I said the colonel wants *you* outa here."

She turned quickly and faced him. "I'll tell you something, for what it's worth to something like you. That prisoner is twice the man that you are. Your only concern is James Hawk. Everything else can go to hell. I'd like to see you hurt. I'd like to see you when they get you down." She thought of the injured men in the hospital ship, pleading for help.

Hawk raised his eyebrows. He nodded. "You won't."

She stared angrily at him. What she had thought was security in the forest looked different here among human beings. If the rest of them *were* human beings.

Whatever they were, he was the worst of them all. She didn't want this terrible thing after all. Hawk's expression did not change. He felt that old, strange and hard divide that kept women away from him. He knew that she had found it too, and that that was the end of that. If it had not been for Taniguchi, it would've taken her a while to figure it out, but she would have. It would have been something else. He was just not the guy you wanted at your tea party. And that would never change.

"I don't know how I could have ever felt anything for you."

"Maybe a Jap bayonet pointed at your stupid skull had something to do with it."

She stared back at him, filled with emotion, mostly hatred, and fighting everything in her to keep from crying.

"Come on," he said. "You're wasting time. The goddam bastards are on their way, get your ass moving." Her face red with anger, she walked down the steps in front of him and stood on the corpse strewn floor. She looked at Taniguchi. The prisoner did not look back. He wanted neither her help, nor her pity. She understood him no more than she did Hawk.

"All right," Dreisen said. "Who wants to go with her?" He said it to Hawk. A rare opportunity offered to a man, who really, had never had any.

Hawk sat down on the stairs, hung his arms over his knees and stared at the maroon floor. He noticed that everyone was looking at him. He knew that he could get back into her good graces, if he accompanied her. A little humor, and a dash of heroics, and she would love him again. But who was she, that he would want to do that? Nobody. Just one more jerk who had stumbled into his life to make it miserable. It would be safer to go with her, of course, and get away from this endless shooting gallery. Koichi waited tensely for some resolution by the door. He whistled through his teeth quietly.

"Let Joe take her," Hawk said. Joe looked at him in surprise.

"Get going, Canlon," Dreisen snapped. Joe picked up his shotgun and slung his M1. He took Ivania by the arm. Koichi stepped outside, quite ready to get out of there.

Ivania stopped at the door. She turned back and looked at Hawk. He was looking at the floor.

"You are not coming?" she asked him. Hawk did not raise his helmet. He was a part of the bloody room. He was the designer of it.

"Got shit to do," he mumbled.

"Go along the cliff, you'll be all right," Baker said, putting a stick of gum in his mouth.

"Okay," Joe answered.

"Watch for mines," Hawk warned.

"Yeah. Thanks, Hawk. Watch yourself." Hawk looked up at him and said nothing. He looked down again and shook his head. *Watch yourself?* The stupid ass.

They left, and after a while Dreisen slapped his leg and laughed. "That eight-ball Canlon gets the girl, and we get eight Japs, men. How is that for justice?" Three or four of them laughed grudgingly.

"Serves the son of a bitch right," Hawk said. Maybe the two of them could talk about the Geneva Convention along the way. She might look like Veronica Lake, but that was as far as it went.

Dreisen reached down and picked up a wallet that

had been blown free of a dead man's pocket. He thumbed through the photographs of the enemy soldier's family.

"You know, Jap women ain't bad looking," Dreisen said, passing the pictures to Breaux. "But these bucks..."

Everyone's eyes suddenly fell at the same time on Taniguchi. He sat well-trussed on the floor with the rusty wire. His eyes narrowed and he looked away from them. They all had the same thought: *she's gone, get rid of him.* It was if someone had said it out loud. It would be stating the obvious to say that they were wrong. It would be explaining the inexplicable to say why they felt that way. Hawk was certain that someone would do it. And if they didn't...

"They're coming this way," Baker said from the doorway. "Two, four, six. Yep, seven of them. I was right." He had a bigger grin than usual. No one remembered if he was right.

Dreisen stood. "Get to your posts," he said. "I want to keep them as far away from here as we can. Hold them off. Help is on the way, and everything. Breaux, cover the door. Hawk, get up on the top."

"Aye... sir." Hawk stood slowly. His back ached from carrying the heavy antitank gun. He climbed the stairs. He found Hai-lon seated in the lamp room. The old man had nine lives. They did not say anything to one another. The monk had his eyes closed. Hawk walked to the wall and saw the paratroopers far out on the plain. He was not worried about them taking the lighthouse. The odds were too even. They had no heavy weapons. He leaned on the wall. He turned around for a look out over the valley. A speck in the vast sky immediately claimed his attention. His eyes narrowed. He had a feeling about it. But no, he was probably seeing, or wishing things. He pushed off the wall and walked to the far side of the room to get a better view. *Yes*, like a summoned evil spirit, the speck rapidly took the shape of the Shiden Kai.

Hawk bit off some chewing tobacco. *The son of a bitch is coming back.* Why? The sky soon provided a possible answer. Two other specks were chasing Zanji. "It's them two assholes," Hawk smiled. He leaned his elbows on the wall to watch. Two against one. This ought to be good. Hawk didn't know enough about Zanji to realize that he would never run from a mere two fighters. He was surprised when the sky dotted with two lines of pursuing Mustangs. He counted a dozen planes, besides the first two.

"They got you now, don't they, old buddy?" He spat onto the floor. He knew how Zanji must feel. He had been there. "Hey, Colonel! Look out your window!" he called. He heard a whoop from below. He smiled. The expression looked unnatural on his grim features. *Dreisen is finally getting what he wanted.* Almost. He didn't catch the pilot himself, but he had a part in it. Before it was over with, he would inveigle himself into the final version of the story. Zanji soared over the valley at an altitude just above the lighthouse roof. Hawk thought of the antiaircraft gun. But there was no sense in pecking at the Shiden. Hawk had already had his chance. The P-51's deserved the glory, and they would do it right, and in short order. Hawk's only wish was that he could see it. Yesterday he would not have cared. Today it seemed important. The planes would probably be far out to sea, on the other side of the island, before the Mustangs caught the Shiden. Hawk sighed and spat. That would be a show. He could see Zanji looking over his shoulder in the cockpit. His movements looked unperturbed. The Mustangs closed in, faster than Hawk thought possible. *Goddam,* he thought, *maybe I will get to see some of this.*

He was wrong. He would see *all* of it. In a maneuver that Hawk had never seen before, Zanji seemed to pivot on his wingtip and streak straight back at his pursuers. He left a white vapor trail that looked like that of a rocket.

Hawk stood up straight. He figured that the Japanese planned to ram an American plane. The Mustangs must have had the same idea. They scattered in all directions, like the petals of an opening flower. The spectator heard a machine-gun rattle from high up in the heavens. They did not sound much better up there. The angry report sounded odd, coming down from high in the placid blue sky. As they scattered, Zanji shot upward, looking for all the world as if he had just launched himself perpendicularly. A white ball of light fluttered from the Shiden's machine cannon. A few seconds later, Hawk heard the report below, as light travels faster than sound. One of the American planes, its nose turned away in an upward climb, began bleeding black smoke. The stricken plane stalled and dropped, the air seemingly trying to break its fall. But it could not. The nose slung itself down and the heavy machinery shot heavily into the treetops below. The Shiden paid no attention to the vanquished. While Hawk still watched the exploding flames on the earth below him, another American plane began a screaming death dive. It had happened so fast, the spectator had missed the cause of the whole thing.

Hawk had seen dogfights before, but he had never seen a contestant of Zanji's caliber. He was amazed by the speed and maneuvering. It was not a cold amazement. His tribal instincts boiled, as he saw American men falling from the sky. The P-51's were flown well, but Zanji's plane seemed to have a mind of its own. There was none of the natural difficulty in making a machine perform a delicate move. To think of an exercise, was to make it for Zanji, as if he were moving his own body.

The Japanese ace was surrounded by them now, and they opened fire. Hawk had no regrets for the underdog. This was life and death, and not a baseball game. Zanji dropped his nose directly at the ground, and spiraled wildly toward it. Hawk thought that the enemy pilot had lost control. None of the Americans could possibly follow him, nor should they have tried. Sixty feet above the treetops, Zanji pulled out of the power dive, exhibiting perfect control. Instead of running, the Japanese flyer swooped up to rejoin the battle. Another Mustang plummeted into the trees. It had been hit by American bullets in the berserk crossfire. Hawk did not realize this, thinking that Zanji must have some sort of superhuman marksmanship skills, with the ability to shoot a plane down during his dive. Hawk was partially correct, in that Zanji had fully expected, and engineered the effect of the friendly fire on the stricken plane.

Above Zanji, below him, and straight for him, the American planes charged with guns blazing. The ace made his hairpin turn once again, dropped for the treetops, and then shot upward. The white light of the machine cannon again fluttered from the Shiden. Hawk winced. He knew that it would connect. A Mustang turned into a smoking orange sunset. But four of the P-

51s swept under the ace to avenge their mate, and to pull the same trick on the Japanese. Their chances of success should have been four times as great. But Zanji rolled on his back and fell on top of them, firing conservative bursts from his upside-down position. He fell through their formation gracefully. Two glass cockpits exploded, flaming Mustangs shot out of sight below the cliff. The two explosions followed shortly after, as they met the rocky earth. It sounded as if they had landed on top of one another.

Hawk sat on the wall now, with an arm wrapped around a column. He watched in disbelief. It was as if this were an air show, staged by the Japanese. It was an unreal display of faultless skill against overwhelming odds.

"Get that son of a bitch." Hawk growled at the Americans. Firing from down below, from his own war, interrupted the show. He ran to the other wall to check on the advancing Japanese. They remained far out on the plain. One looked rather dead. The others were firing on the lighthouse from prone positions. When he looked back to the air battle, the planes were much lower in the sky, and another Mustang was missing.

"That's it, get him low, where he ain't got room to move," Hawk whispered. Although he knew nothing about flying, he had an instinct for any sort of fighting. Zanji turned his wings deftly to a position vertical to the ground. He went into a wide turn. From their position straight above him, the Mustangs had little to shoot at. They tried. Hawk saw bullet holes run across the Shiden's arrogant tail. This would be their best chance to nail him. But Zanji continued flying sideways, in what appeared to be a move of sheer madness.

A well manned P-51 streaked down toward Zanji's exposed cockpit, with his guns spitting a white spray. Zanji went on his back and sliced down in a curved trajectory at the treetops, like he was on a Ferris wheel. He flew as well on his back, as right side up. Hawk was sure that he would crash this time, as the green plane became silhouetted by nothing but the color green. Of course, he did not. When he got to the bottom of his Ferris wheel, he was right side up, and skimming gently across the uppermost treetops. He pulled out of the dive inches above the solid tree trunks. Flimsy boughs hung for a moment on the Shiden's underside. It was a beautiful execution, and even Hawk was ready to admit it, until he saw one, two, and three hotly pursuing Mustangs ram into the trees in a monstrous orgy of explosions. They had been following their enemy too closely, and could not duplicate his escape. Only their skill was lacking, their courage was unquestionable.

Hawk's mouth fell open. He dropped his Thompson and dodged behind the antiaircraft gun. He rammed its bolt back and tried to sight in on the elusive enemy aircraft. It was almost impossible. The Japanese pilot moved at the speed of thought. Hawk could only line up the confused American planes, for some quick practice. Some of the Mustangs had given up. He saw only two left in the sky. The odds now looked bad for those two. Zanji was, after all, human. The exhausting set of maneuvers had left him disoriented. As he cruised and tried to gather his wits, the two attackers dove down for his tail from the rear. It was a perfect kill position. The ace made weak feints to the right and left to shake them off. He knew that they were back there. The American hunters were not fooled. Hawk had a fair shot at the

Shiden as it came toward him. He was afraid of hitting the Americans, or of rattling their demonstrably delicate concentration. He knew that if he hit anything in the vast sky, it would probably be one of his own planes.

Zanji flew for the cliffs. "No!" Hawk gasped. He saw clearly what the ace was doing. The Mustangs did not see it. One of them crashed a wing into the cliff as Zanji barely cleared it. The other plane banked and headed north at the greatest speed he could force from his fatigued aircraft. His was the smartest maneuver by the American planes that day.

The Shiden glided low and triumphantly over the plains in front of the lighthouse. Hawk saw the enemy soldiers waving their weapons at the pilot in exuberance. That is why he came back, Hawk said to himself. He had to have witnesses. At the beginning, the P-51s thought that the ace was running, but in fact, he was only looking for an audience, to report the kills.

Hawk looked for a point of reference. He swung the gunsight to the edge of the cliff. He pressed the trigger before the fast-moving plane got there. The antiaircraft gun recoiled on its springs. Hawk's eyes shook in his skull, and his ears felt a twinge of pain under the noise. He saw huge black holes shatter the metal behind Zanji's cockpit. The plane dove down over the cliff and swooped up again. It was not seriously injured. Zanji made it clear that he could evade the line of fire. The ace looked around in the cockpit, to see where the fire had come from. He was not looking for any purposes of evasion.

"Well, I hit him." Hawk told Hai-lon, quite surprised.

Encouraged by the reappearance of their champion,

the Japanese paratroopers advanced toward the lighthouse, firing their weapons. In their enthusiasm, two of them fell dead from the return fire. The American fire drove them toward the cliff. They fell to crawling steadily forward. Their aggressiveness worried Breaux. He propped his BAR against the wall and began picking up Japanese weapons from the ravaged floor. Ammunition ran low. It was so low, he soon picked up the BAR and stuck in its last clip.

Taniguchi edged across the floor to a gore draped Arisaka rifle. The Americans had left it there, perhaps out of revulsion. The Marines were too preoccupied to notice his movements. He picked up the blood-crusted weapon, and slid it from beneath an intestine. Still, no one noticed. He could shoot one of them, before they could get him. If the one he especially wanted to shoot had been in the room, he would have done just that. But Hawk was not there, and Taniguchi knew that if he could free his hands, he could get even more of them, and possibly get up the stairs, or out the door, depending on how the circumstances fluctuated. The *hancho* decided mobility was the important thing. He had to free his feet first. He could not fight from the position of a tangled crab. As Dreisen blew his last grease gun clip, Taniguchi severed most of the bonds on his feet with a single, indistinguishable shot from the Arisaka. The damage was sufficient for him to rip the rest of the torn wires off. But still his hands were bound.

"Sounds like Hawk is going after that pilot himself," Dreisen told the others, with a proud smile. He was still not worried about the encounter. They were being attacked by about three men now. It looked and it sounded bad, but it wasn't. There was a lot of lead flying in all directions, including up. He hoped for a miracle. He hoped that Hawk would accidentally hit the Shiden. A miracle happened, all right, but for the Japanese. One of their last rifle grenades rocketed through the door. Everyone scrambled in surprise. Only Baker, Dreisen, and Breaux moved quickly enough. They had been in the doorway, and had the most advanced warning. It landed on the floor, right in the doorway, it's shrapnel neatly picking off the unsuspecting men firing from the windows. Taniguchi survived because of his proximity to the floor, and because he was behind the staircase. The *hancho* knew he had to move quickly, while the numbing effect of the blast lasted. He clambered to his feet with his hands still bound by the thick wire. Dreisen and Breaux saw him at once, and charged for him. Baker crawled in a semi-conscious daze for the door.

Taniguchi dealt a vicious sidekick to Breaux's groin, spun around and landed a perfectly executed round-house kick to Dreisen's head. The colonel dropped like a rock. The pirouette had been perfect, except that the burly Breaux absorbed the blow and kept coming. He swung the butt plate of the BAR into Taniguchi's chin, and the *hancho* fell heavily on the stone floor. Bone and cortex may be hard, but not as hard as mindless stone. His head bounced about an inch, and he fell still, with his face in the bloody dust. His hands remained bound.

Dreisen was on his knees, leaning back on one arm when the Japanese burst through the door. They kicked Baker aside like a ragdoll. Dreisen bellowed like a bull, but that was all that he could do. He had no weapon, other than the empty grease gun lying at his side, and it was useless as a club. A bayonet slid into his stomach and pushed him against the wall. Breaux panted, rising on one knee. He raised the BAR and rallied his strength. His trigger snapped back. The Japanese walked right into the fire, falling over one another. The last enemy attacker reached the Cajun and bayoneted him. The Japanese tried to pull the blade out for another thrust. It would not budge. Breaux's heavy stomach muscles were wedged around the cutting steel. Breaux jammed the BAR muzzle into his killer's forehead and dove forward onto him. He fell on the bayonet, driving part of the rifle barrel through his body. Still, he pressed down until he seized the throat of the Japanese soldier. His massive hands crushed the delicate throat. He lost his vision before the man died, but he could feel the relaxed body beneath him. He lay dead over the foe, and almost completely concealing him. The wind blew a gust of rocky dirt through the door.

Baker sat up. He grinned. It was over, and he was alive. Dreisen moaned against the wall. Taniguchi moved only slightly. Baker noticed that the prisoner's hands were bound. He sat against the doorjamb, knocked off his helmet, and covered his eyes with a bleeding hand.

15

JUST THE END OF EVERYTHING

TOTTERING ON THE TOP OF AN ANCIENT SHAFT, BALANCED on the peak of a fragile pinnacle of rock, jutting from the middle of the angry Pacific Ocean, Hawk watched his opponent with stoic fascination. The Shiden banked at a leisurely speed, far out over the valley. The sights of the 13.2 mm gun tried to catch up with it. Hawk pressed the trigger. Tracers arced out into naked space.

"Only missed by half a mile or so," Hawk growled at the weapon. They were a team now, he and this Japanese made machine. He swayed the muzzle back and forth, trying to line up another shot. His concentration was interrupted. The Shiden decided it wanted to take an active part in this contest, too. It turned toward the lighthouse and Hawk became a target for the first time. He heard the plane's motor rev into overdrive. Tons of hurtling metal bore down on the pagoda-roofed lighthouse. Hawk saw the two machine guns on each wing flutter. The huge ringing shells knocked chunks out of the columns. A clump of the wooden roof splashed onto the floor. It lay there, looking like a disturbed eagle's nest. Hawk fought the gun's barrel, trying to get the whirring monster outside into his sights. But the unexpected vision of the oncoming propeller and chewing machine guns forced him to release the trigger and dive to the floor. He heard the Shiden scream just above the shivering roof. There was a rapid, slapping noise, of either the propeller, or the foundation of the building reverberating in an attempt to give way.

Hawk jumped to his feet and spun the gun completely around. The fighter hovered again over the plains. The sergeant had better reference points over the solid ground. He put the knife-bladed foresight on empty airspace in front of the plane's route, and let the fighter fly into one of the horizontal crosshairs. He pressed the trigger. The Shiden glided forward still. Hawk's gun leapt furiously, like a maddened dog, enraged by the postman sauntering just beyond his fence. His eyes rattled out of sync with the gyrations of the weapon. The Shiden floated rapidly out over the valley again. Somehow, Hawk had missed. He now appreciated the scope of the duel. Bullets are fast, but so are airplanes.

"You better move along, Mr. Hai-lon. He's...he's coming back. He's aiming at us now."

Hai-lon stood. "May your God be with you, young seeker," the monk said. They heard the loud explosion of a rifle grenade below.

"Yes, sir." *No shit.* Hawk motioned him downstairs, and glanced at the stairway as Hai-lon descended. It did not sound a hell of a lot safer down there. The simple fact was, if Dreisen did not hold the lower floors, Hawk would be shot in the back by the ascending Japanese infantrymen. He had gotten himself into this other battle, and now felt that he could not get out of it. The fighter would continue to strafe the building unchallenged unless someone resisted. More importantly, there was a chance he could kill Zanji. That was why a company of men had died, wasn't it? That was supposed to mean...something.

Hawk had crates of ammunition for the gun. He decided to try the shotgun approach. Sharpshooting evidently was not going to work; not with a target that fast, and that elusive. Even when his shots seemed perfectly timed, they missed. It would be luck, and the more lead flying, the better his chances would be. He pressed down the trigger with all of his pent-up emotion, swinging the gun behind the plane and trying to catch it. Emotion did not enhance accuracy. The tracers arced over and under and behind the leaping green devil. It was small and invulnerable out over the valley. Its color matched the shadows in the trees. Hawk jerked the muzzle in front of the plane, trying to lead it. Zanji dropped gradually and gracefully, as if he were descending stair steps, and then accomplished one of his hairpin turns. The heavy antiaircraft shells soared always just ahead of him, where he should have been, but was not. Hawk realized that the pilot was delicately waving his altitude up and down, by mere inches and feet, to make himself invisible to the oncoming slugs. Hawk knew that he was no match for such subtle elusiveness. He had never seen a plane do such a thing. The plane's banking aimed it toward the lighthouse. The enemy was coming for his turn at Hawk. The Shiden's machine cannon opened up, and the wings blazed red.

Chunks of the lamp room wall disintegrated into a powdery spray. The tiny pieces of stone stuck to Hawk's sweating face. He pressed down the trigger, trying with sheer force of his will to drill the fire into the center of the Shiden's propeller. Zanji's wings began spinning, tip over tip, until it looked as if a colossal pinwheel of fire were falling onto the lighthouse. The machine cannons poured unchecked bursts onto their stationary prey.

The 20 mm shells rained through the roof and blew craters into the floor. One could see through a couple of them, into the room below. Hawk again abandoned his gun and flattened before the awesome, enlarging specter. He knew that Japanese pilots had few qualms about diving into a target. But Zanji had not made his reputation by committing suicide. When he ditched, it would not be onto a lone man with an antiaircraft gun. He had decided years ago that he would take a carrier or a battleship with him. The Shiden roared beside the lamp room, it's wing barely, but skillfully, missing a supporting column. Sickening exhaust fumes billowed through the chamber.

Hawk stood. He pushed the spring button on the wide banana clip that jutted from the top of the gun. He tossed the spent clip to the floor, dashed to the crates for another, and rammed one into place. He wanted to look down the stairs, to see what was happening down there, but there was no time. The aircraft required only a split second to make a new, unexpected, and deadly attack. It was dangerously quiet below. Zanji was already banking along the edge of the cliff, coasting like a peaceful bird. Hawk had missed his best field of fire, while he had been reloading, with the plane in front of a background of the solid orange and brown earth. Now Zanji would have another turn at bat.

The Shiden swung over the green valley and came from below this time, its powerful engine functioning perfectly and sounding invincible. The machine cannon rounds ripped up through the roof like metal bottles. Splinters fell to the floor. Hawk had no shot at all. He could not aim his gun downward. Zanji swooped up the cliff and showed Hawk the tantalizing under-belly of his craft for only a fraction of a second. But the ace could not score a kill from that angle either. Hawk was still concerned about a crash dive.

With depressing and irreversible certainty, Hawk realized that he had made a mistake. If fourteen highly mobile aircraft with trained pilots could not tag Zanji, what hope did a lone emplaced object have, manned by an inexperienced gunner? Hawk was no longer the hunter, he was the sitting duck waiting for the end. The pilot had known exactly what he was doing from the outset, whereas Hawk had no idea. His only hope was that the fighter would run out of ammunition. It had already engaged the P-51's. How much could it have left? Still, in all of the firing, Hawk remembered, it was seldom Zanji doing the shooting. He was quite conserv-ative with his ammunition. Even so, it might take a while, but he had to eventually run dry.

Hawk considered that. He could let Zanji shoot at will at the lighthouse, and probably save his own life; he should go below for a greater degree of safety, and forget this. The Shiden would have to eventually go away without ammunition. He rubbed the sweat and dust from his eyebrows and blew it from the tip of his nose. His tattered clothing was soaked. It was not in him to quit the fight. This is what they had come here for. This is what the Mustangs came for. Win or lose, fighting was his nature, and this was *the* fight. There was that aggressive meanness and that gambler's madness that said *maybe*, maybe I will win. He had been lucky for so long. But so had Zanji, who also had the ability to give up this struggle with little consequences. But the two killers had now entered into an infernal bargain with one another, and the terms were not yet met.

Hawk would not concede that he was out of his element. He had a gun and a target. He leveled his sights once more at the edge of the cliff, and waited to intercept the Firebolt, who in all of the engagement, Hawk had touched only once.

When he looked up, Zanji had changed direction. How he had managed that was incomprehensible. He would not allow Hawk's best shot at his underbelly. He was a fast learner, and mastering the game. The Marine's gullet constricted. He saw that his opponent had become more familiar with the strategies of the battle. Zanji was doing his homework, and Hawk was not. The enemy ace loomed eerily, unexpectedly, and enormously across the plain toward the front of the lamp room. Hawk had little time to react. He fought the barrel in the general direction of his attacker. This time he stood his ground and fired madly at the nightmare, as it slashed toward him. He jerked the muzzle up and down, and side to side. The burning gun kicked viciously at Hawk, as if it were trying to make him let go of its overworked trigger. Hot vapors rose from its length, the machine threatening to jam. The concrete emplacement at the foot of its pedestal cracked. Splits in the concrete radiated across the floor.

The flashes from Zanji's guns showed through the spray coming from the air defense gun. They were brighter and they blinked faster. The cannon's flashing pulsated on the back wall of Hawk's retinas, brightest in the center and growing dimmer in the afterimages along the periphery. When the firing suddenly stopped, the plane cleared the roof by inches. With stubborn and late futility, Hawk leaned down on the gun with his weight and fired the weapon up through the roof, blowing a great hole in it. Debris fell into his eyes and trickled across his upturned face.

Zanji went into a leisurely loop on the opposite side and returned to the plains in front of the lighthouse. Hawk clawed his fingers over his eyes to clear them of the foreign objects. Always, the sound of the perfectly timed Nakajima engine drilled into his hearing. He blinked pathetically. There was no one to feel sorry for him. He was a cold and murdering animal, who had come to his own lonesome, chosen, and deserved end. His own overconfidence had brought him here. His own foolhardiness, his own refusal to believe that he was only a fallible human being. He wasted precious seconds, batting the gritty boulders out of his eyes. Vivid-colored blood covered his right hand. He had no idea where it came from.

Inside the Shiden's cockpit, Zanji was also a pathetic sight, and a study of sad overconfidence. Yes, he admitted now that he should not have flown straight toward the lighthouse. One of the enormous anti-aircraft shells had penetrated his cabin. He looked down and saw his leg a mass of twisted red flesh. Genius was, after all, a learning process. Zanji had learned from every sortie that he had flown, and retained more of the knowledge than any other warrior. He had committed a major error this time, but he knew that a warrior does not give up when he is hurt. He moved his foot on the pedal. It still functioned. The leg was a horrifying sight, but it did not pain him. Thousands of tiny red dots had sprayed the inside of the glass cockpit, impairing the view.

Zanji saw that the challenging creature in the lighthouse was no longer firing at him. Had he triumphed at last, over whatever this thing was? Had Odysseus defeated yet another unknown mythical monster thrown at him? He could have flown away and claimed that, to himself, if to no other. As on so many other occasions, Zanji sensed the kill. His throat filled. It was a passion stronger than self-preservation in him. He did not know that he had engaged a demon with a similar affliction. He banked and came over the plains again, straight for the lighthouse, just as he had done before. Just as when he had committed his mistake. Zanji was the master, even of mistakes.

Hawk hung his arms warily on his gun and blinked with difficulty. The most important element of this duel was eyesight. He had no idea that he had scored again, there was certainly no indication. He saw that blood ran from a cut on the back of his hand. It was nothing serious. When the plane came at him again, level and like a mountainous arrow, he could hardly move in the face of the sheer speed. He was the weary stag awaiting the executioner. The fiery metal bottles blazed over his head. The chain of them lowered, and knocked down the front lamp room wall. They halved a column. A splintered round from the plane danced down the barrel of Hawk's antiaircraft gun, causing golden sparks to whine and to shower up and over its user. The smell of the cordite, and the flying rock dust choked Hawk. He stood in the swirling maelstrom like a ghostly statue in a morning fog.

At the last moment, when the fury of the fire-burst concentrated on him the greatest, the madness that was Sergeant Hawk leapt into his limbs and he latched onto the antiaircraft gun. It belched a sheet of solid steel at the front of Zanji's plane, but the plane was well-armored, and it was all for naught. The plane shrieked over the roof. This time, Hawk wheeled the gun around. He would not stop. He fired crazily into the vacant valley, chasing the invisible attacker. Rage engulfed his senses.

Zanji saw that his opponent lived, and more importantly, fought. As he looked at his injured leg, he found this enemy infuriating. *You think I will allow this?* He maneuvered into one of his loops, that he might have another fast and rapid spin over the plain. At the top of the loop, he fired from his upside-down position. He let up on the button quickly, remembering his dwindling supply of ammunition. He would wait for the sure kill. He saw his own reflection in the liquid red glow of the glass cockpit.

As he came barreling out of the loop, the full length of the top of his plane was within Hawk's view. The Marine had never released the trigger of his gun. It teetered on its cracking base. It jumped in an uncontrolled frenzy. It eased out of the floor. Hawk continued firing, nevertheless, but he could not hold the heavy weapon up along with the concrete that weighted it. And yet, clearly within his sight, as he stopped firing, it looked like a bright light had been switched on within

Zanji's glass cabin. The tight glass of the cockpit exploded as the Shiden completed its loop. The plane kept coming from the rear of the lighthouse. Hawk lifted the burning and crushingly heavy gun across his leg as he went to one knee. The Shiden grew larger, no longer sporting its allegedly bullet proof glass shield. Its guns were empty and quiet. Hawk could clearly see Zanji's face. It was placid, unaffected. Another day at the mill. Hawk shoved the barrel of the gun onto the remnants of the lamp room wall for some support, and jerked the trigger yet again. The gun fell back on his leg and the fire went wild. He cursed under the crushing weight and the burning barrel.

Ripping his clothes beneath the metal, Hawk pulled his leg free. He saw that Zanji was going to ram him. This time it was not a delusion. He turned and dove for the stairs. He had no desire for the match to end in a draw.

Neither did Zanji. He was alive, though he knew that his plane was dead. He could make a crash landing as long as the steering mechanism worked. He had done it before. He flew straight at the lighthouse and saw that his cannons were empty. He pressed on the pedal to steer around the white shaft of stone. Nothing happened. He looked down. His pants leg and his flesh were torn open, showing the anatomy beneath. He saw the tendon in his upper leg moving, but his foot lay dead and immobile on the pedal. He pressed again. The tendon flexed in a gory frenzy. The foot lay still, its war was over.

The edge of the Shiden's wing hit the roof. The wing sheared off and the ancient columns were knocked over like bowling pins. The pagoda roof sailed far out onto the plains, where it spun and slid asunder. The Shiden cart-wheeled on its side and crashed in red splashing fury before the lighthouse.

Hawk sat dazed on the stairs. He heard the popping and crackling flames of both the Mustangs and the Shiden whipping on all sides in the wind outside. A secondary explosion went off, shaking the lighthouse. He looked up through the roofless building and saw a wide new circle of blue above. He squinted at it and looked down at his hand. He had no recollection as to how that had happened. The bleeding was not serious, but neither had it stopped. It must have been a ricochet. It just had not registered. The past few minutes were lost, like the events of a drunken stupor. He only knew that Zanji lay in the violent and soaring flames outside.

He breathed deeply and clenched his teeth. He could see dead men stacked around the doorway below. He recognized Breaux and felt a pang. Something in his pocket dug into his leg. When the gun had fallen on his leg, an object in the pocket had badly bruised him.

He stuck his dripping red and brown hand into his pocket. He pulled out a small wooden box with a feldspar cover. The relic of Hai-tai within the box also bled. Hawk held his heavy breathing for a moment, as he studied the strange phenomenon. He did not trust his senses. He exhaled harshly. Then he closed his eyes and put the box back into his pocket. His head ached.

He pulled himself to his feet and staggered down the steps. He could feel his heart pounding fiercely. When would it stop? In those familiar nightmares that were his only sleep, probably never. He paused at the second floor, where Hai-lon had taken refuge. The monk stood at the window, watching Zanji's burning plane. The chemical fire roiled furiously. Inside the orange hell, a black corpse, shining with its own iridescence, hung out of the cockpit with its fingers stretched and reaching. There was no discerning who it had been. Hawk stepped into the room and the monk turned around slowly. The burning fuel threatened their ability to breathe. Hai-lon was the first to speak.

"Are you injured?"

"Nothing a little kerosene and Mercurochrome won't cure."

The flashing lights and shadows outside the window were charged with the magical color of heliotrope. Hawk reached slowly into his pocket. He pulled out the relic and handed it to the old man. The monk reached out and took it. He smiled. Hawk looked at him from beneath his brooding eyebrows.

"So, young seeker, we were right. You did find the truth."

"Maybe." Hawk could tell that Hai-lon had known all along where it had been. "I guess it was time that one of us did. Might as well be me." Hai-lon, for all his wisdom, failed to detect the irony of the remark. "Nobody will take it away anymore, now."

"It is good," said the monk, pleased only to have the valuable talisman returned. "Thank you for your protection of it. You are as one of us."

Hawk had nothing to say to that.

"Should we not therefore help the wounded?"

"Yeah. If there is any."

They walked down the stairs and into the butchery-soaked rubble. Three men stirred. Possibly more lay unconscious. Taniguchi tried to sit up. Dreisen lay dying against the wall. Baker looked up silently and grinned.

He was edging along the floor as he sat, slowly, as if in pain, without any specific destination. Hawk knelt in front of Dreisen. The colonel forced a weak smile.

"You got him, didn't you, Hawk? I heard him hit." Dreisen closed his eyes and sucked air through his teeth. "I saw Satan fall from heaven like lightning," he moaned in a loud voice, and then more quietly added, "sounded like an earthquake."

"Yeah. I got him."

"I'll be a general for sure. I won't have to retire to get my star. No, sir. Did you know that, Hawk?"

"Yes, sir. I figured."

"I'll get some medal, too. You can bet on that. They like to give generals medals. I'll get the big one for this. You'll see...because it'll be in the newspapers." Dreisen's voice was crying. He opened his eyes wide. "It's going to be the biggest story of this whole big war. This is...political. Political!" He coughed. "That's marble, ain't it?" Dreisen was looking at the white stone on the wall. It had black streaks in it.

"No, sir. I don't think so." Hawk saw the focus go out of the eyes. The mouth froze. Hawk bowed his head and closed his own eyes. He sighed.

He looked up at the ceiling and shook his head. "I got him for nothing. All of it. For nothing." He was still breathing hard. He clenched his teeth. "All so you could breathe a couple of times and say some horseshit about a wall." Hai-lon stood over them.

"Yes!" the old man hissed.

Hawk looked up at the monk. He had no more patience for the fakir.

Taniguchi sat up. His head swam. He wanted to rub it, but he couldn't. He jerked at the cutting bonds that restrained his hands, when he saw that Hawk was close to him. He forced himself to stand. But he was too weak to fight. He leaned against the door jamb. Baker slid along the wall anxiously now, to get away from the prisoner. He was no longer grinning. Baker likely knew what Hawk was about to do to the captive, and that he probably would not be very careful about doing it. Baker held a hand stiffly away from his body to try to alleviate the pain. He finally settled against the wall at a safe distance, so that he might better watch Hawk kill Taniguchi.

Hawk sighed again and stood. He leaned against the door jamb opposite Taniguchi and unslung his Thompson.

"What am I gonna do with you?"

Taniguchi had no difficulty guessing the answer. He knew Hawk's mind better than did Hawk. He also knew what he would do, if their roles were reversed. The options had been systematically limited to one. But the *hancho* was dizzy and nauseous, and dying seemed like a pleasant thing. Choking, black wraiths of smoke periodically knifed through the windows. He heard the vacuum-snapping of the burning fuel in the wind. It seemed to swirl on all sides, maybe over the entire world by now.

"You must look within yourself," Hai-lon spoke to Hawk, for the staggered Taniguchi. "You must look to the good. What would your own Christ do?"

Hawk looked over at the monk. "He wouldn't be here, old timer."

"That is right, young seeker."

"But I am." Hawk's leg felt as if it were broken.

"Yes."

Taniguchi looked at the hideous face of the eternal killer through his own pain-drunken eyes. Bearded, dirty, degenerate, and twisted, it hovered inches from his own, their backs leaning on opposite sides of the open doorway, but with their bowed heads almost touching. Hawk raised the prisoner's bound hands high over his head and severed the rusty wire with a blinding burst of ear-shattering fire from the Thompson. The blast reverberated through what remained of the lighthouse. The prisoner's hands separated.

What was one more Jap, more or less? The Japanese looked at him with stunned and confused amazement, his freed hands shaking and scorched. Hawk pushed Taniguchi roughly out the door.

"Get out of here, you son of a bitch."